Gary M. Williams was born and raised in Staten Island, New York. He was a teacher and principal with the New York City Department of Education for thirty-five years. He is currently retired and resides in Manhattan and is now assuming a full-time career in writing.

He was inspired to write a historical fictional novel spanning the twentieth century after visits to Newport, Rhode Island, and Europe. After two years of research and eight years of writing, *Gone but Not Forgotten*, the first of a trilogy, along with the second and third books, reached their completion.

In addition to writing, Mr. Williams holds a strong avocation for the arts. His hobbies include theater, reading, and world travel. He is currently working on his next novel and anticipates adding it to his literary repertoire.

Gone but Not Forgotten is dedicated to my beautiful wife and best friend in Heaven, June Battista Williams, who brought me to Newport, Rhode Island for the first time on the occasion of our tenth wedding anniversary. This visit, along with visits to Europe, inspired the writing of the trilogy. June's insight, savoir-faire, and genuine appreciation of the beauty and colors of life had served to paint the backdrops of the novel along with its keen descriptions of finesse and pageantry. Her unflagging support and suggestions were monumental tools for the completion of this work.

Gary M. Williams

GONE BUT NOT FORGOTTEN

AUSTIN MACAULEY PUBLISHERS™

LONDON * CAMBRIDGE * NEW YORK * SHARJAH

Ordering Information
Quantity sales: Special discounts are available on quantity purchases by corporations, associations, and others. For details, contact the publisher at the address below.

Publisher's Cataloging-in-Publication data
Williams, Gary M.
Gone but Not Forgotten

ISBN 9781649791986 (Paperback)
ISBN 9781649791993 (ePub e-book)

Library of Congress Control Number: 2021906259

www.austinmacauley.com/us

First Published (2021)
Austin Macauley Publishers LLC
40 Wall Street, 33rd Floor, Suite 3302
New York, NY 10005
USA

mail-usa@austinmacauley.com
+1 (646) 5125767

I would like to acknowledge all friends and family who have read and supported the drafts of this novel and for always believing that 'I could.'

And once again, I acknowledge my beautiful wife and best friend, June, in Heaven, for assisting me in the writing process and always believing that 'I would!'

Table of Contents

We are but visiting this earth…
It is not the length of our stay which matters
so much as the footprints we leave behind…
The impression we make upon humanity…

A man's value is measured by how long he is
remembered after he is gone…

Tail of the Gilded Age, 1914

All good things come to an end, in order to give birth to new beginnings...

Chapter 1
June 1914 – Newport, Rhode Island

Veda Champion was, if not likeable, a rare and extraordinary beauty. That is not to say she lacked charm, for at seventeen, she was already New York's most desired and sought-after debutante. The photograph taken of her at the city's grand ball that last winter, resplendent in an elegant white ball gown, had made headlines across the country, and arrested the eyes of some of America's most eminent bachelors. She had shoulder length raven hair, violet eyes, rose tinged cheeks, square jaws, and heart shaped lips. She was fluent in both English and French and, though no means a scholar, was sharp of wit and educated—if ill versed in every social grace.

She and her twin sister, Rose, had just graduated from Geneva's most distinguished finishing school, and were home for the summer before they would begin Georgetown that fall. Rose was the younger of the two, and physically identical to Veda, save her soft, gray eyes, and angelic demeanor. Veda was feisty, Rose, meek as a lamb. Yet despite their sharp, contrasting characters, the twins adored one another and remained inseparable.

Today was a most special occasion, the marriage of their brother Marius to Miss Dominique Deneuve, prominent daughter of the founder and president of the Deneuve formal apparel store in Manhattan. Though her dowry was quite significant, Marius was, indeed, the better catch. At twenty-three, he was vice president and heir to his father's throne at Champion Trust, a family-owned bank for three generations.

Traditionally, the Champions waited until the first of July to leave their Park Avenue home and set sail on the thirty-foot yacht for Chateau La Mer, located in South Eastern Rhode Island. But this year, they chose to pack their trunks one month earlier in mutual agreement that the chateau was a more appropriate venue for a late spring wedding reception.

And indeed, it was. Standing at her bedroom window late that morning, Veda marveled at the vast number of yachts docking beneath the hills of the mansion, and the fleet in the distance, sailing lazily on the calm waters of Narragansett Bay. From the clear blue sky, the sun cast silver over the scene, and the water appeared heavenly as did the grounds of the estate.

Above the boulders of the Atlantic, stood the manor house, a twenty-room architectural masterpiece designed as a replica to that of *La Madame* Champion's childhood summer playhouse in Verdun, France. There were fifteen acres of tree-filled property, manicured lawns, and flourishing gardens. Today, the champagne fountains, the tents, and the one hundred immaculately set tables, left Veda breathless.

She looked ravishing in a sleeveless turquoise silk organza dress with layered ruffles, a V neck, and a huge floweret. Her hair was pulled tightly to the back of her head where it spilled over her neck in loose, rich curls.

"Ooooh!" she squealed in shock when a pair of strong hands gripped her waist from behind.

She swung around to meet the smiling face of Theodore Aspan, better known by the young girls he charmed as 'devilish Teddy.' He had golden hair, emerald green eyes, and a heavily muscled frame. He was very handsome, if not industrious. Coming from four generations of wealth, his father, president of Aspan's Fifth Avenue, a family-owned jewelry store for more than fifty years, he was, by far, the best catch of bachelors in New York, and yet, at twenty-three, remained uncommitted to anyone or anything. Having been expelled from Princeton for 'dishonorable conduct' two years before, he entered the American Navy to his parents' chagrin. He had been a grave disappointment to them, unlike his two brothers who flooded Mr. and Mrs. Aspan with pride. Teddy was the black sheep, though the most handsome of the lot. And today, in white tie, he looked dashing.

But Veda would never admit it. Instead, she raised her head haughtily and derided, "Theodore Aspan! Of all your callous pranks! How did you find your way up here?"

But the glint in her eyes and her ill-concealed smile hinted she was charmed.

Teddy fell onto his right knee and flirted as he kissed her dainty hand, "Pardon me, *Mademoiselle,* but my desire to be the first gentleman to rest eyes upon your beauty has prompted me to climb the flower trellis leading to your terrace."

She slipped her hand from his lips and sneered, "Gentleman, indeed! You are a renegade, Theodore, and I being a lady, do not know why I dare even speak to you!"

Then she turned and sashayed to her mahogany wood vanity, flaunting her exquisite dress and the thinnest debutante waist in New York. He admired the gentle curve of her back and the graceful twist of her wrist, as she lifted a crystal atomizer to generously spritz herself with violet toilet water.

"And on that vain, Mr. Aspan, I would thank you to maintain what little dignity you possess by making yourself scarce. If anyone should see you here, they might deem me improper."

Teddy guffawed, and Veda tensed. "Quiet! Someone might hear you!"

He came to her, still laughing. "I don't care who hears me, Veda. And neither do you."

"You are scandalous!" she mocked through the mirror.

He caressed her bare arms, and a wild thrill momentarily paralyzed her. "Which make me all the more attractive to a girl like you."

She suddenly stiffened, and her eyes grew cold as sleight. "Unhand me!"

He obliged, and she masked her relief. She had heard stories about Teddy Aspan, and believed everyone. He was *not* a gentleman.

Then she raised her head and sniffed. "And now you will leave, or I will scream."

He grinned. "Is that any way to treat an old friend who will be at sea in a few short hours?"

She clipped on an earring and gazed at him perplexedly. "What in heavens are you talking about? You have not reenlisted in the navy?"

He shook his head with a chuckle. "Not quite, though the navy days were some of my happiest."

She lifted a silver brush and eyed him though the mirror. "Your father should only hear such mindless talk!"

Teddy stroked his chin, his wide smile flaunting a set of glistening white teeth. "My father, king of Fifth Avenue! Won't he be sourly surprised?"

"Yes, yes!" she droned, bored, and began fluffing her curls.

He grew strangely serious. "If you want the truth, Veda, I have come to say goodbye...temporarily, of course."

"To my misfortune, I am certain," she sniffed, slipping on white lace gloves.

Then she began fixing the floweret on her dress.

He swung her around and took her into his arms. She saw no danger in his eyes, just determination, and a sudden loneliness which nearly warmed her heart.

"I need to tell someone, Veda. And you're the girl I love, the girl I'll take for my wife. I'm going to Africa, on my father's yacht. There are still diamonds to be had there, and by God, I'm going to find them! The Aspan black sheep is going to make an empire of his own, and I'll be brought home in a box first, before I return without a trunk full of diamonds!"

She took him seriously for a short moment before contempt washed over her again. "Theodore Aspan! You have truly lost your mind *this* time! Diamond mining? You, who have not worked a single day in your life?" She paused and added with a smirk, "And to think you would be presumptuous enough to assume I would marry *you*!"

He was clearly insulted, but masked it with arrogance, "You would be a fool not to, Veda! I could make you the richest woman in New York, with or without my diamonds!"

She glared at him, reaching for her picture hat. "Money is not everything, Theodore Aspan, and at the rate *you* are going, you might soon be disinherited."

He came to her with a sideward grin, "Money isn't everything, Veda? Who's the fool? Look around this room; it is straight from a fairy tale. A canopy bed, a Persian rug, hand crafted dolls from around the world, a trunk full of jewels, and armoires stuffed with clothes, not to mention all you have left behind on Park Avenue. At seventeen, you have learned that money *is* everything, and you will need a very rich man to maintain *your* lifestyle!"

"And I suppose you think you are just that man?" she teased, setting the bonnet on the crown of her head.

"Of course," he shrugged. "Who else?"

Her lips curved to form a thin smile. "You are conceited and empty headed, Theodore Aspan, and I would choose to be an old maid before I consent to marry you!"

He smiled with a gleam in his eyes. "You will marry me, Veda, and you will eat your words."

She chortled, knotting the ribbon of the bonnet beneath her chin. "In your dreams, Mr. Aspan."

Then she gripped her parasol and glided to the door. "Good day."

"Aren't you at least going to kiss me goodbye?" he called after her playfully.

She shifted only her head to see him, wearing a shrewd grin on her beautiful face. "Not until you return with a trunk full of diamonds."

An encouraging farewell it was. It was also a dismissal.

Her hand gripped the knob and she opened the double doors short moments after he had exited via the terrace.

She gasped at the sight of her twin sister in the vestibule. Rose, in a yellow princess style afternoon gown, looked nearly magnificent as Veda. She wore an M. Camille Croissant's coiffure, her rich ebony locks pulled back and scooped upward from the crown of her head. Hers was a softer, more subtle beauty.

"Great stars, Rose! You nearly scared me half to death!"

Rose's eyes roved the perimeter of the room. "Veda, did I hear you speaking with someone?" Her manner was demurely elegant, her voice, whispery rich.

Veda beckoned her inside and closed the door. "It was that scoundrel, Theodore Aspan!"

Rose turned to shock. "How did he get up here?"

Veda frowned, but a hint of adventure gleamed in her eyes. "He climbed the trellis leading to my terrace!"

Rose turned ghost white. "He did not!" Then she whispered a question into her twin's ear.

Veda raised her nose. "He did! But I made it quite clear that I am a proper girl and I would scream blue bloody murder if he did not leave at once."

Rose gripped her hand. "You must tell Father right away!"

Veda shook her head adamantly. "A great deal of good that would do! The scoundrel is confiscating his own father's yacht right now as we speak. He plans to sail to Africa and go diamond mining!"

"*No!*" Rose was horrified.

"Yes! He is dead serious. He has completely lost his mind! And what's more, he is convinced I will marry him when he returns."

Rose gulped. "Why, he is not even Catholic! What would Mother say?"

Veda dismissed the notion with a haughty wave of her hand. "Hardly a concern. I would not give that beast the time of day, much less consent to marry him."

Rose was stupefied. "And what will Mr. Aspan do when he discovers his yacht is missing? And the headlines tomorrow? New York society will be stunned!"

"Yes, but not our problem, Rose dear. We will be lounging here in the gardens of the chateau, lazily sipping lemonade, and reminiscing the events of this glorious day," she paused and went to the window. "Oh, look at it outside! Isn't it just breathtaking? The gardens, the tents, the tables! Heaven itself could not be more beautiful!"

Rose came to her and slipped a gentle arm around her waist. "*It is* beautiful, Veda. We are very fortunate to have such a divine summer home. We have grown up here. It has been like a childhood from a storybook. No matter where we might travel, or what we might do, I will always treasure the happiest moments spent here with you."

Veda inhaled the enchantment. "Oh, do you smell the flowers?" Rose smiled and nodded, mesmerized too.

Veda looked back at her dreamily. "I was imagining my own wedding day, or even yours, for that matter. Can you just picture yourself a bride here at the chateau, draped in satin and lace, walking past aisles and aisles of hundreds of New York's finest sophisticates, the princess of this kingdom for a whole day?"

They were startled by an applause sounding from behind them. They turned and burst into laughter at the sight of Marius, dashing in a black tailcoat and white tie. He was strikingly handsome, with jet black hair and soft brown eyes. He was six-feet tall and pencil slim, a bachelor who had broken many hearts in his decision to wed Miss Dominique Deneuve.

"Well done, Veda. There is just one small problem," he teased with a chuckle.

"Problem?" Her face was now red with embarrassment.

"How can you ever be a bride when you are too fickle to choose yourself a beau?"

She laughed again and went to him, setting his boutonniere to perfection. "Well, that *is* a problem; I admit, Marius. But can I help it if the only handsome and charming bachelor I find worthy happens to be my brother?"

She paused to glance at the crystal mantel clock above the fireplace. "And it breaks my heart to know you will be spoken for in less than an hour."

Marius kissed her hand and pretended to blush. "Do not fret, Veda. There are many fish in the sea." Then his eyes swept past her to Rose, who had been giggling on the opposite side of the room. "And how is my lovely, more reserved sister?"

Rose's blush was genuine. Though beautiful, she never quite knew how to accept a compliment. She came and pecked her brother's cheek, expertly knowing how to shift conversation from herself. "You look smart dapper, Marius. I am so happy for you!"

Still holding Veda's hand in his right grip, Marius took Rose's in his left. And kissing both simultaneously, he remarked, "Dominique has quite a task ahead of her after all the spoiling I have received over the years from both of you."

"Are ye three fixin' to be late for this weddin'? Mr. Marius, ye're supposed to be downstairs receivin' ye guests!" It was the voice of Nanny McBride, the corpulent, Irish born perfectionist of a servant who had been in the family for three generations. She gripped a huge vase, sprouting a plethora of summer blooms.

Veda was electrified. "Flowers, Nanny? From whom?"

Setting them on the vanity, Nanny McBride dried perspiration from her brow and scolded, "They're from Mr. Jacques Deneuve, and I'd appreciate it, Miss Veda, if ye was to tell him that with all the servants tendin' to guests and the kitchen, I had no time to make this delivery! If ye was fixin' to be his bride, that's one thing, but—"

"Oh Nanny!" Veda interrupted as she sashayed to the vanity to sniff the bouquet. "Flowers belong at a wedding!" Then she turned to Marius with a smirk, "Remind me to thank your darling brother-in-law, Marius."

Nanny glared at her disapprovingly. "It should be ye own priority, Missy!"

Veda grimaced. "Priority, indeed! Jacques Deneuve is a bore just like his sister, Dominique!"

She had said this intentionally, but Marius was three steps ahead of her. "Mind your manners, Veda. Remember; Dominique is to be my wife."

Veda sighed with a playful spark in her eyes. "But she hates me!"

Marius laughed. "Perhaps if you were more polite to her, she would appear more personable to you. Why not begin by saying something nice to her for a change?"

Veda teased, "Well, only for you, big brother, I will try."

Marius narrowed his eyes. "I'm going to hold you to your word."

Then he added, smiling back at their sister, "Rose has no problem socializing with Dominique. Why, she is even one of her attendants."

Rose blushed again.

"That is because Rose is too polite for her own good. Why, I do not know where she would be today without me to assert myself for her."

"Veda!" Rose gently admonished. "Well, it is true, Rose, and you—"

"That'll be enough banterin', the three of yees! My job's to see that ye're downstairs on time, and I ain't fixin' to have to answer to *La Madame* Champion! Now scoot out the door, and take ye places! There's a weddin' about to begin!"

"A wedding!" Veda marveled.

"Yes, and I am so nervous, that I have goose bumps everywhere!" Rose added.

Marius, the calm and collected groom, steepled his arms and chimed, "Don't be, dear little sister. Now allow me to escort New York's most ravishing debutantes to the front porch."

He shifted his eyes to Nanny McBride whose plump red cheeks swelled with pride. "Pardon us, Nanny! The Champions are passing!"

Both girls laughed as they marched forward. Veda exclaimed as they sailed through the doorway. "Well put, Marius! Champion is our name, and champions we are!"

Chapter 2

As he lay on the chaise lounge in the sun filled room of the Victorian mansion, Hans Wagner pinched himself to ensure he was not dreaming. He was a handsome young man of twenty; a tall, very thin, blue eyed, platinum haired German who had first stepped foot into America just a day ago. He had come with Rudolph Stern, his employer's son, better known as Rudi, who, despite their social contrasts, happened to be his best friend.

He watched the branches of the blooming maple tree waltz lazily with the early summer wind and became hypnotized by the beauty, the serenity, the very scent of America. And as he meditated, his mind drifted back to that last night in Berlin...

"Take me with you, Rudi," he urged, clad in his footman's uniform in the drawing room of the Stern home. A Brahms' symphony drifted from the ballroom, coupled with the laughter of some fifty guests who had come to bid the prominent Rudolph Stern a temporary farewell. He was to depart the following morning to America where he would study at Harvard in pursuit of a medical degree.

Rudi, dashing in a tailcoat and white tie, shook his head confoundedly.

"But I do not understand, Hans. Why would you want to come to America? There is nothing for you to gain beyond what you already have."

Hans grimaced. "What I have here might soon be lost."

Rudi's eyes narrowed. "What are you talking about? Has my father said anything about dismissing you?"

"Of course not," Hans reassured.

"I would hardly think so. Your mother has been the housemaid for twenty years. Your brother, at ten, is already a page here. You have the prospect of one day becoming the house butler. What more could you expect in America?"

Hans shook his head and closed the French doors behind him. "It is a national issue, Rudi. Can't you see what is happening here?"

Rudi drew a complete blank. "You are making no sense, Hans."

"That is because you are not as abreast as I with world affairs. Sure, you are intelligent, Rudi, and you will be a great doctor, but your mind is so filled with classics, Science and the Torah, that you have not been paying an ounce of attention to the dangers surrounding us, orchestrated by our own people."

Rudi raised an eyebrow and challenged. "I know of no dangers, my friend. Germany and all of Europe for that matter, is finally a safe place. There has not been a major military conflict here in nearly one hundred years."

Hans frowned. "That is the problem! People like you have become too complacent. For years now, Germany and France have been building up their armies and their supply of weapons. It is no coincidence! Such action in a period of long-term peace is reason in itself for suspicion. Can't you realize this?"

Rudi smirked. "I am more apprised of current affairs than you credit me. These efforts of army and weapon building are resulting in alliances among countries. True, the German empire is separated from Russia and the rest of Europe, but the country leaders have assured us the alliances have established a balance of power. So long as we maintain this balance, there is no need for concern."

Hans' jaw tightened. "But you do not understand! What government leaders are not telling us is that they are dissatisfied with the empires they already control. They want more and more territory. That is why they keep expanding. They are using economic and political pressures to take over weaker countries. I may be a servant, but I was fortunate your father saw to it that I was educated. I can smell trouble. It is coming, Rudi, faster than you and most others know."

Rudi gazed into Hans speculatively, considering his words. "And what might you suggest could trigger trouble?"

Hans stroked his chin, satisfied that Rudi was hearing him. "Well, the fact that Germany and Russia both have their eyes on the Balkan states is, in itself, a potential problem. The Russians want it because it would give them access to the Mediterranean. Germany needs it to pass to the Near and Far East. I suspect the clash will come here."

"How?" Rudi was now gravely interested.

"That, I cannot predict. But I will say that the people themselves are fueling the Kaiser. It is happening elsewhere too. Ordinary citizens are suddenly overly patriotic. I see it on the streets, in the stores, in places you do not have the need or opportunity to frequent. People believe Germany can do no wrong. It is provoking the Kaiser to do anything he wants."

Rudi turned white. "Lower your voice! Defamation of the Kaiser could land you in prison!"

Hans' eyes hardened into blue ice. "That is exactly why I want you to take me with you to America."

Rudi shrugged. "But how? This is preposterous. What about your mother? Your brother? You cannot just abandon them!"

Hans insisted, "I have already discussed it with my mother. She will not come. She is a devout German, through and through. Gunther is too young. I could never separate him from our mother. *And*, I could never manage to support him."

"And how will you support yourself?" The words were soft, but piercing.

Hans' face glazed over. There was a look of anticipation, a madness almost, like Rudi had never seen before. "I have my passage money. When we get to America, I will need a place to stay just until I find work."

Rudi observed him for a long, pensive moment. "Did you ever hear the saying that the streets in America are not really paved with gold?"

Hans grinned. "Yes, I hear they are actually lined with horseshit."

"Which means?" Rudi quizzed; his left eyebrow raised.

Another smirk, deeper, fueled by an iron will. "Which means, at the very least, I will find work scooping it up. I hear there is a wealth of it to be had."

And in the bedroom of the Newport mansion now, he smelled the sprightly ocean breeze and reflected on that next morning when he had bidden his mother an emotional farewell. But it was not her tears which cracked his heart so much as the helpless abandonment on his young brother's face.

"Do not fret, my dear brother. We will be united once again, soon."

And as he tousled Gunther's platinum hair, Hans knew his brother's words would haunt him forever. "You will never come back to Germany."

He realized Gunther was quite wise for his ten years. Hans had no plan to return to Germany, at least not for a very long time.

"Are you daydreaming again, my friend?" Rudi asked from across the room. He stood in the doorway, clad, once again, in white tie. Only today, it was to attend the afternoon wedding reception of the son of his Uncle Jacob's friend, Winston Champion. They were long-time members of the Newport Golf and

Yacht Club, and socialized regularly at balls and dinner parties in both Newport and Manhattan.

Like many of the guests, Jacob Stern owned a summer house in Newport, and had arrived the day before to settle into the creature comforts of the ocean-lined paradise. Rudolph, his nephew, had taken residence with him for the summer before he would start Harvard in September.

Being a benign man, and aware there would be very little company for his German nephew in the city while he worked, Jacob consented to welcoming Hans Wagner in his home as well. All the courtesies of both the Madison Avenue brownstone, as well as the Bellevue Avenue mansion were extended to the German born servant. But Jacob Stern was undiscriminating. He admired Hans' intelligence and polished demeanor, if not his poor command of the English language. And he was, after all, Rudi's best friend. It hardly seemed plausible that the handsome young man, with his elegant manners and graceful gait, had been born into peasantry, especially today, when he, himself beamed in white tie, having been added to the Champion guest list.

He sprang from the chaise lounge and came to his friend with a broad smile on his face. "I am just thinking of how happy I am to be in America, and it is all because of you, Rudi. I shall be forever indebted to you."

Rudi gripped his arm, and grew suddenly serious, "You owe me nothing. There is no price tag on friendship. I just hope you will be able to make a success of it, here."

"No need to worry," Hans assured. "I am not going to let a tuxedo disillusion me." Then he paused to admire himself in the mirror, and added, straitening his tie, "Although I must admit, it suits me quite well."

Rudi chuckled. "Modesty was never one of your virtues. If you had to, you would even shovel horse waste with your nose up in the air. You have the ability to elevate anything to an art."

"Then why are you worrying about me, chap?"

Rudi laughed again. "I do not know. Perhaps I should worry more about my own hide, with Jews in the minority at Harvard, and I being a foreigner on top of it!"

Hans soothed as he gripped Rudi's shoulder. "You will make minced meat out of them."

Then he consulted the huge grandfather clock. "Now, let's go. We have a wedding to attend, and I do not know about you, but I am planning to brush up on my two step."

Rudi sent a playful left hook to him. "What are you talking about? Every girl in Berlin knows you have two left feet!"

Hans chortled. "America is the land of opportunity. Today will be a fresh new start."

And they exited blithely, meeting Jacob Stern on the huge wrap around porch. Together they gleamed with the brilliant afternoon sun, as the chauffeur came up the flower lined drive.

Chapter 3

The pipe organ at St. Mary's church, and the pair of trumpeters, resounded the first chords of the wedding march at the stroke of high noon. Dominique Deneuve made an exquisite bride, bedecked in layers of jeweled satin, velvet and lace. Her golden locks were stacked delicately upon her head, complemented by a diamond tiara with a history of more than one hundred years and five generations. Her fingertip veil was finished with white crystal lace. Her bouquet was a profusion of stephanotis' and white-collar lilies, and her train ran half the length of the cathedral like edifice.

Veda sat beside her proud parents in the first pew, awed by the sea of white gladioli and tea roses strewn about in splendid arrangements. *La Madame* Champion looked majestic in a formal afternoon tunic dress of soft rose silk, her black hair swept into a stately chignon, her diamond accessories appraised at a king's ransom. Her husband, Winston, was becoming in a black tailcoat, his silver hair receding at the temples, his handlebar mustache expertly trimmed. More than five hundred guests were packed into the candlelit, incense burning church, while the remaining seven hundred non-Catholics were masterfully tended to at the chateau.

Winston himself had been raised Protestant, but agreed to convert on a trip to Paris some twenty-five years earlier where he had been charmed by the beauty and elegance of his prominent wife. *La Madame* Champion had been born Jacqueline DuBois, the distinguished daughter of French aristocrats, and was educated at the most noteworthy schools in the country. Her parents, owners of a Parisian Palais, a beachfront maisonette on the famous Riviera, and a summer chateau in Verdun, could trace their origins back to the French throne. They were, to say the least, displeased when their daughter had chosen to marry an American and abandon her motherland.

But when news of her prominent status in New York society had traveled across the waters, Monsieur and Madame DuBois experienced a change of heart.

Their granddaughters, Veda and Rose, had spent the last three years of their education abroad, and traveled each summer from the eminent finishing school on Lake Leman, Geneva, to the French country chateau in Verdun, sur Meuse.

There were also many holidays abroad, during which the three grandchildren were introduced to the highlights of every noteworthy European city. There were cruises to Egypt and the Far East as well, a living education in culture and history, mostly through which, to their grandparents' chagrin, the children were dreadfully bored.

They sat, Monsieur and Madame DuBois, in the pew behind the Champions. He was dressed in black tailcoat. *She* wore a black broadcloth gown and a triple strand of hand-crafted pearls which sat exquisitely on the black bodice, their round diamond and sapphire clasp matching the jeweled tiara on her crown.

The Cardinal officiated the High Mass after which horse-drawn carriages transported the nuptial couple, their attendants, and both families back to Chateau La Mer. They passed the Vanderbilt's sun caressed Breakers mansion and the palaces standing in their regal splendor along Bellevue Avenue. The Astor's Beachwood, the Vanderbilt's Marble House, and the homes of other prominent gentry greeted them like castles in a fairy tale from an era gone by.

A line of trumpeters sounded as they turned onto the cobblestone drive leading to the imperial front yard. A sea of people waved to them, a congregation of sophisticates, an arena of New York and New England society…blue bloods, everywhere.

"Look at everyone cheering, Mother! It is like we are royalty!" Veda exclaimed from the carriage.

La Madame Champion patted her hand and replied, coolly superior, "You must maintain yourself, Veda, darling. Such emotional outbursts are frowned upon. Just smile and wave. Such is all that is expected of you."

But the excitement of it all had sparked a passion in Veda not even her mother's chiding could control. "Oh, but Mother! The people! The fountains! The music! I have never seen the chateau more beautiful, more alive! It's like—"

She would have jumped from the carriage had her father not restrained her in the next moment. "Come, now, Blossom. It is just a wedding. What might we expect when *you* are a bride?"

She gulped, electrified. "Oh, I can hardly wait, Father! If it is anything like this!"

From the corner of her right eye, she caught a glimpse of her grandmother's disapproving frown. But this too could not stifle Veda's fervor. Her entire childhood flashed before her eyes, the dignitaries who had attended dinner parties and balls in her parents' homes, her schoolmates, playmates and admirers. Seventeen years gleamed like gold, and though she had always been noted for her *joie de vie*, Veda was never happier to be alive.

Marius and Dominique had been riding in the carriage before them, and were the first to emerge onto the steps of the imposing, columned front porch. Veda was supposed to permit the elders in her carriage to exit next, but paid no mind to propriety, and sprang forth ebulliently.

A swarm of young men encircled her instantly, and she expertly brushed them off with casual trifles, coupled with graceful waves of her hand and masterful pleasantries which artfully shifted her from one to the next.

"Marius!" she cried out, strangely envious to see him totally consumed with affection for his new bride. "I just want to be the first to say you are the most dashing groom Newport has ever seen!"

Then she turned from his beaming face to the forced smile on that of her new sister-in-law. "And Dominique, you look darling in your wedding gown! Is it imported?"

Dominique did everything to remain cordial to Veda whom she had long regarded as shallow and patronizing, "It was not. It was custom made and featured, if you recall at the Waldorf's spring bridal show."

Veda emitted a pompous chuckle, feigning a bashful, gloved hand to her lips. "Why, of course! Pardon me for the social faut pas!" then she paused and flashed her brother a teasing wink. "Marius told me I should say something nice to you today, and so I will. You are, without a doubt, Dominique, the most fortunate girl in New York, if not the entire country, to have won my brother's hand."

Dominique was clearly seething. Marius placed a comforting arm around her waist while discreetly kicking Veda's ankle. "We are mutually fortunate for one another."

Veda giggled, waving a perfumed wrist and spinning her parasol in the curve of the other. "You have always had a magical way with words, Marius!" Then her eyes danced back to Dominique. "Marius could charm the devil, himself. It is beyond any of us, how much of what he says is…"

"Here you are, Veda, the most charming, *eligible* young woman present!" It was Chester Worthington. He had said this as a mannerly gesture before the bride, though nearly everyone knew he had been crazy about Veda since the debutante's ball.

He was twenty, and striking. His short, black hair matched the color of his piercing eyes. A set of gleaming white teeth complemented the broad smile set into an olive-colored face for which his mother's Grecian blood was responsible. His father, heir to the Worthington steel empire, had been American born, and could trace his English ancestors back to the Revolution. But Chester's dark, handsome looks had been solely inherited from his mother's lineage, which worked, for the most part, to his advantage.

"Chester Worthington!" Veda flirted. "What a surprise it is to see *you* here! I would have thought, for sure, you would be off somewhere supervising one of your father's steel plants and breaking some poor girl's heart in your spare hours, rather than passing time at something so pure and simple as a wedding on Bellevue Avenue!"

Chester kissed her hand with an amused grin on his face, and a sinister gleam in his eyes. "No place is simple where *you* are to be found, Veda."

She guffawed, "If I did not know you better, I would be downright blinded and swept off my feet by your deadly charm and devilish good looks!"

Chester edged closer, holding her violet eyes in his. "Well, how about offering me an opportunity to redeem my reputation by granting me the honor of the first dance?"

"Why, I would just love to..." Veda crooned and consulted her dance card. "But I am afraid you will just have to wait your turn. My grandfather has been assigned my first dance, and *you*, Chester dear, are number three."

He winked at her with a sudden flippancy in his demeanor. "I will count the seconds until the honor is bestowed upon me."

She charmingly batted her oblique lashes over her violet limpid pools. "You certainly have sugar on your tongue, today, Chester, though I am sure you say such things to all the girls."

Still, his black eyes remained locked to hers. It was as if he were dissecting her, and although Veda silently agreed that Chester was quite handsome, she grew slightly uncomfortable, and was relieved when her grandfather interrupted them.

"Veda, *cher*, I must escort you to the dance floor now. The orchestra is about to begin." His French was eloquent as poetry, his manner, regal.

Veda smiled and slipped her milk white arm through his. "Why of course, *Grand-pere!*" Then she shifted her eyes back to Chester. "Excuse me; I must dance with the most gallant gentleman I know."

On his arm, she sashayed through the gardens, past a sea of admiring guests and garland lined tables heaping with culinary delights. Festivities were well underway; waiters in starched uniforms were serving *hors d'oeuvres* and cocktails, expertly tending to each sophisticate's needs. Strolling minstrels were everywhere; laughter and splendor abounded.

The marble terrace just off the ballroom served as the dance floor, and the large French gazebo directly beyond, housed the twenty-five-piece orchestra.

"Well, I must admit that you are quite a dancer, *Grand-pere!*" Veda exclaimed in perfect French as he twirled her about the floor to the tunes of a Viennese waltz. She, herself, was a pro and relished the attention they were receiving.

The gray-eyed, white-haired man crooned with a broad smile on his face. "Ah, but it is the *mademoiselle* one leads who causes the *monsieur* to shine, *ma cher*. Your dancing is flawless as your beauty."

Veda genuinely blushed. A compliment of such grandeur from a gentleman of his standing was not casually received.

"I am so glad you and *Grand-mere* made a special trip from Paris to be here. Marius' wedding would not have been complete without you."

Pierre DuBois nodded endearingly and held Veda closer as he spoke gently into her ear, "*Grand-mere* and I would go to the end of the world for any of you, *ma cher*."

Veda melted in the safety of his arms, and wished, in that moment, she could remain a girl forever.

The end of the waltz saddened her for the first time that day. Her grandfather kissed her cheek and whispered, "*Merci*, Veda, *ma cher*," before joining his lovely bride of fifty years for the next dance.

"You are an extraordinary dancer! I can hardly wait my turn!" Jacques Deneuve commented from behind her, and eagerly consulted his dance card. Veda swung around gracefully, and offered the handsome, brown-haired, green-eyed Princetonian a gloved hand which he graciously received.

"Why if it isn't Jacques Deneuve! We are nearly relatives now, and this is the first opportunity we have had to talk all day!"

He held her eyes with his lips fixed upon her hand until she artfully slipped it away. "Which makes it all the more pleasurable, Veda. Good things are worth waiting for."

Veda chortled flirtatiously, "You certainly do know how to make a girl melt, Jacques! And to think a minute ago, I was almost upset with you."

"Upset? Why?" Though attractive and intellectually gifted, Jacques was overwhelmingly innocent and naïve to the teasing of a beautiful girl such as Veda.

She lowered her eyes, feigning demureness.

"Well, as I already said, you have been ignoring me all day and after those beautiful flowers you had sent!"

He gulped momentarily at a loss for words. "But, Veda, there was no way I could have approached you at the church. You were sitting opposite us, and then, outside—"

"Here you are, Jacques! I have been searching for you everywhere! I believe we are to share this minuet. You are on my dance card."

It was the voice of Victoria Windsor, the blue-blooded, snobbish daughter of a prominent railroad magnet. She despised Veda, and adored Jacques along with about a dozen other girls present that day.

He looked at the blond beauty nervously, then shifted apologetic eyes back to Veda.

"I am sorry. Please excuse me, Veda. I look forward to speaking with you again later."

Gripping his hand, Victoria sniffed with a thin smile. "Pleasure to see you again, Veda."

Aware that the Vassar honor student was still seething with envy over her having been chosen debutante of the year, Veda raised her nose and rubbed salt into the wound. "The pleasure, as always, is all *yours*, Ms. Windsor."

She sailed away triumphantly, twirling her parasol over her right shoulder. "My, if looks could kill, Veda! What did you say to her?" Rose asked when her sister came to her side. She had been observing the scene from a distance, and marveled, once again, at her twin's ability to both charm and repel.

Veda grimaced. "Oh, that snooty prude! Who cares about her!"

Rose smiled. "Jacques Deneuve certainly does not. Why his face practically dropped to the dance floor when she interrupted you."

Veda glared back at them.

"Thank heavens she did! He was boring me to tears!"

Rose chuckled. "That is just like you to shun the man over whom most girls swoon!"

Veda rolled her eyes. "Well, they can swoon their way right over to him and keep him occupied all day! He is a drip!" Then she paused and added as her lips curved into an impish grin, "Even if he is terribly good looking."

Rose burst into laughter. "There! Even you admit it!"

Veda took her twin's arm and laughed too. "Yes, but only to you, Rose, my darling. And do not *dare* breathe a word!"

Rose's soft, gray eyes twinkled. "My lips are sealed. When have you ever known me to betray a secret?"

Veda smiled and gripped her hand as they walked. "True…If the world only knew half of what I have confided in you over the years…" she stopped and her eyes danced as she inspected the festivities surrounding them. "I am absolutely parched. Let's have some claret cup."

"Lemonade for me, *and*, I suggest the same for you." Rose advised as they started toward one of the countless linen clothed flower lined refreshment tables.

"How boring!" Veda protested, her eyes still fluttering.

Rose teased, pouring them each a glass of iced, cold liquid, "Boring, but ladylike, my dear." And she clinked her crystal glass against Veda's before taking a long, graceful sip.

Veda finished hers in a single, hearty gulp and looked beyond them toward the water, her hair billowing in the summer wind.

"Look at all the yachts, Rose! It reminds me of the French Riviera! Do you remember?"

"How could I forget! With all the mischief you caused—"

Veda interrupted her, suddenly paralyzed, "Rose, who is *that*?"

Rose drew a blank. "Who, Veda? Honestly! I cannot keep up with you! Why, you were just speaking about…"

Veda's eyes widened. "Over there, Rose! That blond-headed man, standing next to father!"

Rose turned her face toward him and was immobilized too. "Why, I do not know. I have never seen him before."

To their amazement, the girls realized that the tall, strikingly handsome young man was smiling at them. It was Hans Wagner, a stunning portrait of poise and dignity. His platinum hair glowed beneath the afternoon sunshine and his blue eyes sparkled with zest.

Veda fanned herself playfully. "I am nearly breathless, Rose, darling! Do catch me if I faint!"

Rose lowered her eyes demurely. "He is looking right at us, Veda! You are making a spectacle!"

"Oh, Rose, really! This is no time to be coy! We must greet the gentleman and extend him the courtesies of our home."

Rose was horrified. "Approach him? Never!"

"Great balls of fire, Rose! Come, now!" Then she gripped her sister's hand and tugged her forward.

They stopped before their father who was speaking with the bearded Jacob Stern. Rose's face was beet red and Veda batted her lashes at the dashing stranger once, before interrupting her father's conversation.

"Father, you must mind your dance card. It will be our turn to waltz shortly. Hello, Mr. Stern," she added, artfully shifting her eyes to him.

He smiled. "Good afternoon, Veda and Rose. The two of you become more beautiful each time I see you." And he received both their hands.

"Here is your claret cup, Uncle Jacob." It was the voice of Rudi who had approached them from behind. He was tall and lanky, with curly black hair and hazel eyes. He spoke with a heavy accent, though his English was perfect, and although he was not very attractive, there was something quite dignified and scholarly about him.

To Veda's surprise, he *and* the blond man were fascinated with *Rose*!

Jacob Stern accepted the beverage with a grateful nod, and took Rudi's arm.

"Ladies, permit me to introduce my nephew Rudolph Stern, who has recently arrived from Germany to spend the summer in New York before he begins Harvard in September. Rudolph, the Champion twins, Veda and Rose."

Rudi's eyes were fixed upon Rose, who was blushing so hard that perspiration beaded her face. He received her hand first, electrified by her meek, girlish beauty. "It is a pleasure, indeed, to make your acquaintance."

His eyes brushed past Veda and then back to Rose. He was clearly swooning, and for the first time in her life, Veda was visibly envious of her sister.

"And this…" Jacob turned next toward the object of both girls' interest, "Is Hans Wagner, Rudolph's friend, who has accompanied him from Germany, also to spend the summer in New York."

And hopefully eternity! Hans thought as his eyes locked with Rose's. *She is the most beautiful girl I have ever seen. So modest. So graceful. So innocent.*

Veda waited for him to notice her, but his eyes never left Rose's. He bowed gracefully and kissed Rose's gloved hand. Then, out of politeness, he received Veda's though his gaze remained fixed upon Rose.

Veda's heart cracked. Though her hand had been kissed by hundreds of men, never had one's mere touch electrified her so profoundly as his.

And before either of them could say anything. Hans turned to Winston Champion and asked respectfully, "May I...em...dance wit you daughter?"

His poor command of the English language made him all the more appealing. Rose could not believe her ears. *And neither could Veda!*

Winston Champion nodded his approval, and moments later, Rose and the dapper foreigner were stopping traffic on the dance floor.

"Your daughter is quite a dancer, Winston." Jacob Stern observed as the pair glided to a Brandenburg medley.

Winston Champion beamed proudly and took Veda's hand. "Both my daughters have had the fortune of being schooled in the arts."

As her face sank, Veda wondered how her father could pass such a casual remark when her whole world had crumbled. They looked beautiful, the two of them, dancing blithely, smiling and staring into one another's eyes.

Veda's heart was screaming out the injustice of it all, but the protests were useless.

"And may I have the pleasure of escorting your second lovely daughter to the dance floor?" Rudi politely questioned; his accent eloquently rich.

"Why, certainly, young man," Winston Champion answered, awash with pride. Of all the debutantes and sophisticates present, Veda and Rose were the main attractions.

But Veda's lips curled downward as she regretfully watched her beautiful sister dance with the man with whom she had suddenly fallen in love.

"I do not believe you are on my dance card," she said in an icy monotone and walked away, dragging her heart to the refreshment table.

Winston and Jacob were dumbfounded, but Rudolph Stern hardly cared. His offer was a mere gesture. He was still arrested by Rose, who, in her yellow gown floating about the dance floor, looked like a princess who had stepped from a fairy tale.

Veda ladled out a generous portion of claret cup, and flinched after her first sip. Then she swung off the rest in a swift gulp, trembling as the alcohol flowed through her veins.

Her eyes sank to the white roses spraying from lead crystal vases, and she fought back tears as they wilted with everything else that had seemed so vibrant mere moments ago.

"Is there a reason why you have chosen spirits over a dance with a becoming foreigner?" It was the teasing voice of Chester Worthington who scooped out his sixth helping. He swayed as he spoke, slowly losing his dignity as drunkenness set in.

Veda glared. "*You* are inebriated!" And she sadly turned her vision back to the dance floor.

Chester snickered after a long, greedy sip. "At least I am having a good time, Veda."

"And what is that supposed to mean?" she snapped back at him, tearing her eyes from the happy couple.

"Perhaps you can answer that question." he mocked, infuriating her.

"For your information, the reason I am not dancing is because Teddy Aspan is not here! I follow my dance card religiously; unlike other people I know!" And she glared back at Rose.

"Are you referring to your sister who is dancing with the dapper German you can't take your eyes off?"

"You are revolting!" she snarled and stormed away.

"Now, wait a minute!" he called after her just as the music stopped.

Moments later, the orchestra broke into a fox trot, and Chester awkwardly came to her, flashing his own dance card before her pouting face. "You're too pretty to look like this." His words were sincere, but Veda was still steaming.

"Oh, why don't you just go away!"

"I can't. We are to have this dance. See for yourself," he paused, and added with a gleam in his black eyes, "You *did* say you follow your dance card religiously."

Veda cracked a thin smile. "It is the devil in you that charms me when I really should hate you, Chester!"

"Oh, no, Veda," he enthused, taking her arm. "I'm too good looking to hate." And he led her to the dance floor.

"Conceited, you are!" she squealed to attract Hans' Wagner's attention, but he was on a cloud she could not begin to reach.

She danced magnificently, if not her partner. When sober, Chester was a master of all steps, but now, he paled.

"You should have seen the old man's face when he discovered that Teddy Aspan had run off with his yacht. You were at church. There was quite a clamor. I thought old man Aspan would jump into the bay and swim after the devil," Chester chortled as they danced.

"Do not make a joke of it, Chester! Teddy was plain out his mind to do such a nasty thing!"

"Aw, common, Veda. It makes him all the more interesting. Look at all these boring stuffed shirts here. Teddy Aspan may have millions, but at least you can have a great time with him. *And*, he has guts!"

Veda frowned. "You run on like an empty-headed fool, idolizing that renegade! He does not have millions; his father does. And at this point he would be better off shipwrecked than to return home!"

"Do you know that you are more beautiful when you are angry, Veda?" he commented, slowing his pace to clumsy twists.

"I have never heard anything so ridiculous, Chester. And straighten yourself up! You are beginning to look as drunk as you sound!"

"Don't you believe me?" he asked with wide, playful eyes.

"I never hold faith in a single word you utter."

"Now, why not?" he flirted, feigning sadness.

Veda raised her nose. "Because bees with honey in their mouths have sharp stingers in their tails."

Then she gracefully turned and sashayed back to the refreshment table, leaving Chester with his mouth agape. She froze as she scooped out another helping of claret cup. To her surprise, Rose was now dancing with Rudolph Stern and Hans Wagner had somehow disappeared.

"Veda, I am so sorry for before. I just could not be rude to Victoria, our fathers being friends and all." Jacques was red faced and choking on his words.

Veda took a long sip and eyed him with disdain. "I am sure it had nothing to do with her being a Vassar girl, and wealthier than the Russian Czar."

The claret cup had loosened her tongue. Her bitterness was a mask for her own envy. Although school held little interest for her, because of its reputation,

Veda wanted to go to Vassar in the worst way, but her mother would not hear of it.

"Fine Catholic girls attend Georgetown University," the French aristocrat maintained, and that was that. Also, whereas her father was quite affluent, his fortune as a bank owner and president was regarded as 'modest' by other New York tycoons, namely, Victoria Windsor's father. At seventeen, in a world where social status meant everything, Veda was inordinately class conscious.

Jacques was clearly startled. "Veda, are you all right?"

She finished her drink and clattered the cup on the table. "I am fine, Jacques, magnificent, as a matter of fact."

Then she paused and questioned guardedly, "Why do you ask?"

Jacques shrugged. "I just never heard you speak this way before."

She smiled coquettishly and her eyes danced again. "That is obviously because you have never paid me much attention."

He gulped guiltily. "Veda, if it seems that way to you, it is only because I am very shy, at least in the presence of someone so beautiful as you."

She stared into his eyes. They were deep, earnest, and filled with love.

How correct Rose had been. Any girl here would have swooned as he voiced such sentiments, but she had little regard for them. If only Hans Wagner were to speak and act this way…

"I love you, Veda," he vowed, taking her hand. "I always have. I always will."

Something inexplicable about him touched her for a fleeting moment and her face broke into a smile. "Those are mighty powerful words, Jacques. How do I know they are coming from your heart and not just stemming from a shallow schoolboy crush?"

He clenched his jaws and edged closer to her. His eyes deepened into green canyons. "I could not be more serious, Veda. And later, I am going to prove it to you."

She waved away the notion with a chuckle. "If you think I will kiss you, you are unquestionably mistaken."

"Veda, may I have a word with you?" They were the icy words of her grandmother spoken in superb French.

"Why, certainly, *Grand-mere*," Veda replied casually, though the stone expression on Madame DuBois' snow white face sent a freezing chill up her spine. "Excuse me, Jacques," she added and took her grandmother's stiff arm.

"You are making a complete spectacle of yourself *and* your parents!" Madame DuBois hissed as she led Veda to a shaded corner of the garden. "Where is your dignity, the propriety you have been taught? You are acting like a low born fool, drinking and flirting openly in public! You must mind yourself and remember who you are!"

Veda burst into laughter. "Oh, *Grand-mere*! Is that all? You truly had me worried for a moment!"

"Veda, mind yourself!" Madame DuBois repeated, her nostrils flared, her gray eyes blazing.

But Veda made light of it, "*Grand-mere*, really! Do be more American! It is not at all like Europe, with all those meaningless rules about how girls and women should act." Then she paused and questioned with raised brows, "Haven't you heard anything about the Suffrage Movement here?"

Madame DuBois froze. Even in this furious instant, she looked queenly, her head lifted, her diamond tiara sparkling beneath the rays of the afternoon sunshine. "I shall speak to your mother about your behavior," she maintained, glaring down her nose.

Veda stroked her breast and chortled. "Oh, now, why would you do that, *Grand-mere*? If you would report anyone to Mother, it should be Rose. Imagine her dancing with strange men who have not even been assigned to her dance card! Now *that*, I declare, is an ultimate breach of formality. Would you not say?"

Madame DuBois eyed her disapprovingly. "Consider yourself warned," she huffed and all ninety pounds of her turned away with the might of a battleship.

Veda laughed her way to the champagne fountain as her sparkling eyes searched through the crowd to catch a glimpse of Hans Wagner. But the sea of merry guests obscured any hint of him.

She raised a crystal glass and with an artful sweep of her hand, set it under the pouring bubbly.

The first sip pleased her. Champagne went down much smoother than claret cup. She acknowledged admirers with smiles and nods of dismissal which seemed to murmur. "Do not approach me, I am not interested."

But one defiant soul was Chester Worthington who staggered back to her and reached a swaying hand under the fountain. "It is so cool and refreshing. And look at the foam. It's like a bubble bath; makes you want to jump right in!"

She frowned and handed him one hundred dollars' worth of crystal. "If you are going to drink yourself into oblivion, Chester, at least have the dignity to use a glass!"

Then she sighed disgustedly when it slipped from his hand and shattered at their feet. In seconds, a pair of servants rushed over and swept the broken glass away.

"You are absolutely pathetic, Chester!"

He smiled back at her and slurred, "But you must admit I am very cute!"

She finished her champagne and refilled the glass. "The only thing I can admit is that you are making a complete fool of yourself, and mortifying your parents!"

He frowned and loosened his tie. "My parents are too busy hobnobbing to pay me any concern." He sounded like a bowery bum now, and it revolted her.

"How can someone so unpolished as you ever expect to inherit your father's empire?"

He snatched her glass and swung off the bubbly in a swift gulp. "I will inherit it, Veda, *and* I'll marry *you*!"

She guffawed. "That will be the day, Chester, my dear! You have so much alcohol swimming in your brain right now, that delusion has become your middle name!"

He edged closer. The stench of his breath nearly felled her.

"Laugh now, Veda, but one of these days, I'm gonna slip a diamond band over this pretty little finger and do you know why? 'Cause we are alike; predators, both of us." And he pantomimed a bite.

Veda pushed him aside. "Excuse me! You are beneath contempt!" Then she glided past him, her eyes peeled in hopeless search of Hans.

Dinner was served promptly at five. Veda was all too glad that her parents and grandparents were seated at the dais with Marius, his new bride, and their attendants. If her grandmother had kept her promise, her mother's silent chides across the table would have been like cannon blasts in her ears.

She sat with her Aunt Mae, Winston's widowed sister, and her three cousins from Maine. There were also distant relatives from Virginia where Winston's family settled when they had immigrated to America nearly one hundred fifty years ago. She nibbled at her pheasant under glass and made polite conversation with everyone, though she knew they disliked her and they bored her to tears.

She only wished she could be speaking with Rose who was perched at the dais like a stunning princess to her mother's right.

Strolling minstrels entertained them throughout the meal. White gloved waiters doted over everyone and rolling bar carts offered free flowing spirits.

Veda indulged in a glass of red wine, ignoring the disapproving stares of her relatives.

Who cares, anyway? This is my home, my brother's wedding, and unlike them, I am having myself a grand time!

Her heart rose when she spied Hans Wagner sitting beside Rudolph and Jacob Stern far in the distance. Her eyes remained peeled to him and she wondered with mounting hope if he noticed her too.

Why is he interested in Rose over me? True, she is beautiful, but I... and then it came to her. *Of course, he cares for me! But Rose is the softer touch, more approachable. Maybe he was afraid that if he had asked me to dance, I might have said no. That is it! Why did I not realize it before?*

"Excuse me," she said, and dabbed her lips with a linen napkin.

She rose at the same moment the orchestra resumed playing, inviting guests back to the dance floor with tunes of Tchaikovsky. She was making her way across the yard toward Hans Wagner's table when her father's melodic voice stifled her in her tracks.

"Blossom, where might you be off to? I have been more mindful of my dance card than you, perhaps."

Veda blushed with a sheepish reply, "Oh, Father! Is this our dance?"

He came to her with raised brows and love gleaming in his dark eyes. "I am afraid it is, my dear...that is, if you have not more important business to attend."

It was as if he had read her mind, and she masked her embarrassment with a wide smile. "Now, Father, you know there is nothing more important to me than a dance with you!"

Then she slipped her arm through his, hoping Hans was watching. They were a graceful pair, though the dance floor and everyone on it seemed to spin like a merry-go-round now that the spirits had fully settled into her bloodstream.

"Are you enjoying yourself, Blossom?"

She adored him. Though a bit rounded at the waist, he was still handsome, his smile generous as his heart, his eyes, zestful as his manner. His handle bar mustache was his trademark, and still, to this day, when they were alone, Veda enjoyed shaping it with her fingers like molding clay.

"Oh, yes, Father! I truly am! We have such a beautiful home. This wedding hardly seems real!"

Winston Champion smoothed his daughter's lovely ebony curls, and she cooed as he spoke. "Ah, but it is quite real, my dear. We have much for which to be thankful. It has been a beautiful life for all of us."

As they waltzed, Veda closed her eyes and took a deep, exhilarated breath. "Oh, Father, if I had just one wish, it would be to stop time and capture this day, this moment forever!"

He observed her endearingly. "You are still very much a child, Veda, my dear. The clock of time never stops. All good things must come to an end in order to give birth to new beginnings."

"Good ones, we hope, Father," she enthused, electrified by his touch, his strength, his scent.

He nodded and nestled her head in his chest as they danced. "We hope and we pray."

The rich green tree tops seemed to sway with the tunes of the music and Veda observed them with wonder in her eyes. The waltz came to a placid end and she found herself embracing her father as guests pranced the dance floor in search of their next partners.

"Excuse me, Mr. Champion," Jacques Deneuve's voice chimed with the first chords of Stravinsky.

"Yes, Jacques?" Winston asked blithely, and Veda uttered a subtle sigh of sadness as she and her father separated.

"If I may impose, sir, I am scheduled to have this dance with Miss Veda." He flashed his dance card, beaming. "I have waited for this moment all day."

Winston chuckled, offering his daughter's hand, "And you shall have it, my fine young man. Enjoy."

And with that, he disappeared, leaving Veda positioned in Jacques' arms. "Jacques, you are quite a charmer," she teased as they circled the dance floor, her head spinning with the scenery.

"But it is true, Veda," he impressed seriously. "I really meant it."

"Meant what?" He was so dashing, and she, so charmed, that for a fleeting moment, Hans Wagner had nearly slipped from her mind.

"That I have been waiting all day to dance with you." He was starched and serious. It was the first time she had known a smile to run away from his face.

Veda flirted, "If you keep sprinkling me with sugar, Jacques, I am just certain I will transform into a pumpkin by nightfall."

"As long as I am here beside you, I don't care if we both turn to stone," he cooed in her ear and held her closer as she did her best to edge away. Jacques was genuinely in love, and it threatened her.

"I believe a pumpkin would be better," she said shakily, wishing the dance would end.

She was delighted when a Strauss waltz came to her rescue and the dance floor cleared to permit her parents to share a duet.

"Aren't they magnificent?" she marveled as Winston and *La Madame* Champion graced the floor. Her mother was a queenly sight, her chignon splendid as it had been that morning, her soft rose dress capturing the essence of the season, subtly managing to singularize her from the rest.

"She is so elegant!" Veda gaped. "I hope to be *just* like her some day!"

She was drinking in the vision of perfection, a woman of culture and integrity, a portrait of grace and elegance, always poised, calm, cool, and controlled.

Jacques took her hand and looked down at her endearingly. "And I hope to be the man dancing with you."

His words cast a film over the scene, and she slipped her hand away from his, whispering, "Excuse me."

As she retreated, he wondered what he had said wrong.

She smiled her way through the crowd, reaching deep into herself for every last ebb of self-command finishing school had instilled as the yard spun before her eyes.

She entered the house through the ballroom where waiters fussed over grandiose Venetian tables soon to be wheeled outside with bombastic splendor.

She proceeded to the powder room and sat at the vanity for a long moment, waiting for the world to stop spinning. Rose appeared as she began powdering her nose, and she smiled through the mirror from where she sat, ashamed of the pang of envy which cut at her heart.

"Well, if I might be so bold, I will declare that you have certainly made yourself scarce since your dance with the *foreigner*!"

Rose came and sat next to her, folding the skirt of her yellow gown neatly over the vanity stool.

"Veda, that is certainly a change of heart. If I recall correctly, you were swooning over him." And she, too, started to powder her nose.

Veda sniffed. "I have never heard of anything so ridiculous. I swoon over no one!"

Rose turned to her with a teasing gleam in her lovely gray eyes. "Really? Am I speaking to the same girl who cried so melodramatically, 'catch me if I faint'?"

Veda stiffened and raised her chin. "It was the heat which had gotten the best of me. That is all." And she added after a short pause, "So, he was quite a dancer; do you admit? Even if he had not been assigned to your dance card."

Rose's eyes enlarged in amazement. "Veda, if I did not know you better, I would say you are jealous!"

Veda laughed, feeling her face redden. "Jealous, am I? Now that is the understatement of the day!"

Rose grinned. "Good. Because I have promised him the next two dances." *Now*, Veda was snow white.

Rose guffawed. "*There!* I caught you! You *are* jealous!" Veda surrendered. "Rose, you are a devil in sheep's clothing!"

Rose winked and finished powdering her nose. "No, I am an angel who can read your every thought."

Veda masked a smile. "Well then, if you are a mind reader, Rose, dear, tell me what I am thinking now."

Rose, too, enjoyed to banter.

"You are wondering why the room is swaying, when, actually, you have overindulged in spirits, against my advisement, I might add."

Veda tensed. "If I have, it is your fault!"

"My fault? Why?"

"Because you have been ignoring me!"

Rose laughed again. "Oh, Veda, you have had half of New York at your feet all day. I would have been lucky to say two words to you after I had danced with Mr. Wagner."

Veda's heart rose at the sound of him, though she feigned ignorance. "Is that his name?"

Rose observed her suspiciously. "Yes, don't you recall?"

Veda shook her head snobbishly. "Hardly...and where is he from?" she added, slipping off her picture had to fluff her curls.

Rose saw the playful glint in her twin's eyes. "I am not falling into your web, Veda. Of course, you remember."

Veda set the hat perfectly on her head and tied it again. There was a short silence before she lowered her guard, and, with the alacrity of a child, shifted her body to face her twin. "All right, then, just tell me! Was he as handsome up close when your faces nearly touched?"

Rose blushed. "He was even handsomer! But we could hardly communicate. He speaks very little English."

Veda rolled her eyes impishly. "With such a dashing partner, *who* except *you*, Rose would care about speaking?"

Rose stiffened. "Mind yourself, sister dear! You really *have* overindulged today!"

Veda stood and batted her lashes. "I am merely having a good time." Then she slipped on her gloves. "Now, come. We would not want to miss Marius and his bore of a bride cut their wedding cake."

"Be good," Rose cautioned, coming to her side.

It was twilight when they returned to the garden where Marius and Dominique were cutting the magnificent wedding cake. Even Veda had to admit they were a sight to behold beneath the burnt auburn sky, silhouetted against the sun setting on the distant horizon. The magical crepuscule cast an orchid iridescence over the calm water and caused the anchored yachts to sparkle like pearls.

"Can I...em...have this dance?"

He had come up from behind them. Veda felt her heart skip a beat. Hans Wagner was clearly the most striking human being she had ever encountered. He stood in majestic splendor, his blue eyes twinkling, the front of his platinum hair falling over his forehead.

The orchestra played Mozart, but Veda only heard rejection resonate in her ears. Again, he was speaking to Rose who seemed a bit uneasy after the conversation moments before.

"Perhaps," Rose stammered, shifting her eyes to her twin. "Perhaps Veda might care to dance."

Veda was red with embarrassment. She wanted to crawl into a sheltered corner in that humbling moment, but armored herself fast and declined with a smile. "Yes, I would, Rose, and I have already promised this one to Jacques Deneuve. Excuse me."

Rose examined her questioningly until she disappeared into the throng of guests who were now sipping dessert wines and cordials.

"In that case..." she said, turning back to the striking German who was feasting upon her beauty with his fabulous blue eyes. "I would be delighted to oblige."

Her whispery voice took his own breath away and she could feel his strong body tremble as he ushered her to the dance floor.

"Jacques, will you dance with me?" Veda firmly questioned, feeling a volcano erupt within her.

Jacques, who had been charming three debutantes, set down his claret cup and nodded with an ecstatic smile on his lips. "Why, it would be my pleasure, Miss Champion."

He bowed to the glaring young ladies and added. "Excuse me."

Then he took Veda's arm and proudly escorted her until she tensed and finally froze. "What is it, dear?" he asked with deep concern, hardly aware that her eyes were riveted on Rose and the man who had both captured and broken her heart in one short day.

"I do not believe I feel much like dancing."

His face went blank. "But you just said—"

She took a deep, pained breath. "I know what I said, but..." And there, glided Rose in the arms of a beaming prince. "I...I feel faint. There are just too many people...too much..." Hans and Rose locked eyes, and then, he held her twin closer.

Jacques grew apprehensive. "Would you like something to drink?"

"No." She was shaking her head as her world shattered. "I just need to sit someplace quiet." She really just wanted to run away.

He glanced around tensely. "*Is* there anywhere quiet?"

She nodded. "Yes, the swing beneath the Oak tree in the side yard."

"Just show me the way." Jacques tenderly soothed and took her arm again.

She led him, though her eyes remained glued to the handsome couple until they were no longer in sight.

As they sat beside one another on the white wooden swing, Veda sadly watched the sun sink beneath the horizon with her dreams of Hans Wagner.

The crickets soon accompanied them and Jacques had a strange glow on his face which she did not notice until he began to speak.

"I am glad we are alone, Veda. I never believed it would happen so naturally. I have something to tell you. I have spoken with your father and he has agreed to arrange a meeting between our parents."

Veda looked at him, stupefied. "Jacques, what are you talking about?"

His face illuminated and his dreamy eyes glazed over. He fell onto his knee, and cupped her silken hand in his palms.

"I love you, Veda. I want to spend the rest of my life with you. I am going into my last year at Princeton. I'll have a few years to prepare before you finish Georgetown."

"Prepare for what?" In spite of her shock, she already knew the answer before it passed his lips.

"For our marriage, of course. I am asking you, Veda, to become my wife. With your approval, our parents can meet and plan our future."

The first stars appeared, and the crescent moon transmitted a silvery gleam over the young, evening sky.

Veda gulped. Her face sank. Her eyes deepened into wells of remorse. "Oh, Jacques, you are so horribly mistaken. I...I never meant to lead you on."

He stood. The enchantment had passed, and his own dream dimmed. "Lead me on? What do you mean?"

She rose and took his hand. "I do not love you, Jacques. I am sorry, but I cannot make it any clearer than that."

His heart shattered. His words cracked, "But what about all you said?"

She tensed. Couldn't he see that she, too, was crushed?

"Please do not ask me to remember anything I said."

His face darkened. Anguish became contempt. "So, you are nothing but a liar, a tease who's been toying with me like a puppet on a string?"

She flinched at the vile description of herself. "Oh, but Jacques, it is not that way at all."

And contempt became fury. "What is it, then? You don't deserve a gentleman like me! You belong with a *drunk* like Worthington! I saw you both before! He's nothing but a bum fortunate enough to have been born into money! But it doesn't change who he is, and it makes *you* no better!"

Veda burst into a frenzy. "Who are you to address me so?" Then she drew back her hand and slapped his face with all her strength. "What makes you think you know the first thing about love or marriage? You are nothing but a silly fool, Jacques! Who are you to judge me?"

He winced, but raised his head nobly as his eyes shot hazel fire. Then he turned slowly on his heels and walked away.

She was alone now, forlorn, and sobbing...

Who could ever begin to understand? But a small voice from deep within her whispered she had to pull herself together. Now, was not the time to shatter.

And so, she breathed deeply, and mustered strength. Moments later, she was carrying herself back to the yard. Her head was high, and she saw no one, ignoring admirers calling out her name.

But she could not tune out the clamor at the height of the ice cream bon bon parade when Chester Worthington dove into a champagne fountain. Blood mixed with bubbly, and red foam flowed everywhere. There were screams and a swarm of gaping people around him. His mortified father lifted him from the mess as servants whisked forward with first aid kits. But the orchestra kept playing, and merry couples still danced under the evening sky.

Veda tore her eyes from the revolting scene and hastened to the house.

But her tunnel vision was broken by the sight of Rose and Hans Wagner strolling arm in arm under the night moon on the path toward the water.

She never heard Marius calling her to say goodbye...she was fleeing the truth, and gunned to her room where she slammed the door and welcomed blackness.

Chapter 4

She was sitting on the chaise lounge, staring grimly into a crackling fire when Nanny McBride came through the door. She had changed into a white satin nightgown with her dress and accessories strewn along the bedroom floor.

The heavy-set head maid was still in her black and white uniform, and large sacs had formed under her eyes from hours of supervising that day.

"Sarah told me that ye wouldn't let her into the room to turn down ye bed, Missy."

Veda pressed her eyes shut and answered, "That is right, Nanny."

Nanny McBride waddled toward her. "Well, *La Madame* Champion is my mistress, and I ain't fixin' to have her speak to me about neglectin' my duties!"

Veda glared back at her. "And just what is that supposed to mean?"

"Like it or not, Missy, I'm gonna see that ye bed *is* turned down!" And she went to the canopy bed fit for a princess.

Veda crossed her arms and turned her face back to the fire. "Do as you please! I do not care!"

"And why'dyer throw ye clothes all over the floor as if this was some shanty shack?" she scolded once the satin sheets had been folded down, and bent to collect the rich garments. "The problem with ye, Missy, is that ye're too spoiled! Ye never stop to think how many long hours Mr. Champion puts in at his bank to keep ye clothed and fed like royalty!"

"Oh, leave me alone!"

Nanny McBride ignored the huff as she hung the dress in a Chippendale armoire, keeping a watchful eye on the brooding young girl she had helped raise. She loved Veda very much. She had always been special to her.

"Well, I hope ye learned a lesson, Missy!" she intoned with a smirk. Veda raised her chin and sniffed. "What in heavens are you talking about, Nanny?"

"Ye know what I'm talkin' about, but I'll repeat it anyhow jus' so ye won't forget it! Words out everywhere that ye were imbibin' in spirits today! What kinda young lady does that? Did ye forget ye're a debutante from a fine family, or are ye fixin' to spoil yer reputation by actin' like some poor white trash?"

Veda frowned. "Be quiet! I cannot stand to hear any of this right now! You have turned down the bed; now get out!"

Nanny McBride shook her head and drew the curtains. "Poor white trash. What'll *La Madame* Champion say in the mornin'? Yer grandparents? How could ye have shamed them all, Missy?"

"I did no such thing!"

But Nanny was relentless. "Back in Ireland, we got names for girls who cast shame on their high standin' folks!"

Veda snapped. Her head was pounding. "Who cares about Ireland? You are in America now and you are making my headache worse than it already is!"

"It's good ye head hurts! It'll help ye remember so ye don't fix to get yerself pickled again!"

"Get out; I said! Go away!"

"I'll leave, Missy, but it ain't gonna change nothin'! Yer'll still have to face it in the mornin'!"

Then she hobbled out. Veda vehemently tossed a pillow after her which bounced off the wall. Her eyes welled tears and her stomach churned. She was too depressed and feeling too sick to consider any thoughts or consequences of her behavior that day.

Knocks at the door added fuel to the fire. "*Go away!*" she thundered as tears streamed down her face.

The soft voice paralyzed her. "Veda, it is Rose. May I come in?"

Veda hastened to collect herself, and scouted for a book in the rack beside her.

"Come in," she called out coolly, and moments later, Rose, in a lavender nightgown, stood beside her with a puzzled expression on her face.

"Are you feeling all right?"

Veda stiffened. She never lifted her eyes from the book. "Now why would you ask such a thing?" her voice was an icy monotone.

Rose sat at the foot of the chaise lounge and smiled. "Well, from the way you shouted when I knocked…"

"That is because I thought you were just another servant pestering me when I am trying to read!"

Rose glanced down knowingly. "Do you make a habit of reading books upside down?"

Veda sighed and dropped it onto her lap. "Why did you come in here anyway? Is it not past your bedtime!"

The words hit Rose like a sharp blow. "What are you talking about?"

Veda mimicked her. "What are you talking about? You are a fairy tale princess; are you not? Which means you require your beauty rest before prince charming returns tomorrow for another seaside stroll!"

Rose gulped. "This is about Hans Wagner. Isn't it?"

Veda was beside herself. "There you go again, playing the coy, innocent sister!"

"Veda!"

"Rose! How could you have mortified me so, in your willingness to relinquish a dance to your poor, rejected sister as if I were some pitiful old maid?"

Remorse hung heavily in Rose's eyes. "Oh, Come, now. It was not that way at all, and besides, you said you had already promised the dance to Jacques Deneuve."

"Are you *that* blind, Rose? Could you not see it was only because I was humiliated?"

Rose went to embrace her. "Oh, you poor thing!"

But Veda backed away vehemently. "Do not pretend to feel sorry for me! You knew exactly what you were doing all along! Finally miss goodie two shoes had her day in the sun, her chance to outshine big sister!"

Rose was horrified. "You could not possibly mean that."

And Veda was a raving wreck. "I do! It's true! I do! Now go away! Leave me alone! I want Marius! I want my brother!" Tears were spilling from her eyes in torrents.

This second dagger cracked Rose's heart. "He is my brother, too," she impressed; her face heavy with pain. "And I am your sister!"

"I do not care who you are!" Veda shouted over uncontrolled sobs. "Just go away!"

Still, Rose tried to soothe her. "Do not do this, Veda. You are tired. You are."

"Do not tell me what I am! Why not just go back to your room and say your prayers!"

Rose sprang to her feet, appalled. "Veda! Mind yourself!"

But she would not be mollified. "Oh, be quiet! You are no fun! You read boring books and talk about boring topics with no interest to anyone! God only knows *what* Hans Wagner sees in you, anyway!"

This blow was slaughterous. "How cruel, Veda!" Rose lamented, tears glistening in her eyes. "I have never had such harsh words spoken to me. And what makes it worse, is that they came from you."

Then she turned with complete dignity and walked solemnly to the door.

It was when she was alone in the hall that she began to weep.

Veda's stomach was churning ferociously. She panicked, feeling the spoilage rise to her throat, and leapt seconds before it disgorged onto the imported Parisian lounge. She darted to the porcelain wash basin and keeled over just in time.

She found herself weeping again when she was through, and with the relief, so, too, came her senses. Reality struck and her heart bled over all she had said to her twin.

"*Rose!*" she shrieked and bolted to her sister's bedroom.

******

"So, she was quite a looker. Wouldn't you say?" Rudolph commented as he climbed into bed.

Hans Wagner closed the English book he had begun studying and smiled at his friend in the bed next to his. "She was more than that. She was beautiful."

Rudi slipped under the starched linen sheets and teased. "And you never thanked me for letting *you* ask her to dance. I was quite swept by her myself."

Hans chuckled. "It was only fair, my friend. I saw her first."

Rudi crossed his arms behind his neck and leaned against the headboard. "All is fair in love and war, and I could have cut in on your parade, but decided to remain a loyal friend."

"And loyal you are," Hans affirmed and grew suddenly serious. "I think I have fallen in love."

"That is dangerous," Rudi cautioned.

Hans frowned. "I know. And it frightens me."

Rudi observed him tensely. "Do not let it happen. It could never be."

A wave of resentment washed over Hans' face. "Why? Because I am poor, and she is rich?"

Rudi nodded sadly. "Yes, unfortunately."

Hans emitted a pained sigh. "Well, it is not just! She is so beautiful, so gentle, so unspoiled, even if she is an aristocrat!"

Rudi reached across the floor and took his friend's hand with empathy in his eyes. "But you still cannot have her. She does not know your station."

A knot of frustration burned like acid in Hans' gut. "Did you ever stop to think that maybe the truth would not matter?"

Rudi felt his friend's anguish. "You are smarter than that, Hans. You know it *would* matter. You are going to see her old man tomorrow. Play your cards right and you will be on your way to becoming an American. But if you rub him the wrong way, even if his daughter loved you, he will have you sailing steerage, back to Germany faster than you can learn another phrase in that English book you are studying."

The words were a bittersweet awakening. Hans' mind flashed back to his life of servitude in Berlin, a peasantry from which he could never consider rising, the political unrest, the inevitable adversity only he and other wise men like himself recognized, but never voiced. He was smart and fortunate to get out while he could, and though he would be saddened in choosing not to pursue Rose Champion, he knew, suddenly, what he had to do.

"You are right, Rudi," he replied. "Sometimes I need you to drill some sense into me."

"I am sorry, Hans," Rudi's voice was a sympathetic monotone.

Hans stiffened. "Do not ever apologize to me. You have given me everything." Then he paused and added as he reached to switch off the lamp. "Now, let's get some sleep."

As they lay awake in the darkness, their minds swimming, Rudi questioned, "By the way, what did you think of her sister?"

Hans pondered for a long moment. "Very beautiful, too. But hardly my type. Too conceited."

Rudi remarked after a short pause. "I thought the same."

"Is that why you did not ask her to dance when I went off with Rose?" Rudi felt his face redden in the blackness. "I did ask her."

"And?"

Rudi was glad Hans could not see him. Rejection was one thing he did not accept easily. "And she said no."

Hans burst into laughter. At first, Rudi was offended. Then, he laughed too.

Veda stormed into her sister's fire lit room and ran to the canopy bed where Rose lay awake with an empty stare on her face.

"Rose! I am so sorry! You must forgive me! I did not mean anything I said!"

Rose elevated to rest her back against the headboard, and her milk white hand beckoned Veda forward.

Veda climbed into the bed beside her and pulled the sheets up to her neck. "Do you feel better, now?" Rose asked with a hint of authority in her tone.

Veda nodded with a sniffle. "Yes. Much better. I became sick, you know."

"Did you learn a lesson?"

Rose, the exemplar was back. Veda gladly welcomed her.

"Yes, I truly did. I do not know what came over me today. It must have been all the festivities. And then, when I saw you and Hans taking a night stroll. Oh Rose! I *am* terribly sorry! I was downright awful! Who am I to say anything cruel about you, when I was the one who made a complete fool of myself today!"

Rose lay beside her, and Veda cuddled snugly in her arms. "Such behavior is unworthy of you, and I am glad you know it."

Veda sighed. "I love you, Rose. I am glad we are going to spend the next four years together. And I hope we never separate. I think I would just die if we ever did!"

Rose kissed her sister's forehead and smoothed her curls. "I love you too. And...I am sorry if I hurt you today. It was the last thing I would ever think of doing."

"Do not, Rose," Veda softly protested, placing a finger over her lips. "You did nothing wrong."

Then she nestled her head in her twin's bosom before a long silence came between them.

Rose cracked it with a sad whisper, "I am sorry, too...about Hans Wagner."

But Veda never heard her. She was already fast asleep.

Chapter 5

Veda awakened at 8:30 the next morning. At first, she did not know where she was…in a foreign room, a foreign bed, with no imported dolls to greet her.

And then the truth struck her. She grimly recollected the events of the night before and cringed. She must have fallen asleep beside Rose, and remained dead to the world until this hour, thirty minutes past the time her mother had established for 'rising.'

Her mother! How would she face her? And what made matters worse, her head still pounded, and her stomach was still churning.

Rose was obviously washed and clothed. She was always a model of self-discipline. In school, she had always been at the top of her class. At home, despite their high standards, she had managed to remain in the good graces of her mother and Nanny McBride.

And what happened to me? Veda glumly wondered.

Knocks on the door triggered a new state of panic. "Who is there?" she called out nervously.

No response. Then, Nanny McBride came into the sun filled room carrying a sterling tea server in her pudgy arms.

"Ain't ye fixin' to get yeself outa bed today, Missy? Has it slipped ye pretty little mind that breakfast is served at nine?"

Veda propped herself up against the brass headboard and squinted as the morning sunshine washed over her face. "I am not hungry this morning, Nanny. Tea will be just fine."

Nanny McBride poured the steaming liquid from the glistening server. "Don't be thinkin' ye're gonna get off that easy, Missy! *La Madame* Champion and *Madame* DuBois are waitin' to tend to ye at the table. So, if I was you, which I'm sure I'm glad I ain't *this mornin'*, I'd rise and shine mighty fast before my cookin' goose finds itself well done!" she paused and added with a smirk, "Get my message?"

Veda threw off the sheets and jumped up petulantly. "I get it, all right! And I would thank you, once again, to stop pestering me!"

Nanny McBride went to the door with a smug expression on her rotund face. "Ye bath's already been drawn, Missy." She intoned over her shoulder and left.

Veda donned her satin robe swiftly and slipped from the room, hoping not to encounter anyone in the floral infused hall.

She entered her own room with a sigh of relief, and emerged some thirty minutes later, bathed, perfumed, coiffed, and clothed in a white linen sun dress, a ritual which regularly took no less than an hour! Amazing, it was, what one could accomplish under pressure. Her hair was fixed in a frontal upsweep, while the back and sides spilled freely in remnant, straggling curls. A white satin bow complemented her ensemble, and she looked spectacular, though she felt abominable.

She descended the grand staircase with a modicum of grace, gripping the bronze and iron railing every step of the way. She heard the voices in the dining room over the clinking of sterling against Minton china. She took a deep breath, pulled her shoulders back, and entered with a nervous smile on her beet red face.

"Good morning, everyone," she managed to chime and took her place at the table without looking at a single one of them. But she could feel her mother's eyes boring into her, her grandmother's profound disapproval, her sister's pity, and the deafening silence of her father and grandfather.

A servant came to pour orange juice, and another to present fresh fruit in a crystal cup on which the family monogram had been engraved.

The dining room was a designer's masterpiece, done in the décor of Hercules at Versailles. The seventy-five-pound chairs were made of hollow bronze, and the brocade cushions were trimmed in fourteen-carat gold. The chandelier presiding over the room was made of Baccarat crystal, and had been imported from France.

"You missed your brother's departure, Veda. He was quite disappointed that you had not been present to bid him and his new bride farewell."

La Madame Champion's words were soft, though abrasive, and out of respect alone, Veda dared lift her eyes from her lap to make contact with hers.

Once again, the family matriarch looked beautiful in a short sleeve cream bolero jacket with turn back cuffs frilled with deep lace, and a tight hobble skirt complemented by a brown tablier. Her face was heavily powdered, her brown eyes wide with disapproval.

Veda trembled. Her voice shook, "I know it was just awful of me, Mother, but I was so tired from the festivities that I overslept this morning."

"And I know why!" Her grandmother, clad in a floor length black day dress, intoned in French with a biting stare.

Veda's head sank. The tension in the room thickened.

"I am terribly sorry for my behavior yesterday. I know I shamed all of you. It was wrong and very foolish of me," she confessed in a contrite monotone.

Rose, resplendent in a pink silk sun dress, and onyx curls floating down her back, leaned forward with a tender smile. "Now, Veda, you must not be so hard on yourself. It was not so bad as you recall."

"That will be enough, Rose," *La Madame* Champion gently admonished, and *Madame* DuBois emitted a sigh of revolt. "Veda *did* shame herself and all of us by her indiscretions as I choose to mildly coin them. They do not warrant qualification."

"Yes, Mother," Rose reverently replied, as Veda tensed in her seat.

Then *La Madame* Champion shifted her stare back to Veda. "And it has been brought to my attention that you were slouching at dinner yesterday, another public disgrace, which offers me no alternative but to assign you to Nanny McBride after breakfast, who will reinforce the art of sitting, which you shall practice for one hour. Is that understood?"

Veda cringed. "Yes, Mother."

And then, her mother's voice softened as her face broke into a tender smile. "Afterward, you will report for your riding lesson."

Veda's eyes widened in astonishment. "Mother? Are you serious? You know I just adore riding, and under the circumstances…"

La Madame Champion interrupted her in a proudly superior tone. "Guilty, though you are, I forgive you *and* trust, you will vow to resume the summer with the same high esteem with which the Times regards you."

"The Times?" Veda quizzed, tickled.

Her father, in a single-breasted morning coat, a stiff turn down collar, and a paisley tie, smiled over the arrangement of fresh blooms.

"My dear, you remain quite a celebrity," he chimed and flashed the front page of the society column.

Veda gasped. There was an enlarged photograph of her waltzing with her grandfather. The headline boasted, *Debutante of the year waltzes with grandfather from abroad, but which American bachelor's hand will she accept?*

At first, she was stupefied. Then, she burst into laughter. "I do not believe it!"

She squealed and looked at her grandfather, who beamed in a black Parisian suit. "*Ma petite-fille*, you were breathtaking!" he affirmed in French.

"*Merci beaucoup*," she replied. "And you, as well, *Grand-pere*."

La Madame Champion observed them pleasingly, as Rose joined her sister in laughter. But *Madame* DuBois remained rigid as stone. "Only in America!" she grumbled in French.

Veda raised her goblet of orange juice and announced. "Forgive me, *Grand-mere*, but I have never been more proud to *be* an American!" Then she paused to glance back at her father. "*And* a Champion."

Winston stood with an endearing wink. "And now, I must excuse myself. I am expecting a visitor."

He pecked his wife's cheek and exited through the French doors leading to his study.

The family finished breakfast and reminisced the highlights of the magnificent wedding which had also been coined by the Times as *The Gala Event of The Year.*

Chapter 6

His legs shook when he stood to greet Winston Champion.

The study was done in Gothic style. The sun spilling onto the carpet through the stained-glass window conveyed a pietistic air which Hans Wagner interpreted as a positive omen.

He wore the one suit he owned, his black footman's uniform which bore no hint of subservience once finished with the Brooke's Brothers' tie Rudi had lent him that morning.

"Em...good morning, sir," he uttered awkwardly, and extended a large, trembling hand which Winston Champion coolly received.

He went around to his mahogany wood desk and sat across from the handsome German immigrant.

"You come highly recommended. Jacob Stern informed me you had worked for his brother in Berlin for several years, and that your mother is an unprecedented housemaid."

Hans stared at him blankly. It did not take Winston long to realize. "Oh, do forgive me for presuming you speak English."

Hans understood, somewhat. "I study, em, each day," he piped proudly.

"Good," Winston replied, steepling his fingers and narrowing his eyes.

"Because I would expect you to become fluent in due time, young man," Hans tensed.

Then Winston broke the ice and conducted the rest of the meeting in German. Fluent, he was not, but versed enough to communicate.

Hans was relieved. They were off to a good start.

If only, it were not for the distraction of Rose's picture on the fireplace mantel behind Winston Champion...

******

"Go, Violet! Go!" Veda exclaimed as her horse made its way to Rose's.

They were racing along the bridle path beneath the dome of sun-soaked leaves glistening on the towering Oaks.

"Oh, no you don't!" Rose cried over laughter and tapped her heel against Black Stallion as a signal to dash ahead, full speed.

She crossed the finish line first and pulled the reins victoriously. Veda sped in seconds later and brought Violet to a smooth stop.

"You think you are so smart; don't you, Rose Champion! I will beat you yet, sure as God made apples!" she vowed breathlessly, her hair billowing in the wind.

They looked enchanting in imported riding suits, straddled on the prized horses their father had purchased them some years ago.

Rose guffawed. "Do not be so confident, Veda! Stallion lets no one beat him!"

"You will be eating those words, Rose, darling! Remember! Slow and steady wins the race."

They were interrupted by Nanny McBride summoning them to lunch. "Coming, Nanny!"

Rose exclaimed, and they trotted forward. Veda saw *him*, and was momentarily dazed.

"You go ahead, Rose. I think I will ride a few more minutes," she mused, and shifted her eyes cleverly back to her twin. "Violet *does* need practice."

Rose observed her suspiciously. "I am sure Violet has had enough exercise for a day."

Veda grimaced. "Oh, Rose! Just go ahead! I will catch up shortly. I promise I will not be late."

Rose saw the determined gleam in her twin's eye and knew there was no dissuading her.

"Very well." And she nodded coolly. "I will see you back at the house."

She paused and added before galloping away. "Remember, Punctuality is nobility."

They were the words of Miss Penda; their finishing school head mistress. Rose lived by her doctrines. Veda made a regular habit of breaking them. Her only focus was Hans Wagner now, and she stared endearingly as he exited the French doors of her father's study.

She cracked Violet's reins, and, moments later, she was galloping again.

She came to a fox trot ten feet before him, and sat there, swooning.

She slipped off her riding hat and cast her black curls into the gentle wind.

Their eyes locked. His glistened like crystals as the sunshine bathed his sculptured face.

"Hello," she said softly as her lips curled into a sweet smile. "Hallo," he replied at a safe distance.

His accent was rich, but thick, and Veda's hammering heart rose to her throat.

"I did not know you were acquainted with my father. Are you the visitor he was expecting?"

He observed her blankly and she realized he understood nothing she had said.

"My father," she impressed, edging Violet closer. "Do you know him?" Hans struggled to comprehend the message.

"Ah, yah. *Herr* Champion. Your Pa Pa…he…em…very kind man."

Veda was melting. "Yes, he is."

An awkward silence came between them.

"Do you like America?" she asked breathlessly.

Hans nodded with a smile. "America? Ya…It is veery nice!" he paused and observed her closely. He admitted she was quite beautiful, and very charming as well.

"And you…" he added, coming before her. "You, veery nice, too."

She was electrified. "Would you care for a tour of the chateau?" she asked with a poise Miss Penda would have awarded a gold medal.

But the moment of enchantment was short-lived when a voice ripped from a distance.

"Mr. Wagner! We must depart! Mr. Stern is awaiting his car!" Hans recognized the bark, though the words were mumbo-jumbo.

He acknowledged Victor, the chauffeur, with a nod, then turned back to Veda and bowed. "Em…I go now, Fraulein. Bye Bye."

Then he turned and retreated as Veda shook with butterflies fluttering within her. She was glued there, her eyes fixed upon him, until he vanished.

There was hope after all.

"Veda!" Her father's voice awakened her from her trance.

He was standing beside her, his ensemble finished with a silk top hat, kid gloves, and a walking stick in his right hand.

Joseph, the stable boy, was there too.

"Father!" she exclaimed, and climbed off her pet horse. "Isn't it a beautiful day!"

He raised his eyebrows and remarked with a thin smile, "A beautiful day for daydreaming, perhaps, Blossom. I have been calling you for nearly a minute."

Veda chuckled nervously. "A minute? Really?"

Then she turned to the stable boy, and artfully changed the topic, "Would you tend to Violet, Joseph?"

He obliged and retreated with her beautiful white horse.

Veda slipped her arm through Winston's, and questioned blithely as they strolled toward the cliff walk. "How was your morning, Father?"

He gazed at her suspiciously. "Since when do the events of my morning hold any interest to you, Blossom?"

She teased with a grin. "You *do* underestimate me! Why, your affairs are valuable to me as my own."

"I am certain they are." He speculated cynically.

"But they ARE! Truly!" She insisted. Then her whole manner changed. "Um…That gentleman who left your study, Father. He looked somewhat familiar. Have I met him before?"

They were by the cliff, fifty feet above the white caps riding the rustic Atlantic waves. The wind blew between them, and Winston laughed as the truth came to him.

"That was Hans Wagner. You *do* recall meeting him yesterday?"

"Hardly," Veda sniffed, turning her face toward the ominously beautiful water.

Winston kissed her hand. "Ah, but you are so transparent, Blossom. Of course, you remember him. And now, I understand why my eventful morning does, indeed, spark your zealous interest."

"I have no idea what you are talking about." She declared, but her face was red with embarrassment.

"Do you not, my dear?" he accused, and thumbed her chin upward so their eyes could meet.

Veda frowned and gave in. "Very well, then. I *do* remember him. Why was he here?"

Winston narrowed his eyes. "It would be a hopeless feat to run after him, Blossom, needless to say, a disgrace for a girl of *your* station."

She was appalled. "*Really, Father*! I hardly equate an innocent inquiry with running after a man!"

Though ten steps ahead of her, Winston played Veda's game.

"Good, then. Because Mr. Wagner's social position is quite different from what you might think."

She felt suddenly betrayed and her face paled. "What do you mean, Father?"

He proceeded to tell her…

******

She entered the grand parlor later, and went to the piano where her sister was gracing the room with a Brahms Lullaby. Rose had changed into a lilac summer dress, while Veda remained in her jodhpurs. She sat on the bench as her twin continued to play.

"I must speak to you!" she insisted. And the piano sang.

"Rose! Stop that noise!" she gushed, snatching her fingers away from the keys.

Rose observed her feverishly. "If you do not mind, I would like to rehearse."

Veda ignored her, impassioned by the news she desperately needed to convey. "You are not going to believe it, but—"

Rose interrupted curtly, "Why did you not come to lunch as you had promised?"

"Oh, blabber, lunch! This is more important!"

"Is it?" Rose sniffed.

"Yes! And after I tell you, you will thank me!"

Rose frowned and folded her hands over her lap. "Very well, then. I am listening."

Veda edged closer until their bodies touched.

"I saw Hans Wagner leaving Father's study today. Then, I spoke to Father. He told me Mr. Wagner is actually a German-born peasant who used every penny he had saved to cover his passage to America. He had worked for the family of a friend, Rudolph Stern. You remember…Jacob Stern's nephew. The two of them came here together!"

"The point, Veda," Rose interrupted testily.

"Well, the point is that Father has employed Hans Wagner as a servant in our New York home!" she was bursting with excitement.

"And?" Rose asked, bored.

Veda turned to shock. "What is it with you, anyway? You *do* remember Hans Wagner?"

"I do," Rose affirmed loftily.

Veda shrugged. "Well, then the truth should change everything."

Rose shook her head. "It should change nothing. I am not inclined to judge a man's value by his social standing."

Veda was astounded. "Of course, you must! Especially if you are to consider him for a beau! I mean…what would Father say?"

Rose locked eyes with her twin. Her expression was firm as her tone. "Whoever said I was interested in Hans Wagner?"

Veda saw victory. Her mind swam…

Well, then, if you are not, Rose dear. *I still am!*

Winds of War 1914–1918

And therefore, send not to know for whom the bell tolls; It tolls for thee...

–John Donne

Chapter 7

It was June 28, 1914. Archduke Ferdinand and his wife, heirs to the Austro-Hungarian throne, rode through the streets of Sarajevo, Bosnia, in an elegant, open car. A sea of spectators had gathered around them. Suddenly, a rebel emerged from the crowd and tossed a bomb into the car. Archduke Ferdinand, in a state of pure panic, caught the bomb and hurled it out into the street. The explosion was followed by a series of horrified shrieks. A shroud of powder obscured the eight victims who lay gravely wounded. Sirens blasted through the air. Pandemonium followed when the haze was lifted and the injured were unveiled.

Little did they all know that the savage act would leave a monumental mark upon the world forever. It was the advent of the century's darkest hour.

Though deeply shaken, the royal couple felt profound remorse for the victims of the explosive aimed at them. In their noble interest, they went to visit a wounded couple that night. While they were returning, a nineteen-year-old student, Gavrilo Princip, fired at their car twice. The archduke's jugular vein was torn open. The second bullet drilled into the Archduchess Sophie's stomach.

Both were viciously assassinated.

When arrested and questioned, the angry student told the police he wanted to avenge the Serbs for the oppression they had been suffering. Though there was no direct proof the assassin had been connected to the Serbian government, Austria-Hungary and Germany accused them of murder.

The Serbs had been a problem for some time. Though Austria-Hungary governed Bosnia, the Serbs believed they had a right to be in control. After all, many people in Bosnia felt stronger ties to them than to Austria-Hungary.

Then came the murder.

"It was no coincidence!" screamed the defense.

It did not take long for their conviction to be confirmed. It was discovered that the Serbian government had prior knowledge of the assassination initiative and did nothing to prevent it.

Germany bonded with Austria-Hungary. "It is now or never! We must finish the Serbs off for good!" wrote Germany's emperor, Kaiser Wilhelm II.

It was all the fuel Austria-Hungary needed to wage a war against Serbia, and on July 28, it was formally declared.

Russia became Serbia's ally. Germany declared war on Russia. On August 3, she declared war on France, and marched into Belgium with a ferocity Europe had never expected. Appalled by her atrocities, on August 4, Great Britain declared war on Germany.

A horror story was quickly unfolding. In eight short days, all of Europe's great powers were engaged in a bloodthirsty war.

Germany executed the Schlieffen Plan which called for a lightning attack on France by way of Belgium. When questioned, they referred to the Belgian neutrality treaty as a scrap of paper, and burned down the village of Lise with relentless brutality.

Next, they took Liege, an old military fortress, and by August 20, Brussels, Belgium's capital, had fallen. In this first month of war, already fifty thousand civilians and soldiers had been killed. And it was only the beginning...

Germans were now in reach of France. British soldiers were sent across the channel to join the five established French armies. Europe waited in a state of terror as the rest of the world sat at the edge of their seats.

******

"What is happening over there, Hans? These are our people turned savage! What has become of our dignity? We are a country of Beethoven, Brahms and Bach!"

Rudolph Stern lamented as he sat across his friend at a West Side café that Sunday afternoon. It was Hans' day off. He had been working as a servant in the Champion House on Park Avenue for two months now. It was a quiet place with the family still at the summer chateau in Rhode Island. Winston was the sole resident, though he sailed his yacht on select weekends to visit the ladies. But when he was in New York, he made himself scarce at the miniature brownstone mansion, merely dining in his chamber, and sleeping until he would head off to his bank at the crack of dawn each day.

But the fastidious house butler advised Hans not to become too comfortable with the situation, referring to the quiet as a mere calm before an untiring bustle. Although Hans' English was improving, at first, he understood very little of what the imposing iceberg had to say. But after unflagging repetition, he grasped the message. *La Madame* Champion was coming, and as with a tornado, they had better be prepared.

Today he wore one of his two white uniform shirts and black trousers. His friend, Rudi, beamed in a tweed suit and foulard tie. Their coffee had just been served, but both continued nursing the vodka in front of them.

"That was the problem, Rudi. I had tried to tell you so many times back in Berlin, but you and your kind would not consider the lurking dangers."

Rudi's right eye twitched in defense. "What do you mean, *my kind*?"

Hans grimaced. "Aw, common...I am talking about the rich! All of you have been lost in the arts and the meaningless graces of balls and dinner parties to recognize what was happening to our own country!"

"And what was that?" Rudi questioned, leaning forward.

Hans tossed off his vodka and motioned for a refill. He did not continue until the waiter retreated. Being a German, now, meant being an ogre. They had been black balled across the globe. And already, these two 'marked' men felt the need to be overly vigilant. Even in this obscure cafe, they had been labeled, as their thick accents had betrayed them. The cool service was rendered with resentment, and the stares and whispers were deadly enough to reduce them to the self-inflicted impression that they were German spies.

"The poor and the powerless were dissatisfied, Rudi. The Kaiser used this to his advantage and made us his pawns! He offered us pride and security in exchange for our brawn! He turned us into monsters, and today, we are lashing out at the world with guns and weapons like uncaged wolves!"

Rudi squirmed in the wooden bench. He gulped as the life and pride he had known flushed from his face and very being forever.

"How did we let it happen?" he asked in a shaky whisper.

Hans' eyes transformed into blocks of blue white ice. His words were marked with bitterness and shame, "Nationalism. It has been the masked demon all along. It fed the complacence of the rich like you, and the starving pride of my class. Now, everyone has become unified in the common belief that Germany is supreme. She can do no wrong. Her soldiers are fighting for the good of the people, convinced that victory is within arm's reach."

There was a long, painful pause. Both of them were suspended somewhere over the ocean separating them from here and a place they were suddenly ashamed to call home.

"But what about our families? I feel as if we have abandoned them," Rudi uttered as tears welled in his eyes.

Hans drummed his fingers on the table in an effort to combat his own fears. "So far, I understand they are all safe."

Rudi snapped back at him. "Well, that is little consolation! Of course, they tell us that in letters! They are fine! We are fine! Everyone is fine, and then there is the truth! They are like sitting ducks waiting to be attacked!"

Hans sighed and reached for his vodka. "No need to worry, *yet*, my friend. Germany has become revered. No one will dare cross her borders in fear of being eaten alive."

Rudi shook. "I never knew such savagery slept in our own backyard."

Hans eyed him keenly, his left brow raised. "Neither did Julius Caesar, and he was king of *his* empire."

A dark foreshadowing flashed before Rudi's face, and he downed his vodka to erase it. The haunting picture spread across his skin and pervaded his person like an infection.

"You do not think that…" he muttered, his voice faltering. "Germany, like Rome, will fall?"

For the first time, Hans the rock, veered its faults.

"I do not know," he grimly murmured and drained the vodka for solace. "I do not know."

******

Berlin, Germany

Frau Wagner called her ten-year-old son away from the window in the servant's quarters of the magnificent Stern mansion.

Outside, the proud band resounded triumphantly as the Kaiser's elite Guard marched through the streets in armored suits and silver pointed helmets on their way to an evening event at the emperor.

"Did you hear me, Gunther? It is time to go to bed."

He remained still, his eyes twinkling with pride for his country and the great cause which had transformed Berlin into a fascinating land of lights and flag waving pageantry for two glorious months.

He was no longer a peasant child. He was a German, good as any rich boy or girl his age. They were all one, unified to win and become the most powerful and revered empire in all of Europe!

Life had become a trip to wonderland, an eager anticipation of the next band and colorful fireworks' display.

"Just a few more minutes, Mama!" he jubilantly protested. "They are marching for our soldiers! They are letting us know we are going to win!"

Frau Wagner came to him with a pleased smile. She could not help feeling proud herself. For once, the working poor had come to see their day in the sun. This war was a path toward freedom, and with Germany's victory, would come a time of revolution, the end of capitalism, and a farewell to privately owned businesses, which would open countless doors for the poor.

She crouched beside him and kissed his tender cheek. "One day you will tell your grandchildren stories about this night, and this moment of history you are living. You will live not only to witness Germany's victory, Gunther; you will grow up to enjoy the beauty of the new empire she will create for you and all the boys and girls your age."

He turned to encounter her once quite pretty face, "Do you think Hans realizes he has made a mistake by leaving?"

The mention of her elder son was an arrow to her heart. Her bloodshot eyes filled with tears, and her voice cracked as she whispered. "I do not know, my darling."

Gunther shifted his baby blue eyes back to the marching band for a long moment, before he turned with another soft question. "If he were here now, Hans would be a soldier; wouldn't he, Mama?"

She nodded, fighting back tears.

Gunther felt a pang of shame. It seemed as if Hans had not only abandoned, but betrayed them as well.

"I wish he had not left! I wish he would have been a soldier!"

Frau Wagner took her son into the warmth of her arms. "Our wishes do not always come true, Gunther."

"Mine will!" he affirmed as he glanced over her shoulder at the proud men in armor.

"And what is that, my son?"

He slipped away from her and stood at attention. The noble gleam on his face tickled her. "I *will* become a soldier, Ma Ma. I am going to make you very proud of *me*!"

******

Newport, Rhode Island

The blaze of candelabras on the dining room table cast an incandescent glow over the cake as the family gathered for the forced eighteenth birthday celebrations of Veda and Rose.

The twins looked radiant in white lace gowns; their hair swept up in rich curls. *La Madame* Champion wore a comely evening gown in soft cream silk, and Dominique, who had recently returned from her honeymoon cruise to Egypt, beamed, too, in a pale green empire gown.

The gentlemen, Winston and his son, Marius, wore white tie.

"Are you not going to sample your birthday cake, Blossom?" Winston questioned as he observed Veda's glum expression.

Veda shook her head sullenly. "I do not feel much like celebrating, Father, with *Grand-mere* and *Grand-pere* trapped over there in France, just waiting for those barbarians to pounce on them like wild dogs!"

La Madame Champion dabbed her lips with a linen napkin, and replied, coolly composed, "I assured you your grandparents are just fine, Veda, dear. Their letter encouraged us to rest our fears. That is why we *shall* celebrate this evening."

Rose, who had been nibbling at the cake simply to please her parents, interjected in a somber whisper. "But we cannot stop worrying. They are our family, and..."

Winston interjected firmly as the tension in the room mounted.

"And the French army will protect its people. They have the British at their side as well."

Marius' eyes shot fire, and his nostrils flared. "I hope they blow those Germans to kingdom come! They deserve it after killing all those innocent civilians in Belgium!"

"*Marius!*" *La Madame* Champion thundered, her face red with rage.

He nodded and demurred, "I am sorry, Mother. This is just *one* topic that incites me beyond reason!"

"Which is *precisely* why it is inappropriate at a dining room table!"

She huffed and lifted her lead crystal glass to take a long sip of spring water. She had been on edge these days, and they all knew why.

Marius turned his eyes to Winston. "Is it true, Father, that you have employed a *German* at the Park Avenue house?"

Veda shifted in her chair. She and Rose exchanged tense glances.

Winston, himself, seemed a bit uneasy. This was becoming a common question. "Yes, and there are thousands of Germans employed here in America," his words carried their usual dignity, and his manner grew overly exalted.

Marius' jaws tightened. "Excuse me, Father, but *this one* is different. He is one of *them!*"

Winston eased back in his chair and observed his son with a challenging gleam in his eyes. *La Madame* Champion glared at both of them. Veda and Rose sat at the edge of their seats.

"He is not responsible for the transgressions of his people, Marius, the same as thousands of German civilians."

Marius eyed his father indignantly. He was fuming, "And those same *innocent civilians* as you call them, Father, are marching off to war. Your German servant *is* of age. And if he were over there right now, he would be a soldier burning down Belgian villages, and heading toward France to attack *my grandparents!*"

La Madame Champion allowed her solid gold fork to drop onto her plate.

The piercing clank was deliberate. The ladies flinched, but the men paid the angry message little heed.

Winston fingered his handlebar mustache. "Ah, but he is not over there, my son. He is here. And I will not cast any aspersions upon him, because he is a hard-working young man."

Marius leaned forward belligerently. "You speak like a traitor, Father."

Winston froze, and his eyes blazed. "Mind yourself, Marius! Remember whom you are addressing!"

La Madame Champion had tolerated enough. She rose from her chair and stormed out of the dining room with the might of a battleship.

The silence which ensued was loud as a cannon blast. The ladies sat tensely.

Winston stood and glared down at his impertinent son. "I shall tend to you later," he intoned with a steely gaze and went off to follow his wife.

Marius, still seething, drummed his fingers on the table.

"I think you owe both of them an apology," Dominique urged, the candlelight illuminating her pretty face.

Marius sighed. "I did not *mean* to offend them. I just cannot believe he is permitting that man to remain employed!"

Dominique stroked his shaking hand. "Your father is a very wise man. You are not in a position to question his motives," she paused and repeated. "Apologize."

Marius nodded sulkily. "All right."

Then Dominique shifted her eyes to Veda, who had been dazed by the whole scene. "I hope you are happy for spoiling your mother's evening!" she hissed with a biting stare.

Veda roused to a petulant defense. "I did not say *anything* out of line! And mind your own business, anyway! She is *my* mother, not *yours*!"

Marius scowled. His wife's and sister's tiffs were become increasingly frequent, and where he had first regarded them humorous, they were now beginning to exasperate him. "That will be enough from both of you!" he ordered.

Veda was not so easily silenced. "No, Marius! I am tired of her insults and reprimands! She has been putting her two sense into everything ever since you married her!"

"*I said, enough!*" Marius growled, his face awash with rage.

"I am going to bed!" Veda snapped and shot to her feet. "Care to join me, Rose?"

Rose shook her head and stared down at her plate guiltily. "I think we had better wait for Mother and Father to return and offer them a joint apology."

Veda glowered at her. "Suit yourself! I am *still* going to bed!"

And she trailed off in a huff, her nose cast arrogantly in the air.

Winston's heart cracked when he found his wife weeping in the drawing room. It was not often that she would err from her eminence to display anything less than grace and perfection. Human weakness was rarely exhibited, least of all, tears.

"It will be all right, my love," he soothed, as he came and knelt before her.

She looked at him, her face soaked from the river streaming from her helpless eyes. "I try to remain strong, to have faith that my parents will be safe, but the truth, Winston, is that I am terrified!"

The words cracked over gushing sobs, and he took her into his arms, appalled, too, that she had lowered her guard to address him by his first name.

"They will be protected, and you shall see them again," he whispered reassuringly, stroking her glistening, ebony chignon.

She buried her face in his shoulder and continued to weep. "How did this ever happen? They were right here in the safety of our home! Why could we not have received a sign, something, anything, to keep them from returning to France?"

He kissed her head and nestled his face against her perfumed, silken hair.

"If only it could be that easy..." he murmured, and held her until her eyes ran dry.

In those somber moments, Winston Champion grimly realized that times were changing. The winds of war were sweeping across the ocean to the shores of the peaceful and the free.

******

Verdun, France

As the rain fell over the hills of Verdun, *Madame* DuBois stood at her bedroom window watching the rich land transform into a lake of mud. The charming town was seemingly asleep. But how many others were staring out into the ominous darkness at the same moment? Never had quiet been so deafening. Never had raindrops tapping on a windowpane been such a shrill foreboding of impending doom. They became the tears of the slain and the oppressed, the tears yet to be cried, and the promise that one day, this evil might all be washed away.

But how long would it take? Each day was a fearful horror. Every second was a torment. Every sound was the footsteps of the German soldiers coming to attack them as they had so viciously slaughtered their neighbors in Belgium.

Her husband, *Monsieur* DuBois, came behind her and swept his gentle lips across her face.

"Come to bed, now, *ma cher*. Everything will be all right. Our soldiers are keeping careful watch over our borders. The Germans will never break through."

His words were hardly a consolation for her trembling heart. The elderly woman turned to encounter him with sheer terror marking her face. "But what if they *do* get through? What will become of us?"

Her shaking words cast an ominous chill across the old man's heart, but he showed no sign of fear. He soothed her face in the solace of his satin robe, and gently whispered as she quaked, "They will not break through, *ma cher*. They will not."

But as his wrinkled hands stroked her head, his weary eyes shifted toward the rain-soaked earth. Suddenly, he, too, wondered, *what if?*

Chapter 8

Hans accompanied Rudi to the train station the following Sunday afternoon. The summer was drawing to a close, and Rudi was on his way to Harvard. Already, he fit the picture of a collegiate in a checkered pullover sweater and red bow tie. Hans wore his regular black trousers and white shirt.

"Well, this is it, my friend. I will not see you again until holiday recess."

Hans was saddened by Rudi's words, but kept the air light, "It will be here quicker than we both know. In a week's time, your head will be buried under so many books, that you will have forgotten I even exist."

Rudi turned serious, "Never, Hans. You are my best friend. We grew up together. You are a part of me, just as if we were brothers."

Hans was deeply touched, and reached out to grip Rudi's palm. "I cannot thank you enough for making it possible for me to come here."

Rudi shook his hand. "Stop thanking me. You have worked very hard. And you are making it on your own."

Hans frowned. "I just hope it stays this way. At the house, there is talk of Mr. Champion dismissing me because I am German."

Rudi's brown eyes enlarged. "Did *he* say anything to you?"

Hans shook his head. "Not yet. But the staff has alerted me."

Rudi grimaced, "Ignore them. It is all just rumor."

"I hope you are right," Hans fretted.

"I know I am," Rudi affirmed. "Just think of me up there at Harvard now, not only a Jew, but a German as well."

Hans' face broke into a smile. "It seems to me that we both carry the same cross."

Rudi smiled too. "It is better than bearing it alone."

And they embraced. When his friend melted within the sea of people, Hans felt a profound sense of loneliness. But he would not exchange solitude for savagery, his only alternative at home. If, home, in fact, it still was.

"Goodbye!" the twins sang in unison, their heads popping through the train window, as the deafening whistle screeched, and billows of steam wafted up into the deep blue sky.

Their parents waved their farewell as the train left the station and made its way south toward Washington D.C.

Veda and Rose settled into their seats afterward, feeling a sudden sense of anxiety. They were heading off to college, embarking upon a new venture, wondering where their girlhoods had gone. Summer's end came with the realization that they were women now, expected to make lives of their own. The mystery of the future was almost frightening. It was a comfort to have one another.

"I am concerned about Mother," Rose said as she removed her sun bonnet and rested it on the lap of her lavender dress.

Veda, in a pink sun dress and matching picture hat, gazed at her twin worrisomely. "I know. Why did those ghastly Germans have to target France of all countries?"

Rose shrugged. "I do not know. But Father said they should reach the French border any day now."

They sank back quietly in their seats as their minds swam. The excitement of starting college, the colorful flowers and swaying trees outside the train window were dimmed by the fear of the unknown in Europe.

They hoped and prayed the French army would be brave and powerful enough to protect and sustain their dear grandparents and the beautiful chateau in Verdun.

******

Kimberly, South Africa

Kimberly is a city in the northern Cape of Good Hope Province. Here lies the big hole, also known as the womb of South Africa. It is three quarters of a mile wide, and some fourteen hundred feet deep. It is the largest man-made hole on the Earth's surface, from which fifteen million carats of diamonds had been extracted for nearly half a century.

Theodore Aspan based himself here, and worked in the scorching heat seven days a week, beside hundreds of other impassioned men with visions of grandeur gleaming in their minds. The labor was torturous, the surroundings, best compared to hell itself. There was little food, limited water, snakes, wild animals, and deadly insects.

Despite the agonies, he worked with unerring determination, never stopping to ask himself why, never considering a surrender to defeat as so many others did each day. He would find diamonds. He would enjoy the glory of self-made wealth. He would show them all at home he was so much more than a spoiled renegade, riding on the strings of his father's coattail. And then, he would tell them all to go to hell!

Chapter 9

The Marne is a river in Northeastern France which flows into the Seine near Paris. The Germans crossed it in September, 1914, and fear paralyzed the French. Sure, that Paris would be defeated, the government was moved to Bordeaux.

The foes met head on, and engaged in the first gore battle which lasted for five days. But the valor and determination of France and her British allies resulted in shocking victory. The Germans were turned back, and France was in the lead.

Civilians who had sat in terror for weeks were beginning to see hope.

The defeat was a great setback for the Germans. Before this, each offensive was a success. Just a few days earlier, the Russians had overrun the Austrian province of Galicia, taking thousands of prisoners. More support was needed, and Germany was all too pleased when Turkey joined the Central Powers in October.

******

Berlin

Dr. Isaac Stern had just finished reading the letter when his wife, Johanna, entered the drawing room to join him for afternoon tea. She was wearing a lovely velvet dress, and he, a sharp blue suit.

"Rudolph is doing rather well at Harvard in spite of the slurs about him being German," Isaac said as he poured his wife a cup of steaming tea.

Johanna sat in the Victorian chair opposite him, and took a graceful sip.

"I am glad. I am quite concerned for him abroad. I understand we have acquired a poor reputation in the states. Even America has begun to blame us."

Isaac did everything to avoid the topic of war. "He expects to receive straight A's. How is that for studying overseas?"

Johanna smiled. Her brown eyes twinkled. "It does not surprise me in the least. He comes from good blood."

"Are you referring to yours or mine?" Isaac teased, stroking his goatee.

"Isaac, really!" Johanna admonished, but held a deep appreciation for her husband's dry humor. He chuckled and lifted a lead crystal decanter to pour two shots of sherry. He presented one to Johanna and proposed a toast.

"To Rudolph's success."

They clinked crystal and consumed the sweet liqueur with dreams swimming in their heads.

"Just think, Johanna. One day, Rudolph will be a doctor, and I will be able to retire once he takes over my practice."

Johanna's face glowed. "Just as we have always planned it to be…and you and I will finally be able to travel the world. Because, we both know this war will not last forever."

Isaac grimaced. "You know, my dear, I never voice my feelings, but I am glad Rudolph is in America. You may regard me unpatriotic, but I say a special prayer each day, thanking God he is not here to fight this war."

Johanna observed him in shock. "Perhaps you should share your thoughts with me more often; I have been doing the same."

As Herr Stern reached across the mahogany coffee table to kiss his wife's hand, Gunther Wagner steamed from where he watched in the vestibule, behind the French doors.

Treason it was! Germany had just lost a battle to France! The Kaiser needed all the soldiers he could get, and these two traitors were proud their son had abandoned his country! At ten, an angry flame had begun to kindle within him. First his brother. Now this! He was helpless as he was irate.

He only wished he were old enough to become a soldier now.

Chapter 10

The twins settled into Georgetown well. With dances, clubs, and academic demands, it was easy to tune out the war in Europe. At first, they shared common interests. There was a party almost every night. Then Rose became buried beneath books and assignments, while Veda remained socially active. Though roommates, they drifted apart, and sadly, an effort to bond was never made.

Rose was now an introvert; Veda, a social butterfly. But Veda's frivolity was not spared its repercussions, and Rose's social withdrawal also collided with adversity.

The climax occurred in December.

"Where are you going?" Rose asked from the desk where she had been studying for hours. She was still in uniform, and her eyes were bloodshot from fatigue.

Veda threw on her school coat and stormed to the door. "I am going out for a walk! I cannot take *this* anymore!"

Rose sighed testily. "You cannot take *what*, Veda?"

Veda snapped back at her. "Isn't it obvious? These books! This pressure! Deadlines! Everything! I feel like I am going mad!"

Rose observed her in shock. "You must not do this. It is final week. In a few days, we will be on our way back to New York for the holidays."

But Veda was hardly mollified. In fact, she was a raving mess. "Don't you tell me I mustn't! *You*! Miss straight A's! Every professor's little pet!"

Rose stood and eyed her twin firmly. "Well, perhaps if you had opened a book this term, you would not be failing every subject."

The truth struck Veda harshly. "I hate books! And I hate this school! I never wanted to come to this second-rate prison anyway! If it were not for the fact that there were men here, I would swear I was locked away in a convent!"

"Veda!" Rose was appalled.

"Do not Veda *me*! I wanted to go to Vassar! That is where all well-bred women are being charmed by West Point Cadets, not these boring squares who dance with two left feet and drink fruit punch at parties!"

It was very rare that Rose lost her cool, but Veda was inciting her to ire. "You are very fortunate that Mother and Father cannot hear you! You know you could not go to Vassar! Catholic women go to Georgetown!"

Veda exploded. "And they might as well all become nuns!"

Rose was silent for a long moment until she gathered herself and questioned in a biting whisper, "And what is wrong with becoming a nun?"

Veda was paralyzed. The anger drained from her eyes, and was replaced with shock. "What are you saying, Rose?" Then she paused and stared at her twin's grave expression incredulously, "You are not actually considering..."

Silence.

"You are not, Rose...you could not!"

Silence... "Are you?"

Rose nodded...She was.

******

New York

The Champion house was a miniature brownstone mansion on Park Avenue and 65th Street. The first floor housed a reception room, a dining room, a pantry, a library and a den overlooking Park Avenue to the east. The ballroom and the servants' quarters were on the second floor, and the bedrooms, guest, and master suites on the third.

It was, indeed, a bustling place, as preparations for Christmas and the twins' return were feverishly underway. *La Madame* Champion immersed herself in holiday drives, dinners, and charities as a means of blacking out the precarious conditions in France. It was working. Giving orders was one of her specialties and supervising a staff of twenty kept her mind well occupied. There was also holiday shopping, menu arrangements for her annual New Year's Eve ball, and plans for her antique show scheduled in January. She seemed herself again, and Winston was greatly relieved. Of course, news of the dauntless French army and its effective defense against the Germans helped matters.

Though a long and tedious task, Hans Wagner enjoyed decorating the twenty-foot Christmas tree in the reception room that snowy December day. As he glanced out the cathedral window onto the white sheet over Park Avenue, he could not help but reflect upon his childhood Christmas' in Berlin. It was always a happy time, a time for family and friends, a holiday Rudi and the Stern's did not share with them. But they never failed to marvel, nonetheless at the warmth and serenity he, his mother, and Gunther had shared.

His mother. He wondered how she was, how she would fare this first Christmas they would be separated. And his mind drifted to Gunther too. He missed his young brother very much, yearned to see his glowing face, and wild, adventurous eyes. He wondered, too, how they were accepting Germany's engagement in the war, what they thought of him far away and removed from it all. Were they glad he was not a soldier like the other young men his age, or did they condemn him a traitor, or, at the very least, a failure?

"*Hans!*" He flinched at the sound of the imperious voice, and sprang to immediate attention on the ladder where he stood, fifteen feet in the air.

His eyes met the steely gaze of Thaddeus, the house butler, and he questioned with unwavering allegiance, "Yes, sir?"

Thaddeus sniffed. He enjoyed needling the German. "Why are you daydreaming? *La Madame* Champion has ordered that the tree be completed by dusk!"

Hans nodded assuredly. "And it shall be, sir."

In four months, he had nearly mastered the English language. His brilliance had evoked admiration from Winston Champion, and resentment from the other servants, particularly Thaddeus, who despised him.

Thaddeus sneered, "I believe you are a bit overconfident, just like the rest of *your people* who are terrorizing Europe!"

Hans' jaws tightened and his face became red with rage. But he choked on his anger and said nothing. Allegiance…always.

"It shall be finished, sir." He repeated.

"*That* remains yet to be seen!" Thaddeus snapped and left, clicking his heels every step of the way.

Hans silently cursed him. But he knew his place as an inferior. An inferior.

But not forever. Winston Champion liked him; he did not know when or how, but one day, it would work to his advantage.

And again, he thought of Rose. She would be home the next day. He would see her again, and maybe…

Stop it, Hans! You are just a servant! he silently scolded himself. *A servant, true, but not forever.*

******

Veda sobbed as she finished packing in her dormitory bedroom. It was their last evening at Georgetown, and it was frigid outside. She and Rose wore flannel nightgowns, freezing from the absence of a fireplace in their room. Just one more night, though. Tomorrow they would be back in their toasty, warm New York house with a crackling fireplace in every room, no drafts, comfortable furnishings, and home cooked food.

Rose's final comforts…Veda's vowed indulgences…

"What is the matter?" Rose questioned softly as she emerged from the bathroom.

Veda sobbed louder, "Oh, Rose! I do not know how I will live without you! This all seems so final! We have never been separated! In just a few short weeks, you will be gone forever!"

Rose came to her twin and stroked her rich black curls. "Not forever. Perhaps a very long time, but not forever."

Veda threw down the top of her suitcase. "How do you know how long it is going to be! Did an angel whisper something about the nunnery to you during those endless hours you spent in the campus chapel?"

Rose sighed. "Please do not do this. It is sinful."

Veda fired. "Do not tell me what is sinful! I have tried to understand what you are doing, Rose, and I am sorry, but I just cannot! You are pretty! You are smart! Why in the world are you becoming a nun?"

Rose looked into her twin's eyes with an angelic glow on her face. "Because I have received a calling."

Veda continued to cry. "What calling? Did God Himself come down to invite you?"

"*Veda!* You have blasphemed!" Rose gushed, appalled.

Veda demurred slightly. "I cannot help it! I always imagined us together! You know that!"

Rose turned her back. Veda came around to see her tear-soaked face and insisted, "Rose, you must try to understand how I feel."

Rose glared at her. "And what about how I feel? Do I matter at all?"

87

Veda softened. "Of course, you do. I am thinking of you, too. I just want you to be happy."

Rose locked eyes with her. "Do you?" Veda was taken aback. "Why, of course!"

"Then offer me your blessing."

Veda fell dead silent. Finally, she nodded, if, begrudgingly.

Rose embraced her. "Thank you! You have no idea how much it means to me! Not even the Germans themselves could hurt me so much as your disapproval."

A light suddenly lit in Veda's mind: *The Germans...Hans...Hans will be there...*

And her world resumed spinning at the memory of the handsome German employee at their parents' Park Avenue home.

Her tears subsided, and her sadness was replaced by exhilaration. "It will be a *wonderful* Christmas, after all, Rose my darling!" she crooned, and resumed packing.

Rose surmised something more than the resealing of their hearts, but could not read Veda's mind at the moment. But she would, eventually. She always did.

Chapter 11

Theodore Aspan straddled himself above the young, African princess, and his blood gorged, vein laced muscle entered her with ease. He rode her slowly, with soft, bestial groans, and tasted heaven.

When he climaxed, the princess let out a cry of sheer ecstasy, and locked her smooth, silken legs around his pelvis to enhance the last seconds of paradise.

For three weeks, they had been at it. She was a gentle, jasmine scented reprieve from the back-breaking hours of labor beneath the relentlessly scorching sun. He was Adonis in the flesh. Though undernourished, soiled, sweaty, and blistered, Theodore Aspan remained ferociously appealing, and never forgot the art of lovemaking he had mastered like a charm.

They had met a month earlier, her father, a Negro descendent of royal blood; her brother, a frustrated, poverty-stricken prince, in search of his own self-made fortune, namely diamonds. He and Theodore shared a common interest and bonded in the heart of the big hole. Simba had invited Teddy to dinner one evening. Hence, the two lovers met, and gave birth, one week later, to a wild flame.

Paradise in hell. It kept Teddy going.

And as the full moon cast silver onto the bed of the six-room shack, as the crickets chirped, and the wild animals howled hungrily in the distance, Tarsheba fell asleep in Teddy's arms, and Simba, unaware of his presence, spoke openly to his father in the next room.

"No one knows I have found them. I will bury them in the backyard until I decide when to declare them."

His father gulped. "So…so many! How will you ever hide them all?" Simba affirmed confidently. "I shall…and there are more."

He told his father where.

By now, Teddy was wide-eyed and standing, his ear glued to the wall.

"But no one must know, Father! No one! It could be very dangerous for us, as natives. It is *our* fortune to claim! We can finally live as the royalty from which you have descended. These diamonds have come from the earth of your kingdom. They belong to us, not to any white man."

You are quite mistaken, my friend, Teddy Aspan sneered to himself, and went back to the bed to slip on his trousers. Then he climbed out the window into the black African night with an even blacker plan in his mind.

Simba was found slain in his backyard the next morning, and the plentitude of undeclared diamonds was a mere memory in his grieving father's mind.

By noon, Theodore Aspan had staked his claim, a chest full of diamonds, and a cave more in the Black Hole. At twenty-three, the family disappointment would return home one of the richest men in America.

Chapter 12

By Christmas, in Europe, the Western front had stretched far from Switzerland to the Belgian Coast. Both sides were several miles of water-logged trenches separated by barbed wire and the uninhabited wasteland in between. Here, lay the scars of machine gun bullets and rattling corpses in shell holes, no signs of life, just cold, wet mud.

Verdun was a comparatively quiet place in view of most other parts of France. War flames kindled around them, and casualties mounted by the thousands, as proud Frenchmen in red and blue uniforms were reduced to corpses on their own Motherland. But the French were putting up a good, dauntless fight, and had managed to prevent the Germans from achieving a total *coup d'état.*

Villages like Verdun were protected, and civilians were beginning to feel somewhat safe again, confident their brave, mighty army would spare them from the atrocities their Belgian neighbors had suffered.

"Joyeux Noel, *ma cher*," Pierre DuBois toasted at the head of the Louis XIV dining room table with a twinkle in his eye.

His wife, clad in black lace, raised her wine glass and smiled. "Joyeux Noel," she repeated, and together they took a long, satisfying sip of cabernet, vintage 1899.

The blaze of candles mingled with the intimate glow radiating from the eighteenth-century rock crystal and bronze gilt chandelier. The tone was peaceful, the ambiance flavored with warmth and love. Beyond them, the crackling firelight further illuminated the candlelit Christmas tree, adorned with colorful glass relics and gold tinsel.

Shadows of servants floated across the African Mahogany paneled walls, and they made a grand entrance with silver domed china on sterling trays.

"*Bon Appetit*," they murmured in unison as the domes were lifted to reveal goose entrees stuffed with apricots and grapes. Then they retreated, leaving the elderly couple alone with the resident bishop who had appeared to offer the grand blessing.

Though pencil slim and hunchbacked, he was an imposing figure, a white-haired prelate who had devoted fifty of his seventy-two years to reflection and prayer. He, too, retreated afterward, despite the couple's countless supplications for him to join them at the dinner table. But the holy man remained steadfast to his vigils. He ate alone, drank alone, prayed alone, joining the family merely for morning mass and blessings. He dissected everyone with an intent stare of his stern, gray eyes, and spoke at a minimum. His voice, on such rare occasions, was a firm monotone, his words, proverbs one had to reflect, at length, to understand.

And when they were alone again, *Monsieur* DuBois lowered his eyes to his linen napkin and feigned disturbance. "*Ma cher*, I believe I have been presented with the incorrect napkin. Apparently, this one is yours."

Then he reached across the table as *Madame* DuBois' bewilderment was replaced by a sudden gasp. The napkin holder was a clever presentation of her Christmas gift, a ring worth a fortune. The blinding array of diamonds was inlaid at 24 carat gold filigree, their blue white brilliance proclaiming flawless clarity.

"Pierre!" she gushed. "You should not have!"

He beamed. "It is just another token of my love for you, a thank you for all the years of joy we have shared."

Madame DuBois studied the ring in awe. Then, her lovely brown eyes rose to lock with her husband's.

"What are you thinking, *ma cher*?" he asked.

She smiled back at him. "You silly old man! You should not be squandering money on jewels when France is at war. We need to save everything we can." Then she grew serious as her face darkened, "We do not know when we might need it."

Monsieur DuBois kept smiling. "This war will be over very soon. We are giving the Germans a harder fight than they had anticipated. They were going to conquer Europe in forty days. After five months, I believe even they can admit they were rudely mistaken."

Madame DuBois frowned. "But there are so many of our young boys dying each day, dying now as we speak. It hardly seems right for me to accept this gift under the circumstances."

He rose from the head of the table, and settled again in the seat beside her. "The circumstances, *ma cher*, have nothing to do with our love. In peace, war, famine or drought, we are one, and shall always be. I would prefer to risk starvation before being convinced to return this ring."

She smiled again as he slipped it over her wrinkled finger, and his lips sealed it with a gentle kiss.

She stroked his face and pulled the chord to summon a servant who appeared with a wrapped gift on a gold tray.

"In that case," she whispered as she lifted the box and the servant disappeared. "This is my present to you."

Monsieur DuBois unwrapped the package, and his eyes enlarged when he beheld the 24-carat gold engraved locket.

"Open it," she enthused, and her own eyes watered with his, as they beheld the picture of their endeared daughter inside.

"So beautiful," he murmured, his heart racing. "And so far away."

Madame DuBois nodded as a tear slid down her face. "She is so worried about us. She blames herself for allowing us to leave the safety of her home last June."

Monsieur DuBois pulled his shoulders back and sat erect in the mahogany wood chair. "This is our home, *ma cher*. And we *are* safe. It will be only a matter of time before our soldiers drive the Germans out."

He paused and added as his eyes sank back to the picture in the locket. "And we *shall* see our daughter and our grandchildren again."

Madame DuBois shifted the topic. It was becoming too painful. "We had better eat. The goose is growing cold."

And as her husband rose to return to his place at the head of the table, she grimly doubted his words.

Chapter 13

The snow fell like glistening crystals from the steely sky that Christmas Eve morning at Georgetown. The twins exited their dormitory for the last time, and followed the driver to their carriage.

Veda sighed in relief as Rose raised her head to allow the snowflakes to kiss her face. "Well, at least it is the last day we must wear these hideous coats! I swear I am going to tear mine off as soon as we get to the train, and burn it in the fireplace tonight when we get home!"

She was referring to the traditional school coat she despised. It was blue, mundane, and standard uniform, quite a contrast to her flamboyant taste.

Rose glanced at her disapprovingly, then lifted her face back to the snow. "Do not swear, Veda."

Veda grimaced. "Well, why do we have to wear them anyway? Neither of us is coming back here!"

Rose answered in a coolly superior tone, "Because it is the dress code, and it is only polite."

"But we are leaving!" Veda protested; her cheeks reddened by the cold.

Rose remained firm, "And we are still on the campus grounds."

Veda would not be convinced, "Oh, what do I care about manners or any of *them*? They were not so polite to me…were they? Failing me as if I were some low born imbecile! I am smarter than every girl at this prison!"

Rose stopped in her tracks with narrowed eyes. "Then why did you not apply yourself to prove it?"

Veda pouted. "I do not have to prove anything! I know I am smart, and that is good enough!"

"You still could have at least tried."

"I did try!"

"Oh, really? When? At the Friday dances?"

Now, Veda sulked. "That was not funny."

Rose eyed her. "It was not meant to be funny, and it will be worse when you tell Father that you have discharged yourself."

Veda's eyes enlarged in shock. "And have *you* not done the same?"

Rose continued walking, all airs and dignity. "Yes, but for a good cause. And besides, I received straight A's."

Veda hastened to catch up with her. "Well, this is one time your perfect report card will not win Father's affection!"

Rose stopped again. Veda knew she had struck a weak bone, and looked at her twin with victory gleaming in her eyes. "Father is not a born Catholic. He will not understand what you are doing, Rose. Face it…you are in quicksand up to your neck…just like me."

Winston and *La Madame* Champion came to meet the girls at the train station late that afternoon. They were all hugs and kisses for the first minutes before settling into Winston's new Ford Model T for the trip home along the snow-covered cobblestone streets of Manhattan.

Christmas splendor abounded everywhere on Park Avenue, from the carolers to the carriages, the shoppers, and the candles glowing in mansion windows. Clouds of smoke billowing from chimneys mingled with snowflakes in the evening sky. Veda's eyes danced as she drank in all the splendor she adored. She was home, and the exhilaration was intoxicating.

The Champion House looked majestic. Lanterns illuminated the pineapple wreath in the center of the front door. Candles twinkled in every window, and the Christmas tree cast an incandescent glow over the foyer as seen through the cathedral window from the street.

Before they sprang from the car, *La Madame* Champion advised the girls they would be attending the Christmas ball at the Deneuve Mansion that night, and had just two hours to prepare for the gala event.

Veda did not relish the idea of seeing Jacques Deneuve again, especially after their bitter encounter at the wedding that past summer. But a party did suit the festive mood perfectly, and she would make the best of the minor drawback.

When she and Rose stepped onto the sidewalk of the Manhattan home, they both cooed as the scent of burning hickory wood, holly, and roasted chestnuts greeted them.

Hans Wagner appeared in the doorway, and froze for a short moment at the sight of Rose. Veda's heart skipped a beat. Rose saw him, and looked away. Her first temptation. Veda's revived obsession.

He looked more handsome than ever in a black footman's coat, the front of his platinum hair swept over his forehead, the rest, trimmed perfectly. His blue eyes sparkled beneath the glowing lanterns, and his tall frame had grown heavily muscled from hard work and the abundance of good, American food. Winston Champion treated his servants well, and Hans was an excellent example of his employer's generosity.

He spoke not a word, trained in the dogma of forbiddance for servants to socialize with superiors. The twins, too, understood it as a rule of thumb as he took their bags and proceeded forward.

Veda's eyes never left him, following his shadow on the wall of the foyer as he ascended the staircase to the third floor. She was never happier to be home. The thought of living under the same roof with Hans was electrifying.

But she maintained herself, squeezing Rose's hand just once at the initial sight of him, and walking with ease toward the vestibule as the dancing snowflakes swept past their faces.

Nanny McBride greeted them with wide open arms, "Welcome home, missies! The sight of yees is the one thing prettier than the Christmas snow!"

Her bear hugs were like none other. Steaming hot chocolate and fresh baked cookies waited for them in their fire lit bedrooms, and hot baths had already been drawn for their arrival.

Miraculously, they managed to prepare quickly in spite of the long journey from Georgetown, and at the stroke of eight on the antique mahogany wood grandfather clock, both young women stood like fairy tale princesses in the drawing room wearing rich satin ball gowns. Rose's was pink, Veda's a striking gold.

Rose had twisted her hair into a tight onyx bun. Veda swept the sides and front upward with a gold bow, allowing the back to drape over her neck in soft curls.

"Mother, you look ravishing!" Veda marveled, as *La Madame* Champion made a grand entrance in a purple velvet evening gown. Her diamonds glistened like a spectacular chandelier, and her powdered face possessed a queenly fairness, prized by New York society.

They were surrounded by 24-carat gold presentation framed paintings and matched the opulent setting exquisitely.

"Thank you, dear," she answered with a smile. "And so do you." Then she shifted her eyes to Rose, the sudden sullen beauty. "Rose, darling, what is the matter?"

Veda tensed knowingly. Rose shrugged with a gentle smile on her lips. "I am all right, Mother. I believe I just require some fresh air," she gently replied.

"And there will be no shortage of that. So long as you do not mind the cold," Winston interjected from the vestibule where he stood beneath the rock crystal chandelier, beaming in white tie. "We had better go, ladies, lest we exceed the limits of fashionable lateness."

Veda waltzed over to him and pecked his pudgy cheek. "Oh, Father! How I have missed you so!"

They rode in a black marble horse drawn carriage. Though motor cars were in vogue, given the snow, the Champions, and most other families opted to leave the marvelous American invention in a dry garage, and adhere to a safer, if more archaic mode of transportation.

The Deneuve mansion was on East 76th Street and Fifth Avenue. It was a limestone palace fashioned in the style of Louis XVIII. Guests arrived by the dozen. Valet men helped disgorge fur and jewel bedecked women and their tuxedoed escorts to the doorstep of the garland lined residence. Orchestral tunes spilled out into the street, and greeted guests with holiday cheer. A line of carriages circled the block, and gaslight lanterns illuminated the sidewalks for those arriving by foot.

Festivities abounded within, where strolling minstrels, carolers, and white gloved waiters bustled, offering every spirit from champagne to wassail.

Veda's first stop was the 'jewel box' of a dressing room where arriving ladies freshened before making their grand entrances. Hers was the most spectacular when she emerged and arrested the eyes of nearly every man present. It felt magnificent to be in the spotlight once again, amongst people who mattered, within a glittering world in which she felt comfortable, and knew she belonged.

Admirers promptly flocked to her side, and she greeted them with a glistening white smile, waves of her dainty hand, expert gestures, and polished mannerisms.

And as she stood in the center of the grand hall, amidst holly, garland and lights, Veda flinched when a pair of strong hands embraced her from behind.

"May I be the first to kiss the belle of the ball?" a disguised voice whispered into her ear.

Veda huffed. "Why, you low bred." Then she stopped in the same breath as her brother, clad in white tie, swung around to face her with a broad, dashing smile.

"Marius! How devilish of you to sneak up on me like that!" he laughed. "You always said I was the devil in disguise."

Veda's violet eyes twinkled. "And the devil you are! Look at you! Handsomer than ever! Though it saddens me to admit, marriage certainly seems to agree with you."

Marius bowed playfully. "It does, Veda." Then his face glowed as they locked eyes. "And you look absolutely magnificent, little sister."

She beamed and span gracefully before him. "Do you like my new dress?"

He nodded and stroked his chin with narrowed eyes. "It is spectacular. I am going to have to keep an eye on you this evening."

Veda waved her gloved hand. "Oh, stop running on! Now usher me to the dance floor for my first waltz," she paused and added with an impish grin. "With such short notice, I never had the chance to prepare a dance card."

Marius grinned. "We shall dance, but not before I take you to greet Dominique."

Veda frowned. "Oh, Marius, must we?"

He winked with a resolute nod. "Yes, my dear. Now come." Then he took her arm and led her to the ornate ballroom which comfortably seated one hundred guests. There were five sets of French windows, each flaunting a massive wreath. A spectacular sixteen-foot Christmas tree sat grandly in the center of the floor.

To Veda's chagrin, Marius ushered her directly to Dominique who looked lovely in maroon velvet.

"Dominique, darling. Veda," he announced proudly, and his wife's smile ran away from her face when she turned to rest eyes upon her sister-in-law.

"Veda." She droned, extending a cool hand. "A very warm welcome home."

Veda accepted the gesture with a forced a smile. "So warm, that the breath from your lips is turning me into an iceberg."

Dominique suddenly enjoyed the banter. "Figurative speech *is* one of your specialties. Did you excel in anything else at Georgetown this semester?"

Veda chortled pompously. "Why, of course! I am not one to boast, Dominique, darling, but I received straight A's in every subject!"

Marius choked on his fruit punch. Veda glared at him, then shifted eyes back to her sister-in-law, feeling her cheeks redden.

Dominique smirked. "Really? No stretch of the truth?" Veda nodded. "Cross my heart."

Dominique's eyebrows rose suspiciously. "Your nose is growing, my dear."

Veda's blood heated fast. "Why, if I don't."

"Hello, Veda," chimed a charming voice, and she glanced over her shoulder to meet the handsome face of Jacques Deneuve. His hazel eyes were glistening beneath the crystal chandelier. His short brown hair was slicked back on his head, and his white teeth sparkled. Clad too in white tie, only Marius, in Veda's unbiased opinion looked more dashing.

"Jacques Deneuve!" she exclaimed, offering her hand. "How history does have a way of repeating itself! I was wondering where you were, *and* waiting for you to ask me to dance."

Dominique rolled her eyes. "Careful, Veda. Your nose might be so large by evening's end that you will not make it out the door."

Veda glowered as Marius shook his head hopelessly.

"Excuse me, Dominique. This foyer is not large enough for both of us," she quipped, and shifted dancing eyes back to Jacques. "I am parched. Will you escort me to the refreshment table?"

Jacques bowed politely. "It would be my pleasure."

Together, they walked arm in arm, capturing the admirable stares of everyone around them. It was widely agreed they made a becoming couple, and many wondered if Winston Champion would arrange yet another marriage with the Deneuve family.

A footman ladled out two cups of holiday punch, and Jacques' face grew heavy with contrite when he presented the first to Veda. "I must apologize for my behavior at the wedding."

She took a generous sip and smiled teasingly. "Come to think of it, you were quite rude, and extremely presumptuous. But I forgive you."

He stared at her with that same earnest gleam in his eyes she had remembered. "Nonetheless, it does not change my feelings for you."

Veda tensed with a bemused grin. "What feelings, Jacques? Oh, yes, that I am low born, and deserve no better than a drunken renegade like Chester Worthington."

He gulped, and his face flushed. "I did not mean it, Veda. I love you! Can't you see that? It is Christmas. Why not start over?"

She finished her punch and thought of Hans as she handed the crystal back to the server. "I suppose we can, but I must warn you, Jacques. *My* feelings have not changed either."

"What feelings?" he flirted.

"That I am charming, dashing and irresistible?" And he did a merry jig which made her burst into laughter.

"Jacques, you are a born clown!"

He bowed, took her hand and brought it to his heart. "No. I am a born Romeo. Now, will you waltz with me, Juliet?"

She smiled back at him as he led her along the parquet floor. "Only if you promise not to climb a ladder up to my window later on."

He shook his head and positioned her for a waltz. "Not a chance for that. The snow is too deep." His words were replaced by the tunes of Tchaikovsky's *Waltz of the Flowers*.

The twins settled back into their carriage at precisely eleven o'clock as Winston and *La Madame* Champion bade their final farewells.

Veda had waited for this moment alone with her sister. "Really, Rose! You could have tried to be a bit more sociable! It seemed as if you were at a funeral instead of a Christmas Eve ball!"

Rose frowned. Pain was spelled clearly on her chalk white face. "I do not understand how you could say such a thing. You know what I am going through!"

Veda frowned impatiently. "You are not a nun, *yet*! You could have at least danced with someone! How do you think it looked for you, a Champion, to deny every eligible bachelor an innocent waltz?"

Tears welled in Rose's lovely, gray eyes. "I did not want to offer any of them the wrong impression."

Veda sighed. "Blabber, Rose! They are all fools! What do you care *what* they think?"

Just then, Rose, the cool, composed model of perfection, burst into a fit of uncontrolled sobs. "Veda, I am so scared! How am I ever going to tell Mother and Father?"

At first, Veda was stunned into silence. Until now, only she had given way to such emotional outbursts. But instinct took over, and she embraced her twin endearingly, nestling her tear-soaked face into the warmth of her bosom.

"It is all right. You will do it the same as you have been successful at everything else in life."

Rose remained frantic. "What will Father say? How will he understand?"

Veda stroked her sister's beautiful black hair. "He will accept it, eventually."

At that moment, she caught a glimpse of her stately parents approaching the carriage arm in arm.

"Now compose yourself. They are coming!"

Rose dried her tears instantly and raised her head. By the time the footman had opened the carriage door, she was sitting like a solemn porcelain statue without a trace of strife on her young face.

Everyone but Veda retired when they reached the Champion house shortly past eleven thirty. She went into the tree lit parlor and settled comfortably into the soft, Victorian sofa. Her dreams mingled with the snowflakes still falling on the opposite side of the cathedral window, and her prince had emerged from them when Hans stepped into the room at the grandfather clock's stroke of midnight.

"Merry Christmas, Miss," he whispered in the eloquent accent she adored, and she sprang to immediate attention as her heart skipped another beat.

"Oh...yes...I suppose it is that time...Merry Christmas," she answered with an awkward smile.

"Were you sleeping?" he gently questioned.

She nodded, dazed. "I guess I must have dozed off for a few moments."

He chuckled and reached for the huge candle snuffer. "It is a good thing I came to wake you. You would have frozen down here by morning."

She looked up at him, awestruck. "You...you speak English. My, you *have* learned quickly!"

He nodded modestly. "It took hours of studying, and practice, but I knew I had to." And he added, reverently, "If I am to become an American."

He wheeled the ladder to the Christmas tree and began to climb. Veda, with her heart in her throat, her body trembling, hastened to his side.

"I can help you..." she enthused breathlessly.

He looked down, reading her mind. The candlelight cast an angelic glow onto his face.

"That is not necessary. I have had much practice alone."

"Oh?" she said, and he stared at her strangely.

Then she added nervously. "I mean...oh...of course. But I would be happy to hold the ladder for you anyway."

"You are very kind, Miss," he answered, and went about his work.

She eyed his every move, savoring the intimacy, the quiet, the seasonal magic. And when he came down, she was there at the foot of the ladder, inches from his strong body, shivering on her thoughts.

Hans studied her awkwardly, well aware of the passion kindling within her. "Em… I must put out the candles on the other side."

Veda gulped, and her words trembled, "Did you think of me while I was away?"

He smelled the essence of her perfumed body, her silken hair, and he tensed, "I…I think we should say good night, Miss."

She edged closer until their bodies touched. All control drained from her as she whispered breathlessly and pursed her lips. "Do not be nervous, please. I have waited to see you. This can be so perfect. I have never kissed a man before." And she froze midair as he gently edged away after a momentary brushing of lips.

He stood, noble and erect, seeming to fight the birth of something new within himself. "This cannot be, Miss. I work for your father. My job is everything to me."

Veda's face reddened with shame. "Forgive me. I should not have done that. I do not know what had come over me."

He observed her, his breath trembling with his heart. He was inches from her graceful neck, her gently curved back, her narrow waist. It was all so tempting to his eyes, but he knew he needed to resist, and he did.

"Good night, Miss," he murmured dignifiedly and wheeled the ladder to the opposite side of the Christmas tree.

"Good night," she whispered back, touching her tingling lips, convinced this was just an awkward beginning to a magical lifetime ahead.

Then she backed out of the room and watched him every step of her slow journey up the staircase.

In her warm canopy bed in the fire lit room, her last thought was the memory of her lips on his before she drifted into a dreamy slumber.

Chapter 14

Christmas in Berlin was comparatively quiet to the festivities in New York. Candles, too, glowed in every Christian window, but the celebrations were more modest, and not just because of the war. It was, quite simply, the German way.

Frau Wagner and her son, Gunther, did their best to enjoy the holiday in light of Hans' absence. They attended mass early that morning, trimmed their three-foot Christmas tree afterward, and feasted on a delectable roast turkey, compliments of their employers, Herr and Frau Stern.

Frau Wagner had struggled to save from her overtime hours to purchase Gunther the train set he so ardently desired. And he was delighted when the Stern's permitted their son, Simon, to enter the servant's wing to play with him early that evening.

"Do you feel left out by not celebrating Christmas?" Gunther asked as they lay on their stomachs watching the toy train encircle the Christmas tree.

Simon shrugged. "Why should I? I am Jewish."

Gunther nodded with a gleam in his eyes. "Yes, but can you not see how much fun Christmas is? It is the happiest day of the year!"

Simon raised his head and replied with a coolness in his tone. "For you, perhaps. We have holidays of our own."

Gunther remained silent for a long moment, considering Simon's words. "But today is Jesus' birthday. Is it true you do not believe it?"

Simon rolled his eyes. "Of course not."

"Why?" Gunther asked incredulously.

Simon sprang to his feet and looked down at his friend with contempt. "Because Jewish people know better!"

And he left in a huff. Gunther was confused, and did not like having his feelings hurt by Simon once again. But *he* should have known better.

"Jews are Jews!" he remembered his school friends tell him. "And they killed Jesus!"

Then he tuned out everything and went back to playing with his beautiful, new train set.

******

New York

Veda woke early Christmas morning with the same memory of Hans' lips on hers. It was so fabulously romantic, the two of them, alone in the reception room amidst glowing candles on the enormous Christmas tree. She thought to herself *Could I be living a dream?*

She did not see him that day. Winston had given the servants a paid holiday, save the few non-Christians, and Nanny McBride, who insisted on adhering to her duties three hundred sixty-five days a year.

The family enjoyed an elaborate breakfast before attending the High Noon Mass at St. Patrick's Cathedral. Then they returned to the house to exchange Christmas gifts before sitting to a five-course gourmet meal, including entrée choices of pheasant, ostrich, and venison.

Marius and Dominique had come to join them, and it was a culinary feast for which only the best crystal, silver, lace, and Ming Dynasty China accompanied a meal fit for royalty.

It was amidst the presentation of the baked Alaska dessert when the call came in from France. *La Madame* Champion, resplendent in a brown velvet dinner gown, her black hair twisted into a chignon, her diamond accessories glistening, tensed for a long moment before she rose to accept the call.

"Excuse me," she said eloquently, and exited the room with starched dignity. The family sat in uneasy silence, exchanging worrisome glances as Winston went to join his wife in the drawing room.

Veda, lovely in a forest green gown, said a silent prayer, and could tell by the expressions on her siblings' faces, that they were doing the same.

Rose, too, looked stunning in plum and Dominique, in royal blue. Marius, matching his father in white tie, clenched his fists tensely, hoping their grandparents were all right.

Every tick of the grandfather clock was a torment. Otherwise, the French Renaissance style dining room was silent as a tomb.

Winston and *La Madame* Champion finally reappeared after what seemed to be an eternity, their eyes sparkling, their faces beaming with broad smiles.

104

"Mr. Champion, you will make the announcement. And, afterward, Marius shall propose the toast."

La Madame's words were a signal of relief. Already, they knew. Their hearts surged with joy.

Winston and his wife took their places at the table. Veda marveled at their ability to maintain themselves at such a glorious moment.

"Children," Winston blithely stated. "We have just heard from your grandparents. They have wished you all a Merry Christmas, and have assured us everything is quiet and well in Verdun."

Veda, Rose and Marius cried out in ecstasy as Dominique took her teary-eyed mother in law's hand.

Moments later, Marius motioned for the servant to pour the wine from the English Georgian style crystal decanter. Then, he proposed a heartfelt toast.

"To our grandparents, and to all of us. A very Merry Christmas." Baccarat crystal clinked, and Marius added as they all took their first sip.

"And also, to the new year…that it might bring an end to the war abroad." Again, they clinked.

Chapter 15

Central Park transformed into a winter wonderland the next day as falling snow added a fresh coat to the white blanket stretching across the earth.

Hans Wagner and Rudolph Stern stepped from a carriage and went to a bench to slip on their ice skates. In front of them, a slew of skaters glided gracefully along the frozen pond.

"I almost thought you had abandoned me," Hans said as he looked at Rudi with gleaming eyes.

Rudi laughed. "Never, Hans. As a matter of fact, *you* are the only reason I *did* return to New York. During my week in Boston, I had met some friends who invited me along with them on a trip to Niagara Falls."

Hans winked playfully. "And so, you chose to visit your pauper servant friend instead."

Rudi chortled. "Who are you kidding? I hear old man Champion pays his employees quite handsomely. Between your regular salary and your Christmas bonus, your bank account is probably bigger than mine by now."

Hans guffawed. "Not quite, but I am working on it. I like to think I am living the American dream. Only, there is one thing missing."

"What is that?" Rudi asked, rising to his feet.

Hans stood too. "A beautiful American woman," he answered, and Rudi slapped him on the back.

"Well, let's get going. The pond is full of them," he enthused, and together they went to join the skaters.

"Veda, I really did not want to come here," Rose protested as they approached the pond wearing fur lined cashmere coats, pillbox hats, fur muffs, and skates.

Veda shook her head resolutely, and tugged her twin to the pond. "Nonsense, Rose! This is probably the last time we will ever ice skate together! Why don't you just enjoy yourself?"

"I cannot," Rose said gloomily. "Why?"

Rose looked at her with pain in her eyes, and the weight of the world on her shoulders. "You know why."

Veda sighed. "Honestly, Rose! Just because you are going off to the nunnery, does not mean you have to stop living!"

"It is not that Veda, and you know it. I am worried about Father. Every time I want to tell him, the words become caught in my throat. I am such a coward! I only wish it were next week already when I will be there. Away from all of this! It will be so much easier!"

Veda eyed her darkly. "What makes you so sure the walls of some convent will satisfy you more than the real world?"

Rose did not take offense. "It will not be to the walls or the darkness that I belong, but to the cause the confinement will represent."

Veda was dumbfounded. "What in heavens are you talking about? You make absolutely no sense anymore!"

Rose stiffened. Her eyes grew cold as the wintry frost around them. "That is because I no longer belong to the world you know."

Veda observed her in sheer fright. "Rose, have you lost your mind completely? What other world is there? Now you are carrying this a bit too far, and I do not know about you, but I feel like skating. Are you coming or not?"

"No!" Rose firmly replied.

"Suit yourself!" Veda intoned and froze on her feet in the next moment. "Look!"

"What now?" Rose asked testily.

Veda's eyes widened in elation. "The figure skaters! It is Hans and his friend from the wedding last summer!"

Rose saw them now as well. They were gliding expertly in the center of the pond, attracting numerous admiring spectators.

Veda was breathless. "Father must have given Hans another day off! Oh, isn't it wonderful?"

Rose, too, was impressed by their talent.

Hans spotted them first, and then Rudi. They had finished their number and were receiving a hearty applause.

"Isn't she beautiful?" Hans questioned, swooning.

Rudi was dazed himself. "Which one? They are both lookers!"

But Hans knew all too well. "Rose! The more gentle one!"

Rudi nodded. "Oh, yes, the one who looks bored out of her mind."

Hans laughed. "I can take care of that. I am going to ask her to skate."

And he started for her, but Rudi restrained him. "Do not do it, Hans. Remember our little talk. You are doing too well. Just another week or so and she will be back to school."

Hans frowned. "Why should it matter? It is innocent, and in the open! The old man will not care!"

Rudi raised his brows. "Really? Do not prove yourself wrong."

Hans knew he was right. He was not impervious to reason. "But who will rescue her from her boredom?" he asked teasingly.

Rudi winked. "I will!" And he skated off, leaving Hans stunned with his mouth wide open.

"Hello, ladies!" Rudi crooned. His short bush of curls had been flattened by the cap he removed. His cheeks were reddened by the cold. His black eyes were wide with zest. "Remember me? I am Rudolph Stern. We met at your brother's wedding last summer."

Veda looked past him toward Hans. Rose was polite. "Yes, how do you do, Mr. Stern? It is a pleasure to see you again."

"Likewise," he replied, ecstatic that she had remembered him. "Care to skate?" He asked, gliding around her.

"Oh, I do not think so," she answered with a demure shake of her head. Veda saw an opportunity and decided to take advantage of it.

"Why, of course she does. Rose is just very shy." And she edged her forward. Rudi took Rose's arm and slipped it through his. "Well, in *that* case!"

And they went off into the center of the pond where they skated magnificently. To her surprise, Rose felt revived. Veda was electrified to see it.

"Quite a pair, aren't they?"

She was paralyzed by the voice. Hans had come over to her, and at first, she did not notice, so engrossed in the joy of Rose's rebirth.

One look at him left her breathless. He might have been dressed poorly in a plaid jacket, an old scarf, and a peasant's cap, but his large muscled frame, his handsome face with its rosy cheeks, and blue eyes bespoke royalty.

She too, looked lovely, with her dainty hands nestled snugly in her fur muff, her face glowing, her eyes radiant with a genuine passion for life. But Hans hardly saw it, so swept by the sight of Rose gliding across the pond like an arctic goddess.

Veda read the obsession on his face, and felt a flash of envy. Her smile faded. Her eyes hardened. "A gentleman would have the chivalry to ask a girl standing alone to skate," she gently admonished, though seething within.

"Maybe I am not the right gentleman." Hans answered, his eyes never shifting from Rose.

Veda's heart cracked. "But you are!" she gushed impulsively, and caught herself in the next moment. "I mean...I would be happy to skate with you. That is, if you."

"No thank you." Cut and dry. His voice was cool, his eyes riveted on her twin.

Veda felt her blood heat fast. "I bet if it were Rose asking you, you would oblige in the blink of an eye." She could not believe she had said it. She, Veda, had never pleaded with any man before him.

Hans blushed and replied politely, "That is not true." He lied, knowing he had insulted her, feeling contrite. And so, he qualified, "But you are also quite lovely."

The pain of rejection had transformed into fury. "Do not patronize me! It is obvious you care for Rose and not me! God only knows why! Try spending five minutes with her! She is so sullen and boring; she will drive you right away!"

Hans grew solemn and withdrew into himself. "It would not matter anyway," he remarked, shifting his gaze to Rose again.

Veda saw the advantage. "No, it would not, because you see, Rose is..." And she caught herself. "Well, let's just say she is not interested in men just now."

"Oh?" He turned back to her, clearly disturbed. There was more. He knew it. "I find...em...it hard to believe that such a beautiful girl does not want to...em...find herself a suitor. And forgive me, Miss...but...you, too."

Insult to injury! She was ready to explode, but did everything to remain composed and dignified. But her tongue sharpened into a sword. "*My* business is none of *your* affair, Mr. Wagner! May I suggest you mind your duties, instead of trying to reason the lifestyles of people out of your league?"

He froze too. She had hurt him gravely, and for the first time in her young life, Veda was glad to have inflicted injury.

His face darkened. His eyes twitched. "Excuse me," he sniffed, and skated away sulkily.

Veda's pain and fury cast a grim film over the winter scene. She hated Hans now, and when she saw Rose skating toward her with a wide smile on her angelic face, she felt her blood come to a boil.

"Veda, I am so glad you encouraged me to skate! I feel so alive again, so happy! You were so right all along! Come now…let's skate together!" Her voice rang with the energy of a child.

"No," Veda replied, pouting.

Rose was taken aback. "But why not?"

"I said *no!*" Veda snapped back truculently.

"But you wanted—"

"I only want to go home!"

Rose was dumbfounded. "Whatever for?"

"I do not have to explain anything to you! Are you coming with me or not?"

Rose observed her in shock. "Why, of course. Anything you want."

But Veda was already ten steps ahead of her. Rose carefully traced every chapter of the day, tensely pondering just what had gone wrong. But it remained a mystery.

The snow had diminished to scattered flurries when they reached the Park Avenue Brownstone, and Veda stormed through the front door in a huff with Rose trailing nervously behind.

"Veda, a word." Winston Champion had met them in the foyer. His face was stone hard; his eyes, razor sharp. But his tone was the worst of all; the frost spewed from his lips could have transformed a balmy summer day into an ice age.

Veda demurred quickly, half stunned, half frightened. "Of course, Father," she replied sheepishly, and followed him into the study.

Rose watched them head down the hall. She sensed the truth, and pitied Veda deeply. How did their father find out so soon? What would he do when he heard of her own plans?

"Have a seat," Winston cracked, and Veda obeyed, feeling her knees knock as she settled into the red Gothic chair.

The crackling fire added no warmth to the frigid room. Veda tensed when her father pulled up a chair and sat beside her.

"So, Veda, since you have been home, you never once mentioned how you were getting along in school."

She shifted in her seat, not daring to look into his blazing eyes. "I…I suppose I have been too caught up with all of the holiday festivities, Father," she answered, her voice shaking.

He eyed her knowingly. "Well, perhaps you might put holiday season on hold for a few minutes and inform me of your progress."

Veda gulped. "Well, it is rather slow, Father."

His gaze sharpened. She could feel the abrasion, though she looked at the floor.

"Slow, Veda, or at a complete standstill?"

The walls of the room seemed to enclose upon her. "I do not understand."

"Don't you? Shall I refresh your memory, perhaps? I received a call from the Dean of Women at Georgetown today. I was informed that you have failed every subject, and had you not discharged yourself at the end of the semester, they would have done you the courtesy themselves!"

Veda felt like crawling under the chair. Her head hung low. She said nothing.

"Has the cat gotten your tongue?" She could feel her father's eyes boring into her.

Finally, she reached deep into herself and groped for words. "Father, I am so sorry. I was too ashamed to let you know."

Winston sprang to his feet and paced the room. "Ashamed, were you? Was it during the recesses of your ballroom dancing, dinner parties and ice skating, or do you have a thwarted way of exhibiting shame through recreation?"

She turned chalk white. Every word was a dagger. "I truly *am* ashamed, Father."

He glared at her from where he stood beneath the stained-glass window. "You speak with remorse in your tone; yet I do not believe you."

"But you must, Father!" Veda pleaded with tears glistening in her eyes.

He remained cool and superior, though he blazed like a torch, "You have the situation confused, my child. *You* are the one to take orders here, not I. And right now, you will offer me a genuine explanation for your failure and the disgrace you have cast upon this family."

She knew she was cornered. It was honesty or nothing now. Winston Champion was too smart to be fooled.

She took a deep, shuddering breath. "I never *did* want to go to Georgetown, Father. I only went to make you and Mother happy, and, of course, to be with Rose. I really wanted to go to Vassar, but knew Mother forbade it."

He studied her intently. As she had expected, he appreciated her candidness. "Am I to conclude, therefore, that your failure was a rebellion?"

She shrugged, defeated. "I suppose it was, Father. But I would be lying to say I would have done any better at Vassar. Forgive me, but school holds no interest for me anymore."

He stared down at her, into her, his wrists crossed behind his back. There was a long, tense silence after which he questioned in a biting whisper.

"And just what do you plan for your future now?"

Her future…a big question mark. It was frightening to realize she was a carefree girl no longer. The future. It was a fog. Rose's was planned. Marius was already married. Where was she headed.

"I…I never gave it much thought, Father," she replied guiltily.

"Just as I had surmised," he observed and came to her side. His eyes narrowed. "I shall intervene now, Veda, for your own good. You will proceed to your room and carry on as if this conference had never taken place. I will ponder a way to apprise your mother of this travesty, and *you* will concede to the plans I shall orchestrate for your future."

"Those being, Father?" She defied to question, testing her limits.

"What else?" he snapped back at her, the firelight illuminating him. "To find you a suitable husband."

She gloomily carried herself up the stairs and into her doll filled, princess style bedroom. She was stunned when Nanny McBride emerged from the bathroom after having drawn her bath.

"Great stars, Nanny! You nearly scared me to death! You could have had the courtesy to make your presence known!"

Nanny McBride waddled to the mahogany wood armoire, and set out Veda's green ball gown for the Worthington party that evening.

"And what would *ye* be knowin' about courtesy, Missy?"

Veda glared at her, finally unhooking her coat. "What in the name of all that is holy are you talking about?"

Nanny replied with a knowing grin, "I been watchin' ye, Missy, and I'm gonna keep an eye on ye for ye own good. *And* for the protection of that poor young footman ye been pesterin'!"

Veda froze. *How would nanny have known?* "How dare you propose such a notion! What footman? I do not fritter away my time with servants!"

Nanny McBride took Veda's coat and began to undress her with a cynical gleam in her eyes. "Like ye time's so valuable these days, Missy? What footman? Don't be coy with Nanny! Ye forget that I was the one who brought ye into the world. Got a crush on him, have ye?"

Veda pulled her slip over her head and fumed, "Heavens, Nanny! On whom?"

Nanny McBride collected the garments and wrapped Veda in a velvet robe. "Yee'd be makin' a big mistake runnin' after him."

Veda tore away vehemently. "I beg your RUDE pardon! I have not been running after anyone, nor shall I ever!"

Then she aimed for the bathroom in a huff. "Now I would thank you to leave me alone! And place another log on the fire! It is like an ice age in here!"

Nanny McBride was relentless. "What are ye plannin' to do now that ye disgraced ye folks, and got yeself ditched from college?"

Veda froze again. *How did Nanny know this too?* She ground her teeth, and shifted only her head to retort. "For your information, I discharged myself! Now I have had enough of this mindless conversation! I would like to take a bath!"

Then she bolted into the bathroom, and Nanny trailed after her.

"No use denyin' it, Missy. The truth is gonna haunt ye day and night."

Veda swept her hair up and sighed. "What truth? You speak like a madwoman!"

Nanny McBride handed her a washcloth as she stepped into the hot tub and settled herself into the blanket of frothy bubbles.

"Ye hurt ye parents bad, and they don't deserve it, Missy! Would ye be thinkin' that ye would be gettin' away with this?"

Veda leaned her head backward and closed her eyes. "I have done nothing wrong! *Au revoir*, Nanny!"

Nanny McBride smirked. "Is that why ye father jus' balled ye out?" Veda glared again. "He did no such thing!"

"Ye lie like the devil himself, Missy!"

Veda covered her ears. "I will not listen to another word!"

"But ye *do* gotta hear ye own conscience!"

Veda kicked petulantly, splashing bubbles onto the floor. "I am *not* in church!"

Nanny quickly laid a towel on the white tiles to soak up the suds. "Maybe that's where ye oughta be…lightin' candles for all the trouble ye caused!"

Veda exploded, "You are hateful! Now get out, or I will hold my breath!" Nanny remained still, and Veda dunked her head under the water.

"Ye can't hide for long, Missy!" she mocked.

Thirty seconds later, Veda came up for air. She was breathless and fuming, but satisfied to see that Nanny had already gone.

Chapter 16

Veda emerged from her bedroom two hours later, resplendent in an emerald green ball gown. Her hair was pulled to the back of her head where it spilled in sparkling curls. As she made her way down the gothic style corridor, she was disturbed to see Rose's shadow cast upon the wall.

She went to the bedroom and was amazed to find her twin in her nightgown, settled in a chaise lounge, and reading a book. Resentment stung as she recalled the episode on the Central Park pond hours earlier.

"Why are you not ready, Rose?" she asked coolly.

Rose looked up at her with a faint smile. "I have decided to stay home."

For a strange reason, this hardened Veda. "Suit yourself," she sniffed, and slipped on her green velvet gloves.

Rose inspected her pleasingly. "You look lovely."

Veda ignored the compliment.

"But I am surprised *you* are going," she added pointedly.

Veda raised her head loftily. "Surprised, are you? Whatever for?"

Rose set the book onto her lap and crossed her slippered feet. "Well, after overhearing Father this afternoon, I would not have expected to find you in party spirits."

Veda observed her contemptibly. "That is the difference between you and me, Rose. A minor tongue lashing can do me no harm…and why were you eavesdropping, anyway?"

Rose looked at her, stunned.

"I was not eavesdropping… I—"

Veda cut her off sharply, "Oh, stop babbling! No need to exhibit your pious airs to me!"

Rose studied her again, and the truth *finally* set in. "This has something to do with this afternoon; doesn't it?"

Veda glared down her nose at her. "I have no idea what you are talking about."

Rose mused for a long moment. "Does it have something to do with Hans Wagner?"

Veda rolled her eyes with disdain. "*That* man is a mere servant! His name shall never pass my lips again! *And*, I will add, I am quite ashamed of myself for having exalted him to being anything higher than his status of peasantry!"

Rose was appalled. "Veda! How unkind, and unworthy of you!"

Veda replied with an impish grin, "You live by your gospel, Rose, dear, and leave me to live mine. Good night." And she vanished, leaving her twin to wonder just what had come over Veda *this time.*

Outside, the snow had begun to fall again from the night sky. Winston and *La Madame* Champion were waiting for Veda in the carriage when she made a grand exit from the front door, sparkling in a green velvet cape and matching beret. She walked without emotion, her nose in the crisp air. She flinched for a mere moment when Hans Wagner came around to open the carriage door. Then she shifted from him and turned to ice. He tried to assist her, but she tugged away and hissed, "No thank you!"

Inside the carriage, tension sliced the air. *La Madame* Champion looked away from her daughter as Winston's hard, unrelenting stare nearly reduced her to tears.

The music from the Worthington house spilled into the snow lined street, but the festivities never penetrated the carriage. Veda was relieved when her parents exited and walked ahead of her. She, herself, stepped onto the pavement and sighed as she took a deep breath of fresh winter air. It had been the longest, most unpleasant ride of her life. Her parents' silence was deadly.

But I am here, now. She told herself. *I am going to have a good time!*

And she started toward the Neo Italian Renaissance mansion with charm school gait in full force.

She entered alone and smiling as a footman assisted her off with her cape. Men flocked to her at once as young women glared. She raised her head proudly, and realized, in that moment, that she did not need a college degree or conformity to a society woman's lifestyle. She *was* already at the top of the world, in the center of everything. *And* she would always be.

As she greeted a host of handsome, smiling rich young men, she stood, her arms, akimbo, and waited for a pair of them to escort her up the winding

Tennessee marble staircase. The unfortunate others trailed behind, and she began her ascent like a coronary march.

Upon spying her from where he stood in the center of the garland lined ballroom, Chester Worthington, in white tie, made a beeline to Veda's side.

He was, by far, the most dashing of the lot; his black hair slicked backward, his muscled frame towering above the others, his dark eyes glistening. His newly grown mustache was perfectly trimmed, adding a somewhat sinister feature to his dark, good looks.

"Merry Christmas, Miss Champion," he droned flirtatiously with a raised eyebrow. "Welcome to the Worthington residence."

Veda beamed and extended her gloved hand. "Why, Chester Worthington, if you are not the devil himself, with that new mustache you are sporting!"

He smiled, and took her arm. "Excuse us, gentleman," he said to the others and ushered her into the ballroom where dancers graced the floor with a sprightly fox trot.

"So, how have you been, gorgeous?" he asked with a wink.

Veda teased, "I do not know why I dare speak to you after your ill-bred behavior at my brother's wedding this past summer!"

Chester grinned. "Oh, that is water under the bridge," he paused, and added with a wild gleam in his eyes, "I spiked the punch, you know."

Veda giggled, bringing a hand to her lips. "Why, you are just scandalous!"

The lights dimmed as the orchestra played the first chords of *Let Me Call You Sweetheart.*

"Would you care to dance?" he asked, beginning to sway.

Veda spied Jacques Deneuve staring at them from where he stood beside her parents and his. She knew what they were discussing.

She looked up at Chester with a bright smile. "Would you escort me to the punchbowl first?"

He grinned down at her and winked again. "It would be my pleasure, gorgeous."

******

It was 10:00, and the snow was falling like cotton balls from the sky. Rose sat in the candlelit parlor, staring at the magnificent Christmas tree, pondering how she would reveal her plans to her parents the next morning.

"Excuse me, Miss," Hans Wagner said softly, and came into the room with a pile of firewood in his arms. Then he nodded shamefully. "I did not know you were here."

She smiled up at him, and modestly arranged the folds of her white peignoir. "Quite all right, Mr. Wagner. Please come forward."

He complied reluctantly; his cheeks reddened with embarrassment. "I must add some wood to the fire," he said, and tended to it at once.

"Thank you. It is becoming a bit cold," Rose replied, and turned her face to the winter wonderland on the opposite side of the cathedral window.

When he finished, Hans studied her for a long moment before mustering the courage to speak, "I know this is not my place, Miss, but why would a beautiful woman choose not to attend a holiday party?"

Rose ran her right hand through her silken black hair. "I suppose I was just a bit tired after ice skating this afternoon. Sometimes the quiet of one's home is more pleasing than the festivities of a party."

He observed her at length. She looked more beautiful than ever on the red velvet sofa, illuminated by the candelabra burning on the inlaid mahogany coffee table. On the wall above her was a Pierre Auguste Renoir painting of Mother and Children, circa 1875. She was a classic portrait herself, and too modest to know it.

"You are so wise," he whispered. "So...different," Rose smiled again. "Different? From whom?"

He had lost control of his tongue for the first time since his employment. "From most American girls. You have everything, and, yet...oh, excuse me. I do not know how to say it in English."

Rose's face glowed with a celestial gleam. He was drawn to her further. The magnetism was more than what beauty could empower, a pure, imperial charisma he had never sensed in anyone before.

"I think you mean to say that I am humble, Mr. Wagner. It is a virtue I always strive to achieve."

He was melting before her eyes. "How did you become so smart?" his words trembled.

Rose shook her head. "Oh, I do not know how smart I am."

He came even closer. He wanted to crouch beside her and take her milk white hand into his calloused palm. But he controlled himself and remained standing.

"But you are!"

Rose waved a hand and adeptly shifted the topic, "You must be quite brilliant yourself, Mr. Wagner, to have mastered the English language so quickly. I remember dancing with you at my brother's wedding last June, when you could barely communicate."

His mind drifted back, and his face radiated as he reminisced. "That was the happiest day of my life."

Rose was intrigued. "Really? Why?"

He looked into her eyes, his own twinkling. "Because it was the day, I met you."

Rose's smile quickly faded. "Mr. Wagner, you must not allow yourself to receive the wrong impression of me. You are a very kind man, but—"

The impact of her words was like a dagger to his heart.

"But I am a servant, and you, are a lady," he concluded gloomily. Rose was stunned. "I was not going to say that at all!"

He nodded, having surrendered to defeat. "I understand the truth, Miss. You need not be polite just for me."

Rose felt his pain. "But, no…" she gently protested, guilt flickering in her lovely, gray eyes.

Hans masked his anguish with a faint smile. "It is all right, really. I was out of line. I have said too much already. I am sorry. It will not happen again."

"Mr. Wagner…" Rose insisted.

But he pressed his eyes shut, and tuned her out. "Please say no more." Then he turned to leave. "Good night, Miss."

And he vanished, leaving Rose ridden with remorse.

******

It was midnight. Veda hiccupped when the knock on her bedroom door sounded. "Who is there?" She was sitting at her vanity, brushing her hair.

The door opened, and Rose appeared in a white peignoir. Veda grimaced, "Oh, what do *you* want?"

Rose's eyes enlarged in shock. "Have you been drinking?"

Veda sighed, glaring at her twin through the mirror. "And if I have, is it any of your affair?"

Rose ignored the question and came to her. "What did Mother and Father say?"

Veda rolled her eyes. "They said nothing. I did not ride home with them."

Rose flinched. "You did not?"

Veda dropped her brush on the glass tray and shifted on the stool to face her twin. "No, I did not. And why is my business so important to you anyway?"

Rose swallowed the sting, and sat on the chaise lounge. "How did you get home?"

Veda raised her head as an impish smile played on her lips. "I had a most enjoyable ride in Chester Worthington's motor car."

Rose turned ghost white. "No!"

Veda fumed. "Yes! Why do you look so surprised?"

Rose could not believe her ears. "Chester Worthington? Veda, do you not recall what he did at Marius' wedding?"

Veda stood and slipped off her satin robe. "Oh, *really* now! That was last summer! Chester has changed." Then she caught herself, "And why am I answering to you, anyway?"

Rose stepped onto her toes and came to her side. Together they glowed in the firelight. "You will be answering to Mother and Father in the morning!"

Veda shrugged defiantly. "I shall, and I hardly care. Mother and Father must accept that I am an adult now, quite capable of making my own decisions."

Then she sat at the foot of her canopy bed as Rose edged backward with a troubled expression on her face. "Veda, what is happening to you?"

Veda's blood came to a boil. "There you go again! Do you know, Rose, you should have been born a nun! Then, perhaps, you would have been unable to lead men on only to unveil the hidden halo on your self-righteous head!"

Rose grew incensed. She had tolerated her sister's abuse long enough. "I will not listen to any more of your insults! This is about Hans Wagner, and do not try to deny it! I cannot help it if he cares for me and not you!"

She could not believe she had said it. What had come over her? She had vowed she would keep the truth to herself.

Veda froze. Her face became flushed. "How do you know that?"

Rose's voice simmered to a whisper. She would tell Veda. There was no retracting it. "He told me…tonight…alone…in the parlor."

And a sudden satisfaction flowed through her. She knew what this new stranger in their lives meant to Veda. And then she felt guilty. This was her lot…a constant admission of sin and silent pleas for forgiveness.

Veda feigned composure. "I see…and, pray tell, what was your response?"

"And why am, I answering to *you*?" Rose defended, reversing the table.

Veda grinned. "Careful…your sudden discovery of a tongue will work to your disadvantage in the convent."

Rose would hear no more. Though it broke her heart to admit, she was losing her sister in these last days at home. But she was not going to do anything about it tonight. It was late, and Veda had had too much to drink.

"Sweet dreams," she said, and walked to the door with a cool superiority Veda both envied and despised.

When she had left, Veda pulled the covers over her face and seethed.

Imagine! Hans approaching Rose and professing his love for her!

"I will get you back, Hans!" she vowed as she reached to switch off the lamp. "I swear, if it is the last thing I do, I will get you back!"

Chapter 17

She was alone at the breakfast table the next morning, nibbling on toast, when Hans Wagner walked past the doorway.

"You!" she called out sharply, and he edged backward, stunned by the change in her manner.

He was tall and stately in his starched uniform, but Veda, in a blue wool dress, spoke to him with overbearing contempt.

"This morning, I noticed the fireplace in my bedroom is filthy! It needs to be cleaned at once!"

He froze and stared at her in amazement. "I…I do not know if I am the one to do that, Miss."

She glared at him. "You *are* a servant…are you not?"

He nodded, stupefied, and remained in the doorway, keeping a safe distance. "Yes, Miss, but it is not one of my duties as a footman, and, if so, I do not know if it is approved for me to enter a lady's bedroom. I shall ask the butler."

"And make it quick!" Veda snapped, raising her tea cup.

He observed her as she took a long, bitter sip, and suddenly read between the lines.

"Yes, Miss," he replied gingerly. "Either way, it shall be done today."

"This morning, I hope!" she sniffed, and set the cup back onto the saucer.

"Yes, Miss," he assured, and turned to leave.

"Not so quick!" she demanded, and he shifted to her again. This time, his blue eyes had hardened into blocks of ice.

"My shoes need to be polished," she commanded, her head raised, her face gleaming with victory.

Hans took a deep breath and maintained himself. Beneath his cool exterior, she could tell he was seething. "Again, I do not know if it is approved, Miss. I shall inquire."

His composure infuriated her, and she lowered her guard, "You think you are so smart; don't you?"

Again, he was stupefied. "Pardon, Miss?"

She glowered. "I know what you are up to! Rose told me everything!" The words paralyzed him. He could feel his body break into a cold sweat.

Veda grinned triumphantly. "Your behavior last night certainly would not have been approved."

He said nothing. He just stood, and waited, gripped with fear. Veda grinned. "You are squirming. Good. You are hoping no one hears me, hoping that I would lower my voice. I could scream if I want to…I could let this whole house know."

Then she paused and sneered, smirking. "I could even have you fired. Then who would hire you? Do you know where you would be? On the next boat to Germany to join the rest of the dirty Huns!"

He was a fuming furnace ready to explode.

Veda cast back her curls and raised her tea cup again. "Approved or not, you will tell Thaddeus I want YOU to clean my fireplace, *and* to shine every pair of shoes by my door!"

Hans bit his tongue as steam blew through his pores. He took another long breath and finally managed. "Yes, Miss. Is that all?"

She raised her eyebrows haughtily. "For now, you are excused." And she looked away from him.

Hans turned and exited, as his blood came to a boil.

Moments later, Nanny McBride waddled into the room. "Top of the mornin' to ye, Missy!"

Veda smiled back at her. "Good morning, Nanny." Her spirits were soaring now that victory flowed through her veins.

Nanny collected the china and gold flatware. "Heard it was a fine party last night at the Worthington's."

Veda fixed the French cuffs on her dress and admired her dainty hands. "Yes, Nanny, it was."

Nanny McBride lifted the 24 carat gold teapot. "Some more tea, Missy?"

Veda shook her head and stood. "No, Nanny. I must go."

Nanny McBride observed her questionably. "Where ye runnin' off to?"

Veda fluffed her curls and marveled at her reflection through the bronze framed mirror.

"Chester is coming to pick me up this morning. He is going to take me on a tour of his father's steel factory, and then to the picture theatre."

Nanny McBride's eyes widened in disapproval. "Do yer parents know, Missy?"

Veda smoothed the wool over the curves of her waist. "No, nor do I require their approval."

Nanny McBride was outraged. "Like horseradish ye don't! Ye march off and get their permission right now!"

Veda swung around and shot her an angry stare. "I will do no such thing!"

Nanny McBride's cheeks reddened with fury. "Ye will, or I'll—"

Veda frowned. "You will what? Send me to my room? For your information, Mother and Father are in the study with Rose, behind closed doors. When they hear what *she* has to say, my riding in Chester Worthington's motor car will be trivial as dandelions!"

Then she turned to leave.

"Ye get back here, Missy!" Nanny McBride called after her.

"Good day!" Veda crooned over her shoulder and sailed off.

Nanny ignited. "Miss Veda, don't ye be walkin' away from me! I ain't gonna stand back and allow ye to ride around unchaperoned with that low-class rich boy, like some common hussy! Miss Veda! Missy!"

She realized it was futile. She was barking into an empty foyer.

******

Rose was clearly terrified. She shivered as she sat between her parents in the study, and did everything to maintain herself.

"Father, Mother...I must tell you something, however painful it might be."

La Madame Champion, radiant in a burgundy morning dress, leaned forward in her seat, disturbed by the distress in her young daughter's eyes. "What is it, Rose, dear?"

Rose drew a heavy breath, and shifted in the chair. "I, too, have discharged myself from Georgetown."

She could hardly believe she had said it, and could feel perspiration beading her face. Beneath her blue satin dress, her body was drenched.

Winston Champion's eyes bulged. His face was distorted with shock. "But that is preposterous! I only spoke to the Dean of Women yesterday. She never mentioned anything of this to me."

Rose looked down at her lap. She could see her knees knocking. "That is because I have asked her not to, Father."

La Madame Champion observed her incredulously. "I do not understand, Rose. You have received straights A's."

Somehow, Rose was managing the courage to speak, "Academics have nothing to do with it, Mother."

Now, Winston was growing agitated. He thumbed the tips of his handlebar mustache, and narrowed his eyes. "Well perhaps you should begin explaining."

Rose did. Her bravery amazed her.

"I have been deliberating for a long while. But it was not until a month ago that I became certain of a special calling I have received."

"A calling?" Winston asked, half shocked, half cynical.

But Rose remained firm. Her fear was diminishing. "Yes, Father."

And she shifted eyes to her mother. "I know you will understand, Mother, given your strong religious background, and having gone to a convent school."

Then she looked back at her bemused father. "And I hope you will come to understand, Father."

She took another deep breath and said it. "I have decided to become a nun."

Finally! It was like a weight had been lifted from her shoulders.

Winston was flabbergasted. "A nun? But why, Rose? You are a beautiful young woman. You have everything. Why would you choose to give up your life?"

She looked at him with a wealth of emotion in her soft, gray eyes. "I would not be sacrificing anything, Father. Instead, I would be gaining the world."

"Nonsense!" he snapped, his nostrils flaring.

La Madame Champion came to the rescue, "Perhaps we should listen, Mr. Champion."

Rose turned to her gratefully. "Thank you, Mother."

Then she shrugged, "I really do not know what else to say, other than to request your blessing."

The room was dead still.

"When do you plan to leave?" Winston asked, having transformed into an iceberg.

Rose felt the horrid chill, and replied sheepishly, "After the new year."

La Madame had been listening intently. She was not surprised, if, silently disappointed herself. She had sensed Rose's piety long before this moment.

Again, she saved the day with a soft smile on her face. "We have been blessed, Mr. Champion. Rose, I am honored. I shall recite an extra rosary today for your intentions."

Rose smiled back at her, then turned to Winston again, "Father, have you anything to say?"

Winston stood. His mind was in turmoil. "How can you cast yourself into this so impulsively? Have you not considered all you will be losing?"

Rose lifted her eyes to meet his. There was an angelic gleam in them. "I am not entering the convent because I have lost something, Father. On the contrary, I have found something."

******

"Goodbye, Chester!" Veda crooned with a wave as he revved the engine of his new Ford Model T and drove away. She hooked her red wool cape, and slipped on her gloves. The air was growing colder at dusk, and it felt, once again, like snow.

The front door was cracked open, and the house butler met her with a perfunctory nod. "Hello, Thaddeus," she chimed, and made a grand entrance.

"Miss Veda," Thaddeus acknowledged tonelessly as she sailed past him and started up the stairs, humming.

In her bedroom, she saw the crackling fire and smiled with a gratified impishness. She was pleased with the colorful richness of the picture-perfect Victorian setting. In some ways, she preferred it over her ocean front chamber in Newport.

But her eyes sparked when she saw her shoes beside the door just as she had left them. Hans did not shine them! I will take care of him! She resolved, and tore off her gloves, cape, and hat.

Just then, the knocks sounded.

"Come in!" she called, unmoved by Rose's chalk white expression and bloodshot eyes.

"Veda! I have been waiting for you to come home for hours!"

Veda inspected her with contempt. It broke Rose's heart to see she still had not thawed.

"So, you told Father," she intoned expressionlessly.

Rose sat at the edge of the canopy bed and burst into tears. "Yes, and it was awful!"

Finally, Veda softened. "What did he say?"

Rose looked up at her twin and replied over shaking sobs. "It is what he did *not* say! He just stared at me in that manner he does when one of us has disappointed him so!"

Veda shrugged and went to her vanity. "Well, I would conclude then, that you were let off easily, Rose, dear." There was a dash of flippancy in her tone.

Rose was beside herself. "Can't you understand?"

Veda looked at her through the vanity mirror. "Yes, Rose, I can. More than you think for your information…and what did Mother say?" she asked, running a brush through her hair.

Rose composed herself and replied, drying her eyes. "She offered me her blessing."

Veda turned on the cushioned bench to face her. Her words were cold, but earnest, "Good. And in time, Father will come around too."

Again, the tears came, streaming down Rose's face in torrents.

Veda frowned. "Oh, stop crying, Rose! You act like this is the end of the world!"

It was very rare that *La Madame* Champion entered Veda's bedroom, and this was one of the exceptional occasions when she came through the door with the grace and might of a queen.

"Mother!" Veda exclaimed, rising in surprised allegiance.

La Madame Champion ignored her, and looked at her younger daughter. "Go to your room, Rose. Veda and I must speak."

Her voice was cool, rich, and superior. Everything about her murmured breeding and elegance.

Rose obliged, and in the next moment, they were alone. "Yes, Mother?" Veda asked, standing at attention.

La Madame Champion came to the center of the room, her head raised, her eyes glaring.

"Your father has sent me to have a word with you." Veda tensed. "Oh?" And she felt herself tremble. The room was dead still.

"It was enough that you had accepted a ride home from Chester Worthington without our approval last evening. Courting him, unchaperoned, no less, is out of the question!"

Veda was caught completely off guard. "But, why, Mother?"

La Madame Champion's face narrowed. "For one thing, he is impertinent. Secondly, he indulges recklessly in spirits."

Veda sighed. "If you are referring to Marius' wedding, Mother—"

She was cut off abruptly, "Marius' wedding, *and* last night, *and* who knows how often in the future! He is unsuitable for you, Veda! You must terminate this at once!"

The demand triggered resentment, and a wave of defiance. "Are these Father's orders?"

"Your father's and mine!" *La Madame* Champion retorted; her voice a blade.

Veda demurred for a moment. "But—"

Her mother fumed. "No buts, Veda! From this moment forward, you are housebound!"

Veda was appalled. "Housebound? I am a woman!"

"Then perhaps you should begin acting like one, instead of gallivanting around the city with some ill-mannered renegade!"

"This is not fair!" Veda protested, thrown into a frenzy.

"Your father and I will decide what is fair, and right now, you will do as we say!"

A cold wind ensconced Veda and hardened her to ice. She stood, erect, rigid, and arrogant. "I am sorry, Mother. But I just cannot agree to this."

Dead silence.

"I beg your pardon?" *La Madame* questioned in sheer astonishment. No one had ever defied her.

Veda could hardly believe her own nerve, and her voice simmered to a whisper.

"I bare you no deliberate disrespect, Mother, but I am not a child."

La Madame was outraged. "Why... I—"

Veda took a deep breath, feeling her heart hammer. "I must begin to make my own decisions."

It hurt to feel her mother's eyes drill into her. "He has made you impertinent as he is!"

128

The hiss stung, but Veda remained firm. "Where is Father?" the arrogance in her voice flooded the room.

"He is in his study, and I shall report your insolence at once!"

Veda raised her head, and locked eyes with her mother, fire meeting fire. "No need to, Mother. I shall go myself."

And she walked out of the room boldly, a stranger now to herself. "Father, we must speak," she said, entering the fire lit study.

Winston was reviewing figures at his desk over a snifter of heated cognac.

His eyes bit her when he looked up over his spectacles.

"I have nothing to say to you," his words spewed frost.

Veda stood tall and pulled her shoulders back, ignoring the pounding of her heart. "Well, I have something to say! It is unfair of you to dictate my comings and goings in this house! I will not agree to become a prisoner!"

He removed his spectacles and stared deeply into her, finding her new found impertinence revolting. He eased back into his tufted leather chair and crossed his arms over his chest.

"You do not have to agree to anything, Veda. There *is* an alternative," He maintained with a superior sharpness in his tone.

"That being?" she asked, suddenly winded.

Winston leaned forward with a shrewd grin on his face. "There is always the street!"

The sting and humiliation of his words had left her speechless. She should have known she was no match for her parents. She had been a fool, and stewed in her defeat as she turned and started for the door.

"Oh, and by the way, Veda," he called, stifling her in her tracks. "Thaddeus approached me today regarding your orders to one of the servants."

The shame was deadly. She looked down at the floor when he came up to meet her beet red face.

"I will state this only once," he intoned, his face rigid and cold, his narrowed eyes blazing. "*You* are not to impose demands on anyone in this house. I employ the servants. They shall answer to your mother and me *alone*!"

Veda gulped, accepting the slaughter. "Very well, Father," she replied, battling to maintain what little dignity she had left. And she continued to the door.

"I have not dismissed you!" he dictated, and she froze.

"Yes?" she breathed with her back to him, her eyes shooting fire upon the French doors.

Winston came around to her again. He thumbed her chin so their eyes could meet. "I have issued an order to the staff. Starting this very day, *you* are to polish your own shoes!"

Embarrassment. Frustration. Rage. Again, she said nothing.

Winston Champion opened the door, eyeing her still. "Now, you are dismissed."

Chapter 18

The news of Jacob Stern's massive heart attack paralyzed the city's financial district. His death curtailed New Year's Eve plans for many New York sophisticates, including *La Madame* Champion, who cancelled her annual ball. His burial took place in Newport, Rhode Island, and the Champions, along with most of Manhattan's upper crust, sailed on a steamship to be there. Summer homes were opened in the dead of winter. Few recognized the mansion lined Bellevue Avenue as it was covered with a blanket of snow, and a top coat of ice.

Rudi, Jacob's nephew, was distraught, though consoled that his uncle's death had occurred before his return to Harvard. His family in Berlin was comforted that he could represent them at such a precarious time with war raging throughout Europe and well into the turbulent Atlantic.

The Champions found themselves taciturn and sullen in the drawing room of the Newport mansion that New Year's Eve night. The air was thick and tense, but it was not Jacob Stern's passing which had caused it. Instead, it was Rose's plans to depart for the nunnery in two short days, and the aftermath of Veda's behavior which had triggered a cold war with their parents.

Marius sat bitterly in a wing back chair in front of the fireplace. The cognac he was sipping relieved only a fraction of his anger after his father had silenced his tirade against the Germans and their savage use of U boats. His eyes blazed as he unhooked his bow tie and flagged a servant to pour him another shot.

Winston, too, imbibed as he sat glumly in black tie, eyeing his three children who had suddenly brought him disappointment.

In a bejeweled black gown, *La Madame* Champion sat beside her daughter in law, Dominique, who looked lovely in burgundy lace. They were reading and sipping port wine as Veda and Rose, in matching ivory velvet gowns, sat opposite them sulkily.

Rose stood and excused herself first. All eyes followed her to the French doors leading to the ballroom. Veda followed her short moments later. In the dark ballroom, she lit a candle, and made her way to the bar. There, she poured two snifters of brandy.

She went out onto the ice lined patio which glistened like silver beneath the glowing moonlight. She walked up to Rose and saw that she was trembling.

"It is freezing out here, Rose! You can catch your death of cold!" Rose gazed ahead into the darkness. "I do not feel cold."

Veda frowned. "Why, of course you do! You are shivering!"

"Am I?" Rose asked, suspended somewhere between this world and her destiny.

"Yes, and I am transforming into an iceberg!"

Rose shifted her eyes to meet her twin's. "Here, let me warm you," and she placed a gentle arm around her waist.

Veda mocked, "What are you talking about, you fool? You are as cold as I am!"

They laughed in unison.

"I poured us a drink," Veda enthused recklessly, extending a crystal snifter.

Rose shook her head in protest. "No thank you."

Veda rolled her eyes and teased. "Oh, really! It is New Year's Eve! In two short days. You will be entering the nunnery! I am sure God will forgive you this one indulgence tonight!"

Rose accepted the glass and sniffed the brandy. The stench of the alcohol caused her to flinch.

Veda giggled again. "Oh, go on and drink it! You will not turn into a pumpkin! And besides, it will warm your bones."

Just then, the distant church bells sounded. It was the stroke of midnight, 1915.

Rose initiated the toast. She clinked glasses with her twin and whispered with a half-smile. "Happy New Year, Veda."

Veda glanced out over the snow-covered earth, onto the glistening black ocean, up into the star filled sky where Orion valiantly gleamed, and then, back to Rose's beautiful face. "Happy New Year," she echoed, and consumed the brandy in unison with her twin.

"There, I feel better already!" Veda exclaimed, caressing her face against Rose's bare shoulder. "I know I have been horrible to you, Rose, but I hope you know that I love you more than anything in this world. And when you go. Oh! I cannot bear to say goodbye!" she lamented, breaking into sobs.

Rose embraced her tightly. "Do not cry. We shall both be fine. We will always be sisters. And nothing in the world will ever conquer us."

She paused to dry Veda's tears with her shivering hands. "And do you know why?" she asked, her voice shaking now too.

Instinctively, they looked up at Orion again, the Hunter, shining in the winter sky.

Veda looked back at her and smiled. "Because we are Champions."

Chapter 19

Rose left two days later. Winston escorted her to the doorstep of the Mother House in Upper Manhattan.

"Are you sure of this?" he asked in a final attempt to dissuade her. Rose looked up at him with a gentle smile on her face. She thought her father had never looked more handsome than he did that morning; in a cashmere coat and a distinguished top hat.

Her words were a rich whisper, "I have never been more certain of anything in my life, Father."

He observed her with a lonely sadness in his eyes. He saw a beautiful, young woman with a wealth of promise being blindly cast aside. He saw the shell of a debutante, clad too, in cashmere, lace gloves and a veiled pillbox hat. She was erect, graceful, and distinguished. *She could have the world in her palm*, Winston thought, *and yet, she was choosing this.*

He opened the door, and together they entered arm in arm. They said nothing, but were thinking the same thing. The stone walls, so stark and cold, the concrete floor, the wooden benches holding a number of timid girls just like her. It was nothing either of them had expected.

A tall, elderly nun came up behind them. "Your name?" she asked in a frigid, biting tone.

They turned to see her. She was stern, steely eyed, and heavily wrinkled. Her coif was stiffly starched, her posture, erect and firm. Her lips were narrow, blue white, and expressionless.

Though he had converted to Catholicism many years earlier, Winston could never understand the reasoning behind this vocation, and yet, this cloaked woman before him commanded every ounce of respect he could offer, "I am Winston Champion, Sister. I present to you, my daughter, Rose."

She looked past him to the frightened young woman clutching his arm. "Have you come on your own will, my child?"

Rose nodded with allegiance, and curtsied before her, "I have, Sister."

Then the rigid nun shifted her icy eyes back to Winston, "Have you a donation to offer?"

Winston hesitated, but after a long moment, he reluctantly slipped an envelope from his coat pocket and placed it into the sister's palm.

He could feel himself burst into a cold perspiration and bit his lip as he watched the stone-faced nun secure the sizable fortune of his daughter's would-be dowry into the pocket of her scapular.

From her opposite pocket, she produced a number, and gave it to Rose. "Take a seat, my child."

And then she walked away.

Winston and Rose both knew the farewell was to be brief and unemotional. They embraced. He kissed her hard on the cheek, and she whispered into his ear, "I love you, Father."

And then she retreated to a bench. Winston looked away and went solemnly to the heavy oak door.

Outside, the cold wind bit his face. He saw other girls arriving with their fathers. He felt so lost and betrayed. His daughter was gone forever. He, a man who had never shed a tear, cringed as he blinked the wetness from his eyes.

******

Back at the Champion house, Veda had been weeping since Rose's departure. She refused breakfast, lunch, and afternoon tea. At 3:30, *La Madame* Champion arrived at her bedroom door.

"Veda, we must speak," she impressed softly, and came to the bedside where Veda lay, sobbing.

She sat and stroked her daughter's dark hair. "You must not cry, my dear. Rose has been called by God. We all must accept His will."

Veda rested her tear-soaked face into the soft satin of her mother's lap. It was the first time they had really spoken since her impudence a week earlier.

"I do not know how I will ever be the same, Mother. Rose and I have never been separated."

La Madame Champion's cotton soft hand stroked Veda's face. "Rose has discovered the path of her future. Now you must discover yours."

Veda continued to sob. "But when I do, Mother, it will not change anything. I will still miss her desperately!"

La Madame Champion smiled. "And so will I, my dear. But separation is a part of life. None of us will be together forever."

Veda looked up at her helplessly. "If this is what growing up means, I do not want it to happen! I know I have been just awful, Mother, to you, to Father, even to Rose! But you are my whole life! I cannot bear the thought of us being parted! I have never even gotten over Marius leaving, but at least I see him! I may never see Rose again!"

Her mother caressed her head into the warmth of her scented arms. "You must not ponder such things, Veda. Instead, you must search to find your rainbow. Your father and I have. So has Marius and Dominique. And now, Rose has discovered hers too."

"And what if I cannot locate mine, Mother?" Veda fretted.

La Madame held her closer. "Then you must look harder, my dear. Search, and you shall find. Ask, and you shall receive."

Veda gloomily protested, "But I have searched! I have asked! I have not found a thing!"

Her mother smiled again. "Perhaps you are guiding yourself in the wrong direction," she paused and added, twirling one of her daughter's curls gently between her fingers. "You are so pretty, so sweet, really. But, too often, you wear the mask of a stranger. Do not permit the stranger to rule you, dear. Cast aside the mask. Let Veda live and glow like the sunshine. She is a beautiful person, you know. I, of all people, *would* know. I have given you life."

The words melted Veda's heart. They were just what she needed to hear, the perfect remedy for her wounds.

"I love you so much, Mother!" she cried, rising and embracing *La Madame* Champion with all her might.

And after the long, endearing moment, her mother gripped her hand, and enthused with a tender smile and a well of love in her eyes. "Come, now. Let's have some tea."

Veda felt much better by nightfall, and so she mustered up the strength to dress and join her parents for dinner. She wore a lovely silver dress and a matching bow in her hair.

The tone was somber. Not a word about Rose was spoken, though the empty chair was an ever-lonely reminder that she was gone. Winston was distant and cool. Veda and *La Madame* Champion engaged in surface conversation until Winston had finished his goose entree and broke the ice.

"So, Veda…"

She was shocked. It was the first time he had spoken directly to her in days. "Did your mother inform you of the arrangements?"

Veda braced herself for the worst. She rested the gold fork onto her plate and folded her hands. She appeared surprisingly obedient. Her eyes shifted from her mother to her father repeatedly, until Winston spoke again.

"Veda, we have decided that since you are no longer enrolled in school, there is just one alternative remaining. We have spoken with Mr. and Mrs. Deneuve. Arrangements have been made for you and their son, Jacques to become betrothed."

The news struck her like a canon, though she remained cool and poised.

Her eyes remained fixed upon the flames of the candelabra as she permitted the shock to penetrate her bloodstream. Then she slid them toward her father and made a feeble attempt to speak until a knot had become caught in her throat.

"Is your silence an objection, Veda?" Winston asked with superior coolness.

La Madame Champion's regal voice sliced the quiet. "Veda and I have had a long talk. She will be most agreeable to the plans we have orchestrated now that we see eye to eye," she paused to glance at her daughter's chalk white face. "Won't you, darling?"

Veda nodded, controlling the volcano erupting within her.

They know better. She kept repeating to herself. But her heart was screaming to be heard. *Quiet!* she admonished. *Where else are you going? You have done enough damage! You cannot disappoint your parents any further!*

"Yes, Mother," she found herself answering. "And, Father…I agree." It had killed her to say it. But it was final.

Chapter 20

They stood at the pier and stared not at the ship Rudi was about to board, but at the German vessels stranded in New York Harbor.

"They are being held here like prisoners," Hans grunted with a bitter twitch of his right eye.

Rudi nodded. "Even though we are not at war with America, there is still a price to be paid. With each day, we are viewed as a bigger threat to the states."

Hans sighed. "How long do you think it will be before it is over, Rudi? Even if they do not say it, I can tell by the way people stare at me that they condemn me; a Hun."

Rudi looked out onto the harbor with hollow eyes. Then, he shrugged. "Who knows how long it will be, my friend. The war was supposed to be won in forty some odd days. Victory is long overdue. I am afraid it could be much longer than any of us had anticipated."

"And what are we to do in the meantime?" There was a helpless ring in Hans' tone, and Rudi placed an assuring arm around his shoulder.

"We just continue to live our lives; you at the Champion House, and I, at Harvard. We cannot change what is happening."

Hans gripped his friend's wrist. "I am going to miss you. It is as though we are always saying goodbye."

Rudi winked with a half-smile. "Never goodbye, my friend. Just until we meet again."

They embraced. Rudi turned to approach the ship people were boarding in droves.

"Rudi!" Hans called out, nearly panicking now that his only link with home would be separated from him again.

Rudi shifted his head to see him.

Hans smiled. "Good luck at school." It was all he could think to say, and moments later, he added earnestly, "I am sorry, again, about your uncle. He was a very good man."

Rudi nodded. "Yes, he was."

There was an awkward silence. Both read the other's thoughts, concern for their families in Berlin; memories of a life in a land at peace, home, so far away, and blackballed around the globe.

"See you in June," Hans said, and Rudi smiled back at him.

"Yes, it will be here sooner than you think." But they knew it was an eternity away.

Then Rudi melted into the crowd, and Hans stared up at the ship as tears welled in his eyes. "Farewell, my friend," he whispered into the cold winter air, and did everything not to cry.

Chapter 21

Veda stared down at the three carat, perfect, blue-white stone as it refracted the rays of the afternoon sunshine spilling through the mahogany wood blinds of the den window.

Why am I doing this? she asked herself for what must have been the hundredth time that day.

Jacques, in a custom-tailored brown suit, sat beside her, dazed and starry eyed, as their parents made the wedding arrangements.

"The date shall be established for the first of May. There will be a High Noon Mass at St. Patrick's Cathedral, followed by a reception at the St. Regis Hotel. As we have inconvenienced many guests to travel to Newport early for our children's wedding last June, I am certain you will agree it would be only polite to see Jacques and Veda wed right here in the city."

May. It seemed so far away to Veda, and yet so close. The snow would be long melted, with the scent of spring flavoring the air, and fresh baby leaves adorning trees.

Winston's words were firm and resolute. The others listened attentively, and Mr. Deneuve replied after a long, meditative silence, "That would be most sensible, Winston. And since Jacques has honored us with the news of his early graduation, the anticipated date shall be splendid. As a matter of fact, we were going to suggest that the betrothal be celebrated as a joint festivity after his commencement exercises later this month. Shall we say. The first Saturday in February, perhaps?"

Winston, in a black tailored suit and tie, consulted his wife who appeared queenly in winter white velvet. *La Madame* Champion nodded her approval, and exchanged smiles with Mrs. Deneuve.

"That will be fine. Under one condition," Winston eloquently proposed.

"That being?" the department store king questioned, easing backward into the tufted leather sofa.

Winston continued, "We insist that the party be held here at our home. My wife still has not overcome the disappointment of having to cancel her annual New Year's Eve ball. A February soiree would please her immensely."

Veda sat in solemn silence as her life was being planned before her eyes. "With the war in Europe, a honeymoon in the States would be more appropriate. New Orleans, perhaps, or San Francisco?" someone said, and the others agreed.

Talk of flowers, photographers, menus, guest lists, and invitations followed.

Veda just smiled and nodded. She was being the daughter she should be, obedient, demure, lovely and ladylike, just what her parents wanted, sitting, permitting herself be married off to a man she could never love. *It was pulverizing her!*

Jacques sensed her uneasiness, but of course, had no clue as to why.

Perhaps Veda was just nervous and overwhelmed as were so many debutantes newly betrothed.

He took her hand gently into his, and smiled as if to say, *Everything will be all right. I love you, darling. I always will.*

But his warm grip chilled her. His smile turned her heart to stone. For the first time in her eighteen years, Veda was truly afraid.

Jacques came up to her in the drawing room an hour later as his parents bade hers farewell in the grand foyer. She was engrossed in somber thought and unaware of his presence, her eyes fixed upon the glazed evergreens beyond the bow window overlooking her snow-covered backyard.

She flinched when he grasped her shoulders from behind. "A penny for your thoughts," he cooed, his face aglow.

Veda sprang to her feet, and snapped as she smoothed the ruffles of her green organza dress. "Do not ever prowl up on me like that again!"

Jacques turned to shock. "Veda…relax. I was just trying to surprise you."

She raised her head icily. "Surprise me, indeed! You are acting like the fool you are!"

He drew backward, assaulted, and exhaled, "I apologize," then he looked deeply into her. "Is something wrong?"

She lowered her eyes to the floor and shook her head. "No."

Then she gulped and looked up at him firmly. "All right, yes! Everything is wrong!"

He brushed up beside her. They made a picture perfect couple against the background of the winter wonderland opposite the cathedral window.

"I…I do not understand."

Veda sighed. "How could you be so blind, Jacques? Can you not see what I am doing? I am agreeing to marry you just to please my parents, when I do not love you at all. And, I am sure I never shall!"

He raised his head nobly, battling the sting of her words. "Love is not important right now, Veda. This union is, a matter of fine bonding. Like my sister to your brother, we are joining with our own kind."

He paused and added, convincing himself more than she, "You will learn to love me…one day…when I father our children…when they grow…when we grow old together…when we live in a house like this, to call our own, and welcome our grandchildren to play."

The intimation repulsed her. Life had to offer more than all he had just described.

She turned to look at him again, and saw he was hurting. To Jacques, love meant everything.

She gripped his arms and pressed her milk white face against his. "Jacques, I told you the truth so there is nothing you can hold against me when we are married and my arms are cold. I can pretend and live this lie if I must, but at least you know, and you will never feel deceived."

He drew away and stared down at her, amazed. "Veda, I can hardly believe this is you speaking. You sound suddenly mature…so serious…almost caring."

She nodded with a canyon of pain in her violet eyes. "I have changed in the past few weeks. Losing my sister and best friend to the convent has left me so lost and afraid. I have disappointed my parents by leaving college, and so I am left with the need to please them. This is the only reason I have agreed to marry you."

Then she gripped his shoulders, with an earnest expression on her face. "But I *do* care for you, Jacques, and would never wish to hurt you!"

He held her closely, enthusing, as she froze in his arms. "And perhaps your care can one day transform into love."

Then he lowered his face to kiss her, and their lips nearly touched until they were interrupted by Hans; so tall, stately and handsome, standing at the arched entrance in his starched footman's uniform. "Pardon me, Mr. Deneuve, but your parents are awaiting you in the car outside."

Jacques nodded and bade Veda a quick farewell. "I will count the seconds until we see one another again."

Then he left. Veda and Hans were alone. He began to draw the wooden blinds as dusk was upon them.

"I suppose you have overheard everything," Veda arrogantly droned.

He ignored her and went about his work.

She glanced back at him. "How long do you intend to go on acting as if I am invisible? It has been weeks now. You must know I am harmless."

No response. He started to build the fire.

"Does it mean anything to you that I am engaged?" She pleaded, coming to him.

Silence, still.

"Oh, Hans, really! If this is about that morning, it is high time to place it behind us! Can we at least be friends?"

He rose and bowed before her. "Good evening, Miss," he muttered and left with starched dignity.

Veda sank into the sofa and stared gloomily into the crackling fire.

Moments later, she found herself weeping in desperate need of Rose.

******

Winston entered his wife's chamber shortly after ten that night, and approached her vanity with a troubled expression on his face.

La Madame Champion, clad in an emerald green peignoir, was braiding her onyx locks, and questioned him through the mirror. "Mr. Champion, what brings you here at this hour? It is past your bedtime. You must be at the bank first thing in the morning."

He ignored the question and stroked his mustache. "I am confused, Mrs. Champion," he said, his mind light years away.

"Confused? Why?" she asked with a soft smile.

"I do not know. Something is amiss and I cannot place my finger upon it," she rose and stood beside him. "This is about Veda; isn't it, my dear?"

He nodded, perplexed. "Yes. She is too agreeable. She has consented to this betrothal without a word of protest. It is too unlike her. It nearly frightens me."

She gripped his arms and assured him endearingly. "You are reading too much into this, Mr. Champion. You are transferring your feelings for Rose to Veda. It is nothing more than that."

"But, why..." he attempted to question, and her soft finger sealed his lips.

143

"Veda is growing up," she impressed. "She is assuming her role as a proper young lady."

He gazed into her eyes and felt his whole body weaken. It had been months since they had made love, but tonight, Winston needed his wife more than he could remember. "Have I told you how much I love you, lately?" he coed, nibbling at her ear.

She felt her heart flutter, and surrendered to the warmth of his arms. "No need, my darling. Your actions speak for you."

And upon her last breath, his lips were upon hers, and short moments later, they were under the canopy of her bed, slipping the wrappers from their bodies, and giving birth to paradise.

Chapter 22

It was noon the next day. Chester Worthington came into the flower filled conservatory with a broad smile on his face.

Veda, in a taupe velvet dress, sneered as she arranged one of the twelve bouquets of roses Jacques had sent that morning. "Well, pray tell, what brings *you* here, Chester? Have you not read the society column of the Times? I am engaged to be married. Your calling upon me might provoke gossip."

Chester unhooked the buttons of his black tweed suit. "I *have* read the Times, Veda, which is precisely the reason for this visit. On my lunch hour, I might add."

She raised her head haughtily. "Am I to be honored?" Then she added with an impish grin, "I hope you have come to congratulate me."

He came closer. He was strikingly handsome in a white shirt and tie, his dark, good looks tickling her, his onyx eyes reading her thoughts. "On the contrary…"

Veda edged backward, shifting her attention to the flowers. "Then I believe we have nothing to discuss."

He smirked. "It was quite a flattering photograph of you, if not the news that you are planning to marry that pansy!"

Veda's face twitched as she fired back at him. "How dare you insult Jacques! You are not fit to shine his shoes!"

He chortled. "I am not fit to shine anyone's shoes, Veda. I have servants to do that."

She glared at him, but a smile played on her lips. "You are conceited and pompous! You might eat those words someday. If your father were ever to cut you off, you just *might* find yourself shining shoes to pay for your booze!"

"I think you imbibe quite generously yourself," he teased, raising his left eyebrow.

Despite the sting, she maintained complete dignity. "We *do* have the tendency to acquire the poor habits of the company we keep, which is precisely why I have chosen to marry Jacques. Good day, Mr. Worthington," and she turned her back to him.

Chester swung her around, into the strength of his heavily muscled arms. He looked down at her, reading her mind once again, and when he spoke, she smelled the faint odor of alcohol on his breath. "You have not chosen anything, Veda. Your parents are behind this travesty. Admit it. You need a *real* man!"

His perception, though amazing, infuriated her. "Unhand me! You are hurting me!" she snarled, struggling to release herself.

But his grip tightened, and he brought his face closer to hers. "Your life will be empty if you marry a man you do not love. Admit the truth. You want me!"

She guffawed, "I have never heard of anything more preposterous in my life! What would I want with a lush like you?"

His arms were smothering her, and his mouth was upon hers when he whispered. *"This* is what you want, Veda."

The kiss was long and powerful and electrifying.

Though it left her breathless, Veda freed her right arm and slapped him.

"How dare you presume your affections upon me! Leave my house at once! Leave, before I have you arrested!"

Chester laughed, knowingly, stroking his reddened cheek. "I was even better than you thought...wasn't I?"

She fumed. "You snake in the grass! Why, if my father were here!"

Having overheard the stir, Thaddeus, the butler, slid open the mahogany doors and appeared in the threshold, "Is there anything wrong, Miss Veda?"

She composed herself with a victorious gleam in her eyes. "No, Thaddeus. Mr. Worthington was just leaving. Would you show him to the door?"

Chester bowed and crooned. *"Au revoir,* Veda," then he threw her a kiss and followed Thaddeus into the foyer.

Alone in the room, Veda trembled. Chester's kiss was like nothing she had ever imagined. Then she stared down at her diamond ring, a reminder of Jacques, the wedding, the conformity, the bondage.

She walked over to the piano and lowered her eyes to Rose's picture. She lifted the gold framed portrait, and wept in dire need for her best friend. "Rose..." she whispered into the empty room over soft sobs. "Rose..."

Chapter 23

She caught a glimpse of the sharp scissors as they came toward her, and then she closed her eyes and bit her tongue as her long, silken, onyx locks were sliced away in four swift clips. Rose, a name to which she no longer responded, remained on her knees, draped in white, beside a slew of other novices partaking in the same ritual.

The three other barber nuns worked adeptly in silence, their shoes, and the stone floor around them covered with a blanket of multicolored locks.

She broke a rule by glancing at the postulant beside her, and flinched at the sight of her bare head. *Mine must look the same*, she grimly thought as the cold shears nipped around the perimeter of her crown.

And then she remembered the words of Sister Athanasius the night before. "The hair," she said in a raspy whisper, "Is the main adornment of women in the world. Having it removed is one's final detachment."

Detachment. It was a word she had learned all too well. It was less than twenty-four hours ago that she had been compelled to make a total severance from all cherished possessions, to destroy all letters and photographs, to deposit any objects which might attach them to a memory into a basket for the poor.

In essence, she had erased everything from her past life, and become an instrument of God. She was named Sister Mary Perpetua, and inherited number *1084*, that of a deceased nun of seventy devout years.

She stood, brought her hands together beneath the cape, and followed the postulants in perfect pairs, her eyes lowered, her body close to the stone wall, as they were led by the steely eyed, elderly sister to the chapel for prayer.

She had been taught well, and was recognized for having the makings of a fine nun. For six weeks, she had learned to keep her hands still and out of sight, except for service or prayer. She and the others had been under the tutelage of Sister Athanasius, the Mistress of Postulants, a firm, elderly vision of unerring self-discipline and piety, who examined them daily to ensure their veils were pinned correctly over their hair, and their capes hooked properly.

She entered the chapel and started down the aisle toward a sea of candles with motionless flames. In a glance of disobedience, she saw some one hundred statuesque sisters praying on their knees in perfect rows. As she sank to kneel, her thoughts journeyed back to Veda, her family, and the culinary feast they had shared on her last evening home.

Then her eyes met Sister Athanasius' chiding stare, the sharp, penetrating gaze which read her thoughts, a reminder that the past is to be forgotten… This congregation of strangers was her new and eternal family, a cloistered world of service and silence, a world and a people she would labor to accept.

Instinctively, she gulped and sank her head in prayer, "Help me, Lord, to erase all memories of the outside world, to become Your humble servant, to embrace and live this life against nature, to forget every material comfort of my past life. I beseech Thee for strength and courage to succeed and become a good nun."

She felt a profound sense of failure. Though obedient from day one, her mind screamed in protest. Her back ached in unrelenting torture that first night she had slept on a straw sac in a large, massive dormitory, shared by two hundred postulants, in semi-separated cells. Her heart froze when at 4:30 am, a deafening alarm shrilled through the room. She had sprung to her feet at the same moment Sister Athanasius began to pray, and automatically, she, and one hundred ninety-nine others dropped to their knees on the cold cement floor.

Together, they recited the rosary.

Then she stripped her bed, arranging the covers in three exact folds, and hung them over the chair, careful to ensure that no edge touched the floor. Then she dressed and glided to the chapel with the others in soldierly pairs.

She hardly believed she could survive in this mirrorless, dawn-less world where speaking was replaced by gestures, and individuality was a word of the past. But she had managed to endure and prevail. *All for Jesus*, she whispered to herself countless times daily. And after six long weeks, she learned to drop everything and proceed to chapel at the sound of a bell, to prostrate before the Mother superior, and hundreds of other nuns as a penalty for lateness, to beg for food on her knees, to record and publicly recite her shortcomings, and to scourge her bare back twice weekly with a pointed hooked chain for a few minutes after lights out. It was a self-inflicted discipline, an eternal penance.

That night, she found herself lying awake in the darkness. She had adjusted to the discomfort of her straw sac, having tuned out the memory of her once soft, canopy bed, her goose down mattress, matching pillows, and duvet. She thought not of the past, but of tomorrow, and the weeks and months and years ahead.

"Perfection," Sister Athanasius assured them. "Will one day become a way of life. It is then that you will know you are a true nun."

She grimly realized she had so long to go. Her actions were nearly perfect, but her mind was sourly tainted. Perhaps it would have been easier if she had been raised poor. But she, Rose, had been reared as a princess. This harsh contrast was difficult to bear. *All for Jesus*, she repeated, and the words resounded in her mind and soul.

As she lay still in bed, she heard the snores of the novices on the opposite sides of the gray curtains around her. She heard, too, the cries from their nightmares, the moans of discomfort, and the soft weeping.

Who was she to singularize herself? They were suffering with her! Every thought led to shame and penance. Once again, she was praying for forgiveness, and preparing herself for the impending shrill of the deafening alarm.

Chapter 24

Veda sat opposite her mother in the drawing room of the New York brownstone that afternoon in a white ruffled dress, and a red bow fixed primly on her head. Her nimble hands were struggling at needlepoint.

"Oh, it is useless!" she squawked, and thrust the canvas aside in frustration.

La Madame Champion, poised and eminent, lifted her eyes from her own masterpiece and observed her daughter compassionately. "You must not surrender to defeat so quickly, my dear. Practice makes perfect."

Veda sighed. "I have been practicing for weeks now! I am no good at this, and I never will be!"

Her mother smiled. "Think positively, darling. In time you will be successful."

Veda shrugged sulkily. "Why do I have to learn this anyway? What good will it do me?"

La Madame Champion frowned. "We have been through this before, Veda. In a few short months you will be a married woman. Needlepoint is the art of a proper society lady."

Veda grimaced. "I cannot think of anything more unavailing than frittering my days away poking needles through tiny holes on a canvas!"

Her mother's eyes sharpened into a disapproving gaze. Veda knew what it meant, and fell quickly silent.

She glumly pondered her future as she made a feeble attempt to return to her work. For weeks now, she had exercised unerring effort to conform to her parents' wishes, to become the 'lady' she knew they wanted her to be.

Only it was killing her. The thought of being Mrs. Jacques Deneuve triggered a consuming depression no one else seemed to recognize.

"I suppose in time I shall improve," she qualified, but knew it would never happen.

"Excuse me, *La Madame* Champion, Miss," It was Hans Wagner standing in soldierly splendor in the doorway.

Veda's heart rose at the sight of him. Each day brought a greater love for him, and a deeper regret that he would not be hers.

La Madame Champion's expression motioned for him to continue. She had mastered the art of never conversing with servants unless it was totally impossible to communicate with gestures.

Hans bowed. "A package has arrived for Miss Veda."

Veda's eyes widened in surprise. "A package? From whom?"

Hans' eyes did not shift from the house mistress. "It has been sent from a convent."

Veda knew immediately. "Rose!"

La Madame's lips curled into a smile. "May I be excused, Mother?"

La Madame nodded, and Veda scampered away like an elated schoolgirl.

She snatched the package from the marble table in the foyer, and carried it up to her bedroom. There, she tore it open and froze for a long moment before bursting into tears.

In the box, lay the silken remnants of Rose's raven hair.

Chapter 25

It was one week later. Veda looked like a porcelain doll as she stood in her flower filled bedroom that evening, one hour before her engagement party. She wore a white princess line velvet ball gown with large puffed sleeves, and a long, graceful train. The heart-shaped necklace flaunted her mother's diamond pendant which sparkled like a miniature star at the crest of her neck. Her dark hair was upswept into an elegant chignon while graceful, wispy, tendrils kissed her cheeks. She lifted the crystal atomizer and daintily dabbed violet scented toilet water behind her earlobes as her eyes glistened in sorrow. Her foreboding marriage was creeping closer. It gave her the chills.

Suddenly, she froze at the sound of a rustle on her snowy terrace. She whirled her head toward the noise, but saw nothing.

Again, it sounded.

Bravely, she proceeded to the ice glazed French doors, and crept one open. "Who is there?" she called into the biting cold darkness, her shaking breath forming rings of white steam.

Silence.

She chuckled to herself, concluding she was imagining the noise.

Then she turned to finish dressing, leaving the door slightly ajar to fill the warm room with fresh wintry air. Suddenly, it slammed, and albeit her fear, Veda attributed it to the gusty winds.

Terror struck full force when a pair of hands came from behind her, one palm enclosing itself over her eyes, and another, over her painted lips.

She tried to scream, and her heart nearly stopped until the familiar voice whispered into her scented ear.

"From the south of Africa, to the city of dreams, I have been deprived of such rare beauty until this moment."

He released his hand from her lips, but maintained his grip over her eyes.

152

Veda was outraged. "Why, of all the ghastly things, Teddy Aspan! Unhand me before I scream!"

He burst into laughter. "Only if you promise to keep your eyes closed."

She fired back at him, "I will promise you nothing, you insult to fine breeding! Imagine! Frightening me half to death! What in heaven's name!"

"Hold out your hand," he said firmly as she struggled to free herself.

"I will do no such thing!"

But he took her hand into his calloused palm and slipped her a cold, heavy rock.

"Open your eyes now, and feast upon the treasure!"

Then he freed her. She looked down at it and gasped. The blinding radiance of the massive diamond moved her to shiver. For a moment, she thought she was going to faint.

Teddy smiled proudly. "It is worth a king's ransom. And this, is a modest one."

Veda was dazed. "So, it is true. News of your return is all over the city. Teddy, you are a millionaire!"

He smirked. "Correction, my sweet...a multimillionaire; at the ripe age of twenty-four."

She looked at him for the first time, but saw not his tall, handsome frame, his golden hair and bright green eyes. Instead, she saw dollar signs, an astronomical wealth she had never deemed imaginable.

Instinctively, she questioned, electrified, "What do you intend to do with it all?"

He reached out and enclosed his strong arms around her petite waist. This time, she melted at his touch. "I intend to marry the most prominent debutante in New York, and not only make her the richest woman in the country, but spoil her to death with everything money can buy."

Veda gaped again. "I...I could never concede to such a thing."

He held her closer. Their bodies touched. His was hard and boiling and hungry, hers, trembling with mixed excitement, avarice, and fear.

"You, unable to help me spend my millions? I hardly believe it."

She whispered in feeble protest. "But you must...I am engaged to be married."

He lowered his face to meet hers. "Engagements are made to be broken."

She whimpered. "But...I..."

He silenced her with his lips. "I brought you back the diamonds, Veda. Now, you must keep your end of the bargain."

Then he kissed her long and hard and passionately. In the strength of his arms, Veda felt the promise of a royal future which erased every other dream she had before this moment. Her mind was swimming, her head pounding. Teddy Aspan suddenly represented power, and everything she would ever need. And in his ardent kiss, for the first time, Veda tasted money.

Chapter 26

In Verdun, France, *Monsieur* and *Madame* DuBois sat in fear. Although the Chateau, with its sprawling gardens, its servants, and creature comforts, was far from the front, the elderly couple grieved for their people being slaughtered elsewhere, the blood of the French soldiers watering the meadows, the widowed women, their orphaned children, the torture, the destruction, the ever-impending threat of invasion. True, they were assured the Germans would never make their way into Verdun, but they were moving through the country with unrelenting ferocity, leaving a trail of destruction behind them worse than any war in the history of mankind. Who could guarantee their safety?

But it was encouraging to know that France was putting up a good fight.

They would not be beaten. National pride abounded everywhere. Only it provided little solace for the countless lives lost.

Pierre DuBois, clad in an ascot and a velvet smoking jacket, heated his cognac in the fire lit parlor and grumbled to his wife, who sat, jeweled, and gown bedecked, sipping brandy.

"Now the Huns have even taken over the waters! A warzone has been declared along the British Isles! All neutral vessels have been warned of the dangers."

Madame DuBois, broken hearted over the war and what it had done to her Motherland, barked a bitter question. "What dangers, old man?"

Pierre grimaced. "I have read about the U boats spying all naval vessels. They are deadlier than cannons. They shoot torpedoes and blow ships to kingdom come!"

Madame DuBois finished her brandy and snarled. "That is despicable! Those subhuman beasts have risen straight from hell!"

Pierre thought for a long moment and sighed as the glowering firelight illuminated his chalk white face. The war had aged both of them a decade already. "And I just read that the British had been defeated yesterday in Belgium. The Huns' new weapon is poison gas."

Madame DuBois closed her eyes tightly and flinched at the thought of such horrendous evil. "I have heard enough about the war for a day..." she snorted, her voice shaking. "We must pray for all of those poor victims. For peace in the near future. And, for the preservation of our country as we know it."

Pierre nodded and took his first sip of warm cognac. "We must offer thanks, too, for the safety of our family in the states."

Then he came and sat before his wife. They joined age spotted hands and sat in solemn silence. This war was slowly killing them.

Chapter 27

Winter passed slowly, and soon it was spring. Leaves were sprouting everywhere, and flowers were in bloom. It was April 30, 1915, the day before Veda's wedding to Jacques Deneuve. The Champion's New York brownstone was shimmering with sunlight. It was a bustling place, as deliveries continued to arrive in droves.

"Are you preparing for an auction?" Theodore Aspan looked dashing in a double-breasted navy reefer, white turn up trousers, and white oxfords. His necktie matched the shade of the bowler hat in his manicured hands. His slicked golden hair glistened, and his emerald eyes twinkled when he saw her.

Veda stood amidst the plethora of extravagant gifts flaunted on antique tables in the drawing room. She, herself, beamed in a pale violet dress, her hair pulled to her crown, where it draped in flowing onyx curls.

Her face illuminated and her heart fluttered. "Theodore Aspan! How dishonorable of you to call upon me the day before my wedding to another man. It is a good thing my parents or Nanny are not here to see you!"

He chuckled blithely. In a few short months, Theodore Aspan had become the most respected dignitary in New York, renowned for being one of the wealthiest men in America, and the most eligible bachelor. Debutantes across the globe swooned at the mention of his name, melted at the sight of his picture, and dreamed of being the fortunate prize he would make his wife.

He had opened his own Fifth Avenue jewelry store, *Exclusively Diamonds*, adjacent to Aspan's Fifth, his parents' famous landmark.

"It is meant to accent, not deter business from you," he assured his disheartened father who offered a limited collection of diamonds, featuring mainly a bright array of gold and semiprecious rubies, opals, and pearls in his multimillion-dollar landmark.

Theodore's gem kingdom was famous before its doors had opened to the public one month earlier. He had plunged into the world of fine diamonds, and lived his life with equivalent extravagance. His picture with the city's most celebrated architect, drawing plans for an unprecedented Fifth Avenue mansion, had been publicized worldwide, along with recent purchases of a sprawling yacht and a glistening Ford Model T.

His largest masterpiece, the Aspan Diamond, weighing more than three hundred carats, was being cut into a gem of inestimable worth. He had brought home new stones in rare and appealing colors. His rainbow of semiprecious gems was being creatively set by expert designers into new pieces of jewelry unseen until now.

Included, too, were exclusively designed chandeliers, tiaras, and decorative fixtures, already in enormous global demand.

From the frivolous family disappointment, to a self-made magnet, Theodore Aspan had plunged himself into a world of colossal wealth, glitter and power.

He bowed patronizingly with a wide smile. "I have come, *Mademoiselle*, to see if you have changed your mind." Then he smirked as his eyes roved the perimeter of the room. "But from the appearance of things, I can judge for myself."

Veda feigned to shift her attention to an arrangement of long stem roses, and replied as she reassembled them, "You are correct, Teddy. I have not changed my mind. I am going to marry Jacques Deneuve at high noon tomorrow."

She paused and glanced at him coquettishly. "It is a pity you have declined the wedding invitation."

But her excitement was ill-concealed. Even an insufferable snob such as Veda could not help swooning in Teddy Aspan's presence nowadays.

He came to her and sneered. "How can you say that with a straight face?"

She looked up at him again with dancing eyes. "Say what?"

His own eyes narrowed in sudden seriousness, and managed to arrest hers. "Profess that you are going to marry a man you do not love."

She grinned. "I do not love you either, Teddy. I would have only married you for your fortune."

He came closer and gripped her chin with a firmness that hurt. "Then why don't you?" His words were biting, but she managed to remain impervious.

She freed herself and stepped backward. Her face grew cold. "We have been through this before," and then she spewed frost. "I will marry Jacques."

He grimaced. "But why, Veda, when I can offer you the world? Give me three good reasons."

She raised her head and stared down her nose at him. "All right, I will. Number one, he is Catholic; you are not. Number two, it is what my parents want, and I must please them. And number three..." she paused at an awkward loss for words. "Well...number three..."

"Yes?" he asked triumphantly.

She huffed and turned her back to him. "Oh, never mind! I do not have to answer to you! Why am I entertaining your fatuity anyway?"

He shifted her to face him. She did not protest. "Because you find me charming and irresistible, and beneath this masquerade, you know you should accept my offer. You want me as much as I do you."

She raised an eyebrow haughtily. "Do I, now? Are you suddenly a mind reader?"

He gripped her arms. She was growing to adore his touch, for it represented a power she suddenly yearned. He observed her for a long moment. "You are very transparent, Veda."

She grinned. "If I am, then you should know that I want you to leave! I must prepare for my rehearsal dinner this evening. I have not another minute to fritter on you!"

Teddy hardened to stone. "If you go through with this, you will be conceding to the biggest mistake of your life. Stop trying to please everyone else! Search to see what YOU want, and go for it!"

She glared at him. "And how are you so sure I want you?"

He brought her closer until their bodies touched. The familiar wild thrill coursed through her again. "Because I can offer you the life you know you deserve!"

She sneered. "Your self-made fortune has made your head larger than this room!" But his arms, his scent, his words were leaving her breathless.

"It is no larger than yours, Veda. Tell me...what is Jacques offering you?"

She freed herself again and battled her emotions. "What in the name of all that is holy are you talking about?"

His face darkened. His eyes bore into her. "Is he offering you the largest mansion the city has ever seen, or a wing in his father's home where you will be no more than an in law still following daddy's rules? Is he proposing to make you the queen of an empire, or to be the wife of a man walking in his father's shadow, heir to a department store to be shared one day with a sibling you despise? Think about it, Veda. Is it worth the price of your happiness to please your parents in marrying this man? Are you not worth more than that?"

She heard him. He was right, and it killed her to admit it. "Why did you come here?" she lamented sulkily. "Everything was fine before you came back into the picture!"

He embraced her again. She wanted to throw herself into his arms and scream for him to take her away.

"Was it fine, Veda?" his words were no more than a whisper, but they penetrated her.

"Please go, Teddy," she murmured, on the verge of tears.

He softened, knowing her mind and heart were at war. Then he edged backward and slipped something from his jacket pocket. "If you should change your mind, I want you to hold onto this."

She accepted it with a bemused frown. "A ticket?"

He smiled softly. "Look closely. It is a boarding pass onto the Lusitania. The Queen of the Sea Set for its Maiden voyage to Europe tomorrow."

Veda gasped. "Europe? Teddy? Are you insane? There is a war going on!"

He emitted a horselaugh. "A war cannot stop a diamond magnet, Veda. I am going to London on business. With, or without you."

Veda gushed. "This is preposterous, Teddy!" But the thought of it actually thrilled her.

He nodded seriously, knowing he had baited her well. "You are entitled to your opinion."

She looked at the ticket hungrily, and then, back at him. "But you cannot be serious."

He put on his top hat. "I will look forward to seeing you, Veda. I have arranged for Captain Turner to marry us. And, I have rented the most luxurious first-class cabin on the ship."

Veda thought long and hard. It sounded almost like a fairy tale. Then she caught herself, remembering her parents, her responsibility, Jacques, and the dreadful wedding. "I will not hear any more of this renegade prattle!" she snapped harshly.

He tipped his hat with a smirk. "Suit yourself. But I will be waiting for you." Then he left.

A storm of emotions raged through her, and she found her tearful eyes fixed upon the boarding pass to the Lusitania.

Then she caught a glimpse of Hans Wagner standing in the archway. As always, he beamed in his footman's uniform, and as always, too, her heart skipped a beat at the sight of him. Life was so unfair!

"Do you make a habit of eavesdropping?" The left-handed insult was actually a vulnerable welcome.

Hans approached her. She could feel her flurry of excitement burst into a blizzard of rapture. He was the closest he had been to her since Christmas, when they stood beneath the candlelit tree, a moment she would cherish always. Her legs weakened. Her head whirled. Hans did to her what no other man had ever done before. If only…

"Pardon me, Miss. I was instructed to make room for more gifts." It was the first time he had spoken to her in months. His words were like a symphony, his accent refining with each day.

"Do as you must," she answered shakily.

"Perhaps I should not mettle," he cautioned. "But all vessels have been advised not to sail into the warzone. I hope you are not planning to join Mr. Aspan. It could be fatal."

Could he possibly care for her after all? She thought of Teddy's words. "Search for what you want and go for it." She did not need to search. She knew what she wanted. Hans!

But how? She looked into his eyes and saw neither love or friendship. They were blue and stoic as an icy sea. His motive was unknown to her, but for certain, it was not love.

She hardened and glared back at him. "Correct, you are! You should *not* mettle! You are only a servant! Now mind your station and tend to your duties at once!"

Then she stormed up to her room and fell onto the canopy bed, succumbing to a long cry.

Chapter 28

Beneath the scorching South African sun, a young princess emitted a shrill of shear agony as she gave birth to a bastard baby, alone, in a barn. She had hidden the pregnancy for seven-and-a-half torturous months. The premature birth was gladly welcomed.

What would she do now? Where would she go? Her parents never knew.

Here, amidst the stench of manure, in a bed of needling hay, she clenched her teeth and prayed to die.

But the baby came, and miraculously, she knew what to do.

The animals lay still, observing in overcurious silence, as nature ran its course, and the baby let out its first cry.

She looked down, tears pouring from her own eyes. A girl. She was a mother, no more than a girl herself.

And as the heat, the stench, and cries intensified to a point of intolerance, she nestled the infant in her bosom and cursed Theodore Aspan.

She thought of her slain brother, the stolen diamonds, and the innocence she had lost in the false name of love. He had brutally destroyed a family and absconded without a trace of remorse. She was ruined. This innocent child in her arms would be labeled damned forever.

It was all his fault!

And in that black moment, she vowed if she had to travel to the end of the world to find him, she would get Teddy back. He would pay. He would suffer. He would curse the day he had darkened South Africa.

Chapter 29

Though she beamed in a silver dinner gown, the sadness in Veda's eyes told the story of her broken heart. For hours, she had sat daintily at the dining room table nibbling at each of the five courses presented to eighteen guests at her rehearsal dinner. Events of the next day were anxiously anticipated by Jacques, their parents, Marius, Dominique, and the other attendants as she sat in solemn silence.

"Are you feeling well, dear?" Jacques had asked numerous times.

To each of which, she offered a programmed response, "I am fine. Just a bit tired."

"And, overwhelmed, I am certain, for tomorrow you will be a bride," followed someone's response which stung her.

Tomorrow, a bride... Marriage to the wrong man.

She gloomily viewed the unhappy years ahead as she stood alone on the moon splashed terrace shortly after the guests had gone.

Her parents had already retired, and the only sounds were the singing crickets, accompanied by the faint clink of china as bustling servants cleaned inside.

"Are you coming in, Miss? I must secure the doors," Hans' voice rose like a melody to her ears, but she kept her back to him in fear that he might see the trembling tears in her eyes.

He came to her as if he already knew. "It will not be so terrible," he soothed, but the words released the tears, and suddenly, a river ran from her eyes.

"How would you know?" she frantically protested. "Have you any idea of how much I have been suffering these past months?"

He nodded gently. Under the moonlight, his handsome face glowed. "I know that you would like to follow your heart, but that cannot be in your world. It is how people of my station live our lives."

Veda cried desperately. "I hate my world, and everything in it! I hate the roles, the rules and the pretenses! I want to escape! I want to run away!"

His eyes sharpened, and his voice grew firm, "I hope you are not considering joining Mr. Aspan on the Lusitania."

She sobbed louder and finally released the words. "Can you not see that I love *you*, Hans? I always have! But you have shut me out! I could make you so happy! I have a small trust fund of my own! It could at least get us started! Oh, we could just live on love! Say you love me, Hans! Say you will run away with me. Tonight! Right now!"

She gripped his muscled arms in desperation, and shattered when he froze at her touch. Now, his eyes were empty and cold. In his heart, he wished it were Rose begging him, and Veda, though forlorn, knew it too.

In mere seconds, he seemed to have traveled light years away. "It is getting late. You should retire now, Miss."

Time had stopped, and her world had come to an end.

Chapter 30

Teddy Aspan had spent the night in the presidential suite of the Ritz Carlton on Madison Avenue. He awakened at 7:00 am, and scowled when he turned his face to the window and saw that it was raining.

"Shit!" he grumbled. "The ship better not be delayed."

He rose, bathed, and shaved. He wore a blue suit and a gold tie. He rang for a bellman and, as he tucked his boarding pass into his jacket pocket, for a fleeting moment, he thought of Veda.

He entered the breakfast room and sat in a black, Adam-style chair. He glanced at his diamond wristwatch and frowned. His father was late.

"Would you care for coffee, Mr. Aspan?" a white gloved waiter asked, holding a sterling pot in his hand.

"Please," Teddy replied, and perused the perimeter of the room which impressed even him. The Ritz Carlton was the latest of the deluxe hotels. He took a mental picture of the Persian carpet and mirrored French doors, and made a note to have a facsimile installed into his mansion. He admired the palm trees on the latticework balcony under a huge glass ceiling which provided an open-air Oriental garden effect, and was glad to be living in such a progressive century.

His father arrived five minutes later, and, as always, Teddy stood to greet the white-haired prig of a millionaire.

"Good morning, Father," he said with polished manners. Not even his own millions could override his feelings of intimidation and inadequacy in his father's presence.

Reginald Aspan sat and cautioned as a waiter quickly poured him a cup of steaming coffee. "Son, I am very uneasy about you sailing on the Lusitania today. Warnings have been issued about proposed entry into the warzone. German U boats have been mercilessly sinking vessels. The seas have become a graveyard. The Lusitania will be a floating time bomb."

Teddy laughed with a gleam of adventure in his eyes. "Nonsense, Father. With all due respect, I will be one of many dignitaries sailing. As a matter of fact, I plan to meet Alfred Vanderbilt for lunch. This is a business journey. A war cannot stop me or others with similar agendas."

Reginald Aspan grimaced. "Your status, *nor* your agenda make you any less vulnerable," he paused and grunted after a long sip of coffee. "With so many Americans sailing, it scares me to think that the Huns might want to retaliate. Do you know that on a quiet day, five thousand men are killed on the front line, more than half of them, by shells and bullets imported from America?"

Teddy's broad smile surprised his father. "And hearing that, prompts me to say that I have never been more proud to be an American."

Once again, Reginald Aspan knew there would be no convincing his obstinate son.

Teddy's chauffeur drove him to Pier 54 where he was met by jostling crowds and relentless traffic. The rain and the fog seemed to have plunged the city into a frenzy. There was a mass of sightseers and newsmen outside the gates, and pandemonium was everywhere.

But he tuned out everything when he saw the breathtaking ship, one like no other his worldly eyes had ever encountered. It was massive, nearly eight hundred-feet long, an elegant, white superstructure over a black painted body, with four giant funnels towering one hundred fifty-feet into the steel gray sky. Two masts at fore and aft rose two hundred-feet, boasting as both a colossus and a portrait of architectural grace; her title as Queen of the Sea.

In that breathless moment, as the drizzle dampened his cheeks, Teddy's mind raced with thoughts of Veda. *She will come*, he assured himself. *She will come.*

******

A royal princess could not have looked more stunning or graceful than Veda that morning as she stood in her bedroom before the full-length mirror, drinking in the incredible portrait of herself as a bride. Hers was a custom-tailored French silk and appliqued tulle gown with a glistening bodice of hand sewn pearls. Upon her crown rested a full diamond crusted tiara supporting a cascade tulle fingertip veil with matching French silk lace. Her hair was twisted into a chignon, and her neck was wreathed with a strand of custom crafted pearls.

She glanced down from where the sprays of stephanotis and lily of the valley of her exquisite bouquet emitted a sweet scent while tears began to slide down her ivory-colored cheeks.

She turned to encounter the rain tapping against the window. It was nothing like the wedding day she had imagined, no sunshine, no sprawling gardens at Newport, no yachts in the distance, and most importantly, no groom to genuinely love.

Her dark future flashed before her eyes; a life of conformity, rules and pretenses, a puppet like existence devoid of meaning. She pondered the senseless prattle at tea parties, the shallow smiles and social gestures, years of sleeping beside a man she could never love, and the eradication of her identity. A horrible entrapment! A fate worse than death! The ransom for pleasing her parents was too great.

She could not do it! The bondage was smothering her!

And then there was Hans, a man who would never love her. Life was so unfair! If only they all could see how fiercely her heart bled. If only they could begin to understand.

Something brought her to the vanity, and prompted her to open the top drawer. She stared down at *it* in teary eyed desperation.

Her ticket to freedom…so bittersweet, and so tempting.

She took a deep breath and composed herself, knowing, as she gazed at the reflection of her new person in the mirror, exactly what she would do…

Chapter 31

As he sat at his bedroom desk at Harvard, Rudolph Stern read his father's letter once again.

To my Dear son:

In spite of the reputation we have earned ourselves, and although I am by no means condoning the atrocities of war, you would be interested to know that national pride abounds here in Germany like never before. Everyone, rich or poor, have united in a common cause. To win. To establish what would be called 'Greater Germany,' where oppression would be a word of the past, and all of Europe would view us as the most powerful country on the continent.

I know that in America you are hearing only negative references to us, that we are barbaric and subhuman. This is precisely why I find it necessary to write to you, to sustain your pride for your Fatherland, and to help you see it from our eyes. Again, I am not advocating war. I maintain myself as a passive man. I need, however, to reach out to you at this time when you are probably being discriminated against because of your nationality. I need to inform you that your people are proud and strong, and out of loyalty to your country alone, you would be proud if you were here, too. We are, in spite of the atrocities resulting from our greater cause, very fine human beings. In war, we have a tendency to overlook the thousands killed at the front each day, and find a glimmer of joy in the knowledge that we are succeeding in becoming great, all that we should be, no more or no less than any other great nation in the world who has gone to battle for a similar cause.

My only fear is that we must be very careful. The tide of American popularity has long turned against us. It would not, therefore, take much to create a demand for America to enter the war. And then, my son, we would all be at great unrest.

We will, however, remain positive. I trust you are excelling, as always, at your studies. Your mother and I are ever so proud of you.

Remain in touch.
Your Loving Father

Rudi's hand trembled as he held the letter, and his mind raced ferociously. He feared for Germany greater than his father could ever imagine. It was a good thing he did not know how much the Germans were truly despised nowadays.

As he glanced down at his Chemistry notebook and saw the words *dirty hun* scrawled on the cover, he knew that if his father could have seen it, his son's studies would have been the least of his concerns. Ignorance, in this case, was bliss.

Chapter 32

Veda emerged from a taxi at 11:00 am, and elbowed her way to the pier, frantically waving the boarding pass in her gloved hand.

"Wait for me! Do not go!" she shouted, jostling, kneeing, nearly trampling her way to the ship where photographers and newsmen flanked. She had changed into a high collared cream length suit with a fitted waist and a lace jabot at the throat. On her head, she sported a wide-brimmed hat with a trimming of standing feathers.

"Teddy!" she desperately called after having cleared passage.

"Your baggage, *Madame*?" a steward eloquently asked.

She cried over her shoulder to him. "Baggage? I have none!"

And as she ran along the deck, she heard someone read aloud from a newspaper, "Notice! Travelers intending to embark on the Atlantic voyage are reminded that a state of war exists between Germany and her allies! All passengers travel at their own risk!"

She ignored the grave voice, and continued on her search for Teddy. She collided head on with Captain Turner who had been making his way to the gangplank to see the commotion. He was a square and solid imposing man, stocky, and grizzly haired. He had square jaws and a craggy face, and if it were not for his stately overcoat and bowler, he would have appeared less than ordinary, until she met his stern, piercing eyes.

"Can I help you, *Madame*?" he asked imperiously, and, for a short moment, Veda was paralyzed.

"Are you the Captain?" she inquired, presuming from his attire.

He formally nodded. "I am Captain Turner. And you, Madame?"

She proudly raised her head and announced, "I am the soon to be Mrs. Theodore Aspan. Can you direct me to my fiancé?"

The Captain's whole demeanor softened, and his face glowed as he smiled. "I and about one hundred others on this ship can do that, Miss Champion. Second to Mr. Alfred Vanderbilt, your fiancé is the most notable personage on this liner!"

Veda turned to shock and blocked out the noise and confusion surrounding them. "How do you know my name?"

Captain Turner smiled again. "Mr. Aspan informed me that he is expecting you. He has also asked me to perform the marriage ceremony on the bridge after lunch today."

Veda glowed. She adored the feeling of rank. It was going to be a beautiful life after all.

Then the Captain flagged another crewman, and asked him to direct Veda to Theodore Aspan.

******

He had been waiting quietly in his stateroom where he sat at the padded window seat and watched the ruckus at the pier. Needless to say, the cabin was sumptuous. It was paneled in neutral walnut, and polished to a lacquer finish.

The red carpet matched the brocade bed covers and heavy drapes. There was a crystal chandelier in the center, and a stocked bar in the left corner on which a sterling ice bucket sprouted a bottle of chilled Dom Perignon, 1898.

The steward had led Veda to the door, and she entered majestically without knocking.

"Teddy, you presumptuous scoundrel! Telling the Captain, I will marry you!"

From the windowsill seat, Teddy became electrified. He sprang to his feet and came to her, gripping her in his firm arms. "And will you, Miss Champion?"

She looked up at him flirtatiously. "Well, for what other reason would a proper girl like me be found unattended on a ship bound for Liverpool?"

And they both burst into laughter. He lifted her into his arms and twirled her about the room.

"Put me down before I grow dizzy!" she squealed, but he silenced her with a hard, heavy kiss. She hung in his arms at length, reveling in the warmth and splendor, the magic of his mouth on hers.

Then he brought her to the window seat and rang for a steward who uncorked the champagne and poured two foamy glasses. He presented each and retreated, leaving them alone again.

"This could be scandalous!" Veda teased. "We are not official yet."

Teddy kissed her again. "Do not worry. I will not take advantage of you. Although I would like to!"

Veda's eyes danced. "Why am I marrying a renegade?"

He clinked glasses. "Because I am irresistible."

And they took a long sip of bubbly moments before the ship set sail. "Why is it so quiet?" Veda asked as Teddy noticed the subdued crowd at the shrinking pier.

He remembered the hawking of a news reporter as he embarked the ship some hours earlier. "Lusitania's last sail!"

But he shrugged and made light of it, "I guess with the delay, everyone has finally become tired."

But Veda sensed more. "And what has happened to the band? Why is it not playing?"

Teddy, too, was disturbed by this, but then the orchestra struck up a medley of Stephen Foster songs, *Camptown Races* and *The Old Folks At Home.*

The young couple exhaled and burst into laughter again. "Bon voyage!" Veda crooned.

Teddy kissed her again.

******

"I see you have also chosen not to retire," Winston Champion commented as he stepped into the parlor shortly before midnight, clad in a satin paisley robe and leather slippers. He clenched a snifter of brandy in his right hand as his wife sat straight backed, fully clothed in a taupe silk evening dress, working diligently on her needlepoint.

La Madame Champion looked up at him disapprovingly. "Have you not imbibed enough, Mr. Champion?"

Winston tossed off the brandy and sat in the Victorian chair beside her. "Now I have," he grumbled, seething with shame and fury. "The invitations, the guests, the plans, not to mention that poor young man standing at the altar of St. Patrick's amidst rows of impatient family, friends and dignitaries, all shot to hell! It could drive me nearly to murder!"

La Madame Champion scowled, "Mind yourself, Mr. Champion!"

But her own thoughts, though well concealed, reverted to the bedroom that morning where Veda's exquisite jeweled gown lay on the floor like rubbish, leaving only her essence and a brief note behind:

I am sorry, Mother and Father. I cannot go through with this. I have decided to join Theodore Aspan on the Lusitania where we will be married.

The words resounded in her mind. Marriage to a non-Catholic! A sacrilege!

Winston observed his wife and knew she was withholding a storm of emotion. "I cannot understand it! I knew she was behaving too agreeably! I told you it was unlike her from the beginning! But this? Running off with a millionaire renegade? It is beneath contempt!"

La Madame Champion closed her eyes tightly in an effort to remain cool and composed.

Winston was relentless. "And to think she is sailing now, heading into a warzone! Has she lost her mind?"

La Madame Champion had heard enough. She stopped her needlepoint, and stood abruptly, "*Now*, it is time to retire, Mr. Champion."

He rose to meet her. Grief was spelled clearly on her face, "Have you anything to say for your daughter, Mrs. Champion?"

She thought now of the hundreds of empty seats in the St. Regis ballroom, the questioning guests, the desperation in Jacques' eyes, the betrayal, the shame, *and* the non-Catholic!

Never had this blue-blooded family seen such disgrace!

She locked eyes with her husband, and for the first time in over twenty-five years of marriage, Winston witnessed his wife turn to ice.

"I no longer have a daughter," she replied from an inner porch of her person, and the words spewed burning frost.

******

At the Deneuve mansion, Jacques had been locked in his bedroom since early that afternoon, despite the numerous protests from his parents and his sister, Dominique.

He had plunged into a well of depression, strangled by enveloping despair. Veda…his dear Veda…she had jilted him at the altar!

He wept for hours.

Then, came the bitterness.

Then, the fury.

And finally, the quest for revenge.

"I hope your ship *does* get torpedoed!" he shouted on the black terrace of his bedroom. "I hope you sink and die!"

Then, he, himself, drowned in sorrow.

Chapter 33

Veda and Theodore Aspan were married as planned that first afternoon.

The ceremony was brief, but the news spread all the way down to steerage. They were immediate celebrities.

The other U.S. dignitaries on the ship included Elbert Hubbard and his wife; the theatrical manager, Charles Frohman; author of the Music Master, Charles Klein; and a young writer, Justin Miles Forman, whose war play had just been performed on Broadway.

And of course, there was Alfred Gwenne Vanderbilt with whom Veda and Theodore had dined twice afterward at the Captain's Table.

For the most part, the passengers had been blessed with sunny weather and smooth seas. By May 4, the Lusitania was in the mid-Atlantic. Here, a submarine was seen off the fast net, but the sighting was kept very quiet, and essentially ignored. By May 5, the ship was coming closer to Ireland. That same day, another sailing vessel was torpedoed and sunk off the old head of Kinsale.

But the Lusitania, believed to be unsinkable, continued dauntlessly on her course, gracefully slicing her way through the sea like an opulent floating city. By May 6, she began to smell land. That same day, Captain Schwieger, German U Boat Commander, sank two more steamers on their way to Liverpool.

Passengers on the Lusitania, though mostly unaware, were puzzled to notice that lifeboats had been uncovered and swung outward. For some, it evoked a pleasantly exciting thrill to experience the faint, distant winds of war as they slowly approached the warzone.

That same evening, Veda and her new husband had dined at a private table for two in the grand first-class dining room. Veda was awed no less each night by the grandeur of the room, styled in Louis XVI, with Corinthian columns supporting a circular balcony, holding additional tables and the orchestra. Above them was a massive glass dome with painted panels.

The orchestra played the 'Kashmiri song' as Veda spread a hearty portion of Beluga caviar on a dainty slice of crisp toast. Theodore observed her with a humored grin on his handsome face. She had to admit he looked striking in white tie, and she, herself, appeared ravishing.

Theodore had taken her on a shopping spree that first afternoon, and already Veda had accumulated two trunks of the boutiques' finest couture. This evening, she wore a gown of dark blue velvet with a chic low neck. Her black hair was drawn elegantly to one side where it spilled richly to the point of her right shoulder. Her neck was wreathed with a diamond necklace, and from her earlobes, draped a pair of matching earrings, wedding gifts from darling hubby.

She glistened, and she knew it. "What are you thinking, Teddy?" she asked, and took a generous sip of champagne.

Teddy smiled with a gleam in his eyes. "I am realizing that you fit perfectly here."

Veda beamed, electrified, "Oh, I *do*, Teddy! I love our life together already! This is a fabulous honeymoon! I never want it to end!"

Teddy raised his champagne glass and leaned forward. "And do you love me?"

With a bright smile on her beautiful face, Veda clinked her glass against his, and replied, "I love your money."

For a moment, Teddy appeared shocked, almost saddened by her candid response. Then he armed himself and assured both of them, "You will learn to love me."

Veda ignored the remark, glancing around her as the orchestra played, and dancers graced the floor.

"Teddy, why must we sit alone this evening? Captain Turner *did* invite us to join him at his table once again."

Teddy's left eye twitched. "I thought one romantic evening alone with my stunning bride was in order. Do you disagree?"

She realized he was offended. "Of course not, darling. It is just that everyone is staring at us. It is almost farcical to think we could be quiet and romantic here."

He kissed her gloved hand. "Well then, why don't we have our dinner transferred to our stateroom?"

Again, she ignored him, glowing with dancing eyes. "Teddy…tell me more about the mansion. Will it really be the largest on Fifth Avenue?"

He eased back in his chair and observed her at length, wondering if he had made a mistake after all. Of course, he had not! Veda was the most beautiful and cultivated woman he could find! She was the only suitable partner for a man of his grand stature!

He teased, eyeing her affectionately. "Veda Champion, always the social climber."

She raised her champagne glass again. "Correction…Veda Aspan…and there is no need to climb, darling. We are already at the top."

He chuckled and snapped for a waiter to refill their glasses. "And what do you intend to do there?" he quizzed, amused.

Veda shrugged. Her face illuminated. Her eyes saw beyond the ornate room to a wonderland she had since painted in her mind. "I want to become the queen of New York City, Teddy! I want to throw parties like no others, to travel the world over, to buy clothes, furniture, furs, to spend, spend, spend!"

Teddy just stared at her in silent stupefaction until a tuxedoed dignitary interrupted them, "Excuse me, Mr. Aspan," then the elegant gentleman bowed before Veda. "Mrs. Aspan," he acknowledged, and shifted his eyes back to Teddy. "May I speak with you for a moment?"

Teddy excused himself and retreated into a corner with this long-faced man who had alarm ringing his dark eyes.

Veda sat alone and uncomfortably, suspecting that something was just not right.

Teddy listened intently as the man spoke, "About an hour ago, a wireless message came in from the naval command in Queenstown, alerting us that submarines are active off the coast of Ireland. Then came a warning instructing us to avoid headlands and pass harbors at full speed, steering mid channel course. Submarines are off the fast net."

Teddy remained cool and composed, "What was the Captain's response?"

The panicking man grimaced. "I conferred with Captain Turner on the bridge. He is paying the warnings little heed, impressing that it will be difficult to leave the Irish coast. He has referred to the warnings as tramp stuff for common captains."

Theodore Aspan's pensive face broke into a smile. "Then there is no need to fret, my dear chap. The Captain is in complete command of the situation, as he should be."

Then he politely excused himself and returned to Veda who appeared quite nervous.

"What is wrong, my dear?" he asked, feigning complete composure as he leaned back in his chair and lit a cigar.

Veda read the anxiety beneath her husband's cool shell. "Perhaps *you* can tell *me*!"

******

Teddy emerged from the bathroom of their sumptuous quarters some hours later, and saw Veda sitting awake in bed with a fretful expression on her face. "Now, what are *you* thinking?" he asked, remembering her question to him earlier.

Veda sighed. "Why have all the lifeboats been swung out? Why are so many people whispering to one another?"

Theodore slipped off his satin robe and climbed into bed beside her, his muscled V shaped frame glowing in the lamplight. "Nothing to fear, Veda. It is just a preliminary precaution as we make our way into the warzone."

Veda frowned. "Was it also a preliminary precaution when that man pulled you aside in the dining room, and you returned to the table with your face white as the tablecloth?"

He propped himself against the headboard and began stroking her perfumed hair. "Veda, Veda…what are you worrying about?"

She grew frantic. "I am afraid that this ship will sink!"

He chuckled. "Nonsense…And if it does, I will save you."

She had worked herself into a frenzy. "How could you save me in the middle of the Atlantic Ocean, miles deep with shark infested water? What good would your millions or your diamonds do you on the ocean floor?"

He made a feeble attempt to solace her. "Veda, you shock me. You never seemed like the worrying type."

She cried louder. "I am scared to death! I am terrified of punishment for what I have done to my parents and to Jacques!"

He brought his lips to her cheek. "It is merely your rigid Catholic upbringing at work, my dear. Cast your fears aside."

"But, how can I?"

"Make love to me," he cooed in her ear.

178

She brushed him away quickly. "I do not feel much like that right now. We have done so twice today already, far more, I am sure, than any wifely duty would require."

He laughed again. "You seem to enjoy it."

She raised her nose prudishly. "A lady never admits to such earthly notions."

He found her protests enticing, and so he took her into the warmth of his muscled arms. "But we need to make a baby, my sweet."

Again, she freed herself. "I do not think I want a baby…not just yet…the thought of stretching my stomach…"

He laughed and slid above her, fastening his powerful hands around her waist. "You will shrink it back to normal. Your will is stronger than the Atlantic, Veda."

One kiss triggered her surrender to his arms. Teddy was, in fact, irresistible, and his lovemaking, she silently admitted, was incredible.

Outside, the moonlight cast an ominous glow upon the ship as it sailed closer to the warzone. Many passengers lay awake in restless fear that night. Veda was not alone.

Chapter 34

Sister Perpetua, formally Rose Champion, was given her nun's underclothing on the night before her vesture. Each piece was stitched with number *1084*.

She slept well that night, as she had learned to do, and awakened ten minutes prior to the shrill bell, another habit she had mastered.

She thought of her parents as the Mother Superior slipped on the black, hand knitted stockings with drawstrings at their tops, and the long-sleeved chemise that came to her knees. She would see them today for the first time since her entrance into the order. She was elated. She only hoped they felt the same.

Then she tuned them out as the reverend mother lifted the black serge skirt over her shoulders and hooked it around her waist as it dropped to the floor. She slipped her hands into the pockets, and marveled at their size. The night before, Sister Athanasius had schooled her and the other postulants as to what they must carry in these pockets, a black velvet wallet which housed her little office, the conscience notebook, a small circular tin box containing a pincushion studded with white headed pins for her novice veil, a small rosary in a leather pouch, a penknife, a thimble, and a large cotton bandanna in blue and white, the only color she might possess.

Then as the Mother Superior added the black gown, the scapular, the veil, and the cape, she wished she could see her image in a mirror.

But she silently chided herself for such an earthly thought. It was the inner spirit by which the nun was embodied. The vesture was meaningful only to the outside world.

The white cotton cap clasped the head closely with drawstrings. As the Mother Superior fastened it tightly as she could, she reminded her that the firmer she pulled it each morning, the more it would help restrain her imagination. "Never forget, Sister Perpetua; daydreaming is a waste of God's precious time."

"And the gimpe is to be pulled up and forward from the back to make a starched frame about your face." She must have read Rose's mind when she realized the shock of having her side vision lost. "This is what the coif is designed to do, my child, to keep you looking in the only direction you should…straight ahead. Toward God." Then she pulled it and added, "In time, it will be all you know."

By 8:00 am, she was assembled with the other postulants in soldierly pairs. She could not help but glance at them, shocked to realize all individuality had been lost. They all appeared to be one and the same.

It took unerring self-control to move in procession down the long church aisle without turning to search for her parents in the congregation. The pipe organ resonated a triumphant march as she approached the altar to be crowned with a wreath of orange blossoms above her veil. The officiating Monsignor recited the Veni Spossa Christi and the choir of nuns sang jubilantly as each new sister was crowned.

Afterward, she embraced all the nuns of the community before meeting her parents in the parlor.

They stood in awe, Winston with troubled, overcurious eyes, as though he were trying to locate his lost daughter beneath the vesture, her mother with a proud, angelic gleam on her face. They were dressed rather simply for eminent people, he, in a black suit and tie, and *La Madame* Champion, in a black dress and lace veil.

They appeared somewhat older and unusually strained. Her mother approached her first and flinched for a fleeting moment when she grasped her daughter's callused hands. "Rose, you are a beautiful nun!" she said, with tears gleaming in her eyes.

They embraced. Rose began to weep herself. "Mother, it has been so long!"

Then Winston came forward. Quickly, she tucked her hands beneath her scapular, glad that it appeared natural. But she was disturbed when he offered her no physical sign of affection. It was not contempt or displeasure which restrained him, but sheer ignorance of how to conduct himself in the presence of such a seemingly unearthly individual who had once been his dear, more reserved debutante daughter.

"Hello, Father," she whispered, her voice trembling, her cheeks moistened by her tears.

He observed her for a long moment. "Rose," he intoned, suppressing a sea of emotions. "Are you happy?"

"Oh, yes," she replied with a celestial eloquence.

And suddenly he found his daughter in her lovely gray eyes which offered him the license to embrace her. She melted in his arms.

"How is Veda?" she asked immediately after the greeting. She saw her parents' faces drop.

"She is fine," her mother quickly replied, refusing to apprise her of the shame.

Winston interjected before she could question further. "She sends her love and pities that today has been restricted to parents and clergy."

Rose sensed the discord, and a chill swept across her heart. "And Marius?" she questioned, already the perfect nun.

How pleased they were that she had shifted the topic.

She hoped they did not sense her disturbance over Veda the remainder of the visiting hour. As do many twins, she felt her sister's unrest. Whatever happened? What was wrong?

Little did she know when she had bidden her parents farewell, that it would be a finality. The truth struck hard through the gentle words of the Mother Superior as they knelt before her seat that night, candles casting huge shadows of their vested figures on the stone wall.

"The farewell to your parents was a symbolic severing of all ties with your past family and your former life. We, the community, are your new family. This order will be adhered to in every thought, word and deed henceforth. Through prayer and holy conscience, the bonding with your new family will occur.

"Tomorrow, each of you will receive your first assignments in the outside world. Remember to touch the world, but never to be touched by it. You are no more than an instrument. However important your assignment might seem, you are to feel no pride, to take no credit for anything you do. We are handmaids of Christ. May we live our lives accordingly."

Five strokes of the chapel bell signaled the beginning of the grand silence. Rose recorded more offenses in her notebook that night than ever before. She tossed and turned in bed later, plagued with the relentless premonitions of imminent danger. "Veda, my dear sister, what is wrong?"

She confessed them publicly the next day at culpa. "I accuse myself of reflecting upon memories of my past family all night. I am guilty of having wept in fear for my past twin sister."

Her penance was ten rosaries and to kiss the feet of every superior nun.

She was then sent to solitary meditation and prayer for three days in a stone walled cell.

Afterward, she was given her first assignment, a student at an esteemed convent in upstate New York where her intelligence had earned her the preparation for one of a sister's greatest honors…to teach.

Chapter 35

It was a foggy morning, and Captain Turner could not determine the exact position of the Lusitania. So, he set his course parallel with the coast, and reduced his speed to fifteen knots which was approximately the same as the surface speed of the German submarines prowling the water.

The U-20, also buried in fog, was less than one hundred miles away. With fuel running low, and a supply of only two torpedoes, Captain Schwieger set his course for home around the West of Ireland. Unaware of one another, the two vessels were brought closer.

As morning wore on, the fog slowly lifted, giving birth to a bright, sunny day, and a smooth, glassy sea. Captain Turner restored the speed of the Lusitania to eighteen knots. At 11:25, another message came from the admiralty: *Submarines active in the Southern Port of the Irish Channel.* But Captain Turner continued onward.

Passengers coming onto the deck for a stroll before lunch saw the line of the Irish coast low on the horizon to the north. At 12:40, another admiralty warning came: *Submarines five miles south of Cape Clear proceeded west when last sighted at 10:00 a.m.* This pleased Turner. Danger could be dismissed. So, he altered his course to close in with the headlands he had been advised to avoid.

The passengers went down to lunch. The new Mr. and Mrs. Theodore Aspan sat like royalty at a choice table in the dining saloon, he, in needle cord pants and a brown check tweed coat over a Brooks Brothers shirt and tie, she in a full sleeved floral cotton print dress and a lovely picture hat.

"To our final lunch," Theodore enthused, lifting a fresh glass of champagne to toast. "Tomorrow we will be in Liverpool."

Veda emitted a sigh of relief. "I will certainly drink to that! I had horrible visions of drowning last night while you just peacefully snored away."

He laughed. Their first course arrived.

"Nevertheless," she continued, gracefully digging into a plate of fresh oysters. "I was deeply relieved to rest my fretting eyes upon the Irish coast this morning."

Theodore Aspan chuckled again. His wife's unfounded panicking was beginning to amuse him.

The ship moved steadily onward as they ate, exhilarated by the fresh spring breeze which shifted through the portholes of the dining saloon, twenty-five feet above the surface of the calm, glistening sea.

Sometime later, Captain Turner shifted his course to the northeast, and steered toward the coast. He scanned the ocean, but saw nothing. Ten to fifteen miles away, men on the low conning tower of the U-20 spied masts and four funnels of a massive passenger steamer appearing over the western horizon ahead of them.

The proximity of the coast was to the Lusitania's advantage. Captain Schwieger, on the U-20, slipped under the surface and moved on a northerly course. The eye of his periscope remained fixed upon the Lusitania.

Both vessels moved toward the coast for an hour, and soon passengers on the Lusitania were coming up to the Promenade deck from lunch.

Veda came alone, successfully escaping her husband's invitation to romantically burn off the calories of their rich gourmet meal in their stateroom.

"I do declare strolling would be a more civilized exercise," she sniffed as they exited the dining salon.

"We have already strolled this morning," Teddy mildly protested. "Now it is time for some fun!"

How vulgar of him! He had had too much to drink. Of the two bottles of Dom Perignon, she had indulged in a mere glass, contending she felt slightly queasy from the excitement. Suddenly, the prospect of life with him worried her. After the honeymoon, his sexual appetite would have to be controlled for sure!

"I think *you* require a nap, Teddy, darling. Return to the stateroom. I will join you shortly."

To her surprise and delight, he agreed. He was stumbling, and slurring on his words. For a split second, he reminded her of Chester Worthington.

She lifted her parasol as she came up to the sun-soaked promenade deck, and smiled as she sashayed past Mr. Elbert Hubbard and his wife who were watching the approach of the low, Irish hills.

The new Mrs. Aspan was the perfect social snob.

At 1:40, Captain Turner swung back to starboard, and sailed parallel to the Irish coast. An attack was now possible.

On the U-20, Captain Schwieger ordered the motors roar full speed. From his eyepiece barely seven hundred yards off the starboard row, he observed the Lusitania gracefully swim directly in front of him.

"*Fire!*" he shouted, and the torpedo crew obeyed.

A hissing rush of air came from the submarine as Schwieger silently stood and observed.

Veda stood at the rail of the promenade deck, twirling her parasol, and drinking in the fresh sea air. The water was calm and placid and beautiful, so still, that is seemed almost like a pond. She smiled, mesmerized. Then she stirred as she caught sight of something highly unusual, a frothy, white line on the surface of the water, making its way on a fast, steady path toward the ship. It ran so straight, so precisely, that it paralyzed her. She glanced around at the others on the deck. No one seemed to notice, so entranced by the warmth of the day, and the tranquilizing ocean breeze.

Above them on the bridge, someone *did* notice, and cried out to the crew in wide-eyed horror, "A torpedo coming on the starboard side!"

Captain Turner was flabbergasted. The threat he had been denying for so long had come to fruition. It was happening! There was nothing he could do now.

Veda's puzzlement had transformed into dismay, and finally sheer terror when others on the promenade began shouting, "Torpedo on the way!"

The eighteen-foot-long torpedo crashed into the starboard side at a speed of over forty knots. The sound of the blast was like that of a heavily slammed door, and at first, the ship merely shuddered until the torpedo's delayed fuse exploded.

Too late to run, too traumatized to scream, Veda pressed her eyes shut and threw her arms over her face at the same moment the torpedo had struck.

What occurred next was a whirlwind. The first explosion had thrown her against the wall of the cabin behind her. The second literally lifted and threw her ten feet to the promenade floor where she lay, in prostration, momentarily dazed.

With the return of her consciousness, she found herself choking, gasping for air as the entire promenade was enveloped in smoke and steam. Nearly suffocating, she labored to her feet, and witnessed the pandemonium surrounding her. This time, it was not a nightmare.

The ship was slowly sinking. Women were screaming frantically, rushing with their children toward lifeboats. Men, in stupefied fear, either stumbled to assist with lifeboats, or fled off to nowhere. Around her, lay blood-soaked bodies with crushed arms and necks, some whimpering in their helplessness, others, still as corpses. Being drenched with water held little impact now as death and horror encircled her.

She covered her ears to block out the noise, crashes, cries of pain and terror, and the relentless destruction. She realized her dress had been splattered with oily coal dust at the same moment heavy timber spars fell and crushed a child before her very eyes.

Then, over chokes and gasps, she struggled to find the strength to speak. No words came at first, just hollow breaths, but then the cry sounded, a shrill, agonizing plea, *"Help me! Someone! Dear God, I am sinking!"*

On the bridge, Captain Turner's first thought was to beach the vessel, and he ordered the helm put down. But too many minutes had already been lost.

The damage was already too grave.

The sound of the first explosion had stirred Theodore Aspan from a sound sleep, where he had lain on the bed, fully clothed. The second sprang him to his feet. His years as a navy diver had equipped him with enough knowledge to know just what was happening.

He sobered up quickly, and fled from the stateroom, thinking not of himself, but Veda.

Perhaps it had been a sixth sense which restored order on the deck.

Passengers suddenly realized panic would do them little good. Crewmen were methodically assembling women and children in lifeboats, and hundreds of others waited in line. Veda could hardly believe her eyes. A ship was sinking, and they were standing as if awaiting their turn on a merry-go-round.

She jolted her way to the front of the line, shouldering, elbowing everyone out of her path.

"Get me off this ship!" she shouted, her eyes wide and petrified, her body shaking fiercely.

Third officer Lewis turned from where he was organizing a group into lifeboat number one! "Madam, you must remain calm."

Veda erupted, "Calm? How can you expect me to remain calm? Can't you see that I am sinking?"

His eyes bulged. Her childish selfishness was intolerable. "You, and everyone else on this ship, Madam!"

"Do you know who I am?" and she suddenly realized how ridiculous she sounded.

How could he or anyone else have possibly recognized her, her body saturated, covered with oil and soot, her hair, a mass of tangles, her hat long lost?

"Restrain her!" the officer commanded to a civilian man, and she was suddenly clawing, kicking, screaming in his arms.

"I am Mrs. Theodore Aspan! And I demand to be let off this boat at once!"

"How about we throw you off?" another man snarled.

This momentarily silenced her.

Theodore Aspan made his way down the sloping corridor and drew aside to allow stewards to usher a terrified group of elderly passengers and crying children past. The angle of the floor suddenly shifted under his feet, but he labored to run, and assisted a few helpless souls along the way.

People were bursting from every corridor, crowding up toward the main hall and promenades. At this point, Aspan began to push his way through.

Strange as it seemed, despite the isolated weeping of women and children, there was, as of yet, no signs of panic. The knowledge that they were on an unsinkable vessel had instilled them with a false sense of confidence. Theodore Aspan knew better.

Will turner, too, had no doubt of the inevitable. The ship would most definitely sink. Water flooding in had collapsed the furnaces, and cracked a few boilers. Four minutes after the torpedo had struck, everyone on the bridge watched, awaiting orders. But he remained silent as his head reeled.

Finally, he issued the command to lower the boats in preparation to abandon ship. Enough people had been assembled to fill the first lifeboats. Veda, in her frenzy, had managed to be one of them. But the boats had swung outward too far for them to step across to board, and even further when the pins fastening the chains were removed. The boats themselves were forty feet above the water.

Terrified, women refused to cross the gap.

Lifeboat number one was lowered to the water. Another rope was tied to the rail, and two young seamen climbed down it to demonstrate.

But still, women refused to slide down.

Third Officer Lewis turned quickly to Veda. "Mrs. Aspan, this is your chance."

She was horrified. "Slide down? Are you crazy? I might drown! At the very least, I will suffer a dreadful rope burn!"

"As you will, Madam," the officer said as Veda's thoughts raced, and she glanced frantically around her.

Hundreds of people waiting to be saved, and *this* was the only way! If she wanted to live, *this would be the only way!*

"All right! I will do it!" she shouted, and her next action stunned them.

She slipped her dress over her head, standing in her slip and panties. "Madam!" the officer cried, but she ignored him, encircling the dress around her hands before gripping the rope.

"You better hope I don't fall!" she shrilled, and ascended into the air. "Tell Captain Turner he should be ashamed of himself for letting this happen!"

Then she slid down painlessly and hit the boat with a thump. "I am safe!" she sighed to the crewmen in the boat with her. They said nothing as they cut the falls and leaped over into the next lifeboat which was still attached to the davit.

Veda, alone, floated away to safety.

Suddenly, others rushed to climb into the remaining boats, no longer fearing risks or obstacles. Women and children were helped into them, and they screamed as the port side sloped back from the water.

From her lifeboat, Veda saw panic triggered by the difficulty in lowering other lifeboats. Already, there was wreckage in the sea, and bodies everywhere as people leapt from the rails of the shelter deck lowering toward the water. She saw women's dresses fluttering, heard the cries of anguish, watched countless passengers make their way toward the upheaving stern. But the titled deck was filmed with greasy coal and dust, and there was a mass of slipping and sliding.

She saw the next lifeboat creak down to the water. When it hit, a massive wave spout about it, but the women and children were steered away to safety.

At that moment, Veda felt proud to have been so brave to be the first to initiate the safety of others. She slipped on her soaked, torn dress, and began to pray.

But success was short-lived, as the Lusitania's stern heaved up higher, and lifeboats, each holding seventy or eighty people, had crashed inward, throwing out most of the passengers, and crashing into the wreckage under the bridge.

At mid-ship, she saw one lifeboat hanging halfway down the cast side. It began to slide slowly, until something happened, and it tipped, tossing half of the passengers out. The others clung to it, screaming, before falling too.

Veda howled and covered her eyes.

On his journey to the deck, Theodore Aspan heard cries of desperation coming from the elevator shafts of people trapped in cages. When he reached the deck, he witnessed the calm transform into pandemonium. Women were weeping at being separated from their husbands and lost children. The liner was sinking faster, and lifeboats were being dropped only to shatter as they hit the water, disgorging seventy to eighty people at a clip.

In the midst of the confusion, the wails, and the agony, an officer made a feeble attempt to sustain order. "Please stay where you are!" he called repeatedly. "Let us clear the deck!"

His words fell upon deaf ears. At this point, it was every man for himself. "Mr. Aspan, we could use your assistance at the lifeboats," another officer said from behind him.

Aspan turned to him abruptly, "Have you seen my wife?"

The officer nodded. "She was on the first lifeboat, steered off to safety."

Aspan should have known. All fear washed from his face and eyes, and he questioned bravely. "Where do you need me?"

As he worked not too far from Alfred Vanderbilt who was also helping to load boats, a burst of smoke and steam shot from the ventilators around the ship's central funnels.

Veda saw bodies tumbling and flogging in the water, and screamed again when the frothy rush of water along the Lusitania's side swept swimmers into the suction currents of vast revolving propeller blades.

Just then, the Lusitania staggered. She quivered, then hurtled again. It seemed to Veda, that the ship was capsizing. People were thrown, tossed off decks and the stern, and hanging boats dangled on their ropes.

Captain Turner, on the upper bridge, observed in disbelief as water spilled onto the ship. He knew the Lusitania had just a few minutes left.

Knowing he had done all he could to help, Theodore Aspan realized the moment had come for him to try to save himself. As the sea poured over the Lusitania's deck, he ignored the fools dangling from the stern's railing, gripping onto what they believed was their last ebb of hope, and dauntlessly dove over himself, into the cold, foamy sea.

He swam away from the sinking vessel fast as he could, aware of the perils of the downdraft. His navy training had won him success, as others less fortunate were already being sucked toward the ship.

Will Turner winced as he watched the water flow over the rail of the starboard wing. His legs were saturated. He was now the last person on the bridge. He propped for a ladder, and began to descend, astounded to see misguided passengers still adhering to the stern deck. The ship was being dragged down faster, and he leapt from the ladder and swam to a life raft paddle floating past him.

To Veda's horror, a hand crept from the water and gripped the edge of her lifeboat. She screamed as the boat tilted, and some water spilled in. Then she saw the wide, helpless eyes stare up at her in deathly terror. It was a man. She had to save him!

There were others they helped onto the boat, and soon the count was ten.

There were a few women, and some children, all gasping, mere moments away from death.

"Aren't you Mrs. Aspan?" someone uttered breathlessly; a middle-aged, debonair man who had recognized her at once.

Veda just nodded. For once in her life, the trauma had left her speechless. "And your husband?" he asked immediately afterward.

Mixed panic and guilt stabbed her when, for the first time since the torpedo had struck, she thought of Teddy. Her eyes swept over the corpses and helpless swimmers in the water.

"Teddy?" she feebly whispered, and her eyes fell upon a struggling woman gripping her dead baby. "Where are you?"

Then she glanced forward and saw what was left of the Lusitania, the divers, the dangling, horrified souls. Was Teddy one of them?

Silence followed as they all gazed at the horrid moment in history being made. Veda gasped as the Lusitania's high reaching stern dropped, and suddenly, the whole vessel heeled over to starboard, causing what seemed to be a tidal wave to pour over her with a ferocity which defied earthly force.

Then she staggered over to an even keel. Giant air bubbles burst from the funnels and spewed everything from them, bodies and debris, like an erupting volcano. People were being sucked into funnels and disgorged again. The explosion was deafening, and there were thick clouds of steam.

Finally, the Lusitania raised itself by the bows, and sank, sweeping everything within its reach into the foamy channel with the relentless ferocity.

As she dropped, there were ominous hisses and moans caused by additional explosions under the sea.

Then there was a somber stillness of the waters followed by a morose silence. "Those bloody Huns!" someone on the lifeboat groaned.

Veda was shivering, panting, biting her fingernails down to the quick. "Mother. Father," she said over more gasps.

She drank in the death and destruction around her. "I am sorry." She sobbed contritely over the hurt she had caused so many people at home. She wanted to erase time, to go back and do everything the way it should have been done. But it was much too late.

"And Teddy... Where are you?"

Her stomach heaved. She remembered vomiting over the side of the boat before fainting into someone's drenched, icy arms.

Chapter 36

The streets of Berlin were in triumph. German men, women and children gathered outside to share their ecstasy as news of the Lusitania's demise spread rampantly across the country.

"Lusitania torpedoed!"

"Americans dead!"

"Hoorah for our U boats!"

Euphoria abounded everywhere. There were kisses, hugs, and cries of prideful victory.

Hundreds cleared the streets and cheered on as a band paraded past, blaring the tunes of the German national anthem. Behind them was another parade of helmeted soldiers clicking their boots as they marched off to war.

Gunther Wagner and his mother proudly sang, waving the German flag in their hands.

"Mother, look! Our Kaiser Wilhelm!" the eleven-year-old child shouted exultantly and began to tremble in reverence and awe.

In regal splendor, the Kaiser rode past them, his horse drawn carriage moving in symphony with the music. How grand this noble man looked in his cocked hat and long skirted, dark blue uniform, draped in old braid and medals, his hand rising to acknowledge the faithful people.

He was their idol, the symbol of bravery, determination and hope.

But there was something lacking in his manner only few were astute enough to recognize. His mustache was fuller today, the upswept ends un-weaved. His eyes, though notably stern and courageous, were glazed with a touch of disturbance and dismay.

Herr Stern noticed it as he stood beside his wife and son, observing from the parlor window of their home.

"Why can't I go outside and join the others, Father? This is a great victory for all of us!" Simon Stern pleaded, and his father silenced him with a gentle hand over his lips.

"I am not certain as to whether the sinking of a civilian ship is something to celebrate, son."

"But why not? Gunther is outside."

Frau Stern interjected, "And your brother, Rudolph, is in America. They consider this a horrendous crime."

But the child's national pride would not be shaken. "So, perhaps they will send him home!"

As he grimly observed the Kaiser go by, Herr Stern acknowledged his son's words as his greatest fear. If Rudi were to be deported, he would have to join these steel helmeted men marching off to war.

The American Ambassador in Berlin, James W. Gerard, was moved by the roars of ecstasy and the German hostility toward the United States, to advise the embassy staff to pack their bags at once. He hoped to hire a special train to evacuate them all to Switzerland.

******

Headlines screamed across the United States. The Germans were murderers! The streets of New York were flooded with newsboys, "Extra! Extra! Read all about it! Lusitania's latest! Americans among the dead!"

News was sailing across the waters in dribs and drabs; the full story was still yet to be revealed.

Ex-President Teddy Roosevelt referred to the sinking as "Not merely an act of piracy, but piracy on a vaster scale of murder than old time pirates ever practiced!"

The furious nation agreed.

The New York Times shouted there must be a demand sent to Berlin that "The Germans shall no longer be war like savages drunk with blood!"

President Wilson, like the rest of the country, was stunned, and took a long walk down Pennsylvania Avenue to sort out his thoughts. It was drizzling, and the sky was an ominous gray. His people were looking to him for some command of action. Reprisal, perhaps? His greatest nightmare was materializing as history was being made.

There was dead silence in the parlor of the Park Avenue brownstone where the Champions sat in frantic shock. Winston and Marius were tossing off shots of bourbon, while Dominique stared at the seemingly motionless clock. *La Madame* Champion appeared coolly composed, fixed in her Victorian chair, draped in chiffon, and working valiantly on her needlepoint.

"How can you focus on that, Mother?" Marius asked with a petulant ring in his tone. "Granted, you are upset with Veda for what she has done, but you *must* care a little!"

La Madame Champion raised only her eyes to spew gray frost. "I care," she intoned, and returned to her work.

Marius loosened his tie and turned to Winston. "Father, I cannot believe this!"

Dominique felt the tension in the room thicken. Even the flames of the candelabras seemed to shimmer.

"Marius, perhaps we should go now."

But Winston mildly protested as he motioned for Hans Wagner to activate the radio for the latest report. "No one is going anywhere." And he drained the bourbon from the snifter as he unhooked his blazer and sat at the edge of his wing back chair.

The newscaster's shaky voice blasted through the speakers. "Of the 1959 people aboard the Lusitania, 1257 of them passengers, 1195 have perished. 124 of the 159 American passengers have been lost. Of the 129 children, 114 have died, 33 of whom were infants. The vessel sank just eighteen minutes after the torpedo had been fired, and survivors have been collected by boats and taken to Queensland, Ireland.

"Elbert Hubbard and his wife have perished, and Alfred Vanderbilt, who was last seen trying to get children into lifeboats along with young diamond magnet Theodore Aspan, are also among those missing.

"Aspan's young bride, daughter of the President of Champion Trust of New York, is amongst the survivors recovering in Queenstown."

La Madame Champion's sigh of relief was the first to flood the room with bittersweet joy.

******

"Veda! Veda!" Sister Mary Perpetua called desperately as she was roused from her sleep by a horrifying nightmare of her twin sister drowning in a turbulent gray ocean. What was happening? Why were fears of her sister's welfare plaguing her so profoundly?

"Sister Perpetua, what is troubling you?" a veteran nun questioned at the door of the chamber through the bars of which Rose could see her candle glimmer.

"I am fine, Sister…" she struggled to mutter. "I was just having a nightmare about my twin, Veda."

The elderly nun understood all too well. It was customary for novices to experience such encounters with the past. "You no longer have a twin, my child. We are your family now. Good night."

And Rose followed the candlelight as it retreated along the stone wall of the corridor until it disappeared, and darkness enveloped her once again.

The past is gone; remember, Sister Perpetua.

But she could not convince herself. Guilt washed over her once again.

She cried herself to sleep, desperately longing to see her beloved twin.

******

"Rose!" Veda murmured as she stirred from oblivion. The huge, gloomy room looked like a terminal. It reeked of rubbing alcohol, sickness and death. A sea of white sheets and gray walls surrounded her. Ceiling fans sliced the stale, tense air hovering above them like fog.

"Go to sleep, my dear. Ye're dreamin'." whispered a gentle voice as a cold washcloth was smoothed across her forehead.

"Rose? Where are you?" Veda feebly questioned, and calloused fingers were placed over her lips.

"Ye need to rest, Mrs. Aspan."

She stared up at the nurse in frantic terror. Who was Mrs. Aspan? And then it all returned to her. The torpedo blast! The sinking ship!

Water! Fire! Death!

She wanted to cry, but her eyes were dry. The nurse seemed to read through her. "It was a horrible disaster. But ye're alive, Mrs. Aspan," she paused and added in her thick Irish brogue. "And so is ye husband. He was one of the few swimmers to make it to shore."

Veda's last memories were the wails of a woman who had just learned of her child's death, and the realization that war extended far beyond soldiers on a battlefield. She pressed her eyes shut, and sank back into a deep sleep.

Anyone who knew Veda well would have understood that morning irritability was a sign of recovery. By 7:00 am, she was unbearable, and the numerous survivors on slumbering cots were awakened by her shouting.

In a simple nightdress, from a wooden wheelchair, she barked tyrannically. "Move this contraption faster! Faster! I want to be out of this dreadful place and on the first *Red Cross* ship back home!"

She heaved a sigh of horror at the sea of decadence enveloping her. There were groans of pain, corpses, bandages, hopeless cries for loved ones, and blank stares of living ghosts.

"I am cold! Bring me another blanket! Why in heavens are you stopping?"

Then she knew. Before her, lay Teddy, weak and helpless as she had never seen him before. His eyes widened pitifully as the nurse edged her closer, and when he illuminated at the sight of her, she hardened to stone.

"*You!*" she bawled, and the room froze. "This is all *your* fault! Only an unharnessed renegade like you would sail through submarine infested water! I could have drowned! Where were you to save me?"

Everyone, including Teddy, was paralyzed by her burst of hysteria.

"Mrs. Aspan!" scolded a white coated doctor who raced across the floor. "Mind yourself! Your husband has suffered a horrendous trauma!"

"And haven't we all?" Veda countered, now weeping.

The doctor's steely gaze was magnified by his spectacles. "Not as much as your husband, Mrs. Aspan. He weathered the currents of the ocean during his swim to shore."

Veda fired back at him, "He should have drowned!"

Her words had the impact of a canon blast. They were all silenced. Teddy Aspan, though barely coherent, heard them, and for the first time in his short life, his dauntless heart cracked.

The doctor's shock transformed into repulsion. Realizing the savagery of the words she could not retract, Veda, too, was taciturn.

"Get her out of here!" the doctor hissed, and Veda was wheeled away before she could do anything to assuage her guilt.

She was offered a room at the Queens Hotel before she would return to America the next day. A far cry from the Waldorf Astoria, but it would do.

197

Anything was better than the ocean floor where the Lusitania now rested, or that dreary hospital of live ghosts.

She was entranced in a chair, staring out the window at the docks where swarms of townspeople stood, silently awaiting the arrival of more corpses.

The room smelled of must. So did her borrowed, shapeless dress, a secondhand oversized garment collected for a female survivor. She did everything to remain composed, and sighed in relief, not fear, when a knock came at the door.

As she walked, she watched her frail shadow travel along the wall, illuminated by a dying candle.

She gulped when she unbolted the door and saw Teddy, weak and haggard where he stood in the vestibule, clad in a shabby brown tweed suit.

His emerald green eyes glared at her. His breath nearly felled her.

"You have been drinking!" It was all she could think to say as a feeble mask for her shame.

He entered and sneered, swaying on his feet. "How very observant of you, Mrs. Aspan."

Veda grimaced and brushed aside a tendril of hair from her eyes. "Oh, stop your fatuity, and close the door before someone hears you!"

Teddy chuckled. "Isn't it just like you, Veda, to still think blue blood runs through your veins while the world's red blood has stained the Atlantic?"

She crossed her arms and snapped petulantly. "Close the door; I said!"

He came to her and took her into his arms. He smelled of booze and the sea.

His unshaven face gave him the picture of a handsome hobo. "No! We are going out!"

Veda tensed. "Have you lost your mind on your swim to shore? Why should I go out *there*?"

He pulled her closer until their faces touched. Fire burned in his eyes. "To learn what it is to care about someone other than yourself for once!"

"How dare you deem me heartless!" And she struggled to free herself.

"Shut up!" he grunted, and, grabbing her arm, tugged her to the door.

"You are hurting me!" she protested.

"Good!" he snarled back.

He took her to the mortuary to encounter rows of shapeless corpses illuminated by the light of gas jets. Around them, people were slowly moving, weeping, as they searched and found bodies of loved ones.

A bunch of children were heaped in the middle of the room, and there was a dead mother still clutching her child for protection in her arms.

"Do we have to see anymore?" Veda pleaded as she shuddered, and felt a wave of nausea stir within her.

"Why, Veda? Have you had enough?" Teddy was furious with her, and she knew why.

"Teddy…I…" she began to whisper feebly.

"You wish I were dead!" he snarled as his eyes flashed.

She shook her head with welling tears. "No…I…"

He was relentless. "You would rather see me heaped amongst corpses, my face green and smeared with blood and mucus!"

"Teddy, stop!" she howled, and her stomach heaved.

He eyed her with contempt. Then he took her arm and sneered, "Time for a drink, Mrs. Aspan."

He brought her into a dark, narrow saloon, and ordered a double whiskey. The bearded bartender laid the drink on the counter and asked, "Are ye from the *Lusy*?"

Teddy nodded.

The bartender smiled. "Drink as much as ye like…on the house!" Then he shifted his eyes to Veda, "And what about the Misses?"

Before she could decline, Teddy chimed, "The lady will have a double whiskey as well."

"No, Teddy."

"Shut up, and drink!" he grunted as he smacked his shot glass against hers. "To life," he added, and tossed it off in a gulp. Then he suddenly grew sullen and snatched Veda's untouched whiskey. "And to all those who have died!"

Tears filled his eyes as he tossed off this shot. Veda's heart warmed and she leaned over on the barstool to permit their faces to touch. "I am so sorry for what I said, Teddy. It was just awful of me! I never meant it! You must believe me!"

He took her into his arms and gave her a long kiss. For a strange reason, she no longer smelled the alcohol on his breath.

Then he whispered gently into her ear, "That was the sweetest lie I have ever heard."

Chapter 37

The sinking of the Lusitania was cause for triumph of the German press. Newspapers proudly boasted the widespread death of American passengers. Hostility toward the United States spread like wildfire, which served as reason for the American embassy to evacuate to Switzerland.

The 'act of piracy' had astounded the whole world. Americans who had believed the United States should remain neutral were suddenly eager to go off to war. Ten days after the sinking, President Wilson sent his first note to Berlin. He impressed that neutral shipping should be left in peace. The Kaiser of Germany, having recognized the atrocity of his country's act, agreed to abide by the order.

Thus, in spite of the mounting hostility and hysteria of his people, President Wilson chose not to declare war.

******

The fanfare of the media was the only warm welcome Theodore and Veda Aspan received on the morning of their return to New York. Both families chose to ignore them in light of the shame of their sudden marriage.

Teddy rented the presidential suite in the St. Regis Hotel, and when asked of the projected length of his stay, he sniffed, 'indefinitely.' In the meantime, he worked on plans for the erection of his multimillion-dollar mansion to be called 'The Diamond House.'

He was impervious to his parents' coolness; certain they would thaw once he returned to his wing of the family jewelry store. Veda was not so easily convinced of her own family circumstances.

She quivered as she entered the drawing room of her parents' brownstone that day, looking stunning in a gold buttoned white jacket, and a cobalt hobble skirt. Her blue velvet hat matched her parasol. She was now a woman, but her parents, glaring at her over the rims of their tea cups, saw only the defiant child.

"Hello... Mother... Father..." she said shakily, and crept gingerly closer as the room filled with frost. "I am home, now," she added, and her heart cracked at the realization that her words had little impact.

Winston, in a black morning coat and tie, sat as an icy statue. *La Madame* Champion, draped in Parisian crepe and linen, rose to greet her.

But the warm arms Veda craved and expected were coldly substituted by a sharp slap across her face.

She fell to her knees and found herself weeping into the tufted velvet of an ottoman. She felt the chill of her mother's breeze as she left the room and the fire of her father's eyes suddenly glaring down at her from where he now stood.

"You have disgraced us, Veda. You may have gained a monetary fortune in marrying a diamond tycoon, but the price was your reputation which makes you poor as a church mouse."

Then, he, too, left her alone and weeping. She would never forget his words, because she knew they were true.

Not even Nanny McBride would see her. Hans Wagner was away at Newport, preparing the summer chateau for the family's arrival. Her favorite place in the world. She would probably never see it again.

It took an age for her to compose herself. And after powdering her nose, she left the house with what little dignity she still possessed, and hastened to Champion Trust before her father would return from lunch.

Thank God Marius was there! She knocked sheepishly on the double oak doors of his office, and was relieved when he invited her inside.

He was handsome as ever in his banker's suit of velvet tailcoat and gold chords. His tie was cuffed to perfection, his jet hair short and impeccably groomed. His patent leather shoes sparkled like onyx.

His office, a potpourri of mahogany wood, stained glass, tiffany lamps, and gold antiques, gave the impression of a prince's domain.

He came to her, and kissed her cheek. "I am so happy you are alive, Veda!" he said, and took her into his arms where she melted and began to weep.

"Oh, Marius! Thank God you are not angry with me! Mother, Father, everyone was so dreadfully awful! I do not know what I would do if you were to reject me too!"

He took a step backward and gripped her trembling arms with a warm smile on his face. "You know it is the role of a big brother to stand by his naughty little sister, no matter what."

"You always have," she sighed as tears slid down her face.

"And I always will," he reaffirmed and gestured her into the room. "Have a seat."

She hesitated, "Oh, but what if Father should return?"

He smiled soothingly. "Father has an afternoon meeting on Wall Street."

They sat beside one another on the maroon leather sofa, and Marius rang for tea.

"Marius, you must believe me when I say that I feel just awful about everything I have done! If I could only reverse time!"

"But you cannot, Veda. You must accept your actions bravely."

She tensed. "But, how can I? Mother and Father, even Nanny McBride, have disowned me!"

He smiled reassuringly. "Give them time. They love you very much. They were beside themselves before they learned of your safety."

The tea arrived. Marius poured Veda a steaming cup and added a lump of sugar as he knew her to take.

Veda took a long sip. The hot herbs soothed her. "I cannot tell you how much I miss our dear Rose."

Marius' eyes traveled light years away. "That makes two of us. Now she has *truly* detached herself from us. It was required by her order."

Veda grimaced. "Order, indeed! Do you suppose God *really* wants that? It is all just some crazy notion concocted by bitter old men centuries ago!"

Marius guffawed. "Veda, I do not believe such talk would be a method of returning to our mother's good graces in the near future. She would condemn you blasphemous."

Veda hardened. "I do not care! I am telling you, not Mother! And as for blasphemy, there is no sin greater than what I saw happen on that ship! People drowning, blown to smithereens, babies dying in their mother's arms, shattered lifeboats, torpedoes, fire, smoke! Oh, Marius! It was so God awful! Thank God I am home! Thank God you care!"

He took her into the solace of his warm arms where she wept at length. He smoothed the curls draping from the rim of her hat as his heart blazed and his eyes transformed into fireballs.

"It is all right, Veda. You are safe now. Home forever," he paused and added, his voice far away, ominous, impassioned. "We will get those dirty Huns back! I will not die a happy man until I blast one of them right between the eyes."

Chapter 38

It was July, 1915, two months after the sinking of the Lusitania, and Mr. and Mrs. Theodore Aspan, shovel in hand, posed for the cameras. Moments later, there were blasts of powder and a slew of flashes as they broke the earth, and scooped out the first pile of foundation of their Fifth Avenue mansion.

The cost would be $3,000,000.00, a phenomenal estimate, but Teddy and Veda were unordinary millionaires whose wealth knew no boundaries. They were famous nationwide, not only for having survived the Lusitania enormity, but for being the youngest, wealthiest, and most dashing couple in America. And today, as always, they looked the part.

Veda wore a formal afternoon tunic dress in soft gray silk with an upper bodice of shear gray fabric which tastefully revealed a pink under bodice. Aspan sported a beige, three button, single breasted lounge suit, a wing collared shirt, a brown necktie, and a bowler hat. Neither the press or the spectators could shift their eyes from them.

To New York society, however, they were considered 'classless show-offs.' Already, their unbuilt diamond lined mansion had been referred to as a 'vulgar display of wealth.'

For their parents, therefore, the notoriety, press interviews, and headlines added insult to injury. Theodore and Veda were a social disgrace. An unannounced marriage, a jilted man at the altar, erratic, defiant behavior, and now a tasteless flaunt of millions! *Unbearable*!

Not one family member had been present. But neither expected otherwise. Teddy experienced little more than cool contact with his siblings at the jewelry store, remaining isolated for the most part in his own domain, and had grown quite accustomed to it. Needless to say, his people despised Veda, and cringed at her periodic visits to Teddy's diamond wing. Her superficial smiles, patronizing waves, and condescending manner were nauseating. But the public adored her, and Teddy welcomed her cameo appearances, coining them to his father as 'great for business.'

Veda had acclimated herself into the role of a perfect society snob quite well. There were charity luncheons, tea parties, dinner parties, shopping sprees, and even political functions. She was socially booked seven days a week, and adored every minute of it. She longed only for her own home. Life at the St. Regis was by no means uncomfortable, and she had already been coined the princess of the palace. But she was becoming bored. She wanted her own kingdom, a palace built just for herself, and Teddy had the money and the drive to do it.

Love was a word she had long forgotten. Money, couture, jewels, cars and other creature comforts had become everything to her. She was a material girl at its finest. It kept her mind stimulated, and off her parents and sister who had abandoned her.

"Thank you," she crooned with a wide smile as a reporter slipped a huge bouquet of summer blooms into her arms and snapped a picture.

Teddy's great arrow limousine pulled up, scattering the crowd. His chauffeur emerged and held the door open for them. The young couple strolled toward the vehicle, waving and flashing smiles at cameras and fans.

Then, Veda froze.

"What is it, dear?" Teddy asked, mastering the perfect social mask. Her smile quickly faded. She said nothing.

Teddy followed her gaze and frowned. "Come, Veda. Do not waste your time on that pansy."

Jacques Deneuve stood at the entrance to Central Park with a forlorn expression on his face. He wore a new tailored suit, and a deep sadness in his eyes.

Veda had not seen him since the night of the wedding rehearsal dinner at the Park Avenue Brownstone. She tossed the bouquet onto the backseat of the car and spoke seriously for the first time that day. "Wait for me, Teddy."

The crowd also froze in astonishment. Teddy did not like it. "Veda, you are causing a scene. Now get in the car."

"No," she replied firmly, then added, walking away. "I owe it to him."

She ignored the people, the stares, the cameras, and her husband's final protest. Then Teddy surrendered to defeat and ordered the chauffeur to drive him away.

"Hello, Jacques," Veda said, and took his trembling hand into her gloved palm.

He had a new ethereal glow on his face, and his hazel eyes looked through, and then beyond her.

"I have come to say goodbye," he said in a gentle monotone.

She had heard of his plans to enter the seminary, and was not surprised.

She nodded as guilt washed over her. "I know. Thank you."

He read her thoughts and attempted to comfort her. "It had to happen, Veda. God works in mysterious ways. It was His method of calling me to serve Him."

Just then, Veda thought of Rose. "Do you truly believe that?" she asked doubtfully, doing everything not to cry.

He nodded.

She gripped his hands tightly and looked earnestly onto his face. Their eyes locked. It was a sudden joining of souls, something she thought she had long lost. "Then you will make a wonderful priest, Jacques."

Then she slipped away and slowly retreated. The tears came with the whisper from her heart, "Forgive me, please."

He peered at her with a well of care in his eyes. "I already have... a long time ago."

She edged forward and softly kissed his cheek. When he purred, Veda knew he would be back...

Chapter 39

The print on the textbook page blurred, and soon, she was fast asleep. A dozen nuns seated around her at the library table did everything not to shift eyes from their studies.

Early that evening, she was summoned to the Mother Superior. The elderly, unsmiling matriarch gave the impression that her wrinkled face would crack when she parted her blue white lips to speak. "It has been brought to my attention that you had given way to slumber in the midst of your studies, my child."

Sister Perpetua trembled on her knees as shame washed over her. The candles on either side of the Mother Superior illuminated the stone wall, magnifying her seated shadow.

"Yes, Reverend Mother...I had."

The ancient nun looked down at her with a steely gaze. "You have recently received a glowing report on a physical examination. Your temperature and pulse were taken this afternoon. There is nothing ailing you medically, Sister Perpetua. Kindly tell me what is troubling you."

The young nun gulped. A sea of guilt raged through her mind. "There is nothing, Reverend Mother," she answered in a shaking voice before being tempted to betray herself. Memories were forbidden. Love for an estranged twin was taboo. An inordinate concern about academics was time stolen from God.

But the cold faced Mother Superior read through her. "You are at the top of your class, Sister Perpetua. Idle hands *are* the devil's workshop, but there is such a thing as an overwrought mind. A good nun is a humble nun. It is wrong for you to possess the urge to outshine your classmates. He who exalts himself shall be humbled, and he who humbles himself shall be exalted."

The young sister was devastated. "Forgive me, Reverend Mother, but that is not my wish at all."

"Is it not?" the question cast the cave like room into an ice age.

Sr. Perpetua sighed forlornly, "I confess, Reverend Mother, that it has always been ingrained in me to excel."

The matriarch's eyes became glazed with complacence. "Admitting our faults is the springboard for correcting them. Our Lord alone is perfect, my child. We merely attempt to emulate Him. Singularizing is a nun's greatest transgression."

Her young heart began to bleed. It seemed as if she was always apologizing, repenting for things her mind could not control.

"How can I correct them, Reverend Mother?" her head was throbbing.

Her knees, so accustomed to the floor, were numb.

The Mother Superior lifted her brass cross for Sister Perpetua to rise and kiss. Then the young nun kissed her feet and awaited instructions.

"Your classmates feel gravely inferior to you. Some have repented their resentment toward you. Humility is the lesson you must learn," then she paused to ponder for a short moment. "A major examination is forthcoming."

Sister Perpetua, on her knees, nodded once again, "Yes, Reverend Mother."

After a long, tense silence, the Mother Superior commanded, "Fail it." Her voice spewed frost.

Rose was momentarily paralyzed.

She never slept that night. She dozed in class the next day, and was sent to meditate for twenty-four hours without food or drink. Then came the exam. She tensed in her seat when she read the questions. She knew every answer like the back of her hand.

And she also knew what she had to do…

That evening, she found herself on her knees once again, encountering the Mother Superior's icy glare.

"You received a perfect score on your examination, Sister Perpetua. You defied my instructions."

Tears slid down Rose's statuesque face. "Forgive me, Reverend Mother, but I deemed it sinful to betray the gift of intellect the Lord has bestowed upon me."

The matriarch's face tightened. Her eyes flashed. She took a deep breath and composed herself. After a long moment, she rendered a reply. It was soft and deadly.

"You leave me no recourse, my impertinent child. You are hereby discharged from your classes. Report to the kitchen after chapel in the morning."

Chapter 40

Veda made a grand entrance through the thirteenth-century German glass doors of Aspan's diamond wing, wearing a tailor-made striped suit, a huge black velvet hat, and a sable boa.

She sashayed toward her husband with an entourage of tuxedoed waiters trailing behind her. "Lunch time, darling," she chimed, and slipped off her gloves as one waiter opened a table, and others tended to the particulars. It was set for two, with Minton china and French lead crystal. A chilled bottle of champagne was popped open, and two glasses were poured.

Teddy chuckled as his wife sat and gracefully folded a napkin over her lap. "Mrs. Aspan, you never cease to amaze me."

Veda grinned coquettishly. "So, I am told, my dear. Care to join me?" and she batted her oblique eyelashes while raising her champagne glass to toast.

Teddy laughed again and sat, tuning out the surrounding patrons and employees gaping in stupefaction.

"To our new home," she proposed, and they clinked glasses. "Pierce at the St. Regis has prepared an exquisite menu, Teddy dear. I know if I had not chosen to come, you would have gone all day without eating."

He eyed her suspiciously as he started on his vichyssoise. "And what else has motivated you other than my nutrition?"

Veda flashed a million-dollar smile. Teddy admitted she was growing more beautiful every day. "Well, now that you ask…"

And she motioned a waiter to produce specs of their mansion.

"I will be visiting the construction site this afternoon and would like to share my latest plans with you."

He snickered, and finished his champagne. "You mean you need me to finance you."

Veda giggled. "How unattractive of a devilishly handsome diamond magnet such as you to reduce this venture to mercenary terms."

He leaned back in his seat and folded his arms. Through the French doors of the jewelry store in the opposite wing, Teddy's family glared at them.

"You have my attention, Veda. But it better be good before I offer you my check book. So far, we have exceeded our budget by a million dollars. Soon I will have to mortgage this store."

Veda waved a patronizing hand. "Oh, Teddy, you know that would never happen! Just keep earning your millions, and allow me to help you spend them!"

He leaned forward and caressed her supple hand. "Is that not what you do best?"

Veda started on her second glass of champagne. "Teddy, really!" then she shifted the topic. "Now, let's begin. My appointment is in less than an hour. I have planned the particulars of the ballroom. There will be a baccarat crystal French glass chandelier, and an African marble floor. The mantel piece will be white Carrara marble imported from Italy, and the wall panels will depict scenes from Greek mythology. There will be circulating fountains installed in each corner, and the ceiling will be the grandest in the city, the honeycomb of neoclassical arabesques and Italian motifs in gold leaf."

She was running on, and Teddy's mind was spinning.

"Now, to review, there will be eight chambers, each with bathrooms on the second floor…oh, and one minor change, darling. I would like two master suites instead of one."

Teddy, his head in a haze, stopped her right there. "Separate chambers, Veda?"

She looked at him in wide-eyed surprise. "Why, of course, dear. All well-bred dignitaries share separate chambers."

He shook his head objectionably. "Not these well-bred dignitaries."

Veda, suddenly cornered, grew shrewdly evasive, "Well, this is hardly the time or the place to discuss such trivia, Teddy…now, to continue—"

He leaned forward and eyed her firmly. "This is the perfect time and the perfect place, Veda. Let's talk. It has been two months since we have been intimate, and…"

She gasped, horrified, "Teddy! In public? Lower your voice! Someone might hear you!"

He intoned with no mistake in his resolution, "I do not care who hears me! I pay their salaries!"

Veda tensed. "Well, then you are obviously not accustomed to being in the presence of ladies!"

His left eye twitched. "What is that supposed to mean?"

She leaned forward; her face suddenly hard as stone. "You read between the lines! Do you deem me a fool?"

Teddy's voice turned to bitter frost, "A man needs to find warmth somewhere, Veda. *You* certainly are not doing the job!"

Incensed, she shot to her feet and tossed the rest of her champagne into his face. "How dare you hold me with such ill regard!"

Teddy, drying the bubbly from his face, rose with forced dignity. "Go home, Veda!"

She fired back at him, stirring a scene. "Home? Now where might that be? The St. Regis Hotel? Or that hole in the ground you leave *me* to monitor while you sit in this store and play with glittering stones?"

Teddy snarled, battling to maintain himself. "Leave, before I have you removed!"

She tossed the sable boa over her left shoulder. "With pleasure, Mr. Aspan!" And she stormed away.

Everyone in the store, including her in laws, still glaring through the French doors, observed incredulously.

Teddy, now furious, turned to the waiters. "Get this out of here!" he snapped, and in seconds, everything was collected and gone.

Veda glided through the grand lobby of the St. Regis Hotel later that afternoon, and turned every head at the elegant grand tea. The harpist played Vivaldi, and waiters doted over tables, presenting sterling pots and triple tiered serving plates of finger sandwiches, scones, and petit fours.

She spied Chester Worthington, beaming in a navy-blue suit and tie, and feigned a frown. "I was informed that a steel magnet was awaiting my arrival. Had I known it was you, Chester, I would have taken the first private elevator to my suite."

And she sat, gracefully draping her boa over her shoulder. But she felt her heart flutter. Actually, she had hoped it *was* Chester. She had missed him. She needed a few diverted moments of adventure in her life.

He grinned, his eyes illuminating at the sight of her. And he raised his whiskey glass as he spoke, "It's wonderful to see you again, too, Veda."

She folded her hands on the table and lifted her chin haughtily. "We must be miscommunicating, Chester. I never said I was *glad* to see *you*!"

He leaned forward with a feverish gleam in his eyes. "You didn't have to. Your manner betrays you."

Veda raised her left eyebrow and grinned. "Still ill-mannered and conceited, aren't you?"

He threw her a kiss. "You bring out the worst in me, Veda."

"Champagne, Mrs. Aspan?" a waiter asked with a glass of bubbly already poured on a sterling tray.

She waved it away. "No thank you. Bourbon today."

The waiter did a double take, then retreated with a "Right away, Mrs. Aspan."

Chester smirked. "I see you change your poison from time to time."

She reached for a scone and whispered impishly, "You bring out the worst in *me*, Chester."

Her bourbon arrived and she raised the glass. "To the good life."

He observed her at length. "Veda, if I did not know you better, I would say you are flirting with me."

She guffawed. "Now isn't that so very typical of your low-grade nature?"

"Are you happy?" he asked, striking the point of his visit.

Her face twitched. She took another sip of bourbon and shrugged. "I am ecstatic. Why?"

Chester's tone grew increasingly serious, "Well, I hear your parents have disowned you, and your in laws despise you. I am concerned."

She hardened and shot him a glacial stare. "You mean you have come to gloat. And frankly, I have not the time *or* the inclination to entertain your fatuity. Given your track record, Chester, I hardly deem *you* an expert on family affairs!"

He flagged down the waiter and ordered another whiskey. "Why are you so coarse? Doesn't a man reserve the liberty to express concern for a childhood sweetheart?"

Veda tossed a lump of sugar into a cup of steaming herbal tea. "I was never your sweetheart, Chester. I was barely an acquaintance."

He leaned forward and took her hand. "We think alike, and we are alike. When are you going to realize and finally admit that we belong together?"

She rose arrogantly and sneered down at him. "When hell grows cold, Mr. Worthington. Good day."

Then she sauntered away, her haughty finishing school gait revved in fast gear.

Chapter 41

Early in 1916, the German army marched across the French countryside to Verdun, one of France's prize, charming villages, the site of legendary battles leading back to the Roman Empire, and the home of *Monsieur* and *Madame* DuBois.

The Great War was becoming a glimpse of hell, a blood bath for both sides. From April 22 to May 25, 1915, the British were defeated at the second battle of Ypres in Belgium. Here, poison gas was used for the first time. It produced horrific physical burning effects.

In October, 1915, Bulgaria declared war on Serbia. The central Powers eventually overran Serbia, Montenegro, and Albania. Romania was also conquered, and the Central Powers turned to Italy.

From December, 1915, to January, 1916, Russians were driven out of Galicia, and much of Russian Poland. Russia lost one million men in prisoners, and there were two million casualties.

As the cold light of snow came through the frost covered window late that February afternoon, Pierre DuBois gazed out onto the white blanketed earth, and grimly wondered how much of it was stained with blood at the borders of the town where the fortress had been built to keep the enemy out. The French Chateau had been transformed into a hospital for the wounded soldiers, and an inn for the cold, the desperate, and the hungry who had been worn to the quick at the front.

The entire neighborhood was now a town of uniformed men, graciously received and doted upon by the grateful inhabitants. Their precious Verdun was being valiantly protected from the Germans whose aim was to bleed the enemy to death, to wear them down, and gain victory over a mountain of corpses.

"*Ils ne passeront pas!*" became the French battle cry, meaning: 'They shall not pass!' And the Germans *did not* pass. They were stopped within four miles of the village and would be fighting here for five months, thus marking Verdun the largest and bloodiest battle of The Great War.

Madame DuBois entered, maintaining total elegance and dignity in a simple house smock. Modest attire was the order of each day now that national pride had been sifted into her blue blood. There were soldiers to be nursed and fed.

Vanity and opulence were things of the past.

"It is time to check on the patients, old man," she said gently and took her husband's frail, quivering arm. She looked up into his weary eyes and questioned, "What troubles you?"

He shivered, and his words shook. "I am cold, ma mer."

The elderly woman forced a faint smile. "We are all cold. Think of our young boys at the front. Come, now. I shall ask Maurice to place more wood on the fire."

"But it is scarce, *ma mer*," he fretfully protested.

Madame DuBois shook her head. "What is one more log to make an old man comfortable?"

And they proceeded to examine the rows of wounded soldiers in guest rooms being nursed by young neighborhood maidens. They extinguished the candles and dismissed the veiled girls as the soldiers were slumbering soundly. The sweet melodies of La Marseillaise were wafting through the door from the downstairs parlor where a soldier played the piano for his fellow brothers. It was inspiring to hear the French National anthem each night, a comfort, a reassurance that France would be victorious.

They offered the soldiers a final round of whiskey and bade them a good night. An hour later, the entire house and neighborhood were asleep.

Shortly afterward, *Madame* DuBois was awakened by her regular nightmare of Germans crossing the fortress and invading Verdun. She lay awake listening to her husband's snores, and watching the snow gust through the icy winter night. The fire had long since burned out, and despite three blankets, stockings and a night cap, she was freezing.

Suddenly, she caught a glimpse of a light in the backyard. She rose from the bed and went to the frosted window. There were two French soldiers holding a kerosene lamp, struggling in the freezing night, seemingly drunk.

"Silly fools!" she grumbled. "They are lucky they have not caught their death of cold!"

"What is it, *ma mer*?" questioned *Monsieur* DuBois, who had roused from his slumber.

"Go back to sleep, old man," she gently chided.

"Who is out there?" he asked, seeing the light.

"Just some drunken soldiers. I am sure they will be looking for shelter," she said with a grimace.

Pierre rose and shivered as he slipped on his flannel bathrobe.

"We cannot turn them away," he said, lighting a candle. "They need rest."

Madame DuBois frowned. "And I suppose they will be wanting a meal."

Monsieur DuBois gazed out at them stumbling over one another on the back lawn. "In the state they are in, *ma mer*, a warm bed and breakfast in the late morning should suit them just fine."

As they walked to the door. *Madame* DuBois grumbled, "We have no warm beds, just freezing cots!"

Pierre took his wife's arm and led her down the dark hall, enveloped by the snores of soldiers emanating from guest rooms. The antique paintings were illuminated by candlelight as was the gold balustrade of the staircase leading to the Gothic foyer.

At the very moment they reached the cold marble landing, the knocker on the heavy oak door sounded. *Madame* DuBois mumbled something under her breath as her husband wearily opened the door. An icy wind swept into the room as the drunken soldiers bowed and greeted them. Though clad in blue uniform, their French was marked with an odd accent, and their features were peculiarly fair and chiseled, their icy blue eyes almost Nordic in appearance.

Monsieur and *Madame* DuBois inspected them suspiciously, then turned to glance at one another.

"Would you happen to have shelter and a cup of hot tea?" one of the soldiers asked, and the elderly couple shook with cold as the glacial wind flooded the room.

"Let them in and close the door, old man!" *Madame* DuBois ordered, and her frail husband obliged.

The soldiers were now in the foyer, seemingly impervious to the bitter cold. "Come," *Madame* DuBois said, and led them into the drawing room.

But something was not right.

"Have a seat," *Madame* DuBois said testily, and then she froze in horror.

One of the soldiers grabbed her from behind and gagged her mouth as the other produced a knife and slashed her husband's throat. She never felt the blade slice through her own flesh, having already fainted at the sight of Pierre's blood pouring onto the floor.

The screaming stress signals awakened the village. Two French soldiers had been slaughtered at the fortress and two Huns managed to cross. They had stolen their uniforms and ran into the town. Police and soldiers were frantically hunting them down.

The Huns were not captured until the following morning when one had frozen in a trench he had built, and the other, half paralyzed by frost, lamely attempted to abscond with the fortune he had stolen from the French chateau. He was spotted on a back road by a merchant and reported to the police. He was apprehended and immediately hung in the square for the villagers to see.

Only it was too late. *Monsieur* and *Madame* DuBois had already been slain. The villagers and soldiers wept for days.

Chapter 42

The Aspan's Diamond House was an architectural wonder. It was a four-story diamond-lined limestone palace with graceful window treatments and orientation. The bronze and iron front doors weighed three thousand pounds each, and a total of five hundred square yards of marble surrounded the forty-room edifice. The entrance hall contained marble floors, marble walls, and a mosaic ceiling. It led to a grand curved staircase with a wrought iron, diamond embossed balustrade. The walls of the entrance vestibule were wainscoted with Votticino marble and underfoot leaf in an intricate pattern of different marbles with a brass leaf set into the floor.

Features in rooms on the main floor included a seventeenth century Herat carpet, a wood paneled library in the grand manner of the French Renaissance, a French gilt metal and crystal chandelier, Japanese Imari porcelains, English Georgian style crystal decanters, and a Dutch brass six light chandelier in the main parlor.

The ballroom boasted six sets of leaded French windows overlooking Central Park, and the richest ceiling in the city.

In the conservatory, a marble fountain added gleam to potted plants, ferns and palms.

The second-floor bannister supported a pair of bronze dore candelabras secured by cornucopia borne by cupids. Each group was seventy inches high.

A baccarat crystal of France chandelier presided over the dining room, decorated with 24-carat gold presentation frame paintings. There were seventy-five-pound chairs made of hollow bronze marble from Africa, surrounding a huge African Mahogany wood table.

The second floor housed eight chambers, each with bathrooms, and two elaborate master suites. The third floor contained twelve servants' rooms, a sewing room, and four rooms dedicated strictly to linens and clothing. The basement housed the kitchen, another linen room, a servants' dining room, a laundry, and rooms for the footman, the butler, the valet, the housekeeper, and the cellarman, plus amenities including the wine storage room, and an iron gate for deliveries.

The Aspans employed three French chefs to prepare four formal meals a day, breakfast, lunch, high tea, and dinner. There was a butler, four footmen, six housemaids, a gardener, a valet, a cellarman, a chauffeur, an errand boy, a caretaker, and Veda's personal chambermaid, Carlotta.

She doted over her mistress in her boudoir that cold February evening, the night of the grand housewarming ball about which society headlines would scream the next morning. It was already the social event of the season, the arena for gold, diamonds and couture to which all of New York society had been invited. Already, chauffeured cars were snaking along the snow lined curbs, disgorging prominent jewel bedecked women and black tied men, draped in fur and cashmere, gleaming in the sweeping spotlights which illuminated the limestone mansion like an oversized diamond embossed treasure box.

Veda wore a crimson velvet evening dress, embroidered in gold with a dramatic low V back. Her hair was swept upward and fell freely behind her neck. Her diamond necklace, earrings and cocktail ring were estimated at a millionaire's fortune.

"My gloves, Carlotta," she pleasantly requested as the young French woman hastened across the room to collect them.

"Thank you, dear," Veda crooned, and slipped them over her milk white hands. "Do you suppose I require a bit more powder on my nose?" she questioned, admiring herself in the huge Venetian glass mirror.

Carlotta shook her head reverently. "No, *Madame*. The *Madame* looks beautiful."

And, indeed, Veda did, beneath the baccarat crystal of France chandelier, and beside the Winterhalter portrait of the empress Eugenie and her maids of honor.

The boudoir was an opulent masterpiece, designed with Louis XIV style furniture, an Aubusson carpet, and lilac fabric on the walls.

Veda fluffed her curls. "And my hair, Carlotta…do you suppose…" she was interrupted by firm knocks on the double doors.

"Come in," she chimed, admiring her reflection.

Teddy appeared in black tailcoat and white tie. His golden hair was slicked back on his head, and everything about his demeanor beamed, save the scowl on his face.

"I would like a few moments with my wife…alone," he commanded curtly.

"Certainly, Monsieur," Carlotta replied with a prompt curtsy, and retreated at once.

Veda dabbed her wrists with perfumed oil and mocked. "Such petulant intrusions are becoming quite habitual, Teddy darling," she paused and added, eyeing him with contempt. "You might smile. You *are* the host of the party. One might think by your glum expression that you were still diamond mining in Africa."

He came to her and snarled, "My diamond mining days were amongst my happiest Veda! Life with *you* has confirmed that!"

She glared at him through the mirror. "Now why does such a slavish remark not surprise me? You have proven that not even a birthright, much less diamonds, can polish a bad apple."

His eyes narrowed. "The game is over! I have conceded to your thwarted request for separate chambers, but I will not be denied my marital rights any longer!"

She laughed pompously. "Marital rights, indeed! *You* the prince of infidelity! How vulgar of you to assume I would share your bed after your arms have been wrapped around some jezebel!"

He glowered at her. His face was long and hard. "Then you leave me no choice but to file for a divorce."

Veda turned to shock. "Is it not just like you to sink to the proclivities of your non-Catholic people in proposing such a vile thing!"

Teddy's eyes shot emerald fire. "You heard me. Make your choice!"

Albeit the sting of panic, Veda maintained a rigid front, "There is no choice! I will never grant you a divorce, and disgrace my name or my people!"

Teddy grinned. "You already *have* disgraced yourself, and your people have repudiated you." Then he paused and added, "Make your decision, Veda. Consider yourself warned."

Then he turned and left.

The truth of his words was a dagger through her heart. She felt suddenly alone and helpless. She had alienated herself from the world. In that moment, she longed for Rose.

Knocks on the door and the cool voice of a servant sprang her back to dignity. "Pardon me, Mrs. Aspan. It is time to receive the guests."

Veda took a deep breath and held her head high. She stiffened her shoulders and sashayed to the door. A Strauss waltz greeted her when she entered the hall which was filled with the highest order of Renaissance style detailing.

She gripped the beautiful wrought iron balustrade at the top landing of the curved stair and beamed at the sight of tuxedoed and gowned dancers, the thirty-piece orchestra, the gloved waiters carrying trays of caviar, canapés and champagne. Wealth and elegance. It was hers…forever.

And when the guests caught a glimpse of her stunning portrait, they froze, one by one, with gazes ranging from awe to envy. She knew she carried the presence of a queen…Teddy would never leave her…

She slowly descended with royal grace as the orchestra began a Viennese waltz. It was one of the greatest moments in her life, being received as the mistress of a palace, hostess of an affair to make all headlines.

And then it all shattered when Marius came running through the front doors clad in his banker's costume and cashmere overcoat. The grand foyer and the ballroom fell silent. Teddy was appalled.

"Marius!" Veda gushed on the staircase, one hand on the balustrade, another over her heart. "You never informed me you were coming!"

But she could tell by the tears glistening in his eyes and his ghost white face, that her brother was not there to celebrate.

"Veda, I think you should come home right away," his voice shook, and his tears fell.

Veda panicked. "Marius! What is wrong?"

He broke down in the next moment, "It is *Grand-Pere* and *Grand-Mere*… They have been killed!"

Veda fainted. The last thing she remembered was strong arms breaking her fall.

******

There was a High Mass at St. Patrick's Cathedral, and a memorial service two days later when mother nature dropped nearly a foot of snow on the city. The grieving family gathered around a monument erected in the names of *Monsieur* and *Madame* DuBois, whose bodies were buried in the French earth they so greatly endeared.

"They have lived and died for their country." They were the only words Veda heard the priest speak as she stood beside her husband in a Russian sable coat. She had been weeping all day, and could not, for the life of her, determine from where her dry-eyed mother had inherited her enormous strength. She knew *La Madame* Champion, though tall, stately, and composed in black mink, was crumbling inside. Her father, Winston, had even removed his handkerchief to dry a few tears that day. Dominique, her sister-in-law, was paralyzed with shock, and Marius burned like a torch.

The snow was falling steadily, and the arctic wind was relentless. Veda's feet were numb, and her tears were beginning to freeze on her face. Rose's absence infuriated her. Order or not, she belonged there with them! She needed her! Did those veiled old women even inform her that her grandparents had been slain by two Huns in Verdun?

They prayed a decade of the Rosary and crossed themselves when the priest offered his final blessing.

"Mother…" Veda sheepishly pleaded as the small gathering of family and friends slowly dispersed.

La Madame Champion looked past her to the ice glazed tree under which their car had been parked.

"Father!" Veda wept, staring helplessly into Winston's eyes.

"Join your husband now, Veda. He is waiting for you." It was all he said before walking past her, *La Madame* Champion in arm.

Veda looked at Teddy. His eyes were warm, his aura beckoning, the expression on his handsome face soft and caring. Ironically, it turned her to stone.

"Marius!" she cried, and threw herself into her brother's arms where she wept desperately at length.

Dominique, nearly frostbitten, had already gone to the car, and it was just the three of them.

Teddy gazed at his wife with a blend of pain and disgust. She had shut him out one time too many. He left, unnoticed, and then it was just Veda and Marius locked in a bereaved embrace.

"Why them?" Veda asked despairingly. "Why does war claim the innocent?"

The fire in Marius' eyes seemed to melt the winter frost. He became glazed, nearly possessed, and snarled as he gazed at the stone monument. "I will get those Huns back! I swear to God I will!"

Chapter 43

In the dead of winter, New York at 5:00 pm is dark as midnight. It was from this, and the biting, blustery cold, that the chandelier lit Diamond House offered Veda a warm reprieve.

She entered glumly, and was immediately received by her chambermaid. "*Madame*! We were *so* worried about you outside in that bitter cold without word for so many hours!"

Veda sighed as Carlotta helped her off with her sable. "How kind of you to express concern, which is more than I can say for my own husband who abandoned me in the cemetery! At least my brother was gallant enough to see me safely home."

She paused to slip off her gloves and hat, then added, "I am dreadfully tired, Carlotta. Please draw me a hot bath, and inform the kitchen staff that I will be dining in my chamber this evening."

Just then, Teddy's muddled voice sounded from the dining room. "Won't you care to join your husband for dinner, Mrs. Aspan?"

Carlotta glanced at her mistress nervously, but Veda quickly placed her anxiety to rest. "Never mind, Carlotta. You may draw my bath later."

Then she passed the huge Chinese vases from which vibrant palms sprang, and inspected her reflection in the 24-carat gold framed gilt mirror before entering the opulent dining room.

Teddy's gaunt face was illuminated by the flames of the crystal candelabra on the table. He had been losing weight in the past few months, and Veda was becoming concerned. She implored him many times to visit a doctor, but he insisted there was no time.

"I am fine, anyway, Veda. Now do not become a nagging wife," he would testily retort, and so she had surrendered to his stubbornness. But tonight, he appeared unusually pale, and thinner than ever. She had reason to be concerned, but bitterness drowned her heart.

The décor of the dining room was French Neoclassical, and Teddy sat in one of the one-hundred-pound head chairs made of hollow bronze.

"Good evening, Mrs. Aspan. I have been awaiting your arrival."

She glowered at him, and bitterly inspected the table gracefully set for two. "The audacity of you to address me after such a callous desertion at the cemetery, *and* in a drunken state, no less!"

He glared at her and snickered. "You would drive any man to drink! Now sit down!"

She was repulsed. "Why, of all the ill based…"

"Shut up and sit down, I said!" he barked back at her. Veda huffed. "No!"

Then she turned and made her way back to the grand foyer. Teddy rose and trailed after her, his head whirling.

"You are my wife, damn it! You're not going to keep running away!"

"Good night, Mr. Aspan," she sniffed, staring forward, her head raised, her shoulders pointed as she ascended the elaborate staircase.

A black rage erupted in Teddy's head, fury spreading through him like acid.

He climbed up after her, two, three steps at a time, and ignited when she slammed her bedroom door in his face.

He kicked it open, and froze, fuming. Sitting at her vanity, Veda stared up at him calmly with fire blazing in her violet eyes.

"So much for knocking, but not a surprise. No wonder you were able to survive in the wild valleys of Africa; you are an untamed animal yourself."

Teddy darkened, possessed by a mix of lust and fury. He gunned to the vanity, seized Veda's arm, and lifted her to face the man turned mad.

She screamed, but he muzzled her mouth with his tie.

She fought him with legs, arms, and fists, but his strength overpowered her, and soon she was trapped in the bondage of his embrace, being carried to the majestic bed onto which he tossed her and prepared to claim what was rightfully his.

He tore off his clothing with a fierce savagery in his eyes, and then hers. She resisted with vehement contortions of her body, but he expertly restrained her, pinned her to the mattress, and entered her with a vengeance.

And as he seized her with fierce, pelvic thrusts, as Veda wrenched to be freed, he cried into her throbbing ear, "You're mine! Don't forget it! You won't deny me! You won't!"

Then he emitted a loud, bestial groan as he exploded, and Veda surrendered to the fervor, electrified somehow by the thwarted passion, digging her fingers into his back, his neck, and coming to a spellbinding climax herself.

He was maddened, ferocious, fueled by months of pent-up rejection. So, he went on, and still, again, exploring, writhing, jolting, as Veda closed her eyes and tasted ecstasy.

Chapter 44

It had been months now, of cooking, cleaning, scrubbing on her hands and knees, setting, and clearing tables, serving, and being regarded by the Mother Superior and the educated nuns as subhuman.

Sister Perpetua and the rest of the lowly kitchen staff outwardly assumed the role of peasantry with grace. Inside, it was gnawing at their bones all too quickly. True, all, except Sister Perpetua had been born into poverty and were merely assuming their rightful role, regarding the walls of the nunnery as a reprieve to stave off starvation and find solace in serving God. But it was anything but pleasant.

Whoever knew there was a class system in the convent? Sister Perpetua never heeded it herself while she was amongst the privileged to be educated to teach. She was laden with guilt to know she had overlooked these poor peasant nuns who had served her as did the maids on Fifth Avenue, and in Newport, Rhode Island.

Perhaps, after all, the Mother Superior had done her a favor in forcing her to experience servitude…

But on a cold winter morning, after she had cleared the breakfast table and prepared to wash the dishes, Sister Perpetua learned by a visit from the glacial Mother Superior that it was more than the need for a lesson in humility which had motivated her to dictate this assignment.

"Sister Perpetua," her voice, though soft, was harshly tyrannical.

Rose thrust her cracked, callous hands from the soapy water, and fell directly to her knees. "Yes, Reverend Mother? How may I serve you?"

The elderly nun's ice blue eyes bit down at her. "I have received a letter from the Cardinal. He has inquired about your progress, and is eager to have you assigned to a prominent parish school."

Rose was flabbergasted. As she gazed up onto the stoic face of the Mother superior, she read disgust.

"Apparently, your one-time father is quite influential He has made the Cardinal his emissary." Then she paused and condemned, "Those of earthly wealth have ways of successfully manipulating even the dogmas of the cloistered which have prevailed for nearly two thousand years."

Rose, still in shock, remained humbly silent and awaited her orders.

The Mother Superior's wrinkled face tightened as she sneered down at her, "You will finish the breakfast dishes, and scrub the floor. Then you will report to study hall. Tomorrow you shall resume your classes."

Then she folded her arms into her scapular and left.

Rose remained on her knees, traumatized. She realized in that moment that for some strange reason, the Mother Superior disliked her intensely. It hurt to recognize offensive human qualities in such a paragon whom they were taught to believe was the closest mortal figure to God.

Chapter 45

Veda sat stoically at the breakfast table the next morning, fully clad in a blue velvet morning dress.

Teddy entered sheepishly in a black business suit. His face was drawn, his demeanor gaunt, his eyes weary.

"Good morning, Veda," he uttered, and took his place at the head of the table.

She glared at him over the gold rim of her coffee cup. It hurt Teddy to see hatred burning in her eyes. She deemed any pleasurable memories of the previous night unworthy of herself. It was bestial, and she, being a lady, was ashamed of herself for feeling anything other than disgust.

"Your audacity never ceases to amaze me," she bitterly retorted.

A servant entered with Teddy's breakfast on a silver tray. He made the formal presentation and hastened to retreat, detecting the steam in the room.

Teddy folded his napkin neatly over his lap. "I suppose I owe you an apology," he remarked guiltily, but Veda remained unmoved.

"An understatement to say the least!"

He gazed at her sadly. "Why do you hate me so, Veda? Haven't I been good to you from the start? Haven't I given you everything you ever wanted?"

She hissed back with a cold venom in her tone, "Are you intimating that I asked you to force yourself upon me last evening?"

He sighed, "You are really impossible."

And Veda fumed, "Am I? And shall I propose a choice word for yourself?"

He stared at her silently again as bitterness washed over him, "Why did you marry me anyway?"

Veda seized the opportunity to wound him. "How quickly you forget, Theodore Aspan. I married you for your money at your own callous request."

The sneer had infuriated him. He shot to his feet and tossed his napkin onto the table. "Well now you can consent to my callous demand for a divorce!"

"I will do no such thing!" she fired back vehemently.

228

"You have no choice!" he grunted, and aimed for the door. He turned once to add, his manner nearly pitiful. "Not that it would matter much to you, but I will not be home for dinner this evening."

Veda rolled her eyes and snickered. "A new jezebel?"

He glared at her. "No…a doctor…not that my wellbeing means anything to you either."

She stared at him silently for a long interval. *Finally…* she thought. If he had done one right thing, he heeded her advice. She almost softened by his weak and tired appearance. Perhaps he was just overworked. But when she saw the hatred in his eyes and thought of the evening before, she iced.

"Correct you are, Teddy. You could die for all I care," and she turned her back on him, beholding the snow-covered park from the picture window.

The words stabbed him. "So could you, Veda…*and* make a beeline to hell!"

Then he left. The slam of the front door was a crack of thunder. Veda remained frozen on her feet.

Chapter 46

The African princess prostituted herself and managed in a short year to save her passage to America.

She sailed steerage with her baby girl en-route New York. They shared a bunk with roaches and rodents with hundreds of other poor souls packed amongst filth, feces, sickness and death.

It was a visit to hell.

The imposing walls and unsmiling faces on Ellis Island were a heavenly welcome.

She made her way into Manhattan, and was greeted by a slew of pimps eyeing young girls as prime meat at the Chelsea Piers. Here, she heard the word *nigger* for the first time. She also learned there was *no* place for her baby on *this* side of town.

The survival theory of the fittest led her to the streets of Harlem where black neighborhoods were beginning to form. She was welcome there, and became employed as a housemaid where she worked for pittance. But it was a living which kept a roof over her little girl's head, and provided three meager meals a day.

But the security came to a quick end when the house master raped her and his wife, upon catching them in bed, accused her of being a 'nigger whore.'

The African princess found herself on the cold, grimy streets once again.

She deemed it a miracle when she found a dollar bill covered with horse manure lying on a cobblestone road. She clenched it, rented herself a room at a nearby hotel, fed her baby, and put herself into business.

'Gypsy,' as she was known, became a popular whore. She was earning a decent living. It would be fine until her daughter was old enough to understand, or when she felt the time was right to destroy Teddy Aspan…whatever came first.

Either way, she was here to ensure Teddy's day of reckoning. She would get him. He would pay. He would suffer worse than she. She was waiting for the perfect moment to strike…

Chapter 47

Veda entered her Fifth Avenue mansion shortly after noon the following day, and was shocked to find Teddy descending the grand staircase, suitcase in hand. He looked emaciated, and his skin had taken on a yellowish hue. He wore a cashmere coat and a derby hat, and grimaced at the sight of his wife in a Persian lamb coat.

"Have you decided to sail back to Africa to revisit your happier days?" Veda scorned, masking her surprise.

Teddy ignored her until he came to the vestibule. The repulsion on his face would make it difficult for anyone to believe he had once loved her. "Unfortunately not, Veda. Just to Newport."

Her eyes widened in shock. "Newport? In the dead of winter, Teddy? Whatever for?"

He glared at her. His eyes were glassy and bloodshot. "I need a vacation…from you!"

Her face dropped. The sting of abandonment struck a nerve. "And what am I supposed to do in this massive house all alone?"

Her reaction had amazed him. He observed her for a long moment. "Always thinking of yourself first, Veda. How considerate of you."

She snapped back at him. "And I suppose you regard it considerate to abandon me? How will the society column read? What will people say?"

"I don't give a damn!" he snarled, and went to the door.

Veda suddenly felt her heart drop too. "I am no fool, Teddy! This is your cowardly way of leaving me; isn't it? Well, I still will not grant you a divorce!"

He came back and sneered in her face, "Careful, Veda. You might just betray yourself and reveal hints that you care something for me."

She hardened to stone, "Do not flatter yourself! A roach means more to me than you do, Theodore Aspan!"

He appeared wounded for a fleeting moment, and she was gratified. "Now why does that not surprise me?" he mocked, and tipped his hat before making his way out into the bitter cold.

It had begun to snow, and it stung Veda to watch his back as he walked away and climbed into his chauffeured car.

She knew it was over, and, strangely, it hurt.

******

1916 would be remembered as the worst year of the Great War. The Allies had lost nearly a million and a half soldiers, and the face of Europe was scarred by the fierce fighting. All soldiers and civilians were weary. One in ten Europeans were now fighting in the war. Those at home were working to supply their countries with guns and machinery.

Ethereal words were quoted and placed into the annals of history... *Never again would Europe know the smell of wet, spring earth. We walk in a darkness, a dumbness, a silence which no voice could penetrate.*

War is a dismal grief, and a purposeless waste.

The situation was severe in Germany. In December, the German government asked President Wilson to pass a note proposing peace talks to the Allies. But the Allies declined, wanting more specific information as to how peace would be organized. Germany refused clarification, and so the Great War's end was nowhere in sight...

******

Veda sat tensely as the doctor entered the office that rainy morning in early April. She wore a brown suede suit and a monkey fur cape.

If not humble, she has developed into a beautiful young woman... Dr. Cannon mused. He had been the family physician for years. He was a short, stout man with tortoise shell framed spectacles, and a bald head.

He sat at his desk and folded his hands with a smile on his face. "Congratulations, Mrs. Aspan. You are expecting a baby."

Veda was stricken with shock. "A baby? Wh...what would I do with a baby?"

Dr. Cannon was well accustomed to women's reactions to notifications of expectancy. Over the years, he had witnessed nearly everything from shouts of joy to hysterics. But Veda's response was most definitely a first...

"You would raise it, Mrs. Aspan." he said, stunned. Veda's face was chalk white. "I know...but...how?"

Dr. Cannon chuckled. "It is not usual for one *to* know how, Mrs. Aspan...at first, that is."

But his words offered little solace.

"I...I never thought much about being a mother."

He stared at her dumbfounded. "Certainly, you expected to have children one day, Mrs. Aspan."

Veda gulped. "No...I mean, yes...but not so soon..."

The doctor observed her for a long, awkward moment. "Well, now you must think more definitively, Mrs. Aspan, because you are most certainly going to be a mother."

Veda was on the verge of tears. "But how? I mean...when?"

He consulted her chart. "I calculate sometime in mid-November."

She fretted. A baby...how could it be? She had just become a woman herself. Teddy's child. A man she did not love! This was *his* fault!

Dr. Cannon read her fear. "Nothing to worry about, Mrs. Aspan. This is all a natural process."

Still, Veda panicked. "But I am not ready to be a mother! What will I do?" And then, she began to weep.

He was numb and speechless. Finally, he leaned forward and reasoned with her, "Mrs. Aspan, you must pull yourself together. Let nature run its course. Besides, I imagine you would find it a comfort for you and your husband to be granted this human legacy in light of Mr. Aspan's condition."

Veda froze. Her eyes enlarged in her face. "Condition? What condition?" Teddy had been away for two months. They had spoken only twice. He insisted it was a prelude to a divorce she would not grant him. Was it more, after all?

Now Dr. Cannon was appalled. He thought she had known.

This would be a much longer morning than either of them had anticipated.

******

Veda insisted that the captain of Teddy's yacht sail her to Newport immediately. It was a long, rainy journey, but she was impervious to weather or inconvenience now. She went straight to Teddy's parents' summer Victorian mansion, and raced up the stairs to his room against the butler's protests.

The sight of him paralyzed her. There he lay, emaciated and frail, a living ghost, existing on borrowed time. Who would have ever recognized the pitiful creature on the bed as the strapping, young millionaire renowned worldwide?

She crept toward the huge canopy bed, and wept when she sat and gripped his limp hand. Nothing, save his emerald green eyes, identified him as her husband.

"So, it is true!" she cried on the verge of hysterics. "They were not lying!"

Teddy's eyes opened in surprise. "Veda, what are you doing here?" his words were weak whispers.

"What brought me here? How could you ask such a mindless question? I came as soon as I heard!"

He was not too languishing to silently admit she looked beautiful in a brown fur cape and matching Cossack. But even her beauty now left him cold.

He gazed at her, dumfounded. "Who told you?"

Veda was beside herself. "It does not matter! What is important is that I am here with you, where I belong! Oh Teddy! You are too young! It just is not fair!"

His face went blank. His voice was expressionless. "How did you know where to find me?"

Veda was frantic. "Stop asking foolish questions! Why did you not tell me, Teddy? Why were you going to let yourself die alone?"

Her words triggered a reflection of the past, that cold winter morning when he had bidden his parents farewell…

"Why are you doing this, Theodore? We are your family; we should be with you!" his father pleaded with tears glistening in his eyes.

His mother was a weeping wreck.

"I want to be alone!" he had tersely replied.

Reginald Aspan tried to reason with him, "I can understand you're not wanting to be with that harebrained wife of yours, but we are different!"

"No!" Teddy adamantly protested. "You asked if you could do anything to make this more comfortable for me. Well, I have stated my wish. Kindly grant it."

His father's tears began to fall. "You are a hard headed boy, son."

Teddy grinned. "I take after my father."

His mother wept louder.

"Collect yourself, Mother," he said. "You must be strong." And he offered her a warm embrace.

Then he turned to hug his father.

"The doctor has promised to contact us at the end, Theodore. You must grant us at least this."

"As you wish," Teddy replied, and valiantly climbed into his chauffeured car.

He held his own tears until the vehicle slid away from the curb. He never turned to wave goodbye. He did not want his parents to see him weeping.

Now, he looked up at Veda sitting on the bed, her drenched face mirroring his in the backseat that afternoon. "I never wished to burden anyone with my problem…least of all, you."

Veda was horrified. "Least of all me? Teddy! I am your wife! I… I *do* care for you deeply!"

He scowled. His words were bitter as his eyes, "Do you? Or is it my fortune you are seeking? I always knew you would assume the role of the perfect widow."

Veda recoiled in shock, "How could you utter something so vile? I know I can be cross at times, but you knew that before you proposed to me!"

He grinned. His infirmity did not drain him of sarcasm, "You will have to do much better than that."

Her eyes enlarged in mixed horror and despair. "Teddy, I do not care about anything right now but you! And I am not going to try to convince you to believe me!"

Then she paused and reflected back to that ghastly day on the Lusitania. "Those dirty Huns!" she snarled. "*They* did this to you! Forcing you to swim all that way in typhoid infested water! You, so strong, and so brave in saving so many lives on that dreadful boat…but you could not save your own! Oh, Teddy! I am so sorry for you! You do not deserve *this*!"

Her words and her demeanor had managed to soften him, and he opened up to her in that vulnerable moment, "My resistance was low from the time I had spent in Africa. I was one of many who had contracted typhoid fever. But at least I managed to survive a year."

Then he caught himself, never heeding the depth of concern in her violet eyes. He hardened again and sneered with a scowl, "But according to you, Veda, I should have drowned."

She heaved a painful sigh, "How could you remind me of that callous thing I said! I admit I was horrible, Teddy! I know I am selfish and pampered and spoiled. I do not know what poison overtakes me sometimes, but I meant none of it, and nothing matters more to me right now than you!"

Teddy frowned in disgust, "Veda, spare us this farce."

She winced. "This farce? Teddy, you are dying! I want to be at your side!"

He looked up at her. His eyes flashed. "But I do not want *you*, Veda."

"You cannot mean that!"

"I do. Now please go. If you want me to be at peace, grant me my wish to be alone."

She glanced out the Victorian window. The spring rain was still falling. Then she looked back at him and felt only pity. "For the rascal of a boy you always were, you certainly have turned into a noble man."

He shut her out, "I do not care to discuss it." And he closed his eyes in an effort to dismiss her.

She sat beside him and gripped his cold hand in hers. "But we must, Teddy! I am going to have your baby!"

He opened his eyes and looked up at her in momentary surprise before he drew back into himself once again, "Would you go to such great length to inherit my fortune, Veda, as to lie about even a child?"

She grew frantic. "It is not a lie! It is true; I tell you! I am expecting; though I regret to say it, especially now when I am going to be forced to face it all alone!"

"I still do not believe you." But he wanted to.

Veda shot to her feet. His words were a dagger. "Damn you if you were not dying, Teddy! Do you not remember that cold, snowy night nearly two months ago? You were very drunk, and I..." Then she broke down again and wept in desperation. "Oh, Teddy! What am I going to do? How will I live through all of this? Do not die!"

He examined her at length. She appeared truly helpless. Perhaps she was not lying after all. "I will need to speak to your doctor to confirm this. If it is true, things will change."

"What in heaven's name are you talking about?" The nightmare was intensifying.

Teddy closed his eyes again and whispered, "You will see." Then he nodded off to sleep.

******

Veda assumed the role of a perfect nurse for three long days and nights.

She hardly minded. It was a shock to both of them.

Then, on day four, Teddy had taken a turn for the worse. Veda summoned the doctor at once, who honored his parents' request in contacting them.

It was a dreadful afternoon as the April rain fell relentlessly from the steel gray sky. Veda sat outside Teddy's room, frozen as a statue, with his parents and siblings surrounding her in the same somber state.

Then the elderly doctor emerged from the room and looked gravely at Veda. "Mrs. Aspan, it is time."

The words were the tolling of a fatal bell. Veda rose as Teddy's father vehemently protested, "But we are his family!"

The doctor gazed at him pointedly. "And Mrs. Aspan is his wife."

It was no time to argue, and they all knew it. Veda proceeded to the door and closed it gently behind her. The dreary room smelled of death, and she was gratified to see that her husband, though in his final moments, appeared strangely serene. She crept toward him and knelt by his side, taking his frail hand into hers.

"Are you in pain, Teddy?" she whispered over gentle sobs.

He shook his head gently. It was clear that he was already at peace.

Veda enthused, placing his hand upon her cheek. "Dr. Cannon told me he has spoken with you…I told you it is true."

Teddy smiled. Then she leaned closer as her heart bled for him. "Is there anything you wish for this child? Summers here in Newport? A pony, maybe? I will do my best alone. I promise. You have always been good to me. You deserve at least this."

There was a long interval of silence before Teddy struggled to speak. "Africa," he whispered, and Veda was deeply disturbed.

"What about Africa?"

"Diamonds…" he muttered, groping for the strength to continue.

Veda was dumbfounded. "Have you left some behind?"

Another feeble shake of his head. He reached deep within himself and labored to go on, "Stolen… Murder."

238

Veda's eyes grew wide with horror. "Teddy, you are frightening me!"

He gasped. "K…keep secret?"

Veda knew Teddy's clock was ticking its last minute. "I promise," she vowed, bringing her face closer to his until they nearly touched. "Anything for you, Teddy."

He took a deep breath. "African man…murdered…diamonds…stolen."

Veda panicked. "Who stole the diamonds, Teddy? *You*?"

He nodded. She was paralyzed on her knees and felt the walls of the room enclose to smother her.

"And…who…who murdered him?"

Teddy gasped again, and gushed his dying words, "I did!"

Veda screamed in terror. She missed the moment of her husband's passing.

******

The rain persisted through the morning of Theodore Aspan's funeral. Veda, veiled in black, stood beside her brother Marius as her parents and Dominique remained in the background. It was over in the blink of an eye, and Veda watched everyone retreat without a word of consolation. The worst sting was seeing her parents depart without a single comforting gesture.

She turned to her handsome brother and remarked bitterly, "This war has taken so much from me! First our grandparents, and now my husband!"

Marius placed a consoling arm around her quivering shoulder. "I am so sorry, Veda."

She began to weep. "I am probably the youngest widow in New York. And now, I am going to be a mother to a child who will never know its father. Why me, Marius? Am I that awful?"

He gazed at her with a canyon of concern in his eyes. "Let's go home now, Veda."

She sighed. "Home? Where is that? The only home I know is with Mother and Father, and they hate me!"

Marius embraced her. It felt so soothing to rest her face into the warmth of his black trench coat. "They do not hate you. And you have a beautiful home."

She released herself suddenly and wept louder. "That is nothing but a dark, dreary museum, and I hate it!"

He gripped her arms. "Veda, you must gather yourself."

239

But she was hysterical now. "I cannot! I do not want to return to that spook house!"

"But you must," he impressed, holding her eyes in his. "In time, things will improve. Think of your unborn child. It will be a legacy."

Veda threw herself into his arms again. "Oh, Marius! Hold me! I am so frightened!"

He gently stroked her head. The scent of his cologne was comforting as his words. "It is all right," he soothed. "Everything will be fine."

As she looked over his shoulder into the pouring rain, Veda desperately mimed, "Rose, where are you?"

******

The nightmare continued the morning Theodore Aspan's will had been read. Veda could not believe her ears when she learned that her husband had bequeathed her nothing but the mansion, having signed his entire fortune over to his parents before he had left for Newport...

"Everything is yours now," he had told them in the family vault.

"And your wife?" his father asked with a grateful gleam in his eyes.

Teddy scowled, "That is why I am doing this while I am alive. She is to inherit nothing."

Remembering this encounter, Teddy's parents grinned in triumph as they sat around the attorney's cherry wood conference table.

Veda, in black, was fit to be tied. "But this cannot be!" she frantically protested. "I am his wife!"

The attorney attempted to reason with her as Teddy's parents gloated. "It is completely legal, Mrs. Aspan. Your husband had no estate because he had turned it over to his parents prior to his death. You have no rightful claim. It was earned prior to your marriage."

Veda remained unhinged. "But what about my child, Teddy's heir?"

Both she and the attorney shifted their eyes to Teddy's parents. They were in command now. But nothing more than a dark, stoic frown was offered by either of them.

Veda fumed, "How could you do this to me? To your unborn grandchild? You are hateful people! Teddy was the best of your whole despicable lot! He must be turning in his grave right now! That is what he meant when he said things would change, but he never had the chance to do it! Curse you! I hope you both die and rot in hell!"

Then she burst into frenetic sobs. Though he felt for her, the attorney maintained professional decorum, "Mrs. Aspan, you must compose yourself or I will have to ask you to leave."

Still, she was a raving wreck, "Compose myself? How could you propose such a preposterous thing? This is *my* life we are talking about! And *my* child's! How will we support ourselves?"

Then the attorney reached for the wood box on the table and removed a velvet bag. From it, he produced the fabulous, glistening diamond. "Mr. Aspan managed to contact me the day before he expired. This was his favorite gem. Originally, he had requested to be buried with it. Now, he wishes that it be passed on to you."

Veda snatched the massive blue-white stone and pointed it at all of them. "This is not enough!" she cried as the brilliant gem refracted dazzling, iridescent rays.

The attorney shook his head, not quite understanding the very rich. That single diamond would have left him and his family set for life. "I am afraid you can do nothing about it, Mrs. Aspan."

Veda fired back at him, "We will just have to see about that! This is war! I will not stop until I get it all!"

Then she stormed out of the office, diamond in hand.

Chapter 48

News of Theodore Aspan's untimely death had spread across the country and eventually shocked the world. Headlines prominently announced Veda's disinheritance, and that the tycoon's fortune had been left to his parents.

Veda became the topic of conversation amongst socialites who gloated over what they considered to be her due comeuppance.

"I know everyone is talking about me!" she lamented at the breakfast table one morning as she tossed the morning Times onto the floor. Then she turned angry, "I will show those proper tea totaling prissies and their potbellied husbands! This is not over yet!"

"Yes, *Madame*," Carlotta replied, as she sheepishly collected the newspaper from the floor, quite accustomed to these regular outbursts.

Theodore! The tragedy was also a chilling reminder that the Great War was beginning to prey upon the country, and that citizens were beginning to wonder just how long it might be before America would be swept into combat.

In April, 1916, the British suffered a serious defeat in Mesopotamia at Kut Al Ilmara where 13,000 men surrendered to the Turks.

All of Europe agreed, however, that the war was too expensive. It cost too much money, and too many lives. War weariness was felt by both sides. Peace seemed possible. But the trouble at sea negated hope.

After the Battle of Jutland, Britain remained mistress of the seas.

Germany's only effective weapon was the submarine which quietly came upon and destroyed merchant ships with supplies for the allies. International law stated that Germans should rescue crews and passengers of torpedoed ships. But as it was impossible for a submarine to do this, Germany violated the mandate.

******

Theodore Aspan's death infuriated the African Princess. The fatal disease was too mild an affliction in comparison to the torture she had had in mind. She would have to alter her plan. His wife was expecting. Hope was not completely lost…

And then, there was the diamond…

As she gazed down at the sleeping baby in the seedy roach infested hotel room, she smiled and whispered with victory gleaming in her eyes. "Mama's gonna make you a rich little girl one day. You're gonna inherit what's rightfully ours."

******

Veda despised every moment of her pregnancy. She lived a life of solitude in her Fifth Avenue mansion with her servants, her chambermaid and her diamond.

"I do not want to see anyone!" she contended, too self-absorbed to realize that very few people cared to see *her*.

Strange, despite its inestimable worth, she opted not to sell the magnificent gem.

Instead, she had it encased in lead glass, and displayed within the center of Teddy's former trophy room.

"I will keep it here as a monument to my husband," she proudly announced to Anders, the butler, one bright May afternoon. "It is the crest of the family fortune."

The pride on her face made it seem as if she had had a marriage made in heaven while Teddy was alive. Strange as it was, she cared for him more now that he was dead. "Our child will respect it as a memorial to his father who died a valiant hero."

And her thoughts reflected back to the first horrid night she had returned to the mansion after Teddy's funeral. She recalled how she had justified his heinous crime as she sat at her Chippendale vanity and unpinned her hair…

"No one has to know how Teddy obtained his fortune…*or* about the murder. That was all the way back in Africa. It means nothing here!" she vowed to the empty room. It seemed so convincing then. Why did she feel a pang of guilt now?

But she had vowed to keep the secret. *And* she would*! She* was innocent!

Veda, however, needed to support herself. It was a problem quickly solved when she realized she was sitting on a fortune. She began with the diamonds embedded in the limestone.

"I want them all removed and replaced with quartz pebbles," she told the quarry man who worked around the clock for three months and charged her a fortune.

She sold them at a great loss. "I know they are worth more than this!" she protested to the gemologist who just shook his head and intoned. "This is my final offer. Take it or leave it, Mrs. Aspan."

Veda snatched the money, and stormed outside into the sweltering summer heat.

In his back office, the gemologist then met Reginald Aspan who had a wide, sinister grin on his face.

"I told you she would accept it," he told the gemologist victoriously. "She is broke."

The man gasped, hardly believing his dumb luck. "Mr. Aspan, these diamonds are worth ten times what I have given her!"

Reginald Aspan smiled in triumph and opened a briefcase which flaunted green. "Yes. Now give them to me, and you will *still* come out a very rich man."

******

Occasional lunch visits from Marius made Veda's day.

"Things are going to change after I have this baby, dear brother," she vowed as she spread caviar over a toast point.

"What do you mean, Veda?" he asked in his banker's costume, slicing hearts of palm.

"The first thing I am going to do is hire a nanny, and then I am going to go out and make a career for myself."

Marius turned to shock. "Veda, that is unspeakable! What would society think?"

She frowned. "What do I care? Look what has been done to me! I am going to make a name for myself! I am not going to sit home and have tea parties and attend charity balls anymore!"

Marius examined her in disbelief. Veda was serious. "But, what will you do?"

She shrugged. "I have not quite given thought to that yet. But I will! Once I get what is mine, I will do something!"

He folded his hands on his lap and smiled at her. "I admire your ambition. Good luck. It will not be the first time you have astounded the city, *or* our parents."

She sighed. "Mother and Father…if only they knew how lost I am without them, and how sorry I am for what I have done."

"They *do* know, Veda. But they still need time."

"How much time? It has been so long already!"

"Be patient," he assured her with a warmth on his face which managed to sustain her.

Then there was a long, solemn silence.

"What are you thinking?" he asked, gazing at her over the rim of his water glass.

Veda's face dropped. "I am thinking of Rose. I miss her so much."

Marius nodded. "So do I. But what can we do about it?"

Veda grimaced. "Nothing. It is hopeless."

"Not quite, little sister," he enthused with a smile. "Have you not heard?" Veda felt her heart rise. "Heard what?"

His eyes glistened. "Rose will be completing her schooling and assigned to St. Mary's school in Newport this coming fall."

Veda's world came alive once again.

There were also intermittent visits from Chester Worthington. Though she feigned repulsion, the attention of a handsome, wealthy, if not sober bachelor tickled her in this period of seclusion from the world.

She received him on the flower filled backyard patio spilling off the grand ballroom of her mansion.

She wore a simple white linen summer dress, and a wide brimmed straw hat. She had gained very little weight in her five months of pregnancy, and Chester thought she never looked more beautiful. But whenever she looked in the mirror, Veda cringed.

"You realize that in a few short weeks, I am going to have to ask you to stop coming," she teased over a glass of lemonade.

Chester drank scotch on ice. He wore a tweed summer suit and sported a fabulous suntan from his recent vacation in the Hamptons. His short, black hair was slicked back on his head, and his onyx eyes penetrated her as always.

"Why, Veda?" he asked with a flippant ring in his voice.

She grimaced. "Because I am going to grow fat. An expectant lady never exposes herself to the public."

Chester guffawed. "Am I the public?"

"No, but you are a man," she replied, glowering at him.

"This is the twentieth century, Veda." And he finished his scotch.

Veda pouted childishly. "I do not care! I am not going to permit anyone, least of all, *you*, to see me swelled up like a balloon!"

Chester reached into his jacket and slipped out a cigar. A servant appeared and lit it for him. Then he poured the young millionaire another shot of booze.

Chester took a deep drag and observed Veda for a long moment. "Does this mean you wish for me to propose to you?" he teased with a devilish gleam in his eyes.

Veda was appalled. "What a callous thing to say while I am still in mourning!"

He chortled. "In mourning?" his words were a sneer.

Her cheeks reddened with fury. "Yes, I am! Now I shall ask you to leave if you are going to let the booze in your head strip you of the meager manners you have to begin with!"

Chester eyed her sardonically. "I think that *does* mean you want to marry me."

Veda glared back at him. "I would rather marry a toad!"

He turned to inspect the mansion. Then his eyes circled the property. "What do you intend to do in this big house all alone anyway?" his concern was genuine.

Veda came to a quick defense. "I will not be alone. I will have my baby." It seemed as if she were convincing herself more than him.

Chester laughed again. "You hardly strike me as the motherly type."

This offended her more than anything, mainly because she knew it was true. "What do I care what *you* think?"

But she did care. He had touched home. He looked her in the eyes and grinned. "I don't know. You tell me, Veda. Aren't I right?"

He was. She suddenly despised him.

And she detested the next four months more so. She did billow everywhere. Her stomach expanded enormously. Her face, arms and legs swelled to abnormal proportions.

She sequestered herself, refusing to see anyone, including Marius. She knew Carlotta had been trained as a midwife, and thus cancelled all doctor's appointments.

Dr. Cannon objected at first, but Veda's vile protests encouraged even him to demure. The fact that she had a live-in midwife convinced him and her family she was under proper supervision.

Only Carlotta knew very little about pregnancy, and her experience in delivering babies was limited to a single breech birth. Veda, in fact, was being neglected, though no one knew it, and she, blinded by vanity, paid the situation little heed.

"I want this to be over with fast!" she cried moments after her water had broken, and the first excruciating labor pain had struck.

After another long hour of relentless torture, she wailed ferociously, "I hate you, Teddy! I hate you for doing this to me! Curse you in your grave!"

Carlotta, numbed by Veda's howls and the overwhelming task ahead, simply smoothed a wet washcloth over her mistress' head and chanted. "Everything will be fine, *Madame*. Everything will be fine."

Veda, drenched with sweat, fired up at her from the bed. "Stop babbling, you stupid fool! Work faster! Get this done! I can't stand anymore!"

But the agonizing labor persisted yet another five hours. And finally, after a volume of savage howls, the baby's head appeared.

"Push, *Madame*! Please push!" Carlotta begged, also sweaty, exhausted, and beside herself.

"I *am* pushing, you ninny!" Veda shrilled, grasping and clawing at the bedposts as perspiration seeped from her like a stream. She had never imagined such pulverizing pain humanly possible. Then, after a long, deafening, bestial screech, the infant emerged from her womb, and Veda, though throbbing, emitted a gasp of relief.

Carlotta cut the umbilical cord in the midst of the breathless silence. The muteness persisted, and suddenly it was like a tomb.

"Carlotta..." Veda whispered, winded. "Isn't it supposed to cry?" Carlotta slapped the infant's bottom. Silence, still.

"Why isn't it crying?" Veda shrieked in panic.

Carlotta grew frantic herself, and slapped the infant again and again. Nothing.

Veda smelled disaster.

"Let me have it!" she commanded, holding out her aching arms. Carlotta obliged, but knew already.

Veda took the child and tensed. Then her heart heaved and shattered. It was a boy. Her son. Her dead son.

******

She was a raving wreck all through the night. "It is my fault!" she cried. "I killed this baby! All my complaints about motherhood! He must have heard everything, and my own poison destroyed him!"

Carlotta, too, was laden with guilt. "I am so sorry, *Madame*. I should have called for a doctor. I should not have done it alone."

"No!" Veda frantically protested. "I am fully to blame! Why would he have wanted to come into this world only to be raised in my cold, callous arms?"

Carlotta tried to comfort her, "You are being too harsh on yourself, *Madame*."

But Veda would not hear it. She wished in that moment that she, too, would die. "I am not!" Then she paused and added over shaking sobs, "I suppose we must arrange for a burial." The thought of it was a stabbing dagger. Throwing her saturated face into her weak hands, she gave way to hysteria once again, "Oh, Carlotta! I simply cannot face it!"

But she did. Once again, she stood, veiled in black, watching the shoe box of a coffin being lowered into the earth above Teddy Aspan's tomb. The boy was buried with his father. Not one Aspan was in attendance. Veda's parents were there, however, and so were Marius and Dominique.

Winston and *La Madame* Champion said nothing at the burial, but Veda was shocked by a visit from her mother late that afternoon.

"Mother!" she exclaimed in shock when she entered the parlor, her eyes swollen from crying, her breath smelling of brandy.

La Madame Champion, handsome and dignified in a black velvet dress, rose at the sight of her daughter, and gripped her shaking hand. "It is time to make the peace, Veda. I have forgiven you. You need us now."

Veda could not believe her ears. She looked into her mother's warm, dark eyes and observed a canyon of care. Her face gleamed with the love she had remembered and adored.

"Marius was right!" she cried, her heart soaring. "He said you would come around in time!"

La Madame Champion nodded with a pitying sigh. "You have experienced enormous anguish in this past year. You have been punished enough, Veda."

"And what about Father?" Veda asked, bracing her heart for a quick plummet.

But her mother's response carried the answer to her prayers, "Your father feels the same."

It was all too much for Veda to control herself. She burst into tears and gushed a plea. "Oh, Mother, may I come home?"

La Madame Champion's words melted her. "Our door shall never close upon you again. We have all sustained great losses. We must bond and treasure what we have left…one another."

Veda threw herself into her mother's arms and wept. "Thank you, Mother! Thank you!"

La Madame Champion, the cool and collected paragon who had managed to remain tearless at even her own parents' memorial service, cracked at that moment. "My dear, foolish girl!" she cried, and gripped Veda with all her might. "My heart bleeds for you!" Then she paused and added as tears slid down her face, "It feels so good to hold you again!"

Veda purred.

Her father's arms were more comforting still when she had met him in the vestibule of the Park Avenue brownstone that evening. "Welcome home, Blossom," he said, locking her in a bear hug.

Veda melted again, resting her face upon his shoulder. His scent exhilarated her. Until this moment, it had been just a memory.

"Father, I have missed you so!"

She felt safe for the first time in a long time.

"Welcome home, Missy! We've been fixin' to see ye all day!" It was the corpulent, red faced Nanny McBride. Veda was in heaven.

"Nanny!" she exclaimed, and ran into her arms.

"We got yer old room all ready for ye, Missy. It's a cry from yer Fifth Avenue mansion; I'm certain. But it's home."

Veda wept tears of joy. "That is right, Nanny! It *is* home, and there is no place like it!"

Over Nanny McBride's shoulder, Veda caught a glimpse of Hans Wagner in the background. Hans, tall, stately, elegant and so very handsome. He looked at her and froze for a long moment.

Veda suddenly felt alive.

She took a hot bath, ate a hearty dinner, and whined to Carlotta in her bedroom a few hours later as she cowered before her image in the mirror.

"Look at me! I am fat and swollen and ugly!"

"Untrue, *Madame*," Carlotta objected as she brushed her mistress' hair.

"It is true! My waistline is gone forever!" Veda protested on the verge of tears.

"In time, *Madame*."

"In time, nothing! There is only one solution to this problem! I will never have any more children!"

"Oh, *Madame*!" Carlotta declared, slipping Veda's satin peignoir set over her shoulders.

"I mean it!" Veda retorted, and she truly did.

Although her canopy bed was sinfully comfortable, Veda was unable to sleep that night. At the stroke of midnight, she went downstairs to sit in the parlor where memories of family gatherings flavored her mind.

But she was stifled in the vestibule by voices emanating from her father's study. She crept closer to listen. It was her father and Hans.

"I thank you, sir, for keeping me on staff in spite of all the opposition."

Winston dragged on his pipe pensively.

"This is my home, and I shall do as I please. You are my best employee, Hans, in spite of your German origin. I am even considering promoting you to butler once Thaddeus retires in two years."

Hans shrugged. "Thank you, sir, but I believe it would cause too much unrest, and eventually, your bank, too, would suffer."

Winston poured two shots of cognac and offered one to Hans who shook his head in decline. So, he tossed off both himself and slammed the snifters onto his desk, muddled. "Damn it, Hans!" he grunted. "If the rest of the Huns are anything like you at all, it would make it impossible for me to believe they are such savage murderers!"

Hans shrugged again. "War brings out the worst in people, sir."

Winston nodded with a grimace and reached for the decanter once again. "I guess you are right."

Hans emerged from the study five minutes later and closed the door so Winston could review figures. Veda spoke to him from the candlelit parlor.

"You should accept my father's offer. To hell with what anyone else says or thinks."

Hans was paralyzed with shock. He entered the room and drew the French doors shut. When he came to Veda, he saw she was drinking brandy.

"Were you eavesdropping?" he asked with uneasiness spelled clearly on his face. In spite of his handsome frame, he appeared timid. Veda was moved, having never witnessed him in this state before.

"It was not my intention," she replied, and sipped from the snifter. "I heard voices in the study, and so I stopped on my way to the parlor."

Hans tensed. "I see." Then he awkwardly shifted the topic, "I am very sorry for your losses, Miss...your husband and your son."

It was soothing to know he saw and accepted her as a woman, and a comrade. Veda was careful not to compromise this new stage of their relationship. If he had recalled anything about her foolish, girlish ways, he pretended not to, or perhaps, even, he had forgotten now that his own welfare preyed upon his mind.

"Thank you," she replied somberly, staring into her brandy snifter. "But pity is the last thing I need right now."

Hans looked away from her into the center of the room. His mind was light years away.

"I guess that sounds foreign to a man who bares the blame for the atrocities of his people."

Veda looked up at him and saw the man beneath the frame for the first time. Hans was no longer just a platinum haired, blue eyed icon, but a human being with trepidations, weaknesses and inhibitions. It made her care for him more. Her father was right. Could he actually be one of the same Huns who had torpedoed the Lusitania and murdered her grandparents? Could the worst have even surfaced from him in such circumstances? She denied it and took another sip of brandy.

"You do not strike me as someone who craves pity either, Hans. But it must be quite difficult for you."

He nodded glumly with the weight of the world on his shoulders. "It is."

She smiled faintly. "Now I am sorry."

He smiled back at her. It had obviously touched him. "Thank you. Good night, Miss."

She called after him. "Hans?"

He turned halfway through the threshold. "Yes, Miss?"

She took a deep breath. "If the worst should occur, and America enters this dirty war, what will happen to you?"

He pondered for a long moment, and finally shrugged, "Your guess is as good as mine, Miss. Good night."

On his way up the servants' staircase to his quarters, Hans thought of his friend Rudi.

Chapter 49

Rudolph Stern was having a difficult time at Harvard as was Hans in New York City. His initial instincts were correct. Being both a German and Jewish marked him twice, and he had become completely blackballed.

He was a loner.

He had been dismissed from his fraternity and barred from all campus events. Racial slurs such as 'German, Jew, Get out!' 'Murderer!' 'Hun!' 'Kike!' were mailed to him, scrawled on the door to his dormitory, on the walls of lavatories with his name beside it, even on his clothing.

Professors, too, seemed to discriminate against him. A's on papers became C's and D's. His index dropped from 3.8 to 1.5. He was risking dismissal. The plummet of his grades had been rendered without the privilege of an appeal.

"But this is a free country!" he contended to a stoic professor who had debased him with a steely gaze. "I shall have freedom of speech which entitles me to an appeal!"

The professor glared at him over his spectacles. "The constitution is for Americans, *not* foreigners…least of all, *your* people!"

Another professor was downright slanderous, "*Your people* even sank the Titanic!"

Rudi was appalled. "Pardon me, sir, but was it not an iceberg?"

The professor snarled in his face, "Rothberg, Silberberg, iceberg…all the same! Are they not?"

Rudi regretted having come to America. Attending Harvard was supposed to be a status symbol for an honor student from Berlin. Instead, it was a living hell.

He did not know how much more he could endure. *They just might drive me out before I am expelled!* he grunted to himself in a hot bath one night after a stone had been cast through his window on which a message had been inscribed. "Kike, Hun! Get out! Go back to Germany!"

And it was only the beginning…

Back in Berlin, Herr and Frau Stern had received wind of the antagonism against Germans in America.

"Perhaps we should have Rudolph sent home," Frau Stern proposed after weeks of fretting.

Her husband vehemently protested, "Why? So, he could return and they could draft him to become a soldier? Never! I do not want our son to become one of these murderers, even if it *is* for our country! One day, this war will be over, and we will be despised everywhere!"

His wife just wept.

Gunther Wagner, now twelve and more patriotic than ever, had overheard the conversation as he polished shoes in a work closet, and greatly resented his employer's national denouncement.

He appealed to his overworked mother that evening. "Is it not unlawful to speak out against the cause? If word got back to the Kaiser, Herr Stern would be either imprisoned or killed!"

His mother's response was a sharp slap across his face.

"It would do us little good if anything were to happen to Herr Stern! We need this job! We would starve without him!"

"But, Mother!" the boy protested; his cheek reddened.

She slapped him again. He winced. "Not another word about it! Forget everything you have heard!"

Gunther stormed out of the room and pouted on a bench in the center square. This was *his* home! He knew he was right! If only he were old enough to fight! He cursed Hans for not being there. One day, when he was older, things would most certainly change.

That night, he lay awake in bed, gazing up at the stars in the peaceful sky, and listening to his mother's weeping on the opposite side of the wall.

Chapter 50

Once the euphoria of being back in her parents' good graces had run its course, Veda grew gravely depressed. The trauma of the Lusitania, and the losses of her husband, her son, and grandparents to untimely deaths had begun to take their toll upon her.

She was embarrassed to be seen until she had lost every pound gained during her pregnancy, and opted to return to her Fifth Avenue mansion until the mission was accomplished. She ate, drank, slept, and existed alone, living a solitary life which terrified her parents. She blamed everything on her appearance, but the root of the problem was much deeper than that.

She was already ten pounds less than she had been before her pregnancy, and never realized it, being so entrenched in her depression. By January, her parents had taken matters into their own hands.

"You need a vacation, Veda," *La Madame* enthused. "With Europe off limits, we have arranged a cruise to Africa for the three of us."

Veda refused. "There is only one place I wish to go," she insisted, still in her nightgown at noon, and ghost white.

"Where is that, Blossom?" her father asked, eyeing a glimpse of hope.

"Newport," Veda promptly replied. "I need to visit Chateau La Mer. You know how much I love it so!"

Her parents examined one another perplexedly. "Why Newport, Veda dear? It is freezing there."

She shook her head stubbornly. "I do not care how cold it is! I want to see the cliffs, breathe the ocean air, savor the beauty of the property and watch winter turn into spring!"

And of course, to see her estranged sister, Rose, but she would not dare admit it, knowing, for sure, her wish would not be granted. Though it broke Winston's heart, even he accepted the rules of Rose's order, when she had completely detached herself from the family. But Veda deemed it all nonsense.

Mr. and Mrs. Champion, though adamantly against the idea in the beginning, were surprised when Dr. Cannon placed his stamp of approval on it, "The ocean is just what Veda needs. Yes, ocean, and fresh air. Newport would be perfect."

She was on the next train.

It was a cold, snowy winter, and the churning waves of the gray Atlantic produced an ominous, yet cozy spirit from the picture windows of Chateau La Mer. Veda found reprieve here, and in spite of the seclusion, she was sustained by childhood memories, the safety, and her plans to see Rose.

******

Sister Perpetua felt profoundly liberated upon her arrival at St. Mary's Convent in Newport, Rhode Island. And in fact, she was. The training of a novice Sister can be compared to boot camp for a soldier. Now that she had been released into the world, discipline was not half intense as it had been at the Mother House. The vow of silence was enforced only after dinner each night and on Sundays. There was no more begging for food on her knees, no more kissing the Mother Superior's feet, no longer wooden planks which had served as dinner plates in the refectory.

Yet many things remained the same, but Rose was unmoved by them now that perfection had become a way of life. Conversation was still kept strictly to matters of general interest, and the past, of course, was never mentioned. She was still not permitted to retreat into a quiet corner, to read a book, to meditate by herself, as such acts were against the dogmas of communal living.

She still exercised self-flagellation as a penance on Wednesdays and Fridays. But this, too, she welcomed. The little chains and sharp hooks striking her back erased the desire for oysters, horseback riding, traveling, and classical music, as well as memories of her family, and a life of luxury.

She had mastered the art of a nun's gliding, sway-less walk; her eyes downcast, and her arms folded perfectly under her new black scapular.

The Mother House was just a memory, and she was glad. She would not return there until she would make her final vows three years later. But Rose felt guilt in never wanting to return. She grimly remembered that last evening when she had been subjected once again to the Mother Superior's caustic tongue.

"Only the wealthy individuals of the outside world could possess the power to orchestrate an assignment such as yours, my child. Returning to the setting of your past life could be perilous, Sister Perpetua. You must pray for your divine soul, and for your earthly father to cease his interference with your affairs. You have been pampered here against my will as you had been in the sinful world from which you have come. You are at great risk. You are the only spoiled sister I know."

Rose lay awake crying all night. How debasing it was to hear that all of the struggling, the sacrifices, the trials and tribulations of her novitiate had been summarized with such ill regard.

She departed the next morning with her head hanging in shame, gripping the papier-mâché suitcase in her weary hand.

But her new Mother Superior offered a warm welcome, and within a week, her dignity had been restored. She began each day with a reflection of her sisters. She was the youngest in the new community, and assumed every duty she saw undone with a wish for no recognition. And above all else, she kept an open heart for her Mother Superior.

"You shall be assigned to the sixth grade, Sister Perpetua," the genteel elderly superior said in a whispery voice the day before school had opened.

Rose, who had wished to work with younger children, replied with a smile, "As you wish, Reverend Mother. I am here to serve."

And she vowed to make a success of it.

Needless to say, she adored teaching, and her students, sixty-five disciplined girls, adored her. The boys were instructed in a separate wing by the older, stricter nuns who taught with relentless force.

Even the nuns in Sister Perpetua's wing were at times brutal. Children were chastised for the slightest infractions of the law.

"Spare the rod and spoil the child!" barked an elderly sister who ruled her classroom with an iron hand. "There is only one way to instill the fear of God into a child, and unless we operate with force, we are doing these flowers of Jesus a grave disservice."

Sister Perpetua, formerly Rose Champion, had been educated in convent schools where the nuns were gentle and soft spoken. It had cost her father a fortune to send her and Veda off to such exclusive learning institutions. It hurt to admit the first Mother Superior was right. Money had spared her the inflictions of rulers, straps and iron hands to which children here, at a local parochial school, were so brutally subjected. It stabbed her with guilt.

And the greatest paradox was how these fierce nuns transformed into meek hand maids of Christ after 3:00, how they spoke softly, and gathered with love around a piano to sing hymns at night, around the dining room table in the rectory, and in the convent gardens. And the same nun who had beaten a child in the classroom, would speak so affectionately to the poor young soul after mass, on the sidewalk, or in the neighborhood square.

Sister Perpetua could not help singularizing herself in this regard. Her classroom was a page from a fairy tale, and the young girls under her instruction were treated with love and care. Education became an adventure. Respect and discipline were elevated to a graceful art. The posture of the students in class was flawless and gracefully mastered in a need for the girls to emulate their heroine. They walked in straight precision without a whisper or wandering eye because they knew it was expected of them, and wanted to make Sister Perpetua proud. Her soft voice carried the weight of a beautiful mountain, and her demeanor was magnetic.

It did not take long for the Mother Superior to recognize her unique talent, and by mid-year, her skillful manner became contagious. There were less beatings, less howls, and even some occasional smiles on the straight wrinkled lips of the most stoic nuns.

Perhaps Sister Perpetua had not been singularizing herself after all.

******

Surprisingly, Veda needed to muster up the courage to visit her twin, and by the third week in Newport, she was finally ready.

It was an early Saturday morning when Rose was summoned from chapel. "Sister Perpetua, there is a woman here to see you," said the Mother Superior with a hint of disapproval in her tone.

"Is it your wish for me to oblige, Reverend Mother?" Sister Perpetua solemnly asked, masking her curiosity.

"The decision shall be yours, Sister, but there are restrictions in this type of matter, and the permission shall only be granted once a year."

Sister Perpetua knew who her visitor was in that moment, and her heart surged.

******

"Why must I speak with you from behind this cage? It is like I am in a confessional!"

Veda squawked, but the sound of her voice was music to her twin's ears. Yet Sister Perpetua took a deep breath and maintained herself., "It is a law by which we must abide."

This riled Veda more. "But why? I do not understand! Why can I not see the Rose I remember, rather than the silhouette of a veiled stranger?"

Sister Perpetua wanted nothing more than to cross the barrier and embrace her dear sister. But again, she adhered to the golden rule.

"That is the purpose," she replied, her voice soft, cool, and angelic. Veda was beside herself. "But it makes no sense to me!"

A long pause. Little did Veda know her sister was at battle with herself.

Then came the dispassionate response. "To us, it makes perfect sense."

Veda anguished. "What us?"

Sister Perpetua trembled on the opposite side of the cage. Please, Jesus, help me to remain strong...she pleaded, fearing at any given moment, she might succumb to the worldly desire.

"Perhaps you should not have come," she sadly whispered, and the words pierced Veda's heart.

"Why not? I am your sister! And I am staying in Newport now!"

Help me, Lord...please! Sister Perpetua silently beseeched. This is my twin, my best friend, a part of myself who makes me complete!

"Our family is our order, Veda," she said, maintaining victory over her nostalgia. "Our past lives have been forgotten." But her shame overtook her as she knew she was uttering a lie.

Veda was numbed by shock, "Rose, if I did not know you better, I would say you have lost your mind!"

A long, tense silence followed.

"Rose is a name to which I answer no longer." It nearly killed her to say it, and Veda was now distraught.

"What has happened to you?" And she began to cry.

Sister Perpetua restrained her own tears and reached deep within herself to maintain strength. "I have become the hand maid of our Lady, and the bride of Christ," she aptly put, but the anguishing young nun questioned her own sincerity in that moment.

Veda exploded, "Oh, stop it, Rose! Stop it! I need you now more than ever! Our grandparents have been murdered by the Huns in Verdun! I am a widow, and I have already buried a son! I am all alone! You are my only salvation! Please do not abandon me!"

The stabbing news of her grandparents' fate was a deadly blow to Sister Perpetua. She felt her stomach churn, and wondered why she had never been informed. *Certainly, a message must have been sent to the Mother House! And then, poor Veda, a widow, and a grieving mother! She needs me,* she contended to herself. *And I need her! Poor Grand-mere and Grand-pere! They were too good!*

Maintain yourself, Sister Perpetua, Her better judgment sternly advised. *Your family is now the community, and the community needs you more.*

She was grateful for the cage separating them when she felt her eyes water.

"I will pray for you, Veda, and for the reposed souls in Verdun. God be with you."

She had exercised an academy performance. Inside, she was deteriorating. Then the bell rang. Their time was up.

Veda ran outside in tears. Rose sat for a long-time weeping.

******

Veda waited until spring to visit her sister again. It was the day before her departure for New York where she would spend the Easter holiday with her family. It was also the last day of school before holiday recess.

She observed from the opposite side of the schoolyard as the stoic nuns dismissed their expressionless classes. And then came Rose with a wide smile on her face, and a cluster of girls who adored her. There were hugs and goodbyes, and even a few tears.

Veda's heart skipped a beat. It was the first time she had seen her sister in a nun's habit. She gasped in shock at first, and then at Rose's inordinate beauty.

"It is dangerous for a nun to be so beautiful," she said at the classroom threshold ten minutes later, after following her into the building.

Sister Perpetua froze at her desk where she had been shuffling through test papers. She knew the voice immediately. Then she shifted her head to encounter Veda who appeared so very thin and dispirited in her opulent apparel of cream satin and lace gloves. Her hair had been pinned beneath a feathered hat, and her violet eyes were dulled with loneliness.

In spite of the hurricane of emotion within her, Sister Perpetua took a deep breath and sustained herself. "You should not have come here."

Veda sighed. "I just needed to see you, Rose, and I believe you, too, need to see me."

How did Veda know? Did she, too, suffer the same nightmare which had awakened her at three in the morning?

But again, the young nun showed no emotion, "We do not pay much heed to our desires. They can only lead us to sin."

Veda came to her with a forlorn expression on her pallid face. "Rose, please do not shut me out. Not today. I promise I will not make a pest of myself, but…" then she broke down and released a tidal wave of distress. "Oh, Rose! I *do* so need you! Can you not see how much I have missed you? Can you try to understand?"

It melted her to witness Rose start to cry. She took her twin into her arms and embraced her with all her might. Fireworks burst from each of them. They were electrified.

"Oh, Veda! How I have missed you so!" Rose exclaimed as tears poured down her face.

Over Veda's shoulder, she witnessed the shocked gazes of two elderly nuns in the corridor. She never knew she had made a grave mistake. But at that very moment, as she purred in the warm hold, Sister Perpetua hardly cared about consequences.

******

"You have succumbed to a forbidden temptation, Sister Perpetua. I have no choice but to send you back to the Mother House for meditation and spiritual cleansing," voiced the Mother Superior in regret that she would be losing her best teacher.

"As I deserve, Reverend Mother," Rose murmured, feeling her heart plummet. The thought of returning to the dark caves under the jurisdiction of the hard-hearted Mother Superior was too much for her to endure.

But she had no choice. She was sent away the next morning. Upon their return from holiday break, her students were heartsick to say the least.

Chapter 51

The African Princess was furious to learn of the death of Teddy Aspan's son.

All hope for revenge had been lost. But it was somewhat comforting to know both had already encountered the fate she had planned for them if, without the torture.

And still there was the diamond she would somehow claim in the near future. Her little girl would not be subjected to a life of poverty or, to being a whore like herself to stave off starvation and keep a roof over her head.

As she sat with the almond skinned, emerald eyed two-year-old beauty on the fire escape of the fleabag hotel that chilly spring night, she nestled her close to her bosom, and sang her an African lullaby.

Dionne looked up at her mother's cracked lip and her swollen black eye.

She remembered the brutal beating her 'uncle' had inflicted upon her mother the night before as she observed, trembling on the fire escape. Some things remain in the immediate memory of even a two-year-old.

And when she finished her lullaby, believing her little girl was asleep, the African Princess gazed up into the starry sky, and remembered the nightmare too...

"You dirty nigger whore! You been pocketin' my money!" It was Sam, her pimp, a tall, well, if, garishly dressed African American who had been in the business for more than twenty years.

"I ain't been, Sam! Business has been slow!" she feebly protested.

"You filthy lyin' bitch!" the pimp growled, his eyes flashing. Then he struck her again and again. Blood splattered throughout the room. Her bestial cries were like something from a slaughterhouse.

He left her huddled in a corner, bloody, numb, and penniless. He had found the jar and confiscated it.

Hope for Dionne's education was lost now.

But there was still the diamond. *Her diamond!* By God Almighty, she would get it!

Chapter 52

La Madame Champion relayed the unfortunate news to Veda the moment she entered the Park Avenue brownstone. Hans observed from the dining room as he polished the crystal chandelier.

"Your sister has been sent away from St. Mary's convent due to your indiscretion."

Veda, in a chinchilla rimmed cape, froze in shock. "Why? Whatever for?"

La Madame Champion shook her head with a scowl and led them into the parlor where tea was promptly served. "You know nuns live in a cloistered world, completely detached from their families. Why did you insist upon seeing Rose? Do you not think I long to visit her as well?"

The shock and the admonishment drove Veda to tears, and made her mother soften.

"I suppose the outcome will be all right, however. Your father has spoken to the kind Bishop, and Rose shall return in three weeks," then she paused and narrowed her eyes. "But you must stay away from her."

Veda nodded forlornly, staring down at the pattern in the carpet. "I promise, Mother," she sullenly murmured. Rose was to be forgotten. It was like burying half of herself.

The Mother Superior at St. Mary's convent was all too happy to accept Sr. Perpetua back sooner than planned. She had sent her away against her own will, responding merely to uphold the integrity of the order.

Things at the Mother House, however, had not been so cordial.

"Once again, your father has come to your rescue, Sister Perpetua. Your past family is your greatest thorn."

But Sr. Perpetua was impervious to the sting of the Reverend Mother's words. She was returning to St. Mary's. She was ecstatic. And so were her students.

Chapter 53

The grand announcement was made over Easter dinner.

"I propose a toast to the future of this family," Marius enthused, raising his glass.

He winked at his wife and smiled. "Dominique is expecting our child."

Over the blaze of the candelabra, Veda could see joyful tears well up in her mother's eyes. Though she smiled, clinked glasses and congratulated them, she, herself, felt a pang of anguish, haunted by the birth and death of her own infant son.

News of Dominique's pregnancy, however, was the only happy thing they could discuss that day. Like a devilfish, the Great War had spread its arms across the Atlantic, and drew America closer to the eye of hell.

Back on December 12, 1916, the central powers had asked the United States to forward a note to the Allies proposing peace talks. The Allies rejected. Then, on December 18, President Wilson asked the belligerents to state their objections in specific terms. Germany refused. The Allies indicated terms in some detail, but the attempt for a negotiated peace failed.

The United States was favoring the Allies. Allied propaganda and submarine warfare stimulated America's war sentiment. Germany was portrayed as a ruthless aggressor, aiming to conquer the world.

On January 22, 1917, President Wilson laid peace conditions which he said the United States would support. Yet on the thirty-first, Germany announced the renewal of unrestricted warfare. America feared control of the Atlantic Ocean might result in a victorious Germany. With an economic investment in the Allied cause, war orders boomed America's business.

Then, on March 1, 1917, the Zimmerman note was passed. In it, Arthur Zimmerman, German foreign minister, offered Mexico the states of Texas, New Mexico, and Arizona if she would align with Germany should the United States join the Allies.

A few days later, news of the Russian Revolution raced across the globe.

Consequently, the overthrow of the Tsarist regime made it easier for America to consider fighting.

Then, Germany declared war on all ships in the Atlantic, military or not.

This ushered America into the Great War.

On April 6, 1917, the United States declared war on Germany, and in doing so, formally abandoned its position as the 'greatest neutral nation in the world.'

Veda and family sat at the radio in the parlor, nervously listening to President Wilson's speech…

"Germany's cruel and unmanly business of submarine warfare against American passenger and commercial ships must be put to an end. The world must be made safe for democracy. The present German submarine warfare against commerce is a warfare against mankind. It is a war against nations. This will be a war to end all wars."

The Champions sat in tense silence long afterward until Marius stood and exclaimed, "Hallelujah! It is about time we blow those dirty Huns to kingdom come!"

His parents were outraged, but said nothing. Hans also overheard from the dining room. He did not know what to feel.

And as President Wilson spoke, the U.S. ships were being sunk by German submarines. It *was* time to retaliate.

The rest happened too quickly. For the Champions, it was a whirlwind. It began with Hans Wagner.

Veda was sipping hot tea in the conservatory of her parents' brownstone that rainy afternoon when the handsome man appeared in civilian clothing, clutching a suitcase in his right hand.

Veda was shocked. Though he appeared just as handsome in a pair of black trousers and a white-collared shirt, she had not seen him out of uniform in years, and astonishment was clearly spelled on her porcelain face.

He looked down at her and smiled. She knew something was wrong. "So, the worst has happened," she said with deep pity in her beautiful violet eyes.

"Not so terrible, I suppose, Miss. Though I have come to say goodbye."

She rose and came to him with the grace of a princess. Even in a simple navy dress and a strand of pearls, he admitted she was regal. In the time she had been home, Hans had come to appreciate small things about her that were grandly monumental...her scent, her spirit, her will, and the seal of approval of his character despite his nationality.

Strange, for a woman he once rejected, he could not wait to see Veda each day, and nearly resented the decorum of her maturity which left him uncertain as to whether her once professed love for him still kindled in her heart.

"Are they sending you back to Germany?" she questioned tensely.

He shook his head. "No."

She sighed in relief. "Thank God! I could not bear to see you become one of *them*! You are so very different, Hans, in spite of what everyone says about you."

He smiled and took her hand as the rain tapped on the window pane. "Thank you. You have no idea of what those words mean to me."

She edged closer to him, and stared into his eyes. Hans, who had not known a woman since he had come to America, felt his whole-body tingle.

"Where will you be going?" her voice was an anxious whisper.

He drew backward, in fear of losing control. Veda understood why. "The government has decided to confine all German citizens living in the states to detention camps. Only those aliens known to have taken part in plots against America have been ordered to be arrested. President Wilson says he has no quarrel with the German people. He believes that we are true and loyal to America."

"Will they hurt you there?"

"No," Hans replied in a reassuring whisper, only hoping he was right.

"What did Father say?" Her eyes locked in his.

Hans took a deep, emotional breath. "He said my position shall be awaiting me upon my return," he paused and added, "He is a very good man." And then his voice cracked, "Almost like a father."

Veda cuddled up against him and rested her face in his chest. Together they stood as statues, watching the rain fall.

"Why did this dreadful war have to happen? It has taken so much from me, Hans. And now, even you."

He brushed his nose through her onyx curls. Her hair had the essence of jasmine. It exhilarated him. He would carry it with him wherever he was sent.

And then, in that warm moment, as the spring rain watered the pavement on the opposite side of the window, Hans grasped Veda in his warm arms and gave her a long, hard kiss. She was electrified, having never known it could be so beautiful, and wished—as she felt his hammering heart, his mouth exploring hers, his arms holding her as a refuge, and their faces pressed together—that Hans would never let go.

But he did when the antique grandfather clock struck two, though his eyes mirrored his heart, and she knew, he, too, wished the moment could last forever.

"I…I think I have grown to love you, Miss," he said breathlessly as a tear slid down his face.

Veda, who had waited to hear these words for three years, felt the rapture explode in her.

"And I have always loved you, my darling. If only…if only you did not have to go. It would all be so perfect. And there would no problems, because Father adores you now!"

He gripped her arms and stared down at her with a helplessness in his eyes. "Wait for me, Veda…please."

Her heart soared as she embraced him again. "I will wait forever, Hans, and even after that if I must!"

He brought his lips to her ears. "Oh, I love you so much! You are so beautiful, so sweet! I want nothing more than for you to become my wife!"

Veda was in heaven. "And I shall be, my darling! When this war is over, we will have a beautiful wedding in Newport! I shall ask Father to grant you a position in the bank. I will sell my home. We will build another one here in the city, and spend our summers in Newport watching our children laugh and swim in a happy world where there are no more wars!"

"I cannot wait!" Hans uttered over gasps, and kissed her again.

He left after another long emotional moment, and Veda watched through the window as he became soaked by the rain. He turned once to bid her a final farewell, and she threw him a kiss as she wept in bittersweet joy. Again, she was watching another man's back head away from her. Only this man would return to her arms, and then her world would be wonderful forever.

"I will be here, Hans…" she whispered endearingly into the windowpane. "I promise."

******

Rudolph Stern's sendoff was not quite so warm…

269

"Be gone with you, you filthy rodent, Hun!" they jeered as he left the campus staring forward and expressionlessly with hollow eyes. And as he continued, his head hanging, his suitcase in hand, he prayed they would not stone him.

After these years of torture and abuse, with his spirit killed, and his homeland possessed by demons, Rudolph Stern wondered if the detention camp would be a warm reprieve.

Chapter 54

American aid to the Allies was slow at first. England, France and Italy were most definitely failing, and Germany underestimated U.S. speed in sending men and resources overseas. It was a grave misconception.

The American draft was signed into law on May 18, 1917. Three million men were enlisted within the first month.

One million volunteered to go. Marius Champion, to his family's great chagrin, was one of them.

"Son, I urge you to reconsider!" Winston's protests were incessant.

As he eyed his father over the blaze of candles on the dinner table that evening, Marius shook his head in firm resolution. "No, Father, I owe it to our country."

Winston grimaced. His son was becoming more obstinate each day. It also did not help to know he would need to assign an outsider as temporary Vice President of Champion Trust.

******

Even Dominique's protests were to no avail.

"But why, Marius? It is bad enough I have lost our child! I cannot bear the thought of you being away!"

To the family's misfortune, she had suffered a miscarriage which plunged her into a grave depression.

That night, as they lay awake in bed, Marius shook his head with a firm expression on his moon splashed face. "I must fight to secure the freedom of our country, and the world for all of us."

Dominique began to weep. He kissed her moist eyes, took her into his strong arms, and made love to her.

But this, too, was little solace.

******

Even his mother's words were impenetrable, "Marius, dear, I cannot help but believe you are doing this to requite your grandparents' death. They are at peace now, and so then, should you, yourself be."

La Madame Champion impressed after summoning him to lunch one day. He gripped her arms with fire blazing in his eyes. "I will never be at peace, Mother, until I, myself, join the effort to conquer the Huns!"

******

Veda made feeble attempts to dissuade her brother as well, "Why do you deem it necessary to risk your own life? You have not been drafted, and given your rank in the bank and society, you will never be!"

Marius frowned, "All the more reason to go on my own accord, Veda."

She fretted, "But that makes no sense at all! I hear those war tanks are murderous robots blowing people to pieces every day! I do not want you to be one of them!"

"No need to fear, little sister," he soothed, kissing her forehead. "It is the Huns in those tanks who better beware of the Champion coming!"

It was little consolation to Veda who shook in fear.

******

The morning of his departure was a somber one. They escorted him to the train station, and his parents and Veda withheld tears until he was gone. Each bade a quick farewell with a peck on his cheek and a grip of his hand in fear of letting emotions get the best of them.

But Dominique was the weakest, and broke down in her husband's arms.

Veda, who had disliked her for so many years, was warmed by the emotional outburst, impressed to witness her sister in law's depth of love, and sympathetic, too, for her anguish.

And within moments, it was over. As Marius' train rolled away from them, Veda took a mental picture of him, his head stretching from the window, his eyes smiling with his lips, his arms flapping their farewell in the breeze.

He was happy.

She thought of Hans and hoped he, too, was well.

Two weeks later, Dominique's mother suffered a fatal heart attack. The funeral was small and quiet, just immediate family. Jacques was not excused from the seminary to attend, and Mr. Deneuve himself, was bedridden by the trauma. Dominique was the heartsick matriarch. It nearly killed her.

Three days later, she arrived at the Champion Park Avenue brownstone to join the family for a Saturday lunch. There was a new light in her eyes, though her face remained long.

"I am going to have a baby," she announced. Then her heart sank with her voice. "And Marius is so far away."

Veda had just arrived, and overheard from the vestibule. This time, she was happy for Dominique. A new life was just what the family needed. She congratulated her sister-in-law when they were alone in the parlor after dessert. Dominique acknowledged the sentiment with a perfunctory nod. It was clear she would maintain the wall between them.

Ten days after that, she nearly lost her child. Dr. Cannon ordered bed rest.

Her father took a leave from the department store, and sailed her to their summer mansion in Newport. Not even the flowers, the ocean, or the vibrant trees could console her. Were it not for the infant growing inside her, with her mother dead, and her husband off to war, Dominique would have lost her will to live.

Chapter 55

U.S. troops arrived in France by the end of June, 1917, led by Major General John J. "Black Pearl" Pershing. American soldiers were fresh and strong, unworn by three years of fighting. Thus, the Allies gained momentum.

Synchronously, Veda and her parents packed in preparation for their summer stay at Chateau La Mer in Newport.

The day before their departure, Veda went to her Fifth Avenue mansion to pack extra trunks, and received a surprise visit from Chester Worthington.

"I have come to steal your heart," he teased in the opulent parlor when she entered in a lovely white linen summer dress. Her hair was swept up on her head, and sparkling tendrils cascaded down the sides of her beautiful face.

Chester was already at ease, sitting with his legs crossed in a wing back chair, his hands folded over the lap of his cream tailor made suit. As always, he looked sinfully handsome in shirt and tie, his skin bronzed, his black eyes wide and mischievous, his mouth flashing a bright million-dollar smile.

Veda was tickled by the visit, but feigned repulsion as he extended an exquisitely wrapped package with a huge red bow.

"How simpleminded of you, Chester, to think a gift could incline me to love *you*!" she paused and added, admiring her reflection in a huge gilt mirror. "And besides, my heart belongs to another man."

He chortled, "Veda, how callous of a *proper* girl such as yourself. Aren't you still in mourning?"

She spun around and snapped at him. "Oh, hush up, and let me have the present!"

He drew it back playfully. "Only if you offer me a drink."

She raised her chin and looked down her nose at him. "And why do I just know you are referring to booze?"

He stood and came to her with a grin on his face. "Perhaps because you, yourself, imbibe, Veda."

She stepped backward, remaining coolly superior. "Perhaps I do, but the poison does not nourish me as it does you!"

Chester emitted a horselaugh. "Oh, and what poison *does* nourish you, sweetheart?"

She glared at him as she poured whiskey from a lead crystal decanter. "Here," she said, handing it to him. "You have your drink. Now give me the present."

He took a long, greedy sip, and grew momentarily serious. "Why are you here today, Veda?"

She fixed her eyes on a Ming Dynasty vase on the fireplace mantel and sniffed. "Why should my affairs be any of your concern?" and she began to rearrange a vibrant spray of summer blooms.

He came behind her and whispered over her shoulder. "Because I am an old, charming friend?"

She slipped past him, enjoying the frolic. It had been so long. A year of mourning the losses of Teddy, her child and Rose had nearly caused her to forget.

"Not convincing enough," she flirted, and poured a shot of sherry, adding after a dainty sip. "However, to quench your curiosity, I have come to collect a few things before I sail to Newport with my parents tomorrow."

"For the summer?" he drained the scotch from his tumbler, and took the liberty to pour himself another.

Her violet eyes glistened in anticipation of the ocean, the flowers, the fresh sea air. "Yes, for the summer," she replied. "And where will you be sojourning? You do not appear to be very industrious these days."

He suddenly changed the topic, eyeing her as he voiced his thoughts, "Why do you keep this big, empty house, Veda?"

She finished her sherry and crossed her arms, feeling a sudden chill. "I do not know. I suppose it is for Teddy…or our son…or both."

She had grown suddenly solemn. He felt for her. "That is convincing. Now open your present."

She snatched the box and tore it open, realizing, too, how long it was since she had received a gift. She gasped at the sight of it.

"Chester! A hat! From Paris? However, did you obtain it? All fashion houses have been shut down because of the war!"

Chester grinned proudly. "I guess I am more industrious than you have credited me, Veda."

She giggled, setting the hat on her head. "Chester, you never cease to amaze me!"

Then she paused and questioned, spinning as she modeled for him, "How do I look?"

He appraised her pleasingly, "Like a beautiful young lady who doesn't know *what* the hell she wants in life."

She tensed and glowered at him. "Isn't it just like you to spoil a happy moment?"

He winked at her and intoned. "To know me is to love me."

She slipped the hat from her head and set it back into the box. "Or to despise you!" she retorted, stifling a smile.

Chester lit a cigar. "Careful, Veda, or I won't bring you anymore presents."

She grimaced, pouring another sherry. "If you think they will bribe me into marrying you, you are wrong!"

He winked again after a long, heavy drag. "I realize you are unable to be bribed. Maybe bought, however."

The flirtatious encounter had suddenly turned sour, and she snapped back at him. "How crude of you! I shall ask you to find your way to the door!"

He smirked. He was feeling tipsy. "I thought you would at least offer me canapés, before giving me the boot."

Veda fumed. "I will offer you something, all right!" and she reached for the decanter.

Chester guffawed. "Easy, sweetheart. I get the message. Great seeing you again. Enjoy the hat."

And he placed on his own, tipping it before he left.

Veda tuned him out the moment he was gone, mesmerized by the stunning Parisian gift.

******

She was so exhilarated the first summer morning in Newport that she had decided to go horseback riding after breakfast. She was even happier when her father chose to join her. This had once been their favorite hobby, a bonding of hearts and souls. Today it helped erase painful memories of Rose.

"It is nice to see you happy again, Blossom," Winston commented as their horses slowly strutted along the Cliffside trail with the glistening ocean below them.

Veda beamed in her black riding suit, gratified to fit into it again after a three-year hiatus. "I finally feel alive, again, Father," she chimed, her dark curls billowing in the wind.

Then she caught herself and added guiltily. "In spite of the war, with Marius being so far away from us." And she wanted to add Hans' name, but did not.

Winston reassured her as they rode side by side, "Never mind the war right now, Blossom. You have been through a very hard time. I was becoming worried about the life you were living, so secluded from the world. It was unlike you. You are finally yourself again."

Veda smiled up at him. Her eyes sparkled with the sunshine. "You are so intuitive, Father. It is a comfort to be close again."

He smiled back at her. "Now it is time to get on with your life. Only this time, we shall plan together."

Veda chuckled. "You are also a mind reader, Father. I was just about to broach the subject."

"Oh?" he asked, deeply inquisitive.

She raised her head proudly. "I have been thinking about my future. I would like to come to work for you at the bank."

Winston's face twitched as he tightened the stallion's reins. Then he froze, gazing back at her in shock, and finally replied, "A woman's place is in the home, Blossom, not a boardroom."

Veda sighed. "Now why did I know this would be your response, Father?"

His stare grew firmer. "Because I have raised you properly."

She rolled her eyes and frowned. "But I do not wish to sit home and just look pretty forever! I want to do something with my life, Father...find some adventure. I may not have finished college, but I am smart. You have always said it. I can be a strong asset to you at the bank. Won't you give me this chance...please?"

Winston shook his head firmly. "No."

Veda pouted and strutted her horse forward. Her father followed, feeling her pain. "Now, now, Blossom. No need to be sore about this."

Veda shrugged sulkily. "Father, you are *so* old fashioned. Not all women stay home anymore. With the war on, and so many men at the front, more and more women are going out to work every day."

Winston's mind remained unchanged, "You should be thanking the Lord you are not one of them struggling to put food on the table and keep a roof over your head."

Veda sighed. "That is not what I mean, Father. I want a career!"

Winston narrowed his eyes. "It sounds to me like you are in need of a husband."

He was shocked by her reaction…Veda stared ahead with a wide smile on her wind-swept face. Thoughts of Hans electrified her. "At least we finally agree on something, Father!" she exclaimed and cracked the reins, increasing the stallion's pace to a gallop.

"Race you back to the house!" she cried, and Winston took her up on it. To his surprise, Veda won.

Chapter 56
France

Marius Champion learned very quickly that a battlefield is no glamorous place. Muddy trenches, gun smoke, and armored tanks raised the very depths of hell to earth, and he found himself lost in the midst of it. He learned, too, that his pampered life had made him a poor soldier. In spite of his tireless bravery and a six-foot frame, his brawn and agility were inferior. But he shared a warm camaraderie with his regiment and they gladly took the eager and dauntless 'little one' as they called him, under their wing.

Today was the worst of all. He, like the others, was worn, tired, hungry and hot. The scorching sun was relentless. The enemy had advanced and was gaining quick victory. The haze of smoke was blinding. The smell of gunpowder made him belch. Fellow soldiers were falling to their deaths beside him as fireballs struck from nowhere. He dropped to his knees and shot his gun into the smoke, hoping each bullet would send another enemy to kingdom come. And then his gun was empty. He had exhausted his ammunition. He was helpless.

Another soldier fell in front of him, and then, two more behind him.

Strange, it seemed, that the 'big ones' were dropping first. The 'little one' was still walking.

He dove onto his stomach and crawled toward a trench where he would be safe. And then, as he groped his way along the muddy path, he was immobilized by the impact of some ferocious element which pervaded and spread through him like a devastating electric shock.

Strange, too, he felt no pain, just a haze, a tranquil delirium, and an enveloping silence in spite of the pandemonium around him.

He smiled, knowing his dream had been fulfilled. He could die a happy man. As his blood seeped from his person and watered the earth of his ancestors, he felt so very proud, grandly victorious in knowing there is no greater reciprocation for nature's bountiful blessings than this. And as he stared up at the cooling sun and the fleecy clouds in the tranquil blue sky, he oddly never felt better in his short life. He could almost hear his grandparents' soft voices beckoning him toward heaven, and he waited with profound exhilaration to flap his wings with the sparrows and carry himself far up, up and away…

******

America

Veda was clipping flowers in the front garden of Chateau La Mer in a bright yellow sun dress and the Parisian hat Chester had given her. Her garments were simpler these days, now that the Great War had had an influence on female fashion. As many women went to work to replace men at war, practical clothing became the norm. Hobble skirts were things of the past. Clothing was free and easy. Modern synthetic fibers were used. Newly created dyes gave apparel a brightness never seen before. Some designers warned these changes signaled the end of femininity, variety and refinement, replaced by dull, mass produced uniformity.

Veda, who had a keen eye and admiration for fashion, encountered this with great chagrin. Still, she did her best to look pretty and elegant, and was, for the most part, doing fine.

The serenity of the moment was short-lived soon as she spied two approaching officers with grave expressions. She waited, smelling disaster.

The uniformed men removed their hats, and one of them handed her an envelope. Not a word was exchanged.

She trembled as she slipped the paper from the fold and braced herself for what she already knew. She slowly lowered her eyes to the print which stung and blinded her. She felt momentary pain, and then, came utter blackness…

******

"Sister Perpetua, Monsignor has summoned you to the church." The young sister looked at the Mother Superior with a troubled expression on her angelic face. It was 8:30 pm. The vow of silence had already been established, and she had been making her way down the hall with the other nuns. This was an unheard action. Like clockwork, the nuns habitually retired to their chambers after chapel. Tonight was different. Something was definitely amiss.

Yet she nodded and gracefully stepped out of line as her mind swam. She began a slow, sway less retreat, feeling the acceleration of her heart along the way. *What could the Monsignor possibly want?*

Strange as it was, she found herself alone in the massive church illuminated by hundreds of flickering, glowing flames. She was motionless at the end of the long aisle, when she spotted a casket at the foot of the altar, and a body being waked. Why had she been summoned here? *Who was this lay person bestowed with the honor of being presented before the altar of God? He must have come from a very influential family.* Should she turn away or proceed forward? She opted for the latter, and edged down the aisle. As she crept closer, she noticed it was a young soldier. *But who?*

When she reached the balustrade separating the body from the marble kneeler, she felt a sudden stab of inhuman pain. Her eyes enlarged in holy horror, and her heart dropped as she stared down onto her brother's young, still very handsome face. Then she sank to her knees, and gently wept.

******

"It was very kind of Monsignor Jarvis to have summoned me to the church, Reverend Mother, and so generous of you to have consented."

After a sleepless night, Sister Perpetua's voice was a somber whisper that next morning. She appeared frail, and her eyes were swollen from hours of weeping. It was a privilege, indeed, to have been permitted the connection with her brother's mortal body, if not his immortal soul.

Again, her father's influence had managed to bend the dogmas of her order. She thought of her days at the Mother House and Mother Ignatius. She was right! And how good of a nun was she anyway, having wept all night over the loss of a brother in her past life? And why, too, should she have cried? Was he not in heaven, enjoying the eternal bliss of paradise?

The gentle, wrinkled matriarch sitting with flawless posture at her desk, managed a compassionate smile. It warmed Sister Perpetua's heart.

"Monsignor Jarvis has granted his permission for you to attend the funeral service this morning."

Sister Perpetua gulped. She could hardly believe her ears. But before she could respond, the Reverend Mother softly foiled the plan.

"You are aware, Sister Perpetua, that although our good Monsignor holds the authority to override the rules of our order, this can be precarious for your spiritual strength."

Sister Perpetua lowered her eyes to the floor. "Yes, Reverend Mother. I am aware," she guiltily replied, thinking of how many young sisters there were so less fortunate than she. She was ashamed to admit that she was a very spoiled nun.

The elderly sister gazed through her knowingly, but her blue eyes were soft and merciful, and in them, Rose could detect a trace of pity.

"I have received a message from the Mother House," she said, folding her hands on the desk as she shifted the topic.

Sister Perpetua fought to conceal her regret, "Mother Ignatius is failing."

Guilt also stung Sister Perpetua for feeling no pain. How could she have when her brother would be buried that same day?

Then the Reverend Mother enthused with a soft smile still on her lips, "You have been offered one of the finest honors with which a young nun can be bestowed. Mother Ignatius has requested your visit to her bedside."

Sister Perpetua's mind raced again. Question marks clouded her thoughts, *Why, of all people, would she have been summoned?* Mother Ignatius disapproved of her intensely, her pampered past, her selfish ways, her father's connection with the church. She was everything the elderly sister frowned upon in a nun, and yet, she had called for her. Why?

"Mother Ignatius' wish is my command," she answered, and again, remorse stung her, knowing she had lied.

The Reverend mother nodded approvingly. "As Mother Ignatius has requested your visit be today, I shall grant you a choice, Sister Perpetua, knowing you will act in accordance with the teachings of our order. You may choose to attend the funeral service of your past life, or accept the honor offered you by the matriarch of our congregation, your eternal family."

Now Sister Perpetua knew why she had been summoned. It was on very rare occasions that she felt fury, and this was one of them. Her heart sank again. She had made her decision.

Chapter 57

The funeral was the saddest occasion the Champions had ever known. Their faces wore an expression beyond anguish, and their bodies ached with despondency. Veda wept between her black veiled mother and her shaking father in the first pew of Saint Mary's church. She grimly wondered how many times a heart could be broken in the same place.

Dominique was a walking corpse, her body frail and forlorn, her own veiled face saturated with tears. She hardly felt the child stirring in her womb. Her father held her motionless hand, barely coherent himself after the pain of his wife's death. A morose cloud hovered over the entire family who had been speechless since dawn.

Veda stared at the closed oak casket and could hardly believe it contained her once dashingly handsome, high spirited brother.

And where was Rose? She knew she had been granted permission to attend the high mass. Why did she choose to visit the Mother House instead? For the first time in her life, she hated her twin. She could never forgive her for this. The three of them had been inseparable, always.

When they marched behind the ball bearers down the long aisle to the vestibule, she instinctively gripped Dominique's arm and was warmed when her sister-in-law did not resist. Together they slowly proceeded, their vision filmed by tears, their minds synchronously reminiscing the happy wedding day here in this same church three very long years ago. As the pipe organ groaned the funeral march, they both silently admitted they would bury a part of themselves with Marius forever. Life was so unfair.

At his grave, they all cast soil into the earth where he would be put to eternal rest. At her turn, Veda transformed into a veiled madwoman.

"You had to be a hero, Marius!" she fired over tears. "Well, look where it got you, you stupid fool! Why did you have to go off and fight? Why? What did you prove? How could you do this to yourself? To all of us? Some hero you are now!"

Nanny McBride was the first to step out from the line of stunned mourners.

She took Veda into her corpulent arms and gently edged her away from the site. "Why, Nanny? Why?" she ranted, still a raving wreck. "How many more of us will this bloody war take before it is finally over?"

For the first time, Nanny McBride was speechless.

******

Sister Perpetua begged for strength and forgiveness on her knees in the candlelit chapel of the Mother House. She pleaded to relinquish her hatred for the dying Reverend Mother whose summoning had prevented her from attending Marius' funeral. She beseeched God for the power to forgive and to visit the failing nun's bedside with a cleansed heart. And when her prayers remained unanswered, she dared to resent her order, her superior nuns, even God. As she glumly exited the chapel with a dragging heart, the anguishing young sister felt herself torn between two worlds, and resolved that this very weakness, the anger, the torment, and the bitterness made her a failure to the clergy. She would never be able to take her final vows.

Huge black wall silhouettes of nuns struck her first before she saw the actual slew of sisters praying at the Mother Superior's candlelit beside.

The sight of the failing woman turned Sister Perpetua's heart cold. In synchrony, the praying nuns came to their feet, folded their arms gracefully beneath their starched scapulars, and slowly exited the room in pairs. Seeing them for once from the outside, Sister Perpetua was overwhelmed with a profound sense of inferiority. Why could she not just exist flawlessly as they? And then she found herself alone, her body quickly hardening as she stood at the door and glowered.

Mother Ignatius' ice blue eyes enlarged, and mysteriously urged the young nun to her bedside. Sister Perpetua, shaken by cold fury, edged closer, and was shocked to see a gentle smile on the woman's ghost white face. In spite of her deathly pallor, her eyes blazed with life, devoid of the icy emptiness Sister Perpetua had known and learned to despise.

"I have come, Reverend Mother as you have requested," she said tersely, gazing at her own shadow on the wall.

The elderly nun extended a trembling hand, and Sister Perpetua fought her withdrawal from it. Begrudgingly, she took the weak palm into hers, and instinctively sank to her knees.

"I have waited for you, Sister Perpetua. Now I can place my mortal will to rest, and ask the Lord to accept my tarnished soul."

Rose felt the nun surface in her again as a soft river flowed through her veins, cleansing the poison. "But Reverend Mother, I am afraid I do not understand. Why of all the sisters have you chosen me? Am I not the most unworthy of your servants?"

Mother Ignatius took a deep breath, and her face glowed when she locked eyes with Sister Perpetua and smiled again. "You, unworthy, my child? I must break a golden rule and speak of a past I fondly remember. There was once a beautiful, young, very wealthy girl with the most desired hand of every man in the county. She went to dances and balls and wore jewels and rich garments. She ate caviar, lobster, and game meat. She drank champagne, and was schooled in Europe. She had planned to marry a man she loved dearly, and to bring his healthy children forth into the world."

She paused and took another labored breath. It had taken great effort to speak. Sister Perpetua, paralyzed on her knees, was both stunned and mesmerized by the catharsis.

"But then, my child, that young girl's life changed dramatically when her father had been stricken with a sudden illness and died. Her mother remarried a gambler who had squandered everything and was sent to debtors' prison. Her mother drank poison one night and took her own life. The young girl was penniless. When she turned to the man she had loved, he had already accepted the hand of another young debutante whose family promised him a more secure fortune. The young, starving girl had no choice but to turn to the church, the convent for refuge."

There was another short pause as she smiled at Sister Perpetua again. "For years, I have fought the resentment. I have prayed until my lips were parched, for the strength to overcome the yearning memories of a life that could have been. I have fasted, and fought sleep with burning eyes as a sacrifice to shed the memories and the desires. I have plead for the fortitude to master this life against nature, and yet, to this day, I long for the banquet tables filled with rich foods. I can still remember the taste of champagne, and still, too, I can remember his name."

Sister Perpetua found herself weeping.

"And then you came along, my child, possessing every worldly gift I once had, with just one exception. You have chosen this life for yourself. You have mastered the battle with nature. I regret to admit that I had resented you for holding all the virtues I could never in a lifetime achieve."

She paused again and flinched at the stab of a sharp pain. Her voice grew weaker, but she managed to finish, "I have summoned you, Sister Perpetua, not only to beseech your forgiveness, but to die with my eyes fixed upon the face of a perfect nun."

Then she expired after another deep breath. Sister Perpetua knelt numbly for a long moment, her body awash with shock, her soul christened with divine inspiration.

She rose and smiled down at the body of a woman who had now, suddenly, touched her forever. With trembling fingers, she closed Mother Ignatius' eyes, whispering as tears streamed down her face, "Sleep well, Reverend Mother…and…thank you."

Chapter 58

Veda went to Dominique that evening. Her parents' summer mansion was a replica of an Italian Palazzo they had seen in Florence and immediately adored.

Two years later, Mr. Deneuve purchased the waterfront property on Bellevue Avenue and erected the architectural masterpiece.

"I am sorry, Mrs. Aspan, but Mrs. Champion is not receiving anyone," the black tied butler sniffed, but Veda was determined.

"She will see me!" and she made her way up the stairs in spite of his protests.

"Dominique, it is I, Veda…may I come in?" she said somewhat tensely, truly unaware of what her sister in law's response would be.

To her surprise, Dominique opened the door, clad in a white satin robe. She looked at Veda blankly, who smelled of brandy, and had not yet changed from her black dress.

Veda gulped. "I…I hope I have not awakened you."

Dominique shook her head, and beckoned her into the boudoir.

She resumed her place in the chaise lounge, and Veda sat at the edge of the canopy bed.

"Well…" Veda said awkwardly. "I really do not know where to begin. I suppose I owe you an apology for my ill behavior at the burial," then she paused to weep into a lace handkerchief. "But I simply could not help it, Dominique! I loved Marius so much, and I know you did too!"

Dominique just stared at her with a twitch of disapproval in her bereaved eyes. "How much have you had to drink?"

Veda sniffed. "I do not know. I lost count." Then she found the need to defend herself, "Well, do not look at me like that… I had to do something to numb my pain!"

Dominique sighed. "There are other ways, Veda. Brandy is not the aid you need. How much of what you say will I be able to accept as truth now that you are drunk?"

Veda looked at her sister-in-law in wide-eyed despair. "Do you consider it a drunken lie when I admit I am simply torn to shreds over my brother's death?"

Dominique shrugged with a scowl, "Oh, Veda, why did you come here tonight?"

Veda quickly protested. "Because I needed to see you, and I believe that you need me too!"

Again, her sister-in-law was silent.

"Oh, come now, Dominique! How long are you going to carry this grudge against me concerning Jacques? It had to be this way! Can't you see it? If I had married him, he would have missed his true calling to the seminary."

Still, Dominique said nothing.

"And besides, what happiness could I have offered a man I do not love? What joy did I bring Teddy? Oh, I have just made a mess of my life; haven't I?" And she began to weep again.

Dominique shifted testily in her lounge. "Veda, this is not the time."

"Oh, but it is! Can't you see that I feel for you? That I understand the depth of your pain? I, too, have buried a husband *and* a child! I know I cannot compare the grief of my widowhood to yours as Teddy and I were never soul mates, but I *do* know what it is to hurt! I have had so many losses…my grandparents, too! And with Rose locked away behind the stone walls of a convent, I feel like an only child right now. You must believe me!"

She stared at Dominique's blank expression. "Don't you?" she asked, and then hiccupped.

Dominique sighed restlessly again, "Even if I did believe you, it would not matter now."

"Why not?" Veda questioned, and blew her nose.

Dominique's words were dark and morose as the expression on her face. "Because I want to die."

Veda turned to shock. "You mustn't say such things! Marius and your mother would never forgive you for losing your own will to live! There is a child growing inside you, the only spirit to carry on the Champion name…Marius' baby, *his* legacy! You must pull yourself together. You owe it to Marius, to the child, to yourself!"

In that somber moment, Dominique broke down and wept. Veda went to the chaise lounge and, sitting on the ottoman, took her into her arms.

"Oh, it will be all right…you will see! The sun will rise tomorrow, and you will live on! I will help you. I promise."

Dominique gripped Veda tightly and sobbed into her shoulder, "It hurts so much!"

"I know it does," Veda whispered, stroking her blond locks.

"Where will I go? What will I do?" She was beside herself.

Veda soothed with a warm whisper, "You will stay right here. And you will have your baby."

Dominique wept louder as Veda continued to stroke her. "I know we have never seen eye to eye, Dominique, but that is past now. We are family, and your child will bring us all joy. I have always admired your proper ways, and your love for Marius. I believe I have even grown to love you."

And she added, drying Dominique's tears with her fingers, "And I suppose you will just have to learn to love me."

Chapter 59

Veda stayed with Dominique until she had fallen asleep shortly after midnight. She strolled the cliff walk alone on the path to Chateau La Mer. Her heart ached for Hans. She gazed up at the summer solstice in the inky black sky and wondered in that solitary moment if her dear love was thinking of her too.

One day this war would be over, and he would return to her arms where she would eagerly await his touch, his lips upon hers, his soft voice whispering into her tingling ear. Yes, life would resume then, when he and their children would help soothe the relentless pain of her losses.

She labored through a sleepless night.

She and her parents lived a sequestered life along with Dominique in their separate summer mansions for two weeks before any sight of a return to society took place. Winston was the first to awaken from his catatonic state after a messenger from Champion Trust had paid him a visit. Before now, he had ignored any correspondence from the bank, but now matters were crucial. He was needed. It was time to get back to work or risk a financial catastrophe.

So, he prevailed as a Champion, although his will was met with strong opposition from Veda.

"Whom do you plan to appoint Vice President now with Marius gone?" she asked with a ring of animosity in her voice as she escorted him to his yacht beneath the hills of the chateau.

"Veda, this is not the time," he droned, but she was obstinate.

"But it *is* the time, Father, and you know it! Soon as you return, you will have to address this matter, and I have a right to know!"

He stared at her inquisitively. In a lovely floral print dress and a straw picture hat, his daughter possessed the beauty of a goddess, and the promise of a perfect society lady. Why then, did she continue to fight her expected role?

Then he sighed and answered, through narrowed eyes, "Though it is a condescension to discuss business matters with a lady, I will remind you,

Blossom, that I have already appointed an acting Vice President. It was done soon as Marius had gone off to war."

Veda shrugged resentfully. "You could not possibly be considering that scrawny fool for your heir!"

Winston's gaze sharpened. "I never mentioned an heir, Veda. On that vain, however, I will state my impatience in awaiting the birth of a grandson. Dominique gleans such prospect. Perhaps you should do the same," Veda felt her blood rush to her head and come to a quick boil. "How could you be so obtuse, Father?"

Now, Winston's tone also sharpened. "Mind yourself, Veda!"

She tore off her hat and threw it to the ground petulantly. "I will not! I should be the one to assume Marius' role!"

Winston chortled, "You? What do you know about banking, Blossom?"

"I can learn!" she protested vehemently.

Winston gripped her arm tightly. "We have been through this before. The answer is no!"

Her eyes shot violet fire. "Why are you so stubborn? And what makes you so sure you will have a grandson, much less run the bank long enough until he is of age to take over?"

They were at the boat now. Winston was slowly losing his temper. He took a deep breath and gripped her other arm. His face blazed with the scorching sun. "Stay out of my affairs, Veda, and start searching for a husband before I find you another. And *this* time, I will not be so forgiving, if you know what I mean!"

She tore herself away with a vengeance, "Do not threaten me, Father! I am not the little girl you think you can wave your hand and marry off any longer! You did not get away with it the first time, and you certainly will not now! Go off! Go back to your bank, and give everything to a stranger!"

"I am so ashamed of you!" Winston snarled as perspiration beaded his face.

Veda fired back at him. "And I am more ashamed of you!"

Then she turned and started up the hill toward the house. Somehow, she would show him. She had lost the battle, but not the war.

******

She stormed down the aisle of St. Mary's church early that afternoon where the nuns were on their knees praying for the reposed soul of Mother Ignatius and the war victims. She went directly behind Rose. Amazing how she recognized her amidst the numerous black veiled statues.

"I need to speak to you!" she said in a surly whisper, and Sister Perpetua, without turning, was paralyzed by the familiar voice.

She kept praying in an effort to ignore her twin, but Veda was relentless.

On her knees, she hissed in Rose's ear. "You better pay me proper mind, or I will make a scene right here and now! I swear I will!"

Sister Perpetua felt her heart hammer, and cringed in shame. The other nuns shifted their eyes in the direction of the blasphemer, as the young nun wished she could crawl under the pew and hide.

The Mother Superior met her shamed expression with compassionate eyes and nodded her approval. Sister Perpetua edged her way out of the pew, and gently motioned for Veda to follow her outside.

In the courtyard, beside the flower lined grotto of the Blessed Mother, she admonished her twin. "Veda, you must never do such a thing again! If not for myself, for your own soul! You have committed a great sin!"

Veda was ablaze. "Do not tell me what is sinful! It is a grave crime for you to remain locked behind the walls of this prison amongst human penguins while your whole family is falling apart!"

Though seething, Sister Perpetua remained gracefully assertive, "I will not hear anymore blasphemy against the church! Your soul is in grave peril. You need to return to God, and beseech his healing grace!"

"Oh, be quiet!" Veda snapped. "It is easy for you to babble these inanities they have taught you in an effort to remain shut out of the world! Don't you know what is happening out there? People are being killed every day! Our brother was sent home in a box, and YOU chose not to be there!"

The sting of her twin's words was venomous. Sister Perpetua was silent for a long moment before she whispered her reply. "You do not understand…you never will."

Veda was merciless. "For the first time, you utter the truth! I *do not* understand! You have thrown away everything! And for what? Look at you! You are a beautiful young woman, masked behind that dreary costume, wasting your best years away until you become old and wrinkled like the rest of them, regretting only *then* what you have sacrificed!"

The venomous notion flowed through Sister Perpetua's bloodstream and stabbed at her heart. She thought of Mother Ignatius in that moment. Was Veda right?

But she managed, as always, to take a deep breath and maintain composure. "I do not believe you should ever see me again, Veda," her heart bled as she said it.

Veda's fiery response shook her. "Do not worry, Rose! I will not! The sight of you repulses me now! Damn you for placing the world before your own people, and for forgetting that charity begins at home! You can be happy now to know that I disown you as a sister! I never want to see your betraying face ever again!"

And as Veda stormed off, Sister Perpetua felt her body weaken. She groped the stone grotto for support, and found herself sitting in the flower bed, panting.

If only Veda *could* understand…

Chapter 60

It was summer's end when the crickets still sang lazily and bees and butterflies slowly disappeared. Newport was quieter now as families packed their trunks and set sail for their main residences. An autumnal chill splashed through the summer wind, and at night, women required shawls, and gentlemen, light sweaters.

It seemed as if Veda and Dominique were the only two persons opting to remain amidst the empty mansions along Bellevue Avenue.

La Madame Champion, clad in a black mourning dress and hat, stood in the vestibule of Chateau La Mer that bright September day and spoke with Veda who wore a riding suit.

"Your father is awaiting an apology," she said in her coolly superior tone.

In spite of the tragedies she had suffered, she maintained the grace and dignity of a queen. Veda envied her composure and self-discipline, and although her mother's radiance had dulled, her beauty prevailed.

"I will never apologize to him!" she firmly protested. "He must realize how much he has hurt me, and that he cannot control me anymore!"

La Madame Champion observed her disapprovingly. "My dear child, what has made you so disobedient?"

Veda shrugged sulkily, "And what has made *him* so blind?"

La Madame Champion slipped on her gloves and took her daughter's hand. "Veda, this is unworthy of you." Then her dark eyes softened, and a loneliness grew in them unlike Veda had never seen before. "Come home now. We need you. With Marius gone, and Rose's cloistered life, you are all we have."

Veda shook her head. "I am sorry, but I cannot come," she was truly remorseful for her mother's sake. But right now, her pride was too great.

La Madame Champion, seeing defeat, eyed her sternly. "And what will you do up here all alone?"

Veda replied, stroking her mother's gloved hand. "I will not be alone. I will be with Dominique."

Another regretful grimace. Mr. Deneuve also had a very obstinate daughter in spite of his numerous urges for her to return to New York.

"She, too, must be convinced to come home. In a few short months, she will give birth. Newport is awfully cold in the dead of winter."

Veda rolled her eyes. "I know, Mother. Have you forgotten that I have spent a winter here?"

La Madame Champion just nodded.

Then Veda enthused with a twinkle in her eyes, "I shall stay with Dominique and wait. I shall wait for her baby to be born, and for this war to be over so I can finally get on with my life."

Her mother gazed at her blankly, wondering what Veda could have possibly meant.

Her mind had shifted to thoughts of Hans...

******

It was an unusually cool autumn, and an icy winter. Though they dwelt in different houses, Veda and Dominique grew close as any two blood sisters could be. Memories of Marius, their childhoods, and the wedding day kept conversation flowing, and exhilarated their minds.

They spent Thanksgiving alone, and planned to return to New York for Christmas where Mr. Deneuve had finally convinced his daughter to remain for the birth of her child. A week before their departure, a blizzard had crippled all of Newport. The arctic winds sweeping off the ocean produced devastating effects from frost bite to death.

Veda managed to weather her way through the storm that blustery day, and was met at Dominique's door by the stunned eyes of her chambermaid, Carlotta, whom she had ordered to stay there the night before.

"Oh, *Madame*! Come in before you freeze to death!"

Veda, shivering in her black sable, matching Cossack and muff, was nearly frostbitten. Her face was beet red, her body, weary. Yet she questioned breathlessly as Carlotta slipped off her coat.

"How is Dominique?"

Carlotta announced proudly, "She is sleeping, Madame. Just like an angel."

Veda dabbed her running nose with a handkerchief. "Has she eaten breakfast?"

Carlotta nodded. "Yes, *Madame*. She had toast and tea."

"Very good," Veda said, and struggled to make her way up the stairs.

She sat at Dominique's bedside and read to her from Dickens' *A Christmas Carol* that afternoon when she was interrupted by a sudden thrust from beneath her sister in law's quilt.

"Dominique, what is it?" she questioned tensely, and seeing water seep from under the foot post, knew just what was happening. But Dominique was barely seven months! How could it happen so soon?

Alarmed and trapped in the last of gray winter daylight, Dominique whispered what they both knew to be impossible, "Call a doctor."

Veda felt her body spring into a panic, and struggled to maintain herself. "Of course," but her words trembled, and she made a beeline to the door.

"Carlotta!" she cried from the vestibule.

"Yes, *Madame*?" her chambermaid answered from the foyer, feeling imminent trouble.

"Come up here, right away!" Carlotta promptly obliged.

"What are the chances of you going out to call a doctor? Dominique has gone into labor."

Terror washed over the young French woman's face. "Oh, *Madame*! I would die out there!"

Veda huffed and shoved her out of the way. "Oh, you are timid as a church mouse! I will go then!"

"No, *Madame*! You mustn't go!" Carlotta fearfully cried. "You won't get beyond the corner, and it will be dark in no time!"

Veda burst into a cold sweat. "But we *need* a doctor!"

Carlotta shook her head, her face drawn, her eyes welling tears. "There is no doctor to be found, *Madame*. No one will make it up here. All roads have been closed."

"*Veda!*" Dominique shrieked from the bedroom. Her wail of anguish resonated throughout the mansion.

Veda and Carlotta exchanged worrisome glances. They remembered that dark night not so long ago when a stillborn had come into the world. And Dominique's baby was premature. A new nightmare was unfolding.

Veda closed her eyes, gripped the bannister, and took a deep breath. Her heart was hammering, her mind racing.

"Carlotta, I want you to go down to the kitchen and gather up everything we need. You have done it before. I am relying upon you."

"But, *Madame...*" Carlotta feebly protested.

Veda gave way to frenzy. "*But nothing!*" she fired. "Now get moving! You are supposed to know about delivering babies!"

"Veda! Veda!" the wails resonated from the bedroom.

"I am coming, Dominique..." she answered, sweating profusely in spite of the cold. "And so is the doctor."

Then she groped her way to the bedroom, only wishing it were true.

Dominique's moans were in somber synchrony with the howling, storm winds. The frozen windowpanes vibrated as crystalized snowflakes shot ferociously against them.

Veda and Carlotta worked laboriously for hours. It was like the blind leading the blind, but somehow, they managed. Strange as it seemed, Veda remembered what to do, and silently prayed that this time, the fragile infant would come out alive.

In spite of her groans, Dominique was an angel through it all. Veda remembered her own grinding and howling, and also knew the pain her sister-in-law was enduring with such admirable dignity.

The baby's head emerged first, and Veda was ever so careful as she eased him into the world. Her body was electrified by the wonder she was witnessing...Marius' son, born into her arms. She held him as Carlotta severed the umbilical cord. Then she struck his backside gently, and uttered a sigh of ecstasy when the young angel began to cry. He was small, but fully developed...alive and healthy.

They washed him together and swaddled him in a heated cloth. So mesmerized by the miracle, they were unaware of the pool of blood gathering on the bed and spilling onto the floor.

Carlotta saw it first, and was paralyzed with fear. Veda saw only the young Champion offspring, and proudly carried him back to the bed.

It was not until she was to lower him into Dominique's arms that she realized with a stab of terror, that the infant would never know his mother.

She was fast asleep...forever.

******

Another funeral. Another circle of black veiled women, and men in black top hats and overcoats.

"God giveth and God taketh away," the priest somberly droned, making reference to the birth of the child and the death of his mother.

They sadly watched Dominique's casket being lowered into the icy earth above that of her young husband.

Two untimely deaths. It had been a nightmare, indeed. "Come, Veda," someone enthused, and took her arm.

It was Jacques, so drawn and weary, with a bereaved white pallor on his young, handsome face.

She wept into his cashmere coat, remembering the day she had done the same in Marius' arms.

Then she composed herself, looked up into his hazel eyes, and uttered in a black whisper, "Sometimes I believe this family is cursed."

******

A whirlwind of events followed. Two days after the funeral, Mr. Deneuve, who had not completely overcome his wife's death, suffered a stroke and remained in a coma. The immature, but miraculously healthy infant was named Alexander, and placed under the care of *La Madame* and Winston Champion.

Veda returned to her Fifth Avenue mansion, determined to establish a career for herself as she awaited Hans' return.

She was visited by Jacques one evening when, he announced in a black suit and tie, his decision to leave the seminary.

"It is not my calling, Veda. I should have known it all along. I only joined to escape my pain."

Veda, perched in a wing back chair beside a crackling fire, frowned as she heated a snifter of cognac.

"I hope you have not come to inflict guilt upon me, Jacques. I simply cannot bear anymore disharmony in my life."

She was very thin and pallid in a black dinner dress, her hair twisted into a chignon.

"I am sorry," Jacques whispered, coming to sit in the chair beside her.

298

As she gazed onto his angelic face, into his soft eyes, and his honest mouth, Veda wondered why she never came to love him.

"I really meant to say that I had entered the seminary for all the wrong reasons. My teachers sensed it. They often told me."

Veda sipped her cognac. The taste of half silk, half fire, numbed her pain, and her guilt.

"And what will you do with your life now, other than assuming your role as heir to your father's fine apparel store?"

Jacques leaned forward. The firelight illuminated his face. "As you know, my father is failing. Doctors give him very little time."

"I am sorry," Veda whispered, reaching out to take his hand.

Jacques shivered. A cold wind swept across his heart at the prospect of losing yet another loved one.

But after a heavy breath, he went on. "We have sold the store and invested all shares of profit into Champion Trust."

Veda withdrew her hand and stiffened in her chair. She tossed off the rest of her cognac and questioned in wide-eyed shock, "Whatever for?"

Jacques was surprised by her reaction. It all seemed so simple. "Now that your father has an heir, Veda, it is time for the family fortunes to merge."

Veda stared at him, dumbfounded, with a hand over her accelerating heart. "And what about you, Jacques? Where do you stand in all of this?"

He gazed at her blankly for a long moment. "Have you not heard, Veda? Where have you been?"

She tensed. "Heard what?" but she already knew the truth.

Jacques leaned closer still, and made the proud announcement. "Your father is training me to be Vice President."

In that moment, Veda despised both of them.

******

"How dare you scorn me so!" Veda thundered as she stormed into her father's office the next morning.

The dark oak walls and matching lacquered furniture offered a heaviness to the room in symphony with Winston's strong character.

He stared at his incensed daughter from where he sat at his throne, his hands folded on his desk.

"Good day, Veda. I was expecting you one of these winter mornings. Do have a seat, please."

He was patronizing her with a victorious smile on his face.

Veda, in her ermine coat, saw fire. "I know what you are doing, and it will not work!"

Winston leaned forward and grinned. "Are you clairvoyant, Blossom? If so, I do not believe you will establish much of a career for yourself on *this* end of town."

She glowered at him. "You think that by appointing Jacques Vice President, I will consent to marrying him!"

Winston raised a finger, and intoned pompously. "Very good deduction, my child."

She came before him, her jaws tightened, her nostrils flared. "Well, I will be the first to foil your plan, Father, in assuring you that it will not happen! Never in a million years!"

Then she swung around and stormed out of the room, slamming the oak door behind her.

At his desk, Winston leaned backward and had a horselaugh. "Not a million years, Veda," he chortled into the empty room. "Much sooner than that!"

Chapter 61

Throughout the winter of 1918, war was brought home to every Londoner as German airplanes regularly bombed the city. Then, in the spring, German troops pushed their way into France. First, they defeated the Allies along the embattled Somme; then they recaptured lost ground. The German army pushed as far west as the Marne River where it had been in 1914. Already, German planes had bombed Paris, killing thirteen civilians. Shock waves ran though the allied nations. It seemed as if the Allies had been defeated.

Then, in July, one million American men arrived like knights in shining armor, and the tide turned. The situation in France improved. The Allied army attacked Germany on the western front. Battlefields in France raged on. Losses were heavy on both sides. French men and women watched wheat fields become plowed with bodies. U.S. losses were running at forty percent. In the battle of Bellevue Wood alone, the U.S. lost seven thousand eight hundred men. By the end of July, however, the Allies were winning.

Then came the battle of the Argonne Forest. Here, Allies used machine guns and cannons. It lasted for forty-seven days before the Germans retreated. Reports came in that the German army was so depleted, it used old men and young boys as recruits.

By September, Allied troops had broken through the Austro-Hungarian defense in the south. Now there was nothing left for the Germans. Kaiser Wilhelm smelled defeat, and on October 14, 1918, he sent word to the Allies that the Central Powers would accept a 'peace with honor.' To his chagrin, the Allies refused. They wanted assurance that if the peace were accepted, German troops would withdraw. There were also hints that the Allies wanted as part of the peace agreement, the abdication of Kaiser Wilhelm.

One by one, the Central Powers fell to the Allied forces in the fall of 1918. Bulgaria and Turkey were forced to sign armistices with the Allies in October. In the same month, the Allies split, and destroyed the Austro-Hungarian armies.

Early in November, the entire Austro-Hungarian Czechs, Slovaks, and Poles declared their independence.

Germany was the last central power to sign for peace. It began on November 4 when the German navy at Kiel mutinied. Sailors who revolted set up councils and were joined by socialists. They called for the Kaiser's abdication and the creation of a German republic. On November 9, Kaiser Wilhelm stepped down from his throne and fled to Holland. With its people angry and hungry, and its soldiers in revolt, the German government agreed to Allied terms.

At 5:00 am on November 11, 1918, the final armistice was signed in a railway car in a French forest. By 11:00 am, guns fell silent. The Great War had finally ended!

Jubilation was everywhere in the Allied countries. Americans burst into an exultant frenzy. New Yorkers filled the streets everywhere and screamed American victory.

"It is over!" Veda exclaimed in the parlor of her mansion where the radio had just blared the good news followed by the national anthem.

She sprang to her feet and whisked to the picture window encountering a sea of feverish New Yorkers on Fifth Avenue.

"And Hans will be coming home!" she gushed into the windowpane with a wide smile on her beaming face.

To be continued...

CPSIA information can be obtained
at www.ICGtesting.com
Printed in the USA
LVHW081232110621
689905LV00004B/316

9 781649 791986